Kata's FATHER

A Bosnian Novel

JOHN M. ZURAK

Kata's
FATHER

A Bosnian Novel

JOHN M. ZURAK

ISBN-13: 978-0-9971748-0-9
LCCN: 2016907173

Distributed by Itasca Books

Cover Design by Biz Cook
Typeset by C. Tramell

Printed in the United States of America

Za Antu Šola, Jagicu Lukenda i moju dragu babu Veroniku Šola.

Contents

Part III: Tito

Part IV: Kuči

Part I

Gora[1]

---

1 Translation for Mountain. (Note: All translations are from Croatian generally spoken in Bosnia, unless stated.)

-Introduction-

Prije¹

The mountain possesses a quiet call that is no more than a whisper. If your mind has the rare gift, even for a second, to stop thinking and be silent, you might be able to hear this scarce and unique voice.

Stop for a second and try to listen. Did you hear it?

If you did not hear it, you might need to close your eyes. Try to block out all surrounding noise, even the beating of your own heart. If you still cannot hear it, you might need to focus your mind's powers in between each breath, for the consumption of oxygen can be quite distracting to the other senses.

If you still cannot hear it, do not be disheartened, because you are not alone in being deprived of this phenomenon. Even if you lived your entire life in the mountains, there is a very real probability you will think this is pure nonsense, and not hear the slightest of

---

1 Before

peeps. Again, do not be disheartened. It is not your fault, because there might be a simpler reason. You might simply be too old.

I do not mean to mock your age, or question your normal listening functions. I am certain your hearing is most satisfactory for your daily requirements, such as listening to conversation or music. I am sure you get annoyed when the neighbor's dog won't hush, or if they are mowing the lawn too early on a Saturday morning. There is in fact, nothing wrong with your hearing, so cancel the ear checkup.

Rather, to hear the mountain call requires a unique skill set that has everything to do with your age. It requires the listener to be young.

More to the point, you need to be a child, and most children are very, very young, unlike the rest of us, who are not. Why can only the very young hear the mountain? Perhaps, the easy conclusion might be a child's ears are simply better attuned to hear the mountain's call, like a dog to a dog whistle. But the real reason might be because this is what the mountain wants. The mountain loves little feet and young hearts. The mountain adores their innocence and their adventure.

Most importantly, it knows it is a child's natural inclination to be honest and act with honorable motives. Because of this, the mountain understands it can trust a child with its treasures and its secrets.

Another justifiable notion to the unique bridge of communication is the mountain's expertise in providing children what they really, really want.

And though, to be sure the initial climatic onslaught that winter brings can provide a brutal initiation for the youngest of souls, but if these newborns can survive this difficult test, the mountains are a paradise ready to be their plaything. The mountain wants children to frolic by its cool waters during the temperate summer months.

The mountain wants children to play tag through the acres of wildflowers. It wants them to hide and seek behind the cluster of biggest oak trees. And then, after their energy-consuming play, the mountain wants each child to relax under the large canopy of refreshing shade. Once they have rested, the mountain wants every young soul to eat, and furnish their appetite with a bounty of tastes that can be plucked or picked from its regenerating shelves.

But, that is only the beginning of the mountain's generosity. The mountain possesses a great gift that only children know how to embrace. The mountain wants each child to personally know that its landscape of hills, valleys, streams, creeks, rivers, gorges, and high up out of the way peaks has no fences. No fences mean no barriers and no cages. No fences mean they can go where they please. No fences means that the mountain cannot nor will not keep anything in or out. In the mountains, each soul is given the opportunity to go where it pleases. The mountain is free, and it wants all of the little ones to know this freedom too. The mountain has seen what freedom does to the little ones. It is a perfect picture of joy.

The mountain feeds off this perfect picture, and feels even freer, even grander. According to the mountain, freedom is a group of children belly laughing. Freedom is children playing where they do not know that time exists. Freedom is a deep sleep in the great outdoors, away from the false safety of blankets and walls. The mountain knows this. It wants others to know it too, so it whispers it, hoping for someone to hear it. It hopes someone will hear it, and claim it. The mountain is ready to give it to whoever wants it.

If it could go further, the mountain would give even more of itself than freedom. Because freedom is only the beginning. There are even greater gifts than freedom. What might the mountain give, you ask? If it could choose, firstly, the mountain would even allow itself to be owned by each child who heard and answered its call. However, the mountain knows this would never work, because children do not stay children in the mountains for long.

-1-
Šta je?[1]

Have you ever heard of someone being bitten by a bee in the dead of winter? In the middle of the night, no less? Mijo Pavlović had.

According to the only witness, the strange phenomenon occurred in his own house, just minutes before he was informed. Cynically, Mijo refused to believe it. Bees don't venture out in the winter, his logic protested. It would be unexplainable, his logic continued. The Papacy might have to investigate it as a possible miracle, his logic mocked. A little miracle, perhaps insignificant, but one all the same. Mijo had seen a lot in his life, but never a miracle. Not in his house and not in his village.

So, logically, it could not have happened. Mijo's mind was made up. It did not happen, so cancel the telegram to the Vatican. Truth be told, if Mijo's eyes met theirs, or if his ears heard buzzing, or if his skin felt the swoosh of their droned haste; he still might not have believed it. That's the interesting thing about miracles. They only occur if you are looking for them.

Mijo was not seeking miracles in his mountain, but rather he was panning for silence and peace. On this night, however, he found neither, and as a result missed finding the golden nugget. You

---

1 What is it?

shouldn't blame him though. The only witness account was given by a four-year-old boy, and who really dares to agree with the ramblings of a little child, especially in the middle of the night?

But, there was one problem that Mijo's logic could not explain away. His only child Mirko was adamant and refused to be swayed. He was a true believer. According to the little one, not only did he see the bee, he was bitten by it, and no logic or presumptuous reasoning was going to change his mind. Not even his father.

"It happened, Tata. It happened," Mirko wailed. "A big buzzing bee! It happened. I saw it. It stared right at me and it bit me. Right next to my belly button and it itches. You need to scratch it, until it feels better."

Mijo was not convinced. He squinted and strained his pupils, to see what Mirko spoke of. Even with the dull luminous glow of a kerosene lamp, and Mirko's pointing finger directing his eyes to the region of the supposed attack, Mijo could not see a sting, a bite, or any other visible markings.

"Where's the bites, son?" Mijo demanded. "I can't see anything."

"It was one bite, and it's right there," replied the four-year-old, motioning to his abdomen.

"You're just having a dream, Mirko," demanded his father. "Go back to sleep, child."

Mirko shook his head, sobbing. "I can't Tata. It was here. The bee got me! I saw it. It could come back. It will come back and it might bring friends!"

Mijo quickly understood this was a losing battle. His skepticism was not winning him his evening back. He needed to placate his son and fast, or it was going to be a painfully long night. "If I kiss it better, will you be able to go to sleep?" pleaded a growingly desperate father.

Mirko quickly understood that trying to convince his father in the middle of the night was never going to end well. And so, despite his fears and tears, he relented. "Da," consented a still weeping Mirko.

Mijo kissed his sobbing child, and roughed up his hair. Mijo waited for his son to obediently close his eyes, removing himself from

Mirko's room and into the darkened hallway with the traditional good night greeting of "laku noć."

Closing the door behind him, Mijo shook his thinning scalp, dismayed. He considered his one and only child, and what it might be like with multiple Mirko's. A stressed shudder came over him. So much time lost on silly little things, thought Mijo.

While wading through those waters, Mijo was startled back into the hallway's reality by his wife Mara, who thrust open her bedroom door with haste. "What was the matter with Mirko? I heard crying." she asked, concerned.

"Nothing," Mijo responded emphatically.

Hearing commotion created by voices outside her door, Mijo's mother Vjera was next to abruptly enter the already crowded hallway, startling the couple.

"He was having a vivid dream. He's fine," pronounced an exasperated Mijo. "I told him to go back to sleep. You both should too."

"Vivid dreams, about what?" queried a weirdly-smiling Vjera. Mijo sighed and shrugged his shoulders, hoping his vagueness could end this unwanted late night roundtable conference. It was very late, and he was tired. Not for sleep, but tired all the same.

Mijo peered over at his grandfather clock. He strained his already squinting eyes in a lost cause to make out the time. Moving closer towards its tick-tock, the hands pointed to twenty-three past one.

"Boy, don't shrug your shoulders and walk away from me," Vjera ding-donged, alarming both Mijo and the grandfather clock. "Oh and when are you going to sleep?" Mijo turned to answer his bellowing inquisitor, to apologize that his fatigue dominated his manner. But before he could, his mother interrupted, "I know, I know," she chortled. "You don't sleep." Mijo relaxed, quickly realizing his mother was not annoyed, but rather toying with him like a wolf might a mouse.

"That's right; I don't sleep," Mijo agreed, playing along. "And it appears no one else in this house does either. Laku noć."

Mara, smiling, closed her door, content to rest now that her son was peacefully sleeping once more. Vjera closed her door, content that she could still put her son back in whatever place she deemed necessary. Mijo, content that things were put back in some semblance of order, returned to his chair, stationed by the flickering combustion that was charring the hunks of spruce his ax split months earlier. He sat quietly, rubbing the stubble on his chin, listening to flames cackle like his mother and wife just did. It was true: Mijo rarely slept. "Why sleep if you don't need it?" he reasoned to himself and the fire.

His entire life Mijo never needed much sleep. By the time he was eleven months old, he did not take an afternoon nap. As his age reached beyond double figures, while teenagers around the world snored away years, Mijo never wanted more than a few hours. The ability to defeat this need was a gift that stayed with him as he became a man.

And now, surrounded by responsibility, he loved the freedom it provided him. While others were handcuffed by daily honey-do lists and overt daily weariness, the world was at Mijo's beck and call. He could do as he pleased, knowing he had all the time in the world. He could work when he wanted. He could rest if he felt the need. His only problem was finding something to fill all the extra conscious eye blinks.

He did his best to keep busy. Like his father and grandfather before him, he was a pretty handy woodworker, so on other nights, Mijo might carve a little trinket he could give as a gift, such as a pipe for one of his friends, or a pencil box for one of their children.

Currently, he was building a chess set as a gift to himself that one day he would pass along to his son. Other times, though he was not much of a writer, he could craft letters without rush to relatives that he hadn't seen for days, months, or even years, such as his second cousin who lived in Chicago, America. When his hands wished to rest and his feet wanted to do the work, he might take an evening hike around the village perimeter. This civic duty was especially valuable in the winter months, when he could ensure a retaining wall had not fallen smack bang in front of any neighbor's door.

However, the problem was Mijo got his lists of things-to-do done so quickly, he found he had too much time on his hands.

He always needed another list of additional distractions. Mara had suggested trying to sleep for a change. She never quite understood Mijo's disdain for sleep. So Mijo tried to be like the rest of the world, but he just couldn't do it. He could do anything he put his mind to but sleep. He earnestly tried, but he ended up just lying there as still as possible so as not to awaken his wife. Hour after hour, he lay motionless. But, to keep that still for that long is unnatural. Even when Mara was asleep, she could sense his stillness and it weirded her out, disrupting the deepness of her slumber.

"Why don't you find another hobby other than sleeping?" she had suggested lately.

So he did. At first Mijo had attempted to disrupt the sleep of others by organizing late-night *Tablić* card games. And though cards were a popular village past time, Mijo's late-night games were always sparsely attended, and then eventually not all. The village wisely considered Mijo's unnatural nocturnal preference a real card-playing advantage their fatigue would not overcome. So to ensure they kept their *dinar* in their pockets, they began to ignore his invitations, again leaving Mijo needing to find other nightly occupations, alone.

After weeks of frustrating experimentation with vocations that bored him and annoyed others, Mijo stumbled across a beautifully simple discovery. The discovery was Mijo loved sitting and thinking about whatever crossed his mind. He found it especially enjoyable in winter, where he could play with the fire, recharge with the occasional clinking glass full of *rakija*[2] and really ponder his place in his mountain.

This made him and Mara chuckle. A fourth-grade educated mountain man's mind pondering the world and its reason as if he were Aristotle or Socrates. Still, this nocturnal vocation was productive in sweeping out the dust that settled on this thinker. The more he sat with his newfound friends *Silence and Thought*, the more he realized there was much to consider in his corner of the world.

This corner was well hidden from almost the entire world, situated in a small alcove high above the valley. So high you could

---

2 Plum brandy

stare flying eagles straight in the eye. The mountain village of Pavlovići was founded by Mijo's family many generations ago, before the Ottoman Empire came to stay.

Currently, seventy-six families nestled against the obtuse-angled walls of this portion of mountainous Kraljeva Sutjeska, a region known for the Franciscan church and monastery founded centuries earlier that shared the mountain's name. Mijo's village was within walking distance of the famous church, and was within earshot of the local *tamburica* players that earned their keep in the valley in the town of Čatići.

The closest village below was Veliki Trnivci. A few miles of wild flowers above them, in the higher altitude were the lush grounds of the smaller village of Kopjari, famous for the regional spring waters and wild strawberries that were large enough to feed giants. Further away, but part of their greater circle, were the towns of Vareš and Kakanj, which owned a healthy industrialized infrastructure.

Mijo rubbed his hands together, reacquainting himself with his evening blaze, and also to warn off further disruptions of felonious bees attacks. "Oh well, not every evening can be perfect," Mijo sighed, still hoping that his new evening friends would pay him a visit. He also rubbed his hands together to ward off the low temperatures that permeated his outer extremities. This night did possess an abnormal chill. To be sure, the cold at this time of year was an expected guest, but this year the *Sjeverac*, the Northern Winds, hit harder than a headmaster's strap. Even the most ardent felt its whip.

Padanje[1]

Alone at the foot of her bed, Vjera pondered the day's earlier conversation. As the family discussed the bitter weather, she, as older folk can, taunted them with stories of harder winters that lived long ago. "When you were a little lad, Mijo, perhaps five or six, it snowed so much and so often, we forgot what the sun looked like," she had mocked. "The snow reached beyond the roof of the smaller village houses. You're lucky your great-grandfather built this two-story beauty."

She continued, "There was the winter a year before your birth. It was so cold the snow dare not fall. The ground was ashen and ugly. It was as if death took a hold of everything. At least we are getting a pretty blanketing this year."

But now that she was alone, with the One Who Made Everything, including thought, Vjera spoke whispered truths, admitting her comments were bravado. In actuality, her hidden concern over the difficult conditions was growing daily.

Vjera sighed. This year's blanketing had been severe. The sky always seemed gray; everything else was white. The sky-scraping trees that surrounded their homes did their best to hold off invasion, but

1 Falling

there were just too many flakes enforcing the territorial occupation. In some places, five feet of extra mountain height plonked itself down, becoming a constant winter squatter, eagerly stealing the lush green fields from each villager's mind. The need to shovel just to get out the door was a real, nightly fear. Earlier that day, Mijo mentioned that the snow had been falling for twenty-three consecutive days. That amounted to a lot of digging.

Though she did her best to ignore it, the cold had transposed into Vjera's bones. She barely thawed last summer before the tundra returned. Vjera wondered how many winters she had left, leaving her additionally afraid. Not for herself, for she knew what the gift of forever sleep would bring. No, she worried for others in a way increased age made you reflect on the mortality of others. She lamented mostly for the welfare of her son, his wife, and their young family.

"*What might find them?*" she pondered. The awful weather reminded her of the recent brutality of the world. This hurt had tormented many other places far worse than her little alcove, but sad tidings still haunted her. "*Was no one left untouched by the evil men and women show each other?*" Quickly she concluded, "*Not anymore!*" Even a place in the middle of nowhere, between Catici and Kopjari, was not spared.

With this understanding, Vjera also fretted that her village was changing, moving quicker every year. Lamentably, the village could not hibernate until spring like it used to. A growing trend witnessed more husbands seeking additional work to supplement the growing list of needs that their once productive little farms now could not provide. Each year, these lists would find their way to the factories and mines in Vareš and Kakanj. The gusts and biting cold made these treks hazardous, almost as hazardous as the work that would find them at the end of their travels. This type of weather was not built for walking meters, let alone multiple kilometers. Though Vjera rejoiced that Mijo's full larder meant he did not have to make the journey, she knew a large number that would trudge for hours in the deep slosh.

But Vjera had a plan. To combat this increased worry, her prayer time was growing too. Alone with her vocal rustlings, her faded red rosary beads, and memorized "Our Fathers," Vjera battled on with another marathon genuflecting session. For one hour, two hours, three hours and more, she was in her quiet place, repeating each prayer over and over, even though these sessions would leave her in great pain. Her arthritic hands, moving over each bead would throb stiff. Her feet and knees would swell, leaving her unable to walk for hours after. Undeterred, she kept on. Like most recent efforts, Vjera knew tonight was going to be a long night.

Everywhere Vjera looked there was required prayer. And as Vjera knelt late that evening, she was reminded that prayer was needed most during times of darkness. It did not have to be nighttime for Vjera to see how truly dark it was.

Yet, while being aware of the worst, Vjera prayed for the best. Each day Vjera prayed that the Sutjeska could be the place, for even a brief time that did not have to face hate's storms, its stings and its winters. Vjera prayed that maybe she might be allowed to soak in the smiles of peace from the faces of the children, and the children's children. Fifty-six years she had waited to see that dream fulfilled, at least for one moment. It had not happened in her lifetime. At least not yet. She always believed it could happen, that somehow, one day it would happen. She just would need to be patient a little longer. Her body, however, was unsure how long Vjera could wait.

Each snow day produced a different result within Mijo. As his father and grandfather before him, Mijo proudly refused the elements entry into his home. Despite the devil's howls, his family slept in their house and roared back. They did not live like kings, but thankfully, the four of them ate well enough. The larder held a healthy level of provision; enough to feed the many visitors that came to their front door. Whether guest, or unexpected empty stomach, God had provided enough for every additional mouth. This was a good thing too, because another baby was on the way. Vjera was adamant it was another boy. She said she could tell. Mara and Mijo did not argue with her and her ways, because you just didn't argue with your elders. Besides, time would tell them soon enough either way.

This was another reason why Mijo loved his quiet nights. He could ponder his growing family and his place in the mountains. As a boy, Mijo was enraptured by old family stories, particularly about his great-great-great grandfather Pepan, who had killed a wolf with his bare hands. With the same blood running through his veins, the youthful Mijo ventured all over Sutjeska, regardless of the time of the day, in all weather conditions to explore his mountain.

Though he was now older, Mijo still knew this place was a divine birthright. And perhaps because of this, sometimes, as he sat, when most beguiled by his aloneness, Mijo could almost hear the mountain wisdom being whispered by his ancestors. And in those brief seconds, Mijo felt worthy of his name of Pavlović, like a conquering hero of old.

He was proud that his history was secure, yet tomorrow left him so uncertain. Mijo wondered if the next generation would be able to battle the elements as his forefathers did. Was it too soon to doubt his son? Mirko was only four, but Mijo did not appreciate his young son's sense of folly. This did not make him mean, or a cruel father. Perhaps Mijo at worst was simply too serious. Recent times and the most recent events that reshaped Eastern Europe and the very world could be blamed for some of this. It was just that Mijo saw the mountains as a serious business, for serious people.

In those moments, opinions other than his own would creep in and also sit by Mijo's fire. Many of the village shared Mijo's belief, or maybe fed his concerns. Most of the comments were light in nature, but words spoken can float on the breeze, and dangerously go where they please, even to foreign ears. "The boy is silly," they would say with a laugh. "He is a *budala*[2]," or "He is *blesav*[3]," they would state.

Mirko didn't help matters. He often would be found standing on

---

2 Fool

3 Stupid

his head, singing songs of pure nonsense. And when not performing his acrobatic musical act, Mirko loved to also spend his free time running into neighboring chicken coops, yelling at the top of his lungs, while dressed in only in his underwear and a woolen hat. Be it summer or winter, there was Mirko in his uniform of choice, invading the peace of these poor birds, and loving the moment far too much.

"He is too silly," they would comment. "Perhaps he is even *lud*[4], like Marshall Tito is lud."

And though the village and Mijo agreed, he was outnumbered in his own home. Mara would tell him not to worry, reminding him they could do with some silliness after everything everyone had been through, and were still going through.

Anyway, Mara thought her son was funny. Mara found it funny when he would bark like a dog, or howl at the moon before bedtime. She thought it funny when the boy would ask older children in the village if they knew where his sheep had gone. The joke was, there were no sheep, though of course, they did not know that. As these unsuspecting folks prepared to assist the cheeky blighter find his ewes, he'd run away cackling.

Vjera's thoughts on Mirko were similar. Unfortunately for Mijo, she would express them in more blunt terms, perhaps in a way only a mother is allowed to.

"You're stupid, Mijo! Mirko is *slatki*[5]. There is a sweetness to your son," she would state firmly.

Vjera saw beyond Mirko's cheeky disposition in a way Mijo could not. She saw much more. In his quieter moments there was a softness in his tone. There was a natural charm and hidden depth. On the occasion the young boy sat silently, it looked as if he was pondering great thoughts. It was at these moments, Vjera loved nothing more but to pick up her grandson, hold him close with her eyes closed, and soak those thoughts in. "Pure sweetness," she would

4 Crazy
5 It is the male possessive to the word slatko, used earlier to explain sweetness, kindness, etc...

proclaim. Vjera especially loved the way he looked back at her, with a piercing stare, which owned a deep love. All could see, even Mijo, that Mirko loved his grandmother. When he wanted a hug from his grandmother, which was often, Mirko would charge at full speed, unconcerned about how her aging body might fare from the crashing collision. Mijo once demanded that Mirko show extra care, but Vjera would scold Mijo for interrupting and tell him to "get away" from both of them. The young boy placed a mark on his grandmother far deeper than some simple bruising. Before the young lad was born, since the death of her husband, her heart did nothing but ache. But Mirko had helped heal this, and Vjera loved him for it.

"Pure sweetness, do you hear?" Vjera demanded.

But the echo of these words did little to calm Mijo's nerves. The mountains were harsh on most men who are made of harder stuff. This place could do real harm to those who are too silly, or too sweet. This type of damage could not be fixed with medicine. Mijo's father was a colossus and the mountain had defeated him too soon. But, while wrestling with these jangled thoughts, Mijo reasoned that those who were a little crazy had a chance, giving him some comfort.

"A bee sting in winter," Mijo chuckled. "Silly, maybe crazy."

As Mijo sat and thought about all of this, he rubbed his chin with his left hand, while his right tussled against a three-legged side table. On the top of the table sat a white embroidered tablecloth, given to him by his grandmother. Though this cloth was dulling the *tappitty-tap* of Mijo's fingers, its force clinked a small glass and a half-drunk bottle. Without thinking, this noise reminded Mijo to refill a glass that was already three-quarters full. And yet, as he sank deeper into his chair, he promptly forgot about his drink, though he was still holding it.

As Mijo lost himself within future possibilities, his eyes scanned the differing corners of the living room area that held the history of his life. Through the scope of scattered candles, oil lanterns, and darkness, you might see the handiwork of Mijo's family. A carved table from his grandfather. The clock from his great-grandfather. The chairs from his great uncle. The wooden paneling on the walls provided by his father. The upholstered red chair stenciled with yellow wild flowers scented by Vjera's grandfather's tobacco pipe, and recent fire ash.

While the first floor was a sparsely affixed working environment with simply a picture of the Pope, a Catholic calendar, and a crucifix, the second story was a cozy environment that nightly protected each set of slumbering toes. From this seat, like a Lord of the Manor, Mijo could see all and soak it in. And yet tonight the view strangely was unsatisfactory. He could not settle. His mind was in flux, and he unusually needed motion. His eyes were scanning with unnatural haste, seeking something that was not there. "Bee stings. Silliness!" he muttered.

Frustrated, he jumped up, zipped down the stairs, and with an outstretched left arm flung open his front door. His feet followed, he reasoned, so to make sure they were not snowed in. In truth, Mijo went outside in hope that the fresh air would repair his jangled nerves. Now outside, he stood surprised, for the snow had stopped falling. "Wow, respite! Maybe that's all the mountain's got?" Mijo wondered, somewhat hopefully, somewhat arrogantly, as if his years in the mountains ensured he knew what was to come tomorrow.

Mijo took a depth breath from his vista. Consuming the cold air was a wonderful food substitute if the cupboard was bare. Like everyone else, Mijo had eaten that type of mountain cuisine a time or two. On this night Mijo was hungry, but not for food. Strangely the freezing air did not provide the usual satisfaction. It tasted different. Mijo did not like it at all! With expectations unmet, this curious air created unease. Rather it had none of its usual clean crispness, but rather a tangy sourness, providing an awful dry aftertaste. Mijo quickly drank from his glass that he only now realized his right fist was still gripping. He hoped that it would wash away this foreign odor. It did not. Far from removing the mouthed muck, it exacerbated it!

He took another big breath of the mountain air to make sure. Dreadfully, the air's taste was still there, and now it further invaded him. It was in his nose, quickly obeying gravity's laws by traveling into the throat, and in an instant, it was in his stomach. Its rapid plunge left Mijo queasy. He wondered if perhaps he had drunk some bad rakija. He remembered that Josip, a neighbor, and Mara's cousin who lived four houses down, made the bottle he was drinking. He promised himself that this would be the last time he took a bottle from that incompetent.

Mijo took another taste of the air. His stomach was still unhappy with the world, but more so. Though this additional breath made him feel worse, thankfully it confirmed it was not the rakija. Mijo was glad for that because Josip had given him two other bottles that were currently unopened, nestled safely on the first floor shelf near the crucifix and the calendar.

Losing interest in drink, Mijo dropped his glass and its remaining contents in the snow, and staggered a few steps beyond his door, hoping to clarify what was happening to his mountain. Mijo was shuffling only a few paces away from his front door, and yet for the first time in his life there was unease to his mountain travels. Was he afraid? Maybe. Why? He did not know.

"Bee stings in the winter?" Mijo mocked, equating his foolish behavior to that of his small child.

As he chided his own behavior, Mijo's mind spun at a worrying pace. Each revolution motioned faster than a pinwheel in a gale, leaving Mijo's small comfortable world feeling off-kilter and vast. Mijo did not like it at all! It was as if he had an acute case of vertigo.

"A bee sting in winter? Crazy," he muttered once more, as he had a dozen times.

Staggering up to his water well, he leaned against its sturdy structure, worried he might be blown over. Using the structure to prop himself up, Mijo huffed and puffed, completely exasperated while staring at the surrounding strong cluster of similar homes. Each had its thick, strong-built mud brick walls, and its blackened roofs. All hardy enough for whatever elements dare to come he thought.

And yet, as he readied himself to further test his senses that he was not trusting, Mijo froze. Something captured his attention! The 'something' was brighter than white; a blur of light, perhaps. Tiny in size and ultra-fast, and about forty paces away, the entire moment was less than a second, giving Mijo little time to comprehend the illogical glimmer captured by the corner of his right eye.

"Mijo, what are you doing outside?" asked a familiar voice.

Mijo hesitated in responding, still fixated on what he did or did not see. "Nothing Mama," he replied finally.

"What is the matter, son?" she pressed, knowing something was troubling him.

"My stomach hurts a little. It's nothing," said Mijo. "Why aren't you sleeping?" he asked, to change the subject.

"Old women don't need sleep," she replied, hobbling closer. "Maybe that's your problem all these years. You are just a *stara baba*!"[6] She continued to chuckle. "But really," a serious concern returning to Vjera's demeanor, "What is it?"

"I thought I saw something," Mijo muttered, half to his mother, half to himself.

"Oh? What was it? A wolf?"

Mijo shook his head. "Nah, no wolf. I haven't seen a wolf around our village for a long time, Mama. It was nothing. Strange sky tonight, I guess. A shooting star or something," he reasoned. "It was nothing. What are we doing out here?" he continued with a rhetorical chuckle, as he headed back towards the house.

"Maybe the snow will return tomorrow. I need to go to bed. Good night Mama."

"Are you sure you're alright?" Vjera asked one more time, noticing her sons unnatural wish for sleep.

"Yes Mama. *Bog*."

"Yes dear. God be with you too," Vjera replied.

"And son?" she continued with a laugh, "be careful not to be stung by any bees while you sleep."

"Right," Mijo muttered, half to himself. "Crazy kid," he continued.

✳✳✳

---

6 Old grandmother

Chapter 2

But Mirko was not crazy. He was not quite correct, either. Don't fret for the lad though. Most of us will find ourselves living between being right and being crazy. He is luckier than most to start learning this lesson at such a young age. But, to repeat, Mirko was not stung by a bee. Bees sting to hoard what they have. It was not a bug either. Bugs come to pester, and Mirko's evening guest did not arrive to agitate, despite the protestations of both father and son.

No, the thing that 'bit' Mirko was a far better thing. If Mijo knew what disturbed his son, even he would have agreed. Europe's mountains, and its tree-lined landscapes, are full of the unknown. In a feeble attempt to explain, famous scribes and poets write of gnomes, goblins, witches, and ghouls, and winged fairies. Those stories are pure gibberish.

The Sutjeska had their own stories of legend and fables too that scratched around truth's surface. They attempted to remind the people of better days and past glories, before the Austro-Hungarian Empire, and before the Ottoman came to stay. The most popular stories centered on kings like Tomislav, the greatest of Bosnian rulers. The stories say that under their king's rule, the people were rich beyond their dreams, riding Arabian horses bred in their own fields, wearing tasseled gold that was as pure as the August sun. Their garments had so much fabric they wore extra around their necks to show off, calling them *Cravats*. During their time, the legend was, that the place was once a flat land, until King Tomislav read a passage where it was said that the faith of a mustard seed could move a mountain. He wanted that type of strength, so he went to find a mountain to bring back for his plains. It was said he rode many months, but he finally found one that had a very old forest full of mystery and misunderstanding.

But, this mountain was bought at a great price. The wealth was gone, replaced by harsh winters. Perhaps because of this, the stories, like the old kings and their colts, nowadays do no more than fertilize the soil, leaving those who remain not knowing the difference between fable and non-fiction.

But thankfully, that very evening was about remembering, proving its events were not a fabrication. The creatures in question were a real gift, because they bring treasure. The type of treasure that people live and die for. No, they are not bees, not gnats, not bugs or flies to swat at. Nor are they goblins that crawl out of dark holes at night. Their names are far better fitting, monikers long ago given by the mountains. They are known as Dreamers, or Figments. However, they are best known as Wisps.

You scoff, thinking I jest. I do not! Wisps are as real as me, and the people they find. They are more than just an old Baba's bedtime fable created to scare the out of wits of children as they go to bed. They are realer than most things you see in broad daylight, though they come in the night, as it is easier under the cover of stars for them to complete their work. They come to grant gifts to whomever they deem worthy. What do they gift? More than just themselves, though after they plant their one and only kiss, they live no more. They gift the one thing that keeps all freethinking creatures alive.

Dreams! They give dreams, because even Wisps know, though hearts pump blood, and the brain monitors your need for oxygen, it is dreams that stir the soul as a reminder that something greater created us. And at differing times upon a generation, when they deem it right, the Wisps move.

Excited, they move readied to change a single soul, or a complete civilization. But isn't that the same thing? They move in unison, singing beautiful tunes. But alas, we who they visit cannot hear them. There are millions of them, but we cannot see them. Only the ears of the mountains and the heavens can hear them. Only the angels can sing with them. But if we were to take a deep breath, we could taste and smell them. Especially at this time of year, when the snow is at its whitest, their flight adds additional crispness to the air, perfuming and even changing its texture. To some, the change is unpleasant, but to many the Wisp's create a meal so good, food need not touch your lips for a week.

And on this night, the air was especially scrumptious. The Northern Winds whipped up a strong cold push to ensure the perfect dancing weather - in the midst of dancing mountain people. The Wisps were readying the *Folklor* once more. The Kolo was about to be danced.

Chapter 2

The *Folklor*, the mountain people say, was created by King Tomislav. That is not true either. In reality, it was a gift given by the Wisps for the people to dance their troubles away. But people have a habit of carrying troubles, and forgetting to dance. Thankfully, the Wisps on this night, returned to show the next generation how they were supposed to dance. In the midst of the falling snow, the Wisps begin their intricate patterns with the unique song in their heads, each as unique as your thumbprint. Each Wisp is a graceful Bolshoi, dancing on the grandest of vistas. With each spin, pirouette, and tumble, the Wisps showed that there was much for them to celebrate.

Beyond their tasks, there was an additional reason to cheer. Indigenous to these mountains was the *Tisovina*, the Magic Tree. The holiest tree to the people of these mountains was holy to the Wisps too. The Wisps believed that simply a small morsel of the Tisovina would enhance the power of each of their dreams. Like a sugar-covered bonbon to a child, it gave the creatures a rush, making their flight even more beautiful, in colors created only for angels, on the holiest of nights.

The Wisps' time was now. The Wisps could smell the trees, and it sent them into a joyful frenzy! Generally, the Wisps would soak up the entire night, flying as high and far as possible. After all, they are built to fly and parade.

But this night was different. They were placed within reach of the grandest of trees. This left them a difficult choice. They could dance as high and far as possible before the sun arrived, or visit the Tisovina, eat from its sap, and further empower their gift.

But if they chose the tree, there was a risk! One night of life is so short, and yet there was so much to accomplish. What would each of them do? The Wisps knew only too well that there are only so many children to visit in this region, and only so much dreaming they can take in an environment so harsh. They all had to choose what to do, because if they did not decide before sunrise, their gift would die with them. This was unacceptable to a Wisp. If there was one Wisp mantra, it was a dream wasted was truly a terrible thing.

People are blessed and cursed by dreaming. Hopes are lifted by it. Societies rise and are crushed by the expectations of them. With each dream, the next generation has a chance to make something of itself. There is a risk too. Either they will show they are better or more arrogant than the last.

Mirko knew nothing about societies being shaped, and ideals being transformed into action. All he knew was the night was cold and his sleep was interrupted by something, and then his father scolded him for it. He could never have guessed what it was. He supposed it was a bee.

Well, this "bee" gave Mirko a gift. For the first time, this child of only five winters, whose eyes had only known mountains and peaks, snow-covered beech and Norway spruces, visited faraway places he didn't know existed.

On this particular night while wrapped in soft cotton blankets and wool, Mirko received a gift of ships and ocean cruisers. For the first time, he heard terms like 'starboard,' 'port' and 'aft.' For the first time, a boy who knew only sheep bleating and cows mooing, saw dolphins cackling, cutting through waves the size of Silver Firs, while being chased by great whites. He saw whales maundering in the warmest of bays with their newest calves. A boy whose stomach rarely knew meat that night feasted on barbequed barramundi, steamed cod, and fried catfish. On this night, this boy giggled while being tickled by the water's spray. On that night, Mirko learned of a happiness he did not know existed.

The mountain smiled too. Not just with Mirko, but also with all the children who slept sounder than ever before over its landscape. Mirko was not the only one to dream new dreams. The Wisps created many figments of vivid imagination across this Eastern European night. All of those receiving gifts would dream dreams of places that seemed warmer, happier and freer. However, something else happened that night that was exciting, and terrifying at the same time. Mirko was not the only one in his father's home to be nibbled at by phantoms buzzing.

With one unexpected kiss his unborn sibling, who up till that moment had rested peacefully for almost its entire forty weeks, allowing his mother the easiest of pregnancies, violently jumped and kicked. The child stomped so hard it awoke his mother, and even his father, who unexpectedly had dozed off.

"What is it now?" bellowed Mijo, his evening further ruined.

Looking at his now standing wife, he felt aggrieved at asking what appeared a stupid question. But like most things that evening, the appearance of things and its reality make fools of everyone. If all had known what just had happened, Mijo could have said it was the fairest question he had asked of himself or anyone else that night. After all, something out of the norm should be questioned and better understood.

The complete answer to Mijo's question was this: firstly, the Wisp that visited Mirko had drunk a little too much from the Tisovina and was almost seen, which would have been unfortunate. He got lucky, despite his sloppy stomach bite that should not have been more than an unnoticeable peck. But what had happened to the unborn babe was that the child was unfairly disrupted by an overzealous and out of control Wisp. Yes, the unborn babe was given a gift by a Figment. Though not a written Wisp law, it was a generally accepted rule that the unborn should be left alone. The offending Wisp would have generally agreed. Each Wisp knew unborn children have the gift to dream their months away, without the additional assistance. But the Wisp had drunk too much from the Magic Tree. He had made its choice to stay and consume from its trunk, and then took too long to find the right child to give his dream to. So he did what he thought was best, despite his inebriated state. All that the Wisp could think of as he flew erratically was that a dream was a terrible thing to waste.

Was this supposed to happen? Who knows? Fate and coincidence are strange bedfellows, and exuberance and impetuousness are blood brothers, unwilling to live peaceably on their side of the line. Why did this happen? Perhaps the answer simply is sometimes those who can go too far, do. And when they do, something that might not have occurred does.

✳✳✳

Mijo wondered if peace and quiet was ever going to return to his home. After tossing and turning for what seemed hours, he got out of bed and placed his face as close to his clock as he could. Even without any light, Mijo could make out that the time was now sixteen past three. He could not believe it; he had been asleep less than an hour. He continued to stare at his clock, just to make sure time was still moving.

Mijo went towards his son's room, having a powerful, unshakable urge to make sure he was okay. There, he found his boy sleeping soundly, with a large smile on his face, and his backside raised as high as it might go, in a way only children can comfortably sleep. Seeing how happy his son looked, Mijo took a deep breath. As he consumed this oxygen, Mijo realized his stomach was untroubled, and the recently awful taste in his mouth was gone.

"Sweetness," Mijo muttered to himself about his son. "Pure, crazy sweetness."

And with everything seemingly back to normal, Mijo returned to his room, fell back asleep and dreamed.

-3-
Magla[1]

Mijo awoke shivering, startled. He had no idea where he was. He was not in his room, nor in any part of his house. He was not even in the surrounding areas of his village, or at least he did not think he was. Worse still, he couldn't recall how he was snatched from his home and put in this foreign place. His primary senses were further disorientated by an immensely heavy blanket of fog blinding him, making understanding his surroundings a frustrating impossibility. Without his eyes, he felt helpless, hopeless and paralyzed by the uncertainty that a million valid questions could bring. Where was he? Was he taken? Did he sleep walk? How far could he have gone?

The clouded cocoon made him question whether he was even on his mountain. The entire situation made him question his sanity. He asked himself, how does someone just go from one place to the next, without knowing how? Fear had engulfed him. What was going to happen to him? Unfortunately, there was no guide to enlighten this wayward traveler on where his feet or state of mind were.

Mijo yelped for help, thinking even if nobody could find him in this mummified tomb, at least they all would know they were lost together. He called over and over again, but the only voice he

---

1 Fog

heard was his own. Not a soul replied. Not a bleating from a lamb, a mooing from a calf, or buzzing of an insect. Nothing! It was as if this fog perfectly insulated all noise. He attempted his desperate call again and again, without reward. Only once his voice became hoarse did Mijo accept the strange reality: he was all alone.

Thoroughly petrified, little of what was occurring made any semblance of sense. All he could recall was being in his son's room moments before, then asleep in his bed next to his very pregnant wife. And now he was here, wherever here was, outdoors covered in dew, cold, and confusion. With the sun and moon perfectly hidden, he could not even tell if it was still nighttime or if a new day had dawned. In this fog, time lost meaning. It could have been minutes, hours, or days since his last conscious thought. If he wore a watch in this place, it might have started spinning anti-clockwise, so surreal was the entire experience. Despite actual evidence, his mind stubbornly insisted that he had to still be on his mountain. It had to be, right? However a stark truth remained: anybody who might know his voice had yet to answer any of his persistent cries.

Mijo closed his eyes and consumed multiple long breaths, readying himself for what he had to do next. He had to move from the place, despite nature's blindfold, and he had to go right now. Mijo could sense that danger lurked. He attempted to quickly calculate what he knew, before traveling with the haste required. Desperately, he knew little. Mijo found himself still dressed in his sleeping attire, and he did not have his shoes, leaving his feet exposed to the elements. He was out in the middle of somewhere, which might have been smack bang in the middle of nowhere and he knew not how he got here or how he was going to get out of here, wherever here was.

And yet, while surrounded by the awful uncertainty, Mijo found something positive to cling to that surprisingly made him smile a very big smile. On top of the sturdy soil, his toes were wiggling in the grass. He felt grass, and if he felt grass, most joyfully, that meant here was no snow. To make certain he quickly crouched down to the ground with his hands. Blissfully, his feet were not liars, for

Chapter 3

as soon as his knees and fingers connected to the ground; they dove in lush green clover. "Grass, grass!" he laughed. He put his nose in it, and its freshness made him sneeze. He laughed a long, clean, loud laugh of happiness that left him winded, and gasping for breath. He did not realize how tired he was of the wintry battle, and how happy he was that at least another year was defeated.

Mijo could have lain in these peaceful surroundings forever, but the urge to move on returned. He did not know what was driving his senses from this place, but he did not doubt them for an instant. He had to move, and it did not matter in which direction.

As he rose from the turf, he attempted to swipe a handful of the fresh green grass, as a comforting keepsake. But as hard as he might, Mijo could not rip a single blade free from the ground. He pulled and tugged. He ripped and yanked, but the blades refused to cooperate. He gripped a tuft with both hands, and strained with all of his might, collapsing backwards from fatigue still clutching nothing but the fog. Frustrated, Mijo stomped his feet, cursed the ground below him, and cursed his predicament. Crawling away frantically in a crabbed like manner, Mijo wished that that he had never found the grass in the first place.

"Help, help!" over and over he called as he moved, tears traversed down his face, and wetting his neck.

His despair was a greater shadow than the fog, and it engulfed Mijo. The unanswered questions brought on by this wicked blindness swelled up within him. He hated this moment more than any he had in his entire life. So open was his wound it reminded Mijo how he felt when his father died, but remarkably, this hurt him more. "*This could not be home,*" Mijo agonized. His home would never do this to him, could it? Just entertaining this betrayal was too awful. Mijo was almost ready to just end his quest and curl up in the fetal position to be found by whatever created this mess.

But with each humbling despair, a small flicker of resolve was born that kept him moving. He had to get home. His movements were small and slow, but he was moving. The further Mijo moved, the more his senses calmed, and refocused to the challenge before him. Excited, Mijo realized he was not just moving forward, he was traversing an incline. Mijo's smile returned, realizing if he was going up, he might be traveling up his mountain, and back home.

After a period of serenity, if by magic after traveling on all fours like a dog for minutes - or was it hours? Again he was not sure. Mijo's hands ran into a solid structure, almost butting it with his head like a ram. Moving his hands across it, Mijo recognized rock and mortar. It was about six feet wide, which was only slightly smaller than Mijo's present smile, because he knew with almost certainty what this construction was. Moving up against it, the building was approximately four feet high. Beyond the rock and mortar's highest point there was a wooden bucket hanging below a roof type enclosure. It was a well. It was his well! He had found his home. He was standing right in front, some fifteen feet below it. Relief and panic swept over Mijo simultaneously. If he was home, where was everyone else? Why was it all so silent? Did this fog consume and confuse everyone in his entire village? Was his entire family lost to it too? He yelled out, fearing the worst.

"I am here!" he yelled over and over again. "I am here! I am here!"

Faintly, in between his desperate calls, Mijo thought he could hear soft murmurings in the relative near distance. Leaving the safety of the well, Mijo scampered recklessly towards the newly discovered sound. By moving towards it, quickly Mijo discovered the noise was coming from within his house.

"Oh God," Mijo whispered in prayer, fearing the unknown.

With his hands and the newly found wailing as his guide, within seconds Mijo hit his front door in full stride. Painfully, his lips, nose, cheek, and right ear became one with the house's main entry point. Mijo shook off the painful cobwebs, and realized the noise he heard was the soft, dull cries of a woman he did not recognize. He quickly found the front door handle and yanked at it. It did not budge. Violently he tugged at it, but it refused to comply. The door was locked.

"What is this?" Mijo questioned loudly.

Chapter 3

His front door had never in his entire life been locked, but today it was. Mijo pounded on the door, demanding its opening.

"Who's in there?" he protested. "Let me into my house!"

No one answered his question or demands. Not the door, not the fog, and not the voice inside. The muffled cries simply continued repeating, like a recording. Mijo cupped his right ear to the door. Finally, he could hear what was being cried.

"Mijo, help. It's mine," muttered the distant voice. Over and over it repeated, "Mijo, help. It's mine."

"What's yours?" asked Mijo.

"Mijo, help. It's mine."

"Wait, I'm here," Mijo said awkwardly. "I'm coming."

Mijo was desperate. He needed to get to that mumbled, confused voice. It was the only voice he had heard other than his own during this entire bizarre episode, and it was coming from inside his home. Maybe it would have answers to all the questions he had: about the fog, the locked door, and how the voice knew his name and where his family was. So he had to get in, locked door or not.

With his entire might, Mijo forcefully rammed his right shoulder into the door to ajar it open. Over and over he hit it, with everything he had, shaking the wooden structure. But his effort was foolhardy. The door was built to last forever. An ox with an ax would have struggled to break through.

"Mijo, help. It's mine," rang in his ears with each unsuccessful barge upon the door.

"Wait, I am here," Mijo whispered, his resolve breaking into tears that returned to his cheeks.

Mijo slumped to the floor, feeling bankrupt. With his head and ears in his hands, he wanted nothing more than to block out the woman's voice. Everything hurt. His head. His feet. His shoulder. His heart. He noticed his lip was bleeding. His eyes felt bloodshot, having worked so hard to see through the fog. But amazingly, this action to block out the calls proved feeble. His futile attempts to close everything out only increased its volume. The woman's voice was coming through clearer and louder. He could not keep her out! The more he tried, the more her voice and the fog tightened their grip. Mijo was trapped. There appeared no solution to break him free of the thick mist. There was no way to get into his home, and no way to keep the voice out of his mind. Mijo was miserable, desperate, cold and in pain.

Suddenly, someone hit Mijo in the right shoulder. It was as if he was still hitting the door. Then it hit him again. Lost in his self-pity, Mijo shrugged off the strike by refusing to acknowledge it.

"Mijo, get up and help me," the voice commanded.

"Wait, I am here," Mijo muttered, blubbering spit, snot and blood, totally defeated.

However, the voice was not done with him. It was coming through so clear it now sounded as if it was outside, though the door had not been opened and was in fact as Mijo found it, still locked. Someone hit him again, in the exact same point of his shoulder.

"Mijo, don't tell me to wait. It's time!"

"It's time?" he blurted. "Time for what?"

Suddenly, Mijo found his surroundings changed! His eyelids blinked rapidly, attempting to adjust. His eyes could no longer see any fog. It was all gone, replaced by pitch darkness. He realized he was now lying down, in his bedroom.

"Mijo, you idiot!" yelled a distressed Mara. "Fine time you start snoring. Mijo, it's time. *The baby is coming!*"

Reality returned with breakneck haste. "Oh," was all Mijo could mutter. Embarrassed and disorientated, he quickly scrambled out of bed to get help. Groggily, he ran into the wall, bruising his right leg before entering his mother's room, and in a most incoherent manner blurted out what was occurring.

Understanding perfectly, Vjera pushed past him, leaving Mijo standing in her room, dazed. Trying to shake off the overriding fatigue, Mijo looked at the clock. It was only fourteen minutes to four. It felt like hours and hours since he first freely lay in his bed, but his entire slumber was a total of only twenty-four minutes. It felt like the deepest, longest sleep of his life, but it was barely the duration of short afternoon nap. He sighed and wandered back towards his room. Before Mijo could enter, the door was slammed across his face.

Chapter 3

"Get Andja, from four houses down, you fool!" yelled his mother through the door.

The door quickly opened again, and out poured his mother's smiling face.

"And Son, get some water and towels ready too, dear." as the door slammed again.

Over the next few hours, village matriarchs came and went, mostly to attend to Mara's needs, but also to ensure Mirko was fed, and that Mijo was staying out of the way. Occasionally, they would ask Mijo if he was doing okay. He would nod, providing the appropriate polite partial answer. He was anxious for his bride and child, but having been awoken in the most disheveled state, it left him feeling inappropriately disjointed. More so, the fog that horded around him as he slept remained in his thoughts, leaving him exhausted.

As he sat, he concluded that he hated sleep more than ever. Mijo was uncertain what to do and where to be. His comfortable chair was uncomfortably too close to the action, so the Lord of the Manor sat downstairs amongst the masses and beyond his comfort zone. Mijo realized he really did not like sitting on the first floor away from his creature comforts. A few of villagers sat at the table with Mijo, surrounding multiple plates of cakes, egg and cheese pita, and an unopened bottle of rakija as the centerpiece at the ready to celebrate the imminent arrival of the newest mountain resident.

Mijo was not thirsty or hungry, and was feeling very distant. At that moment, he was lost in his thoughts, and though Mijo had known each person currently in the room his entire life, they all felt like strangers.

He was about to be a father again. What would this child grow to be, and was the child a boy or a girl? A girl or a boy? Was his mother right, or did fate wish to hand them another turn? Girl or boy? Boy or girl? He just had to wait. It had been hours. Or had it been minutes? It had been forty weeks? Or forty winks? The strangeness of the entire night had bewitched him. He felt sorry for himself. His lip hurt, as if he bit it while sleeping, and his right shoulder was sore, making him wonder momentarily where Mara had learned to punch. But mostly, Mijo's mind was wrapped in a bouncing collective of uncertainty, which he wished would roll away. His eyes were open, but he just could not awaken from his dream. Though he had been awake long enough to leave it behind, he still felt the presence of the muffled voice repeatedly begging for help.

"*What is taking so long?*" he argued within his frustrated mind. He needed something real, to end these successions of the abstract. "*Patience,*" he reminded himself.

Girl or boy?

Suddenly, as his great-grandfather's clock ticked over to six past one in the afternoon, in the distance a new voice could be heard. Muffled, but constant. Beautifully, the voice spoke with the softest wailings, of the newest kind. The like only spoken when breath hits ones chest for the first time, and yet has the power to bring tears to the sternest of eyes.

Mijo jumped.

"Is it a boy or a girl?" he asked instinctively to a room full of people who could not know the answer. The room laughed without laughing at him.

"Mijo!" Vjera called, peering from behind the second floor door. She was smiling. Mijo could see her smile was full of joy and confidence. Smiling in a way that told him she knew all along.

"I have a second son," he told his mother.

"You have a second son, my son," Vjera confirmed.

"I'll be right up to see Mara and Mato," Mijo said announcing his newest son's name.

Vjera returned to Mara. The room erupted into back slaps, songs of thanks and praise and yelps of glad tidings. Mijo took a moment of aloneness in the midst of the crowd, sitting back down, and letting his head rest on his fists, elbowing his grandfather's table. Mijo took a deep breath and showed the room his large smile and red cheeks.

"Mato Tomislav Pavlović," he pronounced to the room. "My son!"

And with that, he leaped to his feet and up the stairs towards his future.

-4-

Vrijeme¹

Time either moves too fast or too slow for the anxious. For Mijo on this day, both were occurring in unison, finding him sitting somewhere between certainty and fluctuation. It also found him outside, holding a chair.

Glumly, he sighed. Mijo did not have anything to do but wait, but he did not wish to miss any more of it. And "it" was outside! Time was ticking. Mijo missed much of the morning by pottering around in circles. Circles! Mijo did not like moving in them. As he sat and breathed, Mijo pondered that circles were becoming more and more a part of daily considerations. The world, Mijo knew was full of circles far bigger than his, but now it seemed more things were annoyingly reminding him of it. That was why Mijo was sitting outside on a chair that was generally made for inside comfort. He was keen for his circle to begin dominating the day. He, in fact, hoped this day would never end.

This mountains vista found Mijo dressed most formally, different from his typical day-to-day attire. If the mountain wished to comment, it would have mentioned how impressed it was, as Mijo was wearing in his traditional best. Black pants, made from woolen

---

1 Time

cord, his best white shirt under a black vest of a similar fabric to the pants. Covering his almost-bald head was a small black Homburg, with a red macaroni.

Mijo was never much for overdressing, even with the beginning of cooler weather, but his attire was befitting the day. There was a wedding to be enjoyed. The bride was the daughter of Josip and Andja, the same Josip who lived a few houses down. The groom was from a good family from Veliki Trnovci. The happy couple had met at the *Kraljeva Sutjeska*. They fell in love, courted, became engaged and were to be married all in less than two months. Many thought that was not long enough, but Mijo noted to himself, when pondering the quickly arriving nuptials, "*Ko zna, zna.*"[2]

Mijo surmised the "I do's" were probably occurring at the Kraljeva Sutjeska at that very moment. For an instant, Mijo regretted he did not go along. But this thought was fleeting. Earlier, when he was given the option, Mijo had been most adamant about staying home. Mijo surmised both Mara and Vjera were there to represent the family and provide the happy tears first hand. He also had done his duty by reminding them to bring their handkerchiefs, so why else did he need to attend?

Because of this, Mijo was allowed to sit and wait in quiet solitude. This was not the general course of things during sunlight hours. It was especially peaceful as both of his sons, Mirko and Mato, were currently nowhere to be found, though they were expected back before midday. Mijo's right hand dug into his left side vest pocket, and pulled out a once gold-colored pocket watch. He knew time was running out before everyone would return, and his nerves jangled like the pocket's contents.

Flipping the timer's flap, his eyes met with both hands on the timepiece. It read twelve minutes to twelve. Impatiently, Mijo tapped his right foot. The festivities, he feared would arrive too soon for the entire Pavlović family to properly greet them.

---

2 "Who knows, knows." This delightful little phrase explains it's only the wisest that know things. This of course implies that those who don't know aren't too bright.

Chapter 4

"They'd better be here," Mijo sneered.

It wasn't like he did not know where they were. Both of his sons were creatures of their unique, if somewhat baffling habits. Mijo knew Mirko, his eldest, was by one of the local rivers, probably immersing himself. Mato, now thirteen – fourteen by next winter was a blur of speed and haste – most likely, Mijo mused, winning a race over a nearby hill. It had been that way ever since Mato took his first steps. It was if he was running that very same day, and both had been roaming ever since. Since Mato's feet learned to fly, twelve calendars have come and gone. Twelve birthdays. Twelve winters. Twelve saint name days. Twelve additional Central Party anniversaries. Mijo shook his head at the difference of his two boys and their preferred vocations.

Mijo looked at his watch once more to further confirm his annoyance. It was almost twelve.

Observers would doubt Mijo's vexations were completely the boy's fault. Lately, Mijo often personified agitation. What made it difficult was Mijo knew why. It was the growing circle's fault! On the appearance of things, his corner of the Sutjeska had not changed much, but in reality, Mijo knew much had, and little for the better. The annoying thing was it seemed like he, alone, had noticed.

However, today, Mijo needed to ignore these nagging concerns. Though each day brought its own troubles, todays were thankfully simpler. Easier to understand, and much easier to traverse. Today the concerns could focus on whether the wedding festival would be enjoyed by all. Or which long lost faces would Mijo get to see first? Or would the weather hold? Or other silly things, like whether his wife or mother would cry first at the ceremony. Or would there be enough rakija? Yes, Mijo chuckled, there was always enough.

The most troubling question, if Mijo chose, would be if both of his boys would return at the promised time of twelve? To that question, he was not so sure of the answer.

And yet, as Mijo pondered all of these little questions created just for today, other issues made for other days lurked in the shadows. They lurked beyond the *Dol*, their little valley. They lurked beyond the *Gaj*, the oak-treed bushlands just minutes from his home.

These other issues lived in dark unspeakable places, having first festered in larger circles far away. These shadow lurkers, were now tempting Mijo to condemn himself with problems not made for today, and what was worse, Mijo's own left hand was doing their biding, tempting him to look deeper. They all knew what tomorrow's problems were and where they lived. They lived in Mijo's right hand vest pocket.

Thankfully, Mijo's mind was still in control of his left hand, and it was able to shake it off. The hand, for the moment, complied. "Not today!" Mijo muttered. The item in his pocket could wait for the proper time, he reasoned. It could wait at least for a few days, his common sense chimed in. At least until after the wedding was over, Mijo concluded. That would give him three days to see both Mara and Vjera celebrating, and maybe for those three days, Mijo could also forget tomorrow's troubles.

Though Mijo left the pocket's contents alone, the shadows were not convinced. In the pocket was a letter. A letter addressed to Mirko. Mirko was now seventeen, a strapping lad, full of might and high ideals. Mijo had not opened the letter. That would not be right, but he had an idea what the letter was, and what was in it. He knew it was not a personal letter. Mirko got the occasional personal letter, from cousins or friends, but this was not one of those. This letter was different. The envelope and type font had an impersonal formality not associated with friendship. Furthermore, Mijo had seen these types of letters before. Their contents were not meant to be happy.

Mijo again urged his mind to be forgetful and ignore the coming winter. He closed his eyes and exhaled once more. First, he would enjoy today. Today would bring smiles and merriment, he concluded, almost to convince himself, and anyone else who might be listening. And even then, after the wedding party, the coming storms would have to wait for this season's harvest.

Reopening his vision upon the world, Mijo was glad to be struck with the gleaming bounty of Autumn's parade. As it stood at attention, fields of pleasure were waiting to be plucked, prepared, and cultivated. Feverish activity in a few weeks would overtake the

Chapter 4

entire landscape. Everyone who was capable, from the youngest child to the oldest baba, would allow the mountain to place sweat on their brow. This year's crop perhaps was not the best, nor the largest the village had even seen, however, the weather, praise be to God, had been kind to ensure a proud bounty. A royal return that any market square would be pleased to display.

Beyond this cultivated village soil and its soon to be harvested bounty, Autumn's majestic decay was in full color. What a sight it was! For multiple decades, Mijo had viewed the splendor of the fall season. Never did he tire of it. Sutjeska's vista had spent weeks perfecting its attire for today's celebrations, as if it was not to be outdone by Mijo's traditional garb. Towering timbers swayed in the softest of breezes, each playing a magnificent game of one-upmanship. The forest provided a marvelous mixture of plumes, with each dressed in an array of unique hues. Summer and annual greens of fern, forest, hunter, dartmouth, and dark spring were mixed appropriately with differing reds, yellows, and oranges of burgundy, saffron, jasmine, amber, mustard, gold, sunglow, crimson, carmine, maroon, auburn and cardinal and many other shades without proper names. Each species of tree, it appeared, was clothed by a master tailor who created its finest garment.

As Mijo soaked in his opulent surroundings, he finally felt alive. He grinned. He felt ready to embrace the festivities. In close proximity, the smells of his homeland were mixing perfectly with their wedding traditions. By this, his eyes confirmed what his nose smelt hours ago; three of the fattest sows roasting on an open fire. These pigs were being closely guarded by twelve disciples of traditional slow-cooking methods. As each swine gently spun on a spit so to ensure a journey from pink to crackling, Mijo could hear the twelve consuming newer tasks. A more odious but unfortunately more prevalent one around these parts: they were discussing a newspaper from Vareš that explained how Tito was marshaling each of their lives for the better, with new agriculture planning programs.

With fingers plugging his ears, Mijo purposely ignored the men and their decrees from Belgrade and focused on the smells of today's feast. Today smelled wonderful, and it made him smile a naturally crooked smile.

As Mijo's grin continued to be paraded before his small world through the throng of lazy smoke, he caught a flash. A blur of motion on the mountain's horizon. Pulling it out of his ear, Mijo placed his left hand above his eyes so to better shade his vision. By this, Mijo could see a young whippet, slender and strong, effortlessly gliding across the landscape making quick work of the undulating hills. Mijo knew from the speed and free moving hair, it was one of his sons, the youngest, Mato. As Mijo looked down at his watch he ceased smiling. Mijo muttered disdainfully, "About time."

-5-

Ples[1]

Down the mountain, Mato galloped. He had been running all morning racing kids from the village, and beating them, too. Even those a few years older. However, the older kids kept egging him on to race one more time, and although victory was sweet, these endless calls of one more time had made him lose track of it. Being on time was the one thing his father asked him to do that morning. He wanted to do that for him. But not all was lost. Not yet! Mato knew if he ran as fast as he could, he could find what he had lost, and get in front of it and the possible scolding from his father. With the need to make amends, Mato cut across the landscape, his father's voice chasing him over the last furlough. Even without having a watch, he knew he was cutting it close. Seeing that his father was sitting outside further enhanced Mato's nerves. Mato noted that his father never sat outside. As he returned to his doorstep, Mato noticed his father looked stern and cross. He might have been additionally worried, except his father always looked like that.

"Sir, I made it back in time, didn't I?" the youngest asked, arriving without even a loss of breath.

The question prompted Mijo to look again at his watch. It read

---

1 Dance

four minutes before noon. "Barely," he replied, nonplussed. "Where's your brother?"

Happy to have avoided the calamity of being late, whether real or imagined, Mato shrugged his shoulders.

"You haven't seen him?" pressed Mijo.

"Not since Mama and Baba left this morning," Mato noted.

"Well, then," his father replied confidently, "You know where he is then."

"I do?" said Mato, somewhat confused. "At the Trstionica?"

"Yes," began his father. "Where the creek meets the river."

"Really?" whined Mato, disappointed. "That's four kilometers away."

"It's more like five," replied Mijo. "You better run if you want to see any of the parade. *Brzo*². Make haste!"

Knowing an order was an order, Mato was a fired bullet. Mato really did not have to ask his father where Mirko was. Everyone who knew his brother knew he was at the edge were the local creek called the Potok, met the always frigid Trstionica River. The Trstionica was a fast moving mid-sized river that fed into the powerful River Bosna. Mirko spent all of his free time in what he called his Mississippi River. Ever since Mirko was a small boy, his only dream was to sail all the oceans. But lately, Huck Finn's time on the water had diminished because of his work commitments in Vareš. Five-days a week in the city left Mirko restless, meaning any free moments, would find him by the water.

As Mato ran towards his certain location, Mato knew Mirko would be either tinkering with his raft, or he would be making the newest toy model. Or he was fishing for trout. Mato hoped Mirko was fishing for trout. As Mato traversed downward, a flock of geese could be heard overhead. The birds were leaving the Sutjeska wedding party early. Mato stretched out his arms to mimic his flying friends. He loved all types of birds, whether predator or prey. He was envious. They were not restricted by laws of gravity or borders.

By the time Mijo's watch ticked to twelve past the lunch hour, Mirko was within Mato's sight, right where his father expected him

2 Quickly

to be. To Mato's disappointment, he was not fishing, but rather building his raft. The Titanic II, Mirko called it, with mocking derision. This was because the last raft broke into a thousand pieces on rocks further downward. Mirko said it was not the rocks that did him in, but his lack of boating education. The village gossip found Mirko's raft building and his reasoning hilarious. The mountain people worked the mountain and used the water. Mirko worked the water, using the mountain. While they all waited for this mountain lad to grow out of building toy boats, Mirko's imagination instead grew each year, just like a small stream finally reaching the River Bosna. Toy boats were not big enough anymore. He wanted to build something bigger, something better. He did not care that the few friends he had mocked him, calling him Noah. These friends would ask him when the flood was coming. He often would retort it already had, and his boat was the last chance to get out.

Mirko could see his brother rushing down the mountain towards him. Mirko knew why Mato was coming. He was late for the party. He promised his father he would be there to see the procession. But now that it was time to go, Mirko did not want to. He simply changed his mind. He felt old enough to do that. Without looking up from his efforts, Mirko happily greeted his younger sibling.

"Hello, *Mali*," he said.

"I'm not that small," Mato said, defending his stature. "You're late. Tata wants you back."

"I know I'm late," Mirko replied. "Did you see the birds fly overhead?" he noted, changing the subject.

"Yes, they were geese, about forty of them. Tata said you needed to come back with me." Mato replied, returning to the topic at hand.

"I will be there in a little while," Mirko said mater-of-fact. "I've got to get this finished."

Mirko attempted to further change the subject, pointing to a tree, about seven feet to the right.

"I caught a couple of trout. Take them to Tata."

Probably for the first time, Mato did not care about fish. "No! Tata said you need to come back with me," he protested.

"Sorry little one," Mirko noted, apologetically. "I can't right now. Tata will understand."

Mato chuckled. "Oh, c'mon Mirko. No he won't. He'll yell at me."

Mirko knew his brother was right. "Okay. Tell Mama. No! Actually, tell Baba, and she will tell Tata. That will get you off the hook. Now run along, or you'll get in trouble."

Mato knew there was no reasoning with Mirko. He was lost in thoughts of ocean spray as if he was Magellan, Columbus, or Heyerdahl. Giving up, once more Mato rushed to his village, and back towards his father's anger. Mato did not want his father to be angry with him. It wasn't his fault, right? He was only thirteen, he reasoned. And though worrying about what his father might say, as Mato got closer to the village, he could hear joyful yelps and cheers, and he forgot what he was worried about in the first place. With each quickening stride, he could better hear the songs. Glad tidings were following each note. Mato looked up at the horizon. On the dusty road, a procession of feet and tradition could be seen. The pomp and festivity had arrived.

Within moments, Mato was in its throng. He passed tables laid with rows of sustenance created by every village family. Hungrily, Mato told his stomach to wait. Soon, he could feast. Though his stomach grumbled, Mato believed everything had its proper time, and this was not it. His own mother and grandmother had been busy little bees for days, creating pans and pans of pita. Much flour had been thrown on the cooking tables and rolled into cakes, and other treats. Beyond cakes and pita there were cuts of cold and cooked meat. There were soups sitting near bread and butter. There were sweets and sugar treats. All waiting for him and everyone else. And though the cupboards had been barer this year than years before, today the sufferings could be defeated, making it all worth it.

Controlling his cravings, Mato met up with the throng on the main road entering Pavlovići just arrived from the Kraljeva Sutjeska, Mato witnessed the procession's order. At its front, it was led by the children, chaperoned by a small group of teenage girls, followed closely by a larger group of married-aged women. Behind them, taking a position of respect came the senior matriarchs. As he ran closer to the parade, it was the baba's that Mato heard singing. They were leading the wedding procession songs, as was their right. As the procession continued, Mato could see both his Mama and Baba out in front of the senior matriarchs. They were beautifully dressed in their *nošnje*, traditional dresses of wool, in black and white. Each nošnje had commonality, as they all were garnished with richly-colored threads of the most colorful kind, embroidered with patterns of beauty. In the old days, when Mato's great-great grandfather traversed this path on his wedding day, it was said all the women had pure gold hanging off their nošnje. These riches were now gone, so now it was mostly the striking colors of differing reds and the darkest, strongest blues that continued to convey the pride the mountain people had in these warm garments.

Each head was held high, as if this day were their day. In addition to the nošnje, each woman wore a headscarf of cotton to cover her hair. These were black. White socking covered the legs, and their feet were in traditional shoes. Each person who traveled down the path looked so regal. Mato imagined the kings and queens of old, and he could not believe they could have looked any better. And though their appearance pleased Mato, it was the songs that truly stirred his soul and made his heart race quicker than his feet. Song after song was sung, with the collective voices refusing to allow silence to take part in their joyful day. Their voices spread traditional songs of love and joy,

> *"Trepetika, trepetala puna bisera*
> *Aj ovi nasi bijeli dvori puni veselja*
> *Sta se ono gore bijeli, gore u gori*
> *Aj ono majka sina zeni pa se veseli"*

With the song's verse, the onlookers waited to sing it back to the parade. Each knew the words well, having heard these tunes as soon as they left the womb. Mato saw his mother stride by, so he waved proudly, singing. His mother, singing, smiled as she also waved back. Mara's heart swelled from seeing her son.

As she ventured down the road, Mara was basking in the glow of a beautiful wedding day. She knew the young bride well. She had changed her diaper once or twice and had fed her belly a number of times more than that over the years. And now, she was a woman, about to begin her own family. Mara did not have a daughter of her own, so she treated the young bride as if she was hers.

Mara had had a daughter briefly, but not anymore. She had been born three years after Mato. She had lived long enough to be named. They'd named her Kata, after Queen Katrina. But like Katrina, Mara's Kata had left the mountains too soon. After only ten days of life, God had taken her home. That was ten years ago.

For only ten seconds on this day, Mara allowed herself to think about her beautiful little one. But through this moment of reflection, she knew she was happy. She had two beautiful sons. They would provide her daughters, God willing. Mara started to tear again, but refusing to feel sorry for herself, she pushed through with a smile, glad she could sing and again share in the celebration,

> *"Savila se zlatna zica sa vedra neba*
> *Ah savila se mladozenji oko fesica*
> *Aj sa fesica djul nevjesti oko duvaka*
> *Svi se svati veselise, majka najvise,*
> *Aj doveli joj djul nevjestu, djulom mirise"*

Suddenly, through the singing, one could hear the clip-clop of hooves. The groomsmen arrived on horseback with a rush. Mato watched in awe, while wondering where they got those horses from. Traveling with such haste and power they looked so much older, wiser, and more important, even though most of the riders were around Mirko's age. Mato wanted to be able to run that fast, with that type of strength and power. He promised himself one day he would.

Lost in the fabric and color and noise of the procession, Mato did not notice his father calling him. Exasperated by Mato's

Chapter 5

ignorance to his persistent calls, Mijo unwillingly marched closer to the procession and towards his youngest, sternly tapping him on the shoulder.

"He wouldn't come," Mato sheepishly replied. "I tried."

This exasperated Mijo further, but he understood. He knew his oldest was stubborn. More so each month. But Mijo was stubborn too. Refusing to take no for an answer, he commanded his poor message courier to try again. "I need to see him now," Mijo confided. "I have to tell him something. He will want to know what I have to say."

"But the *Kolo* is about to start!" Mato defiantly replied, to his father's cryptic message.

"It will be going for the next three days, son. Plenty of time to dance and eat," Mijo sighed. "*Idi.* Make haste!"

Angrily, Mato trampled back across the five-kilometer journey. This left Mijo alone, to let out another sigh. Today had been a trying day. More than Mijo could have wished. Unwillingly, Mijo's left hand had overruled his mind and tunneled back into his right hand pocket. Mijo had planned on waiting to break the news, but now he was not so sure. Three days would be a long time to let anything burn a hole in ones vest pocket, especially since it was sitting so close to his heart. Mijo thought he could wait a little while, but now he knew he was wrong. Mijo reasoned with his new decision. He would keep the news from his wife and mother, at least during the wedding festivities. This way, he would not be breaking away from his original decision. They could have the next few days of merriment, but Mirko will be glad for the news. *"Why should I keep a good thing from my son?"* Mijo's mind chimed in. Perhaps, Mijo imagined, when Mirko hears the news, he will decide to enjoy the next few days with his family and not the water's edge. At least, Mijo hoped that might be his son's reply. He hoped his son might understand how important this was to his old dad. How he hoped.

✸✸✸

Mirko could see his brother returning once more. He wondered what he had to do to be left alone. In the past, his hide would have been sorely reddened for his defiance. Still, he did not care. Mirko concluded the party was three days long, and he would visit soon enough. He had work to do before he had to return to his employment two days from now. The family troubles and his need to travel down to Vareš had kept him from what he considered his most important work. "*Why can't everyone just understand this?*" pondered Mirko. He wanted this craft completed before the winter came. Time was running out! He could smell change coming. But here came his doltish brother, bringing unwanted messages. "I told you, I would be there later!" he yelled towards his younger sibling.

Mato ran up to the craft, right below his brother who was on its deck. "I know," he gasped, red faced and out of breath. "But he, Tata, said he has something important to tell you. He wants you to come now."

Mato did not care about this back and forth any longer, the message or anything else. He wanted to get back to the party. Back to the people. Back to the food. Back before the Kolo arrived.

The Kolo was a whirl of motion and color, music, and song. Accompanied by multiple tamburica players, two circles would be formed of varying size. Firstly, a group of young women holding hands would weave their procession line into a circle and start to spin and step with beauty and grace. On their lips would be songs of love and joy, similar to those heard in the wedding procession. In turn, a group of young men would place their arms on each other's shoulders. They too would spin and step, but with power and purpose. With each patterned step, they would sing a reply to the ladies, worthy of their beauty, worthy of their culture, and worthy to their families' name. With this dance, the courtship of the Kolo and their basis of Sutjeska's society would be in full elegant view.

Chapter 5

But the Kolo would just be in its infancy at this point. The fun was only beginning! In unison, each of the circles would spin separate from each other. A matrix of steps and the pattern of song, perfectly weaving, slowly gathered speed. Each member of the village would take part in the dance at some point. Mara would dance many Kolo's over the next few days. Vjera's feet and mind would overrule her aging body and dance as well. Even Mijo, though preferring to watch, would dance because of nationalistic pride. Mato, though very young, and not at all skilled in the patterns of the Kolo wanted to dance, too, and be a part of it. And right now he was kilometers away. It might as well have been a thousand. "C'mon Mirko. He wants you there!" Mato pleaded.

Mirko understood why his brother was being so persistent. "Am I making you miss the party, little brother?" He jumped off his craft, rubbing his brother's head mockingly.

"Yes you are. Let's go Mirko!" begged Mato once more.

In the foreground, if the two brothers could have ceased their arguing, they would have heard the tamburica players quicken their pace. The Kolo was gaining and at that moment, the two circles would become one! At this moment, the untrained eye might fret the circle's momentum appeared reckless. But each dancer knows what will come next. A smaller circle will break out and converge within the greater, larger circle with two men for each woman. Then the speed would gain some more. The young ladies will be picked up off the soil and fly. Yelps of joy will be heard. Delirium will be embraced. The onlookers will become drunk from the cultural sparks, flying from the dancer's effort. Like most of the village, Mato loved to watch the flight. And now he knew he was missing it. His brother was driving him to frenzy. Impatiently, Mato reached for Mirko's hand, attempting to head him back up the mountain. The bigger and stronger Mirko could not help but laugh, while fending off his younger brother's feeble attempts to arrest him.

"*Stop*! I said in a few minutes," Mirko reasoned, unwilling to move on his brother account.

"No, you won't," Mato blurted, unbelieving. "Why won't you come?"

Mirko looked at his brother. He saw his youth. He saw his face. He saw parts of himself. Parts of their mother, parts of his father. Parts of other relatives, long past. Mirko wanted to explain, but was unsure Mato could understand. Mato was so much younger, so much more innocent. It was more than the silly boat. Time was running out for him. One day it would run out for Mato too. "Because, I don't have to," he blurted.

Mirko's defiance burnt within Mato. He did not like it. It made his brother look ugly, and in turn made him look ugly. Mato reached for Mirko's arm once more. But Mirko slapped it away, harder this time. "Stop it little brother," Mirko demanded with an unfriendly tone.

Mato really hated being called little. "You should want to come!" responded Mato, loudly.

Mirko could hear the disappointment in his brother's voice, and it hurt him. Tired of the bickering, he relented. "I spend my weeks doing what others want. What Tata wants, what Vareš and the Sutjeska wants. What Tito wants."

"You don't know Tito," Mato interrupted, confused in Mirko's meaning. "C'mon, what does Tito want?" Mato asked.

Mirko sighed, knowing it was no use. "Everything." he answered directly. "Come on," Mirko relented. "I shouldn't make you wait any longer. Let's go."

"Really?" Mato blurted, excited.

"Yes, let's see how fast you really are," challenged Mirko, smiling. "Let's run, before the Kolo ends. Make haste, little brother."

Otjerati[1]

Nations remember peace like your stomach remembers being full. Whether international or internal peace, all is safe and sound until the growls return.

So it was during the wedding feast. For three days the entire village - including the Pavlović family, their local and far flung guests from around the Balkans sang, danced, drank and ate, and thus kept their stomachs quiet. But that was then.

The wedding party was over!

Truth be told, there were a few families still in the square, finishing up the last morsels of festivities, but in the Pavlović household, attentions had been diverted from the happy nuptials for hours. Replaced with wedding hospitality, there was hostility. Replaced with wedding peace, there was war! Faces were red, hair was disheveled. Insults were directed. Feelings were hurt. Tears were falling. The two oldest men of the house were dug deep into their trenches. Both sides seemed in it for the long haul. Mijo was adamant. Mirko was defiant. A quagmire was developing, and each believed they had enough ammunition to win. Like most battles, there was much at stake. Many hurts were going to be inflicted in this personal battle in the Sutjeska.

---

1 Marching orders

"There's no more to be said, huh? Huh?" derided Mirko.

The entire house knew this was a false statement encased in the shrapnel of a sarcastic question. They were going to battle on, even if they hurled the same insults at each other, over and over again. That generally explains what every argument, in the history of arguments has ever looked like: the same accusations, though phrased a little differently, shouted over and over again, until one side is totally worn down.

"There's nothing that can be done about it," reiterated Mijo, for the fourth time. "It's not my fault."

Each time Mijo made this pronouncement, it further fueled the scorching blaze shooting up through Mirko's feet, into his belly and further north up his chest and throat. The only thing stopping a rapid explosion of anger was Mirko's clenched jaw and a wall of teeth.

"Not your fault!" Mirko seethed. "Of course it's your fault! If it's not, whose fault is it?"

"Pick someone!" demanded Mijo. "The Chetniks, the Muslims. Tito! One of them, all of them, I don't care! Everything has changed, because of them!"

"Not everything old man," Mirko quickly replied. "Not everything."

It had been two months since the final night of the wedding. Much had changed. For example, the snow had returned. Its return, currently, was ensuring Mato's feet were making the most rapid crunch-crunch commotion, heard hundreds of yards away, even by the deafest ears.

Mato was running hard, and his breathing was heavy. He was running further than he ever had, and this additional effort was straining him. It was evident his lungs were still not acclimatized to the challenge it provided, as he had yet to complete the entire trek without stopping. This bothered him because how could he consider himself a runner and not finish? So tonight, Mato would not give himself a respite, even if his body screamed murder. He would challenge himself. The test was not just from the length of the run, but where he was running. Just as he did the previous Monday and Friday, on this night Mato had taken a harder trail, off the main road, through the forest. And he was doing this without company, all on his own.

He did not realize that he missed being alone so much. Mato found the best thing about being alone, was you could be yourself, and be whatever you wanted to be. If he wanted to run a straight trek, he could. If he wanted weave in and out of the trees, he would. If he wanted to imagine there were bears in these hills chasing him, he could run for his life. These moments of imagination also allowed Mato to really explore what his heart was set on; to find out how fast he really was over this difficult terrain, and over this longer distance. Someone had mentioned the distance was just over 20 kilometers. "*Almost half a marathon,*" thought Mato with glee.

As he ran, Mato pondered over how much had changed. It had been six Mondays and six Fridays since everything became different. Mato could not believe how much had altered. Everything became new, or at least what he knew, was being forgotten. And though Mato did not wish to forget, the fact is, everything had flipped. His daily chores had changed. His daily interactions had changed. His family had changed too, and most recently, Mato also found out, the country had changed as well.

This transformation all started because of a letter. A letter that first sat in a right-sided pocket, sent by those who wanted something, and would never take no for an answer. It continued with a huge argument, centered on much sadness, and ended with much upheaval.

The letter was sent to Mirko, but it affected the entire family. Mirko had been invited, and by invited the letter stated it expected Mirko to attend military service. This requirement was old news to the village, the region, and the nation for that matter, as this law had been established for long enough, but it was always a startling new shock when it personally reached within one's home.

But debts needed to be paid. Every Bosnian, whether Croatian, Serbian, or Muslim, had to pay this debt to the new nation, and their new leader. The other states of this nervous alliance, known as Yugoslavia, would pay too. Each young male, before they reached twenty-one were required to provide two years in the Army, Navy, or Air Force. The leaders would say that it was for their own good. That this service ensured the people their protection from the surrounding nations, hungry to conquer them, just like the Austro-Hungarians and the Ottoman Empire once had, or as the people whispered, the Communists had. The people would continue to whisper into the wind, that the only people who would wish to fight Yugoslavia lived within their borders, and not out. Furthermore the people joked the protection the leaders talked about was a precaution to keep the combined states from each neighbor's throat.

This would not be surprising, if you knew a little bit of Balkan history. The peoples there had always been destroying each other, while building hate and distrust. The tiny region was admittedly dealt a difficult hand. Its fate was to be in middle of everything! Bosnia was where East met West, on faith, finances, and geography. Over the centuries, valuable trade routes were established across its lands. As a result the new leadership of Yugoslavia, led by Marshall Tito, like the old leadership, had much to gain from the wooded mountain land and therefore had much to protect. Protecting it, and ensuring its peace was harder done than said. History had shown everyone over time had failed.

But Tito had told the world he had a perfect plan! The world was sick of the problems of this little place in the middle of everything, and was glad that a crazy Croatian who fought the Nazis was willing to take on the awful challenge. Tito would play both sides of the Cold War, greasing America by annoying Stalin, while still sleeping behind the Iron Curtain.

Closer to home, propaganda and strength was the key to making this plan a success. Tito told the people that it was his destiny to lead them. To convince the people, his Communist hoards took this message to the city streets and to the villages in the mountains, demanding the people believe him. Surprisingly, exhausted by the heavy losses during World War II, the people were complicit.

But even Tito knew this would not be enough. To make it work, Tito needed the nation to get to work as a collective unit, even if it did not want to. Even if they hated each other. To do this he needed strong backs, which would carry the nation's weight. Strong backs like Mirko's. In turn, this idea ensured Tito was powerful enough to hold the reigns of his unbroken colt that was Yugoslavia.

"The Navy wants me!" a very excited Mirko pronounced, to a startled household. "Can you believe it? Boats, ships, cruises! Oh, submarines!"

Mirko could not withhold his glee. Not that he was trying. To be sure, the entire household knew that one day Mirko would board a sailboat and float away, "but Tito's Navy!" They did not know Tito's Navy were where dreams came true. Required service, by all sensible accounts was not created to be easy. All had heard the stories of mistreatment. The stories of empty bellies. The stories of smiling boys going into service and returning to their villages as stern faced men. Mara had heard those stories. That's why she was crying. Vjera had heard those stories. That was why she was in her room, as always, praying. Mijo had heard those stories too. That is why he would not stop arguing. He needed Mirko to hear him. He needed Mirko to hear those stories now, before it was too late. Unfortunately, deep down, Mijo knew it already was.

"I'm signing up tomorrow Tata, and leaving as soon as I turn eighteen," repeated the defiant firstborn. "It is my duty. It is my right."

"Duty? Your right?" barked Mijo "You're talking like the Communists own you. They don't own you. We own..."

"We?" butted in Mirko. "Who is 'we?' Don't you mean you, Tata? You think you own me, but you don't! *You don't!*"

The words were taking their toll. Hearts were being visited by hurts that would never want to leave. Chests were heaving heavily from the weight. Tears were welling up in eyes that were not accustomed to channeling them. Each was saying things that a clearer head would want to take back. But the tongue is a slippery slope. Words were cascading with rapid haste. Each man was at a disadvantage. Neither was well practiced in the rules of engagement for this type of warfare.

"I'm going, and that is it!" repeated Mirko.

Mijo did not understand why Mirko wanted to leave right away. There was plenty of time. He knew Mirko would have to leave eventually, before turning twenty-one, but that was over three years from now. Tito's nation could wait. Mirko was needed here now. Mijo was frustrated that either his eldest son was too stupid or too selfish to see that. The family needed Mirko's help. That was his first and only duty, right? Mijo was not getting any younger. He was not as spry as he once was. He was not the only one. Vjera was visibly starting to show her age. Her eyesight was fading. Her feet moved a lot slower, if not at all. She barely ate. No one knew how long she had left. Mato too, was not a baby anymore, and would need his brother more than ever. Furthermore, Mijo was concerned with Mara. How would Mijo console her if he left? It would change everything. And not for the better.

"But why are you in a hurry?" asked Mara, saying something for the first time.

"Yes!" Mijo agreed. "Yes, why can't it wait? You have time!"

Mirko seethed. This was supposed to be a joyful occasion for him. For years, he had dreamed of nothing else. The sea! Open waters were within his grasp! He could taste the salt water. This is what he had always wanted. He had paid penance for almost eighteen years in the mountains, and his patience was being rewarded. And yet, his family, who were supposed to love him and know him best were attempting to thwart his dreams coming true. He could not believe it! For three days, Mirko could not understand why his father had asked him to keep the news hush-hush. And now that the reasons behind it were being expressed, it made him rage! He hated having to explain himself. He could not understand why they would want to stop him. Surely, each family member knew how much this meant, and why he needed to go. Surely, they had seen how he spent every free moment by the water's edge. Surely, they knew this was his destiny.

"I can't wait," Mirko replied.

✱✱✱

Mato loved maps. He loved to pour over them. It did not matter what the map's focus was. Local maps. Regional maps. International maps of faraway places. Mato was fascinated by all of them. One birthday, Vjera had bought him a map of America. He treasured it, and took it everywhere. He was fascinated that people lived in the places dotted on them, far away from his little village. He was fascinated they lived speaking different languages, in different climates, while eating different foods. He was even fascinated by the shapes of different countries, and how each of them came to be.

"You know the borders of these countries change all the time?" Mijo had once informed his youngest son.

"Really?" he replied, somewhat surprised. "Why?"

"Because of battles and wars. The winner gets to change them."

"Oh," Mato replied, thoughtfully. "Like the war your Tata fought in?"

"Yes," Mijo answered, quietly. "Just like that one."

✱✱✱

"You know your decision changes everything," proclaimed Mijo to Mirko. "Mato!"

Mijo turned to his younger son. Tears that were welling up in Mijo's eyes flowed freely. Mato looked at his father. Mato had never seen his father cry before. As Mijo teared up, Mato noticed how much older his father looked to his younger eyes. He felt so bad for his father, though he did not know why. "My son," he stammered. "My son..."

That is how it all began and ended for Mato. And just like that, he was not a child anymore. He was now a man. He had to be. Six weeks after the war of words, Mirko packed up a small bag of belongings, a few articles of clothing, his small toy boat and set sail the new Yugoslavian way. And then, a few days later, Mato, not yet fourteen, took over Mirko's responsibilities in Vareš to work in the steel mill. Though the war of words was mainly about Mirko leaving to join the Navy, Mato joining the work force, set off a new front in the verbal warfare between Mirko and Mijo, ensuring many further sleepless nights. And no, neither side asked Mato what he thought.

Many weeks later, as Mato trekked across the snow, though there were many fights between his father and brother on his behalf, the last one, the night before Mirko left for the Navy, stuck in his mind. "That's not fair. He's only thirteen!" protested Mirko. "I didn't start until I was fifteen."

"If you go, there is no one else," Mijo retorted.

Angrily Mirko responded. "Why don't you go, Tata?" he yelled. "You're only doing this to get back at me," he barked. "Why don't you go? Aren't you the father? You should go, instead of leaving your job to a little boy."

This hurt Mijo terribly. This opinion had bubbled close to the surface for years. Ever since Mirko first carried the mantle of a full-time employee.

"Why don't you go?" Mirko continued, mockingly. It was if he was calling his father a lazy coward.

Mijo did not have a ready reply that would satisfy the taunts. Instead, he looked so ashamed and naked in front of his family. He was hurt, defeated. The war was almost over. "Because, I cannot," was all he could stammer.

"Oh, I forgot. That's right. You can't, Tata," continued Mirko. He was now a river out of control. There was no going back. "Everything changes, except you old man, and we all have to pay the price, right?" Mirko won the fight, and everyone, it seemed, lost the war.

This left Mato in the forest, running back and forth to Vareš. And as he pondered the imaginary, he also remembered the first day of his new reality. On that first cold, dark morning, Mato walked with trepidation down the stairs from his room. He walked past his father, who was nervous in his chair by a confident fire. His father refused to make eye contact, looking crushed. Mato remembered how he needed his father right then, but no help was forthcoming. Mijo believed he had nothing to give his son but shame.

As Mato continued down the stairs, he could hear his mother singing. Sadly, there was no happiness in her song, nothing like the singing heard at the recent wedding. This song was solemn and forlorn. Seeing her son, Mara held Mato tight as if this was the last hug she would ever give him. Mato allowed himself to be lost in the moment, as if he understood his mother's pain. After a few minutes, or was it an hour, because Mato could not be sure, with tears in his eyes, Mara handed him his knapsack that contained food and a change of clothes, and wished him on his way. As he took the bag, Mato slipped his favorite keepsake of his map of America inside, and headed towards his new life.

Before he could leave, Vjera was waiting at the door. Her lips forced a smile, but her eyes betrayed her pure sadness. She had said goodbye to Mirko only four days before, and now Mato was going too. As Mato leaned in to embrace his grandmother, Vjera stood on her tippy-toes, so as to reach the cheek of her fast-growing grandson. It was then she whispered the same thing that she had told Mirko only a few days earlier, "Do not let what's out there take you."

And with that, Mato ran towards his future.

What found Mato was a wall of heat and noise. A world of responsibility and deadlines. Bells ringing. Whistles blowing. Hard steel and harder men. Men from different walks of life. Different ideals. Different hopes. Different experiences than Mato understood. Mato ran into a world that cared for itself, and not a lick about what he thought, or what he believed. This was because, though the mountains saw him as a man, the city, even one as small as Vareš, saw him as nothing.

"You're Mirko Pavlović's smaller brother?" the steel mill foreman said sternly, on meeting his newest untrained employee.

"Yes, Sir," whispered Mato.

The foreman sighed, disapprovingly. "Let's learn if you'll fit in."

Putting his knapsack down in the corner of the foreman's small office, Mato found out his job was to be a runner. His role basically was to get whatever was needed, as fast as he could. Water for the men. Water for the steel. Run buckets of slop. Remove the trash. Whatever loose ends needed to be completed, it was his job to do it.

"Is this what Mirko did?" Mato asked the foreman.

"No!" shot the foreman. "We lost a steelmaker, and got you instead."

"What do I do?" asked Mato, eager to impress.

"When they yell for you," the foreman began to explain, "Make sure you come. Especially, if I yell."

For the rest of the day, Mato was yelled at more than he had been in his entire life. Yelled in different dialectics of Serbian and Croatian. He was yelled at by people from his village, and from villages that shared his father's mountain. Mato's mind was spinning. He needed very much to sit down, but he was not allowed to stop. It was his first day, but no one cared. The hardness of hot steel, coupled with grim faces and stern voices, left Mato feeling overmatched.

Up until that first day, Mato only knew of sporadic sounds. The church bell on Sunday. The stream a mile off the village square. The happy cackles of children's invention, or the voices of men and women singing, while they swung their sickles. These sounds were simple interludes where silence was king. But now, sound was an invading hoard, a million chaotic instruments playing out of tune and out of unison. Each barrage was an unwanted plight on his ears demanding his utmost attention.

Mato tried to cope by listening to the stored remembrances of quieter days he enjoyed so much, but it was no good. Even though he lived them just the day before, all he could hear now was the shouts of "Boy! Hurry up! Move quicker!" Mato had never been told to move quicker before. He heard it a lot that first day, and the proceeding weeks. All the noise made his head hurt. His ears felt as if they were bleeding. His nose was running faster than his feet, with a disgusting hot stream of snot flooding the neck of his shirt, as if his body was rejecting this ghastly new reality. Outside, it was a chilly new winter day. Inside, it was Hades. His heart was tired, and his mind exhausted. He was hungry. Mato felt as if lunch time should have been called hours ago, but he was not sure, because the foreman told him he could only sit and eat when he said, and he had yet to do so. The fact is, the foreman should have called lunch for Mato an eon ago, but he did what he always did to newbies; he worked them as hard as he could, so he could learn how much they could take. The foreman was impressed with his skinny new recruit. Mato could take a lot.

"Boy!" motioned the foreman. "It's almost time to go home, and you stupidly haven't stopped to eat. Sit for a few minutes, before you pass out."

The day was almost over! "At least time doesn't stop here," thought Mato. He followed his foreman to the office to grab his bag. In the future, he would have a locker and a room for his belongings, but on his first day, Mato brought everything to work like he was told to. He left his bag in the corner, thinking it would be safe. It was not. Leaving it there alone all day, the rats believed it was safe for them. And it was! The rodents took what they wanted, leaving Mato nothing but his change of clothes, and his map.

"Noooooo!" Mato whimpered.

The foremen laughed. "You have fifteen minutes, and then one more hour of work," he chortled.

As Mato ran on this Friday evening, he thought about how he survived the rest of that first day, and the rest of his first week. He thought about how the rats feasted on his weeks' worth of food in minutes, and how the men from the village ensured he did not starve. One of them even taught Mato to make some inexpensive noodles, known as *pilav*. Up until that day, Mato had hated the stuff. It is amazing what you will put up with when you have no choice. So much so, pilav soon became one of Mato's favorite daily pleasures.

As Mato ran, he thought of the simple food he had eaten each day. The simple room he rented. The building was old and small, but thankfully cheap. After that difficult first week, the older men kept an eye on Mato, but gave him his space while he learned how to withstand his new obligations. They were glad, that at least on the surface, Mato appeared to handle it well, like a man from the Sutjeska. But in the quieter moments, when he thought no one was looking, Mato would sob, longing to return home to the mountains. This was the greatest adjustment of all. Not the work, though that was unpleasant. Or the traveling, because that was fun. Nor was it being away from those he loved, though he did miss them. It was the fact that he had to be here, in Vareš and not in the village, and in his mountains. Mato learned that for the first time in his life, he could be in prison, simply for the crime of getting older.

Surprisingly, Mato learned he was not the only one struggling to adjust. Each worker pined for their chosen homes, and their families. Mato saw how they attempted to handle this. Some prayed, but more drank. Others gambled. Others smoked too many cigarettes, coloring their teeth a bruised orange. Others spoke with a foulness he had never heard of before.

This created concern within Mato. Would this happen to him as well? Would he grow up to be a foul-mouthed drunkard that gambled on card games? Thankfully, during those times, when fearful thoughts attempted to penetrate his mind, Mato would lean on the last words his grandmother gave him on his first day, and he remembered what he loved to do most; run!

He would run, and run fast. Mato would run as fast as he could at work and then he would run even harder every Friday night. And as he ran, he would let his mind run far away; to places on maps he used to have time to study. You see, though the world was demanding this thirteen year old be a man, something inside of him reminded him, that acting like a boy was alright too. And so, when he returned home after another hard week, though exhausted, he would tell his excited mother and grandmother where he had been.

"I went to Guam," said Mato the third week.

"To Tonga," he said the forth week.

"To Ethiopia," he exclaimed the fifth week.

"Why Ethiopia?" said Vjera, playing along.

"I went to bag me a lion," Mato roared. "And, to meet women that are so pretty that the Old Testament Moses married one of them."

This is how Mato successfully coped. On this night, for example, he was going to tell them about his trip to Australia and how he outran a mob of jumping kangaroos. That was why his lungs were burning; because of the kangaroos.

That's why Mato ran alone. To run with kangaroos. To think about how he was following in his brother's footsteps, while Mirko followed his dreams. Soon, maybe Mato might further follow his. As Mato ran alone, his dreams went with him. Here, Mato ran alone so could imagine that his father was not sad for sending him to Vareš. In the forest, as Mato ran, his mother wasn't crying and his grandmother wasn't aging. Here, Tito did not exist. Nor did Vareš or anything else he did not want. Here, Mato was who he wanted to be.

And yet, though Mato felt like he was alone, much lives in the forest. As Mato ran, he thought the forest was a quiet, beautiful place.

It was not. It was a place of noise and disturbance that shared many similarities with his steel mill in Vareš. It was just that Mato's ears could not hear the forest's millions of organisms. That was because they were trained in stealth and guile. They knew its secrets, and Mato did not. Some of these creatures lived alone and eked out a semblance of living. Those creatures were hard to find, for it is their pleasure to hide. But not all creatures live alone. Some live with others. These creatures, who lived in bunches, did not need to hide. Rather, their numbers granted them confidence in their collective size. The bigger the group, the more forceful the instinct. The larger the instinct, the greater this pack thirsted and hungered. The greater the thirst, the greater their ability to sense new blood.

Mato was only a few miles from home. He was running at a good pace. He felt like tonight he was going to finish the entire trek. It had been a long week. After six weeks on the job, he thought about how he was starting to get the hang of his role. He was hardly being yelled at, and the rats had not been at his food. He felt as if he was getting stronger. So much so, instead of sleeping Sunday away, he was going to hang out with his friends after church during the exchange of languages, known as the *Hasikovanje*, even though he thought the entire game very silly.

As Mato looked out at the horizon, he noticed the sun was almost disappearing for another day. Soon the dark sky would invade the forest. Mato was not worried though. In his backpack, if he needed, Mato carried a very small lamp just in case it got too dark for him to see where he was traveling. As the sun said its "laku noć," thankfully, the white snow on the ground gleamed against the moonlight, making visibility most comfortable, and the lantern unnecessary.

While lost in his own world, Mato's surroundings continued to be very quiet, except for the aforementioned crunching of feet. Strangely, for the first time, he thought that the forest was too quiet. It was if for the first time Mato recognized the forest for what it always was, an eerie, almost spooky place, not built for unnecessary adventures. With these thoughts pressing on his mind, Mato noticed a trio of finches flying off a branch high above his head and into the vast horizon. The appearance of these flighty creatures made Mato feel like a jittery rabbit.

Mato quickened his steady pace. And then, after a further few moments of uneasiness, he quickened it again. He did not know why he moved quicker, but yet, he knew. Though everything seemed as it had always had been, it was not. And though his mind attempted to reason with his feet, this proved pointless because his pace quickened some more. Something was not right, but what was it?

Mato's feet knew why he was running as fast as he could. His feet sensed that the forest had tricked him into believing that he was alone. What Mato did not know is that a king is never alone in his

Chapter 6

castle. There is always someone else lurking to overthrow them, and take their place.

What Mato did not know was the forest considered him an invader. That he was the one lurking, trying to take the rule of others. This was their home, not his. While the mountain is a child's play thing, the forest has no masters except hunger and thirst. This master demands a penance from its miscreants. Hunger eats at their stomach. The thirst owns a set of hands that chokes their mangy necks. This need hangs over them, tormenting them with constant howls. This call becomes unbearable at night, as thirst and hunger never sleep. So they hunt in packs, with green eyes that pierce with vengeance. They hunt to seek and to destroy. They hunt to kill. To murder. And with the victim, the demons of the forest hope to finally to quench their master's wants. Perhaps, on this night, they will eat like kings and not like rogues. A million times over they have killed and hoped for this. But they are still hungry. They are still thirsty.

Sensing all of this, Mato was frantically trying to move even quicker, but snow was falling once more, slowing his feet. For the first time since his first day in the mills, fear was fettering at Mato's heart. He knew what was behind him. He knew without turning to look. The truce between him and the forest was at an impasse. The evil with fangs and teeth were out to play. Four weeks earlier at the steelworks he had found and killed a rat. He had imagined it was the rat that had eaten his food. On that day, he claimed vindication over the thief. Now the wolves were playing cat and rat with him, while taking back the trees that Mato had dared to tempt with his childlike dreams.

Požuriti![1]

"Make haste!"

It is a phrase Mato's ears had heard a million times before. From his father. From his mother. From his grandmother. Whether it was to pass along a message in the village, or to borrow a cup of flour from a neighbor, or to once more summons his brother from the water, there was always some great need. Now, as a man, Mato had heard the phrase enough these past six weeks to last a lifetime. The steel mill inhabitants were always demanding greater swiftness.

"Make haste! Make haste!"

Moving fast was a commandment of Mato's young life. Especially since his reputation followed him. After all, he had defeated young men of sixteen or seventeen years of age consistently in foot races. It did not matter whether the race was over a short distance on the flats, or a cross-country caper over the jagged terrain, Mato could and would smoke them all. Mato ran fast because he could. Mato ran fast because he wanted to. Mato lived to make haste!

But at that very moment, Mato had never needed to make haste more. His life depended on it! Mato was learning the truth. His perceived snow-covered forest friendship was a sham. The beasts had

---

1 Make haste!

Chapter 7

finally trapped him! What Mato did not know was they had been on his trail since the first Monday he dared to venture out alone. The shadows were quick to sniff him out, and now they were quickly closing in. They had lurked long enough. They were ready to show their teeth and celebrate their perfect hunt.

"Make haste boy, make haste!"

Mato was a mess of motion and panic, desperately trying to cut through the fresh powder that surrounded him. He could feel them on his tail. Their breath, spit and heightened anticipation was fouling the clean wintry air. Moans of hopelessness filled Mato's vocal cords. "Anywhere, please!" he begged the forest, as he looked heavenward for a vantage place.

Quickly, a tree with a lower branch presented itself, giving Mato a chance to be Edmund Hillary and climb what was there. Behind him, furious teeth pulsated at full speed. The devils knew their catch for the day was trying to get away. Up Mato jumped, his arms straining, hoping to get as high as they might. "Oh, no!" The limb he reached up for was beyond him. The tree he chose to be his savior was a false idol. Gravity brought him back down into his personal hell. He looked around for the first time. The devils were within fifteen feet, right within striking distance. Mato risked life and limb, knowing he had to take his eye of the brutes for a second, to find a perch of safety. He needed a tree, a branch, even a twig to grab a hold of.

To Mato's advantage, the wolves too had ceased their breakneck pursuit. They were certain of victory now. They were stalking their prey, slowly circling in an anti-clockwise direction, drinking in the moment. They had won. Euphoria was theirs, and they would savor it.

"Make haste, boy, make haste!"

Mato was surrounded. There were at least a dozen of them. There might have been more. As he looked upon them, they stared back at him, as if he was the only creature in the world. Mato, strangely gained confidence from this, as if he was very important. An entire civilization existed in their pack. They would live and die with each meal. He was the meal they needed. Mato laughed, and thought how they needed him. Mato looked with greater intensity at the hoard. They appeared tired, and hungry. They looked as if they wished the chase to be over.

Each breath further delivered calmness to Mato. More importantly, the wolves noticed this rising composure. They all believed the race was over - after all, the creature had stopped running. He had given up, right? But the captured creature was not crying or bleating. Many of their kills had done both before they began to feast. But this one was not even shaking. He was just standing there, grinning. Their captured creature was increasingly making the wolves edgy.

But what the wolves did not know was that Mato lived for the race, regardless of what the *peloton* was made of. He lived to be chased and get away from man, and as this situation needed, beast. Mato had been chased hundreds of times before. He had been chased all over the mountains and won. He had been chased from one end of the steel mill to the other, and survived. Mato knew this was not over, and this realization brought forth a healthy laugh, as if he was mad. Staring at death could do that to you, but he was not mad. Madness arrives after fear has had its way with you, and Mato was not afraid. He was resolute. He felt like he was going to get out of this predicament. He knew he would, he just did not know how: at least, not yet. The cards in this pack just needed to play themselves out and show him trumps.

But, Mato was fully aware that the pack still owned the upper hand. They after all owned the sharp knives. He knew he had to make the next move, and the next move had better be the winning one. Mato knew they soon would have to lunge, fear or no fear. Their hunger would eventually lead to a brutal strike. Mato knew what he had to do. He had to fight.

"So Mato," he began to ask. "Where did you go this week?"

"That is a good question," he started to respond, while pulling his lamp out of his knapsack. "I went to a place not on maps."

"Oh, really?" Mato replied. "Where did you go?"

Chapter 7

"I went to a white planet and danced with the devil."

"Oh, how was it?"

"Intense," Mato calmly replied, as he readied his new weapon by turning on its light.

Mato's continual smiling and laughing was making the pack overtly tense. They sensed no fear. *"What is this folly?"* they asked. *"Does it not know it has lost?"* they speculated. *"Where is the fear?"* they inquired. As much as they wanted meat, they also craved the smell of fear. Fear can feed an empty belly too. The fangs needed to eat. They had waited so long. But the pack now realized this meal was not going to come easy. Mato was not afraid. He was ready.

Mato stepped forward, as if to entice some of the pack to break ranks and charge. It worked! One of the younger, more foolish members took the bait and lunged towards the boy. Mato swung his lamp, and then his entire knapsack, colliding with the jaw of the younger brute. He connected perfectly with both weapons, bruising its throat and jaw, sending the wolf flying with a high pitch whimper, back amongst its kind.

A second lemming did not learn from the first, following suit with an erratic lunge. But this one got closer to the mark, almost nipping at his right thigh. Mato sharply pivoted on that very leg and kicked the brute with the full force of his left foot, right into its rib cage, while smashing the lamp upon the wolf's head.

A rush of power and strength swept within Mato. It's funny what you think of at certain times. Mato thought how, up until this night, he had had no use for his lamp, despite carrying it back and forth each of the past six weeks. Well, Mato was certain he was going to get his money's worth now. He swung the lamp a second and then third time, thwarting a larger beast from tasting his flesh.

While wiping multiple beads of sweat from his brow, it was then that Mato saw it for the first time. Mato viewed a massive dog, almost twice the size of the rest of the pack. Its eyes were greener. Its snarl louder. Its disposition far more menacing. As Mato fixated his stare upon the large dog, the beast trod on the most recent would-be-attacker while bellowing with a loud and disapproving growl.

Then, it looked at Mato, who was breathing heavy, adrenaline at its highest point. Mato reached down at his right calf. It felt hot. The most recent attacker did get a small taste of skin, but the pain was not stronger than his will to fight. Thankfully, the brute had gotten more of his pant leg, than the leg itself.

Mato could not believe it. Remarkably, he was still there! He was still alive! They got a taste of him though. Mato knew time was running short. They would not be so careless at the next snap. Mato stole a quick survey of the scene of trees. *"Make haste boy, make haste!"*

Mato, once more, was on the move. Tonight, he knew he would learn how fast he really was! He looked to his left and decided that about twenty yards beyond existed the tree that might save him. Without hesitation, Mato charged towards it. Stride after stride, he kept his eyes on his prize. The wolves, dismayed that the race had resumed, followed suit. This time however, the largest of the pack was leading the charge, ready to right the wrongs of the tribe's pawns.

However, the wolves miscalculated! In a flash, Mato hurdled himself for the second time up towards a tree. He placed his foot into the trunk, and it catapulted him towards the needed overhanging branch. This time, both hands surged towards their goal with confidence, as if he was an acrobat in the Moscow Circus, flying without a net. He had to get it right this time. To miss would have meant death. Both hands clung on for dear life. Success! Mato tussled himself upon his new found perch, while the hordes snapped at his steel-capped boots.

"Make haste! Make haste! Make haste!"

Mato climbed further in and higher up into the tree, looking to find a suitable branch to sit on.

The commotion below was a perverse vision of evil and foulness. The smallest pup that first attempted to claim Mato's hide, could be heard squealing in pain. He was being punished by the larger dogs, with bites and scratches for his overeager petulance. Seeing this, the second brute that had gotten a piece of Mato's apparel ran away, before they might punish him as cruelly. Finally, the pack got bored with the little one, and let it go. It too ran away, licking its wounds.

Chapter 7

The fangs had erred. They were patient, but not enough. Their haste had given Mato enough time. Enough time to climb far enough away from the howls and teeth. Up the tree, the young climber went, in a crab-like manner. Up an up he went, because a thousand leagues beyond the teeth would not have been high enough. But thankfully, to his tired body and mind, he was sufficiently safe. Mato might have been out of breath, but thankfully, he had proven he was not out of time.

As he looked down, he did not realize how high he had climbed. The mixture of surprise and fatigue made him dizzy for a moment. Mato had climbed many trees in his life, but never that fast, and never that high. He did not think he could have scrambled more that fifteen feet up, but looking down it appeared he was more than fifty feet beyond the ground. He was so dizzy, Mato needed to close his eyes. "*Wow, I'm fast!*" Mato thought to himself.

Mato looked around at his new environment. Mato could not believe it. "Make haste, make haste," he muttered under his heavy breathing. He had won! He had outraced a pack of ravenous wolves! He began to cry, as relief welled up within him. The therapy of those tears however, was chum for those swimming in the water below. Mato had yet to notice that the largest of the beasts was whipping up its troops into a rallied frenzy. Some the larger minions, longing to impress their leader, were hitting the base of the tree, in an attempt to shake their cornered captive from his perch. Others were roaring at full speed, attempting to vault up the tree and make the impossible climb.

The wolves' efforts made the tree sway slightly, forcing Mato to look down. "Make haste!" he yelled at the pack. "Wa-Whoooooooooo!" he cried, while raising his arms aloft in triumph.

"*Hoooooowwwwwwwwllllll!*", the largest of the wolves bellowed back.

This shocked Mato, almost dislodging him from his new perch. The largest one's response was so loud, and menacing, that it clanged around within Mato's heart and mind. What was even more frightening was it seemed the wolf's howl was a direct reply to his victorious taunts.

"*That's not possible, is it?*" wondered Mato.

Put Do Vrhunca[1]

Two hours had vanished since Mato scaled the zenith of his newly-favored summit. As hard as he would try, Mato's imagination could not fathom Everest, Kilimanjaro, or McKinley's vista being as sweet. His happiness was beyond his wildest dreams.

But this was no dream. His eyes were open, and even in the darkness Mato could see them. The wolves were still there, lurking in a vicious silence, as if they still had a redemptive chance. Not that Mato could see how. After the initial burst of energy from the frustrated group of hunters, their recent efforts were sullen, and owned very little commotion. During this slowdown, Mato had counted as many as sixteen dogs guarding him. But what Mato did not initially notice during his headcount was the lead wolf had in fact disappeared. Relief further swelled over Mato. It was gone! When it had left, Mato could not say. It seemed ages ago.

With its departure, and with each passing moment, the pack appeared calmer, almost at peace. Mato thought they looked like a placid group of pets at rest, at the foot of their master. With the apparent truce at hand, with great care, Mato finally captured enough courage to maneuver his knapsack. Up until this time, it had

1 Higher ground

Chapter 8

been wedged between his back and tree trunk, making it dangerously difficult to get to without risking tumbling downward.

But other needs were overriding his preexisting fear. A lack of activity was causing his limbs to become painfully numb. Worse, the temperatures were reaching freezing point. His fingers were bricks attached to his wrists. Hunger was also lurking. Thankfully, his knapsack held solutions to both of his needs. Inside, were a small blanket, and a smaller amount of bread that Mato regularly kept for the journey home. Mato didn't know how long this food needed to last, but since his stomach was growling louder than the beasts below, this internal rumbling ensured it was time to eat his victory dinner! Mato concluded there was no point saving it anyhow. What if he became too weak and fell from his safe landings? To get back to Pavlovići, he needed to stay put in his perched place.

"So where did you go this week, Mato?" he asked himself. "Hopefully, home," was his earnest reply.

Mato's mental meanderings ventured towards his loved ones. They would have expected him to be back by now. Mato hated being the cause of their worry. This mixture of concern, cold and hunger, made Mato cry and laugh at the same time, as if he were a May Day sun shower. Scornfully, Mato grabbed at a handful of acorns that hung on a nearby branch. As forcefully as he could, he hurled them as rocks down upon the beasts.

"Yes! Success!" Mato bellowed, as he struck one of the smaller minions. "Ko zna, zna," he taunted, congratulating his arm's strength, which in reality was not that great, as the struck wolf barely budged.

His game of skipping stones completed, Mato quickly finished the bread. Lamentably, he was still ravenous. He looked around his surroundings, hoping to find a runaway crumb. Surprisingly, something was tantalizing his senses. It was substantive, more than some pungent plume.

"Flowers in the winter? Hah!" muttered a doubtful Mato.

But despite his disbelief, Mato's smeller could not stand the lingering scent any longer. He had to find where it was coming from. So very carefully, Mato reached up to the branch above his head to stretch. Skillfully, his hand reached toward this northward limb.

As his fingers met the bark, Mato noticed its surface had the stickiest matter sitting there. Putting his hands to his nose, Mato quickly discovered the odor he believed was conjured by his imagination, was real! He dared to sample it. It tasted delightful, and more surprising, very filling. He reached up again, this time with his right hand, his taste buds hoping there was more. Delightfully, there was! Mato grabbed a handful, and ate the entire amount in one greedy gulp, making sure to lick every last amount. It was the most delightful honey-like concoction Mato had ever tasted! What was most amazing was how full it made him. Mato had never eaten a more satisfying meal. If he were offered a full plate of lamb and pita, for the first time ever, he would have refused it. Mato was full, he was safe and suddenly, he felt very strong, ready to take on the entire world. *"First the wolves, and next, whatever,"* thought Mato triumphantly.

Suddenly, Mato noticed movement both below and above his station. New snowflakes were falling, but more startling; the pack was back into action. Within moments, the large group was disappearing. Sixteen became ten, then seven. Then the seven became three. Then finally, one by one, the last of them slipped into the shadows.

"Maybe they have finally gone?" wondered a hopeful Mato.

Just then, Mato heard the largest, longest howl! It shook his eardrums and the sound quaked his soul. Quickly, Mato regretted pondering whether his evening was concluding, for the howl told him otherwise. The evening was just about to begin, for in ventured the largest wolf, returning with two of its more impressive bishops. Though, not as large as the leader, each were imposingly menacing in their own right.

The One, as it was called, looked like it held a very scornful grudge. Mato did not know it, but it was the One that first picked up his trail, some six weeks earlier. It was the One that picked up his fresh scent earlier that evening, and it was the One who now had the scent of rage hanging from its nostrils. What Mato could tell however, was that it led the pack. It fed the pack. And on this night, it had failed the pack. There was a cost to failing the pack. Leaders cannot lose too many battles. It was then Mato concluded both had much to lose and gain from the evening's outcome.

Again, the One blasted a very loud howl! And again, and again, and again. Then for a fifth time it bellowed, as if it was a trumpeter out of control. When the One finally stopped, it was only to allow its minions to join the fray. The orchestra created a maddening cacophony, each taking turns to bluster Mato's ears with their song of terror. As their instruments played, the other wolves returned. There was far more than sixteen now. Stunned, Mato quickly counted over forty of them! He had never known a wolf pack this big. It was if the One had called other groups to join in the fray, which is exactly what it had done.

The noise was becoming deafening. Dozens of howls at the same time can make an awful racket. But the commotion did not concern Mato. After six weeks on the job, the steel mill had prepared his senses for much worse. His smile returned, further alarming the One. The One looked frustratingly at Mato, startled that its plans were not working. Desperately, the One began to circle faster and faster, and in turn, the noise of its minions become louder and louder, and then louder still. But to no avail! In fact, Mato was so comfortable with his perched surroundings, the heavy want of sleep was availing him. But before his eyes drooped shut, the last thing Mato saw was a growing smile upon the One's face.

The howls of the wolves had been heard so often that night that they were now no more than a background lullaby. The fight to stay alive became the fight to stay awake. The wolves were now humming in perfect unison. They stalked Mato's tree with a greater swiftness, united once more, sensing a weakening prey. Mato rubbed his eyes, and then slapped his face. Anything to keep him from Nod's door. Then, Mato heard a whisper. He put his freezing fingers into his ears, in an attempt to clean them, because he thought he heard the beasts whisper out his name.

"Mato. How is your brother, the *blesav*[2]?"

"What?" Mato replied, stunned. "What did you say?"

"You know, the blesav," repeated the One. "Or your father, the coward. How is he?"

"What?" barked Mato.

"You know, the coward? The coward who thinks he can talk with his dead father. Tell him I have a message for him."

"What are talking about?"

"Tell him, the mountain never sleeps," chortled the One.

"What does that mean?" yelled Mato.

"Don't worry," said the One. "He will know."

The wolf began to laugh. It was enjoying its personal joke. Suddenly, the One once more became ferocious and serious.

"Let me make it plain for you, fool. Mato, you are mine," the One menaced. "You were won at a great price."

The One voiced its last claim over and over. Mato was questioning his sanity. But, each deviled announcement was clear to hear.

"*What price?*" Mato thought to himself. The One somehow heard his question.

"Pepan, Pepan Pavlović tasted rather nice," the One began to mockingly sing. "But, he was mutton: old and tough. Mato, Mato Pavlović will be a great lamb chop on my plate. I'll chomp, chomp, lamb chop!"

With the One's words, the pack continued to howl. Louder and louder they became, their presence encircling the entire forest. "You are mine, Mato Pavlović," continued the One.

The noise completely overwhelmed Mato. He could do nothing but cover his ears with his hands, though, that too brought no respite.

"Howwwwwwwllllll!" Mato frustratingly growled. However, Mato's feeble effort did nothing but bring further derision from his would be attackers. Laughter now filled each of their voices, as if they were part hyena. Mato did not know they could do that.

"I don't believe this is happening," muttered a now weeping Mato.

---

2 Stupid

"It isn't, you foolish boy," retorted the One. "You are asleep. We almost have you. Arise from your throne and bow before us. Howwwwwwwllllllll!"

Mato's eyes opened, alarmed at the clearness of the retort. But, the wolf's words were true! Awaking from the devilish dream, Mato found his legs dangling dangerously off the tree. The shock of being awoken so high off the ground pulled from his vocal cords a giant yelp for all his unwanted guests to hear.

Thankfully, he woke up just in time. As Mato pulled himself back up to safety, the young lad saw the pack bustling with a rapidly renewed vigor, in some kind of feeding frenzy.

"Oh no, my knapsack!" Mato despaired.

Mato had paid the price for his dozing. His blanket, pack, and all of its contents, including his map of America, were no longer his, but rather files sharpening teeth below.

It took a good while for Mato to regroup his frayed senses. Dusting of the snow sitting on him, Mato noticed the dark cloud cover that had brought the cold white, had moved on towards Belgrade. The clouds were replaced by a million stars. Mato smacked his lips. Surprisingly, though he had not eaten or drunk for hours, he was not hungry or thirsty. Nor did his body ache from lying on his branch. He mused at his strength, for he guessed it must have been born from an alert need to survive.

Time was moving slowly and boredom was setting in. What was Mato to do? He was still stuck so far up the tree. The beasts were not going away. The night was not leaving either. He had never wanted to be home so much in his life. Pavlovići was only five, maybe six kilometers away, but it might as well have been a million. Too far away to call out. Too far away to see. Mato thought of happier times of running in the fields, and defeating Mirko's friends in foot races, while his older brother stood bare toed in the stream catching fish by the dozen.

Those thoughts warmed his cold body in a manner that his lost blanket could not. He thanked God for those memories. Mato shook his head. After what must have been seven, perhaps eight hours of perched safety, only now did he remember to give his thanks. He closed his eyes for the first time that night without being afraid, and tried to thank the One who had spared his life.

Mato was not sure how he was supposed to say his thanks. Sure, he knew how to recite both the Our Father and Hail Mary, but he had said those a million times before, without feeling anything. So he improvised. Mato spoke about how he survived the possibility of being eaten alive. Finally realizing this made Mato sob.

"Thank you," he muttered through tears. "Amen."

As he opened his eyes, Mato heard the One below let off another howl. But this howl was different. This howl was strange. It was high-pitched. More of a whine than a call of strength. Mato thought the wolf sounded frightened.

The One looked up at Mato, and Mato stared right back at him. The once piercing green eyes were not piercing anymore. The wolf that had tormented him now looked like a scared little wet puppy lost in the snow. And though he did not know why, Mato continued to stare at him with force. The wolf had to look away. The One attempted to howl once more, but nothing left its mouth. Startling itself at this, the One hurried off! Its minions ran after their leader, and within a few moments, the entire pack, all forty of them, followed suit. For the first time that night, Mato knew he was all alone. But, in his high perch, he did not feel lonely.

This silence however was only a brief respite. A loud, muffled noise could be heard in the distance. Mato, at first could not make out what it was. Not that he was that adventurous to find out. He knew it would be crazy to get out of his tree so soon. He would sit and make sure the pack had left for good. Perhaps they were setting a trap and hiding behind the bushes, hoping he would return to the ground and then they could have the last laugh. After a night in the trees, paranoia was a reasonable friend to have.

Whatever it was, Mato's focus was distracted by the morning

Chapter 8

sun ready to make its daily appearance. The sun is a slow riser in the winter, but it quickly thawed Mato's frosty limbs, removing the unwanted night dew. Mato could hear the Cuckoos chirping their hello to the new morning. Noticeably, his heart was singing with them. Mato smiled. His shoulders dropped. He relaxed. He put his hands behind his head, and crossed his feet, content to sit a little longer, and enjoy the moment. The sun reminded Mato of the gift of another day.

With this additional light, only now could Mato properly view his tree and its surrounding areas. He could not believe the thinness and small stature of his selected tree. The branched perch was no thicker than his leg and its length was of a medium-tall man. The night before, he was certain the tree owned a stronger appearance. Now Mato learned he was wrong.

Nor did Mato climb as high as he had thought. At the time, he believed he was at least fifty feet up. Mato wasn't. He was perhaps only twelve to fifteen feet above the ground. Mato looked around. Furthermore, he could not believe he picked this little sapling, considering there were numerous large oaks standing nearby. "The night can really play tricks," Mato concluded.

Standing for the first time in ages, Mato climbed down one branch. Not to get down. He was still not ready for that, but rather to mark his territory, as a remembrance of this day. After an entire night facing the wolves without a weapon except his wits and his lamp, Mato remembered the switchblade he had in his right pocket. Part of him was glad that he had forgotten about it. It might have made him feel braver than he should have. In any regards, the rusty thing would have its purpose on this day. Mato drew out the blade and marked the tree forevermore, with his initials and a short statement.

M.P > WOLF

Today, Mato did feel greater than the wolves.

After he was done scrawling his memento, Mato sat back upon

his branch. This time, not because he was frightened of what might be lurking, but because he wanted to. He was not ready to leave. He liked it here, on his tree. Mato sat and pondered his bizarre experience. He pondered what he had been given. He still could not believe what he survived, but survive he did.

Then once more, Mato heard a distant sound. It was different than the sounds heard the previous night. It was more inviting, even friendly. Finally, he could make it out. The sounds held a word. One he had heard a trillion times. "Mato!" the sound called. "Mato!"

Mato realized what or rather who it was. It was his father, with others from the village, echoing his father's call.

"*Mato!*" they yelled.

"Over here! Over here!" he laughed, over and over again, till the new pack arrived to his evening dwelling.

Within a few minutes, staffs and guns in hand, the troop arrived to the spot where Mato was stationed. The pack of men had heard the wolves and feared the worst. But on this night, the wolves did not get to eat. Their hunger was to brood for another day, while Mato's would soon be filled with bread.

-9-

Odmaranje[1]

Life is made up of millions of thoughts, all running at a million strides an hour. The mind can't help it. It never stops. It's always chasing something, even while we sleep. It is surprising then, though it is powerful enough to conjure millions of recollections, the mind feebly focuses on only a small handful of ideas. Over and over again, the persistent focus on this small list nauseatingly proves how singular we, as people are.

And that is how it was with Mato. He had millions of thoughts ruminating on a handful of ideas and memories that in summary centered on one thing. Each remembrance, in their own way counted down the last twenty-one months since the wolves. Yes, almost two years had come and gone since the great escape! That equaled a lot of running, a lot of steel production and millions of singular notions.

While every day was filled with the same thoughts, some things did change, like Mato's foreman. The previous mean brute was thankfully gone, making work far more pleasurable for the entire crew. Nico, though born in Germany, spoke perfect Croatian, except for a Bavarian twang, which amused Mato, as he'd never heard a foreigner speak Croatian before. But what Mato really appreciated

---

1 Rest

about Nico was he encouraged the entire crew to learn new roles in differing departments. Currently, Mato was learning to drive the cranes, an extremely difficult and important job for someone so young. Not that anyone gave that a second thought, as Mato proved he was a natural with machinery.

Beyond the mill, millions of thoughts went home to Pavlovići. A million thoughts each were spent on his father, mother, and especially his grandmother. Each winter, Mato, like the rest of the family worried a million times over if it would be Vjera's last. And yet, after each winter, the tough old bear would emerge from her den and taste another spring. Mato pondered a million times how Mirko would be glad to see her again.

Twenty-one months had gone, and over a million thoughts were spent on his brother. With the two years' service almost complete, Mirko would be home soon, for at least a furlough, as all expected Mirko to make the Navy his career. How Mato missed Mirko. This longing cost Mato another million thoughts. Sure, Mato wrote all the time and even got the occasional letter in return, but sadly, Mirko's replies never said enough. Truthfully, they said very little. Each note was always short, and very to the point. They would rarely comment on what Mato had written in the preceding letter, and more frustratingly, Mirko gave very few details about his new adventures. This always surprised Mato. He thought those living their dreams would have much more to say. The short notes would simply repeat that he was doing well and was enjoying himself. There was little of Mirko's charm and personality in them. Mato sometimes wondered why he bothered to write them at all.

Still, Mato knew Mirko would be home soon, and then things could go back as they were. Then they could talk face-to-face and share millions of thoughts. Mato was especially eager to talk about his fateful night when he defeated the wolves, just like his great-great grandfather Pepan.

Mato thought a lot about that long night. Millions of thoughts on one night. He thought about the chase, how fast he had been and how quickly he climbed. He thought about the wolves that raced after him and then questioned him in a haze of a dream. But most of all, Mato thought about each hour spent in his amazing tree, and the weird tasting nourishment he found there. Knowing it was not honey, Mato had spent a million thoughts trying to figure out what the stuff was. Even after all this time, Mato could still taste its sweetness on his tongue. He still craved more. Eating anything else, even his Baba's pita now felt like a chore. He had gone back to that tree, of course, to seek for more of the delightful food, but there was none to be found. That surprised him because the tree looked very healthy, though curiously it had not grown any taller.

Mato's lack of appetite was not the only change. Sleep seemed even less important than food. Mato would often stay up half the night. Others noticed it too. His father and mother at first worried about Mato, but Vjera knew better. "He gets stronger each week," the old baba reminded them. "So don't worry."

Vjera was right! Mato was becoming more powerful. Though you would not see it from his slender appearance, Mato was an ox that could haul more than his body weight. He was also faster than ever. No one could catch him. Mato now competed against and defeated adults regularly. Most of these races were not even close. Mato was not only healthier, but he was happier. He especially enjoyed his Sundays. He had a million thoughts for each of them. Being that there were eighty-four of them these past twenty-one months ensured a lot of introspection.

Mato had another million thoughts at the ready when he awoke to enjoy another Sunday: the eighty-fifth since that night in the tree. Mato was home, and he was glad for it. With millions of thoughts focused on work and the Sutjeska, naturally Mato thought less and less about faraway places. His grandmother and mother had long ago stopped asking him where he had been that particular week, for the answer was always the same: Vareš! Mato would then start boring them about machines, conveyors and other contraptions that they cared little about.

And though Mara and Vjera missed Mato's verbal journeys, they were glad too, because they understood it meant Mato was further accepting his life, which then lessened the sadness residing in Mijo's heart. It was undeniable, that the more Mato morphed, the more Mijo returned to being his old self. As Mato slept less, Mijo also slept less. As Mato ate less, Mijo drank less. As Mato ran faster over the mountain, Mijo ventured a little further beyond his tight circle. The more Mato discussed his machines, the less Mijo worried about the future, for he knew his son was slowly conquering the mountain.

Not that Mato knew much about all of this. He was simply glad to get up each of the previous eighty-five Sunday mornings, with his family, sans his older brother, for the hour-long journey, and place their feet on holy ground. Like all the other Croatians in the region, they flooded two by two towards their Kraljeva Sutjeska.

Built by the Franciscans in the 14th century, the Kraljeva Sutjeska was a monument to the Catholic faith that would have befitted any grand city in the Western world. Situated a short amble from Bobovac, a small town from where Croatian kings once ruled, it was now the heart of their faith. From all over the Sutjeska they would migrate, to pray, praise, play, and delay tomorrow's worry. Each time he arrived to the foot of cathedral, Mato was awestruck by the majestic white stone that adorned the exterior facade. Beautiful regardless of the season, Mato especially loved it in the winter, as its appearance conjured images of what heaven might look like.

As much as Mato enjoyed the exterior, he was amazed by its apse. The structure was held up by a vast array of columns and arches of Gothic proportions that went as far as his eyes could see. But what Mato was beginning to understand, for each visitor the greatest gift given during this weekly pilgrimage was not the building. It was rather, every week, each was the given a comforting reminder that they were not alone. Whether from Aljinjići, Bulčići, Bjelo Polje, Dujmovići, Grmace, Lučići, Pavlovići, or any of the other high places, at least on Sunday, they were all together. Well, mostly together. Mato wondered why the priests looked so stern.

"They look so cross," Mato remarked, while sitting next to his mother.

"You know, a long time ago the monks were revered, because they refused to convert when the Ottoman came," Mara began.

Chapter 9

Mato looked puzzled, as he wondered what that had to do with his statement.

"But that was a long time ago." His mother continued. "Now all that is left is the burden. It's a heavy burden to carry that cross for Christ all day, my dear," she remarked, looking up at the statue of the beaten and scared Savior, depicted in polished wood.

"They have to carry it all day?" Mato queried, startled by the idea of constantly lugging anything so cumbersome.

"Most of the priests come as just boys, not knowing that the comfort of a meal will come at the cost of a lonely, unmarried existence. Sometimes this is a dangerous way to live," she lamented, her son totally oblivious to her meaning. "It is a heavy price," she pondered with sadness.

"It's dangerous not to get married, Mama?" Mato asked. But by then his Mother's mind was elsewhere, thinking about a million other things.

Mato scanned the cathedrals pews. Like every other week, they were filling quickly. From Čatići, Govedovići, Lukovo Brdo, Ratanj, Tesevo, Veliki Trnovci, Zajzda and more, they came. They came from their farms, the factories, and from the mines. They even came from the growing politburo. Together, each family would stand and sit. Sit and stand. Open their hymnal. Worship and pray, and remember what they were, and what they might be. Sing and stand. Sit and read along. Look at the decorations and colored windows. Sit. "This is the Word of the Lord," they would recite and then stand. And then sit and listen to the Father teach what they just read. Stand and stretch. Amen. But with Mass completed, it signified only the beginning of the Sabbath festivities. After all, the people of the Kraljeva Sutjeska did not need an excuse to celebrate. And besides, it is easier to ignore the chores if they were an hour away.

In Kraljeva Square, families would sit and eat, sit and talk, and catch up on the news of family and friends living in nearby villages, from Prapatno, from Kopjari, and so forth. Conversation of life would hum throughout the vast crowd, with a cavalcade of stories coupled with free-flowing laughter. How's your son in the Navy? How's your mother? How's your sickly cow? How, how, how, and more how's. Others would tempt fate, and share whispered thoughts about government business. But this was rare and generally unwanted, even by those from the politburo. Rather, the gathering would be about the sounds of voices, piano accordions and tamburicas, daring the first of many Kolos, which would not cease until the Hasikovanje for this Sunday was complete.

Though Sunday mornings were about Mass, and the afternoon about gathering, the evenings were always about the Hasikovanje. The Hasikovanje were a Sunday tradition even before the Friars came. It's ritual older than its current name. A million thoughts agreed the Hasikovanje was older than the largest trees found in Kopjari. Whether this was true or not did not matter; the Hasikovanje was as uniquely Bosnian as the mountains themselves. It belonged to all the people, but especially the younger souls who were preparing for their final rite of passage. And as it should be for those growing souls still considered children, their rite of passage was based on a game.

Not like games they played before. While other mountain skills valued craft, guile, and tact, in the Hasikovanje you also needed wit and charm. You needed to understand the value of the exchange rates of words, which was worth more than paper money, they whispered, "Especially since the paper now had Tito's face on it." After all, like paper money, not all words were of equal value. To perfect the Hasikovanje, one needed a sharp mind and brilliant tongue. You needed to understand the value of poetry, like a farmer might a sickle.

In the game, boys and girls would pair off at the Sutjeska square and *"the Talk"* would begin, though it was more than just talk. Each speaker was expected to conjure sonnets, and give verbal gifts from the cusp of their mind. The best talkers would weave verse that they learned from all genres, everything from the traditional farming folklore to Shakespeare, to give their verbal music a chance to dance. This was a serious business. In the Sutjeska, the most popular youth were the best talkers. Success one week would make you most desired the next. After all, nobody wishes to be stuck talking to a gray wall.

Chapter 9

Regardless, the Hasikovanje allowed the girls to find out which boys were not only capable farmers, but which ones valued testing their mind. Furthermore, the young ladies could learn whether the young men were made of hot-aired bravado, or a mixture of wisdom, wit, and innocent charm. The boys in turn, would find out which girls would respond to their complements with either intelligence or vanity. And through this little game that had been around for centuries, with each new week both the boys and girls had an opportunity to learn to like each other before lust and responsibilities dared to get in the way. In reality, the Hasikovanje was not about talking at all. It was a game of life and love. Other than crops, what else should matter, especially when one is so young?

On this eighty-fifth Sunday, the families of the mountain had spent a good amount of time together. Food had been eaten, and conversation had been had. The children had consumed cakes and sugar treats. For the bookends of age, both oldest and youngest, it was time to head home. In fact, Mato noticed that his mother, father, and grandmother had already started to leave. Mijo said they needed to, as "Baba is not feeling very well."

"I'll come too, and help get her home," Mato suggested.

"No son, you stay," replied his Tata. "Your grandmother likes to know you're having fun. We'll see you later."

"Okay," was all Mato could reply.

As Mato headed towards the square, he waved to his smiling grandmother, and she in turn, feebly raised her hand. Vjera was happy to see her grandson embracing the mountain life. Mato had only recently begun to join in the parade of words, although anemic at the art. For months his grandmother had plotted to involve him into the fray. He naturally was reluctant. "You mean I have to talk to them, them girls?" Mato blurted.

"Yes," replied Mara. "How'd you think your father courted me, and your grandfather netted your grandmother?"

"But I don't think I want to," replied Mato, nervously.

"Why not?" mocked Mijo, "You're willing to take on a pack of wolves, but you're scared of some little girls?"

"Oh, stop that, Mijo!" fussed Vjera, slapping Mijo's back. "Don't worry about all of that silliness," offered Vjera to Mato, knowing her young grandson was not quite ready. "Sit, relax, and get away from us stupid older people and all of our troubles, okay?"

That advice was given over four months ago. Mara wanted to push Mato to stay and play right away, but as always, both Mijo and Mara deferred to the wise old owl, and left Mato alone. "You wait and see," Vjera began. "You plant a seed and watch it grow."

As always, Vjera was correct. About ten weeks later, a nervous Mato sprouted from the mountainous soil. Just as the summer months were slowly beginning to cool, he did not go home after the festivities with the rest of his family. He stayed and dipped his toe into the Hasikovanje. Mato would say he could not help it. A pretty girl he had not seen before caught his eye. He was hoping she might give it back.

Part II
Žene[1]

Predahnuti[1]

(Lumen est)[2]

I was brought to the banquet.
Me, the mountain's young charge
To be nourished
By a banner that spoke so large!
About who we longed to be
In the Sutjeska!
The table was set.
Decorated with cakes, pita and promise.
Because verse and supper are always prepared.
And I wanted to eat deeply
For I knew I needed to.
And though not young anymore
I was homesick.
Before I sipped from our cup
An evil did erupt!
We learned.
Oh, we learned.
All of us were had!

---

1 A short breather
2 Latin for purgatory

The banquet was a sham.
We all could now see
Once the blanket was pulled back.
With haste
The awful dance commenced.
Defined by cast lots
A battalion quickly lost.
So many dreams jostled and tossed!
Each drowned in blood.
Though fear found us
Finally, valiant swords and spears
With righteous banners did appear.
Upon each was written;
Lies, truth, bravery, fear.
Battling against every foe
that swooped and veered
I stood there.
A simple, foolish mountain servant
Alongside each fellow
A brave soldier, peasant and artist
We charged our hearts out of their fortresses.
Against every demonic darkness.
Into our pillaged fields and desolated forest.
With baited breath.
I, a fearful servant
though grateful for sweet bloodied toil
Needing respite,
I waited.
But, before our righteous banners could strike
The vulture,
A friend of rogues and shams.
Fluttered forcefully out of its once mighty cage.
It flew over the flowered fields
And highest mountains range
To hoard over my, a young charge's frame.

And plagued me with woe!
Powerfully, and quickly so
It was satisfied
With my lowered place
The terror sat upon the jester's lap.
It pestered with agitating quips,
that all could mournfully hear
"Death is done!
Get ready!
You're all as good as dead!"
So I, the young fool who followed folly
I cowered and hid.
That is shamefully what I did.
But I strengthened myself,
Believing it could not be helped.
For I, was wintered by sadness of fight.

Lamentably, I anguished
With the painful question I pondered
To which garden has she gone?
I cannot see her, the Lovely Sutjeska!
Her wild flowers of peace
Of pinks, oranges, reds and blues.
Oh pain!
The vile brute
Would not listen to me.
I despaired.
Oh where, oh where could she be?
This young maiden of mystery.
I hear your voice Sutjeska!
I hear your song over the drums.
My youth once drank a cup of honeycomb.
Let me once more be refreshed
By the mountain's forthcoming snow
So I might remember which way

I am supposed to go.
Verily, the sun did return.
I, the mountain's peasant
Was awakened from the terror of one's sleep.
The banquet,
Its sham and vultures death
All appeared done.
Though, I thought all was lost forever
But here I sat, safe
Naturally questioning my fate.
Was I, the last lost explorer
Still in Sutjeska's realm?
And was the blood of battle
Won or forever lost?
But chance!
The mountains brought forth a new road
That felt good to my feet.
And delivered me, a humble servant
A horizon
I had never known.
That coupled with good rest,
Might allow me to dream mightily.
So I, the young charge
followed this new path.
And happily
Began eating pitaya,
Cut from a newly discovered tree.
Each taste removed fears
That I did not know I owned.
With a pocket knife
I, the mountain's young charge
Went further
Cutting down a jackfruit
While a Jumbuck
Peacefully drank from a pond with coolibah.

Then thankfully
It was then
I and my beloved Sutjeska,
were once more reunited.
There we waltzed fleetingly.
Beyond the mountains so blue
seemingly for only us to view.
But I, the young mountain adventurer
Foolish and wrong
Took an ill turn.
I viewed
"Oh, not you!"
I darted for the hills.
Exclaiming with dread and fear, shouting
"You cannot catch us, wolves, you cannot!"
It was then I truly knew
Better than the brave soldier, peasant and artist
How I needed my Sutjeska!
And yet
The evening hangs.
A remembrance of the price.
Till the day breaks
I will go my way.
Into the mountains and foray.
With hope not provided
By swords or spear
Or victories cheer.
But by a new stronger banquet
Of the first and the final tense.
And without blood on my hands
Satisfied.
I can run
And perhaps once more a Kolo I will dance.
However, beware!
I say Beware!

For I have learned first hand
The shadows
Is only a day away.
Unspeakable vultures, wolves and crows!
Longing and yearning to take flight
With a new fear.
On the lips of the unknown future and the foregone.
If you dare to listen,
Listen, Listen, Listen.
They mockingly proclaim,
"Nothing is going to be the same!"

Govoriti[1]

The night can change your perception. It can change your vision. And if you are not careful, it will reshape what you think you see. Up until tonight, Mato had little appreciation for the Hasikovanje. The past few weeks, at the behest of his eager family, Mato had forced himself to at least stand around its very edges, hoping in vain to decipher what the fuss was all about. His previous efforts seemed a waste of time.

But tonight was different. Tonight, Mato was there because he thought he saw, well…something! He was certain of it. Something caught his eye. A glimmer that sparkled. Though he did not get a fix on it, he believed he saw something, because when he tried to remember what he saw, it made him smile in an embarrassed, but uniquely honest way. Mato wanted to find that glimmer, so he might smile like that again.

However, doubt lurked, suggesting, he did not see a thing. This doubt dashed Mato's weakening confidence against a stone. His innards created a buzzing canister of nerves and confusion, as if he was walking into a personal Sjeverac. His mind developed excuses for his nerves, suggesting food would settle the multiplying butterflies.

---

1 Talk

But as Mato walked and munched into a healthy piece of pita, it did not end the wanton curiosity. What was Mato to do? He thought he was going to be sick all over himself.

"*Really, this couldn't be over…*" Mato began, while he shook his head. "*No, it couldn't it. Could it?*"

Mato looked at the swaying trees. They told a story. The coolness had come early, and it gave Mato a shiver. He regretted not bringing his coat and gloves. And yet, with winter approaching, Mato was reminded and glad his simple life held its comforts; like that missing pair of dry gloves and warm garment. Even the routine of the past two hectic years, owned a comforting daily similarity to it, which made him look forward to tomorrow. All of these thoughts magnified his discontent for the Hasikovanje. "*Oh, what am I doing here?*" he pondered.

But try as he might, Mato was not ready to leave just yet. Mato's feet were not listening to his innards want of usual comforts. To his annoyance, his feet were sending him in the last place he wanted to go, into the throng of chaos and noise. Into the midst of anarchy. Mato's feet were bringing him into the Hasikovanje!

Mato's body was in the midst of a complete civil war. Mato's innards had tried reasoning and attempted logic, but his feet just would not budge. In protest, Mato's mind did the most mature thing he could think of; childishly mockery! He mocked everything about the evening. The number of boys and girls there. The way they swooned before each other. But especially, Mato mocked "*the Talk*" he heard. Oh, the awful talk! Mato's stomach churned at each churlish verse of supposed poetry. Mato thought they sounded awful. As a child, he was told that during the Hasikovanje, he would hear Shakespeare. Or perhaps Bryon and Keats, being woven with peasant-speak. Dismayed, Mato heard none of the classics, but rather a mixture of confused babble about how each boy wanted to give the weirdest gifts, like tropical fruit to each girl. Any fruit that was not grown naturally in the mountains was almost impossible to get, but Mato thought the constant use of it in folksy verse was beyond ridiculous. In fact, Mato believed everyone sounded, well…really stupid. Each failed sonnet, each broken song, made his ears twitch, and his vocal cords snicker.

Instead of seeking the glimmer, or worrying what he might say if he did play in *"the Talk"*, Mato created his own game, he found immediately satisfying. His invention was to try to memorize as many awful attempts as possible, so to make fun of his pals later. With each line, laughter was building. Mato scoffed with each given pineapple, banana, and orange. The only thing Mato could not understand was why he was the only one having fun in this way.

"Why do people sound so dimwitted when they are attempting to be so smart?" he opined, while listening in on a private conversation.

"My dearest," Mato heard a chap pronounce.

"I would purchase a fragrant bounty of fruit,
From distant sands.
If I might be allowed to hold your hand,"
Mato cringed. *"What is he talking about?"*

"And what would my father think?" Mato heard the maiden reply.

"No problem," the boy sighed. *"Here is my father's gift of rakija for your Tata. Please drink."*

"Really? That's his response?" Mato laughed.

"That is quite a forward notion, dear boy," the lady in waiting mentioned.

"To offer my father a cup to get drunk.
My mother would not approve a tongue so rude."
"Or dumb," Mato smirked.

"My pardon,
But don't make haste," the boy motioned, and they continued to walk.

"Don't dismiss a humble gift.
Understand,
I too am chaste."
"Ha!" Mato started, biting his hand to stop the laughter becoming too loud.

"And of mountain stock.
But my dear,

Kata's Father

Tonight as you sleep,
Understand the truth.
My heart will be awake,
And wander in gardens,
Built for you.
Searching for one so sweet,
Under the light of a full moon."

"*Yuck!*" Mato's mind spat with disgust. "That was yuck!" he lips muttered. "Yuck, yuck," Mato continued in a most boorish fashion, unable to remove the taste placed in his gob by their private words.

But this couple, like all the others surrounding Mato, took no notice. They were too busy being amused at each silly statement. They were too busy laughing at themselves, as if laughing at each other was the most natural way to learn to about someone. They could not see nor hear Mato's stinging critique, so much was their enjoyment. They could not hear Mato because the Hasikovanje was doing its magic, breaking barriers, and building a foundation. Mato did not understand, but why would he? He was still confusing a childlike game with being childish.

But as Mato quibbled at the lack of literary genius that was in the Sutjeska square, luckily not all of him agreed with his opinion of *"the Talk."* His feet, once more were one step ahead, ready to answer questions his mouth, ears and innards did not wish to know.

Mato's feet made a beeline for a mountain flower, now, perhaps only thirty yards in front of him. She had disappeared while Mato played his game, but to his surprise, there she was once more. He smiled the new smile for the second time that evening, building a need he had never known. Happily, Mato stepped towards this new frontier, but inadvertently, it also led him into a mass of ill-disciplined giggling young humans. These talkers, showed an unthoughtful disregard, thwarting a new adventurer's commanding stride. "*She's getting away!*" Mato's mind bellowed. "*Where's she going? She is not going away, is she?*" he fretted.

Chapter 10

He had never seen so many people his age in his entire life. Frustrated, his voice wanted to call out beyond the masses, but what could he shout? "Hey you!" What would that do? Nothing! Though exasperated, Mato found some humor in his situation, laughing when he imagined he was like Livingstone cutting through the fringe of forest to get to his mapped zenith. But the forest kept growing and growing both in size and noise. Amazingly, Mato could now hear music.

As if on cue, a Kolo, with its whirling dervish surrounded Mato from all sides, further barricading and tussling his every move. An older, uncaring brute, without noticing Mato, hipped him of balance, without even a halfhearted attempt to make amends. This left Mato to the effects of gravity and the evening's dampening turf. Now on the ground, to Mato's dismay, instead of slowing, the Kolo began to pick up speed. Sprawled out beneath them, painfully, Mato found himself being stomped on by the unwitting dancing throng.

But suddenly, a saving arm reached out towards him! Instinctively, Mato grasped the salvation that the hand was providing. With great force, a slender arm and a small hand propelled him out of the quagmire. So eager to rediscover the girl he had being following all evening, Mato did not even remember to thank his rescuer. Mato jumped quickly up and down on the spot, hoping to catch a glimpse of his lost target, and while doing so, he missed who or what is in front of him. "Are you looking for someone?" a girl's voice, near Mato, asked.

"Um, yes, someone," Mato responded while continuing to look beyond the throng. But as he answered, Mato's eyes finally met the voice and learned the awful truth; that his object of pursuit was now standing directly in front of him. "Oh, yes," he croaked, a toad unable to gracefully reply. "Yes, someone."

"Well, aren't you going to say thank you?" the girl stated, sternly.

"Um, yes" Mato stuttered, embarrassed that he was rescued by the very person that placed him in this new danger.

"Well?" the young girl no more than sixteen years of age demanded forcefully.

"Well, um, what?" Mato retorted, as gracefully as a three-legged bull. In the background, Mato was certain he just heard the couple he was mocking earlier begin laughing at him.

"What do you want?" the girl asked bluntly. Mato gulped. He was taken aback by her impatient nature, though he kind of liked it.

But with her continuing stern demeanor, Mato's smile quickly was replaced by a rapidly drying and frowning mouth. This made Mato angry with himself. Angry that he even came to this Hasikovanje. Mato had suspected he was ill fitted for it all, and now he was certain. What made everything worse, Mato was also sure, that the younger version of himself who dreamed and traveled to far off places nobody heard of, was far better equipped for the daunting challenges now before him. Just over two years ago, "*the Talk*" would have come so naturally, the young lady before him would not have gotten a word in edgewise. He would have offered her all types of fruit, from places she had never heard of, his imagination had eaten a million times before.

Time was ticking! Mato's brow was flooding with perspiration. He needed to say something, but what? Mato did not know where to turn. His recent experience gave him little space to move. What was he going to talk about? Machines and steel? Boring! Mato needed the old Mato back, but he knew the explorer was lost. And now, out of the blue he was asking himself to find him without a map. Mato felt lost.

Wasn't what was lost, lost forever? Doesn't a violin that is not played lose its ability to make music as it once did? Tonight, for the first time in a long time, he set out for adventure, and all he found was that he had little confidence in himself anymore. And because of this awful find, Mato realized he was afraid to chase. He had not run after anything except work since that night he flew from the wolves. It was if Mato realized that though he survived that night, the old Mato did not make it out of the tree. Again, Mato was certain the young lady standing in front of him, would have preferred to chat with the old him. For the first time, a long while, Mato realized that he preferred the younger version as well. What made Mato feel worse was it was he who had killed him.

Chapter 10

"Hey, you! Where are you going?" the young lady asked.

She could see Mato's fears and she could see he was edging away. She felt kind of special because of his nervousness, which calmed and strengthened her focus, for she was there for a reason as well. She too was looking for something, and needed a question answered. A question that she was certain only the boy before her knew how to answer. It was a question that has been eating at her insides for much of the evening. To learn the answer, the young lady was even willing to thwart the boy's escape.

"You do not have to be afraid," the girl noted, while grabbing Mato by the arm, in a duel attempt to reassure him and stop him from departing. "I saw you looking at me. I didn't mind it. I don't expect you to say much. I can see *"the Talk"* does not come naturally. It's okay. Maybe, we can say just a little. It might be nice to chat, you know?"

Talk? What was Mato to say? How do you start a race you are not prepared for? Did the starter pistol go off? What could he note that might impress her, and be worthy of her? He knew nothing. He felt like nothing. He was an ignorant peasant. A steelworker. A child. He was not his brave brother, nor his loving mother. He was not his wise baba. He was not a shadow of his father, who was the mountain and he a pebble to kick into a stream.

"You should say something. It's alright, I won't laugh," the girl said hopefully. " I think we could be friends, you and me."

This made Mato smile, though nothing more than this. How long, he wondered had the silence continued. Two seconds? Two minutes? Two lifetimes?

"I will start," the girl continued, determined.
"I am Verka, from the higher mountains I live.
Strawberries there,
Grow real big."

Mato laughed. He let out an unwanted blast, loud and uncontrolled. He didn't mean too. But he did so anyway. The girl blushed, embarrassed. "Well, it's not like you are saying anything better!" she protested.

"Here's another one," she continued with consternation, her insides now demanding she flee.

"Did a wolf catch your tongue?
Are you stupid? Are you dumb?
Whatever, Stupid.
Have a nice night.
I'M DONE!"

"No, don't, please!" Mato stammered as Verka stepped away. Mato finally stopped thinking, for at least a second, and stepped towards her, with forlorn, apologetic eyes. He wanted to tell her he was not laughing at her, or making fun. He was giggling at himself. But, he had giggled too soon. The laughing is supposed to come after both have talked, after both have played. As yet, Mato was not a participant, but only a spectator. He had yet to combine words to stoke heights that might sore beyond the magicians, and word wizards; or at least peasants with fruit fetishes. And yet this for him was a breakthrough. He was ready to maybe have fun. To be silly. To be young.

"I'm sorry," Mato blurted. "I thank you for telling me something about yourself because I wanted to know your name. Verka," he said through a smile, signaling his approval. He liked saying her name.

"I have not seen you before," Mato continued, outside the rules of *"the Talk"*.

"Oh no," Verka protested.
"You have to create a verse anew,
So, I might laugh too."

Mato did not wish to be laughed at. But he knew he had to act, and soon. Regretfully, all Mato could think of was all the awful lines he had made fun of earlier that night.

"Pineapples and bananas are stupid," he muttered, not realizing he spoke out loud.

"What? What was that?" Verka asked, bemused.

"Nothing," Mato replied, further embarrassed by his ineptitude.

"Well, I'm waiting," Verka demanded, placing her hands on her hips. "If you don't say something soon, I am going to call you a mean liar, and say you were laughing at me. I'll tell everyone!"

"Something, huh," Mato asked, rubbing an imagery beard.

"C'mon!" Verka, protested. "You're stalling."

"Yes, yes, I am," Mato, laughed. "Something."

"Hurry up!"

"Shush," Mato calmly whispered, putting his finger to his lips.

"Did you just shush me?" protested Verka.

"Yes," Mato answered, "But let me begin. Okay, ahem," Mato closed his eyes and coughed, clearing his voice for what felt like the first time in two years.

"I could offer you bananas,
And other items
That around here
Are considered a rare thing.
But what would that bring?
Not a lot.
A moment's blot,
That gives a stomach minor comforting.
So perhaps,
I might mention,
Fruit of distant lands.
From Asia like rambutan.
But honestly,
This is what I think.
When I sit and ponder,
In between each eye blink,
That maybe one day,
One pleasant day,
I might find,
With one to pair,
And share "the Talk"
About the scariest place,
That I hide,
Deep inside,
A beautiful place where my true dreams reside."

The two young people stood there startled. Mato was far more surprised. His innards were in complete shock, his lungs out of breath. His mind was in a vacuum of silence. Though the throng was clustered around them, at that moment, both Mato and Verka were alone. Mato heard nothing. Not words. Not laughter. No sounds except his heavily pounding heart.

"He is not dead," Mato muttered, he thought only to himself.

"Okay, I guess he is not," Verka, finally mused, slightly weirded out by the fact Mato just acknowledged either an imagery friend or perhaps a split personality. "I was hoping you might have rhymed your name with something," she laughed as she grabbed the stunned boy's right hand.

"Oh, sorry," Mato blushed.

"Mato is my name.

I like to run,

In the snow, sun, or rain."

"That's better," Verka replied, laughing. And with that Mato laughed too. A big very happy laugh, and then he laughed some more. After this the two of them said nothing for an hour. All they did was giggle, and giggle, like two silly, but very happy kids. And the best thing was, neither thought there was anything more appropriate.

Mato ran all the way home, gleefully euphoric! He had never arrived back from church faster, though he had also never stayed back later. He was most satisfied with himself, and his evening. He could not wait for next Sunday, where both new friends promised to meet again. After this solemn pact, the two of them just sat there, holding hands and watching the rest of the Hasikovanje. It was as if what they had said was enough. With this knowledge and promise, Mato burst upon his home, bringing with him the hope of tomorrow.

But as Mato open the door and stepped upon the house floor as he had a million times before, a terrible heaviness invaded his belly, which left an awful taste in Mato's mouth. The air on the first floor held tears and worry. It had his mother sitting at the table, red eyed, her face puffy from distress. The wall hit Mato hard, and terror stomped upon his mind.

"Mama, what happened?" Mato asked fearfully.

It took all of Mara's strength to lift her head and answer her son.

"Baba, is… she is…" Mara stammered, unable to finish her sentence.

From upstairs, a creaking of a door and Mijo's footsteps could be heard below.

"Son," Mijo began forcefully, but with care. "You better come upstairs. Baba wants to see you."

-II-

Soba za goste¹

Mato wanted a lot more stairs, but there would never be enough of them. Logically, Mato realized a million stairs would not delay the truth, or thwart the grief. Nor fear.

With each step northward, up the millionth stair in his mind, the unknown haunted him. Mato had yet to witness death. He did not know what it might look like. He was afraid of what he was going to find. He was afraid how much this was going to hurt. He wanted to see his baba, but not like this. He was too afraid to go in, but too scared to delay seeing her one more time. Mato wished to go back in time. To go back to church. Back to the Hasikovanje. Back to a time when everything was comfortably the same.

But the steps ran out. Mato shook his head. Dread filled his heart. So much so, he regretted the entire evening, feeling now that he should have gone back with the family, as he had originally suggested. Had he not listened to them, then he could have helped his baba back home. Mato felt guilty for listening. Tears were already welling up inside him. His feet were made of heavy iron, refusing to move him any closer.

And yet, the stairs ran out, and he made it to the door all the

_____

1 Guest room

same. Mato closed his eyes, and took the longest breath of his life, gently tapping the door's surface.

"Come in," chirped Vjera, from behind the old wooden door.

Mato timidly peered into the room. He observed his father sitting beside his mother's bed, looking as grave as he felt. Mato could only see Vjera's head and neck, the rest hidden under a mountain of warm blankets.

"Here I am Baba," Mato whispered nervously. "I am sorry I took so long to come. To come home, I mean."

"Nonsense," Baba retorted with zeal. "I know you were having fun this evening. I could feel it," she noted with complete confidence. "Where is my son?" she asked, turning her head, while coughing through the words.

"Here, Mama," Mijo stammered. "Do you need something? Anything?"

"I need you both," Vjera wheezed. "I need you both to come here." The two generations of Pavlović men shuffled nervously closer, each scared that each breath Vjera blew was going to be her last. "Come here now, I have something to share with both of you," she whispered.

"Don't talk, Mama. You need your strength," Mijo began.

"Son, sometimes you do sound stupid!" Vjera laughed, through a painful, hoarse cough. "What do I need strength for? Listen!" Vjera fussed with the blankets. They were so heavy, but in her frail condition, the cold beyond them was far worse. She had never felt a harsher winter. She knew life was leaving her. Yet, this realization created a wonderful large smile that could not help but get bigger and bigger. Though the cold made her miserable, she was content, but she needed to do one more thing.

"My boys, I beg you. Listen!" Vjera continued. "The mountains. The mountains have been good to me. Good to both of you."

"Yes Mama," Mijo answered.

"Be quiet boy! Just, listen," Vjera, wheezed.

"I am, Mama," answered Mijo.

"Not to me, son. Not to me," replied Vjera as she began to raise her frail body. "I want to sit up."

Both Pavlović men jumped from their hypnotized positions, hoping to aid Vjera's last wants in any way.

"I am thirsty," Vjera pronounced.

Mato grabbed a small cup of water, and placed it to his grandmother's lips. He looked upon Vjera's thankful eyes, noticing for the first time how deep and powerful they looked. Colored with the most striking pale blue, like the freshest water of the River Bosna. Mato thought his grandmother looked beautiful. He pulled up Vjera's blankets, in an attempt to further comfort his grandmother, but Vjera resisted. With whatever strength she had within, Vjera pointed an arm and her boney index finger towards her sparse bookshelf. "Over there, Mato," she whispered. "Get my Bible. Get it for me."

Mato sped over and brought it back to his sickly grandmother. The old book was tattered and frail, just like its owner. "Have you got it?" Vjera chortled through the phlegm and pain.

"Yes Baba," Mato replied.

"Good, give it to your father, and then come closer," she commanded. "Both of you, it's getting hard to…"

"Please Mama, just rest," voiced a scared Mijo.

"I will, I will. Soon. Don't fret yourself, my boy. My beautiful man," answered Vjera. The old lady stopped talking for a second, pausing purposely, so that she might gaze upon them. She loved them so. Vjera looked upon them proudly. She looked at the both, and remembered what she had prayed for all these years; to see hope in the mountains. She nodded to herself, approvingly, and then continued with what she needed to say. "The book, the mountains, can help. All of you, if you want." Vjera stopped short again, this time by an agitating attack of the coughs. Both could tell Vjera was frustrated. There was so much to say. Once more, Mato brought forth the small glass of water, in a hope to relieve his grandmother's suffering, but he was thwarted by a persistent old bird who wished to finish her thoughts. "Full of song is our Sutjeska, isn't it Mijo?" Vjera asked.

"Yes Mama," Mijo responded, not really understanding her point, but willing to agree to anything at this moment.

"Lots to see as well, right Mato?"

Chapter 11

"Yes Baba," Mato replied.

"Boys, the book has answers to its songs," she continued. "For all three of you. For you and both your boys, Mijo. I found 'em, I found 'em."

Vjera's voice was no more than a mouse sized whisper, her vocal cords stretched and dry.

"Mato, your brother. He will need the book too. Will you look after my book?" she asked them both.

"Yes," them answered in unison.

"Good," Vjera replied. "Now," she continued, with a cheeky look appearing on her wrinkled face and in her pale blue eyes. "Mato, come closer my boy. Really close." The lad moved closer and leaned in. He thought of the numerous times Vjera had asked him to lean in. He wondered what wisdom she might pass along. He hoped it would be wise enough to comfort him at this time. "My boy, let me ask you. Is she pretty?" she asked.

Mato was startled. Vjera chuckled, and asked again. "Is she pretty? I can see it in your face, so just tell me. Is she?"

"Yes, Baba," Mato answered, his voice choking up.

"Good," she nodded to herself. "Good. My boy, one more thing," Vjera continued.

"Yes Baba," asked Mato.

"Mato," she began. "Tell me sweet boy, for old time's sake. The night of the wolves. When they thought they had you. Where were you going?"

Mato seemed confused. "What do you mean, Baba?"

"C'mon boy," Vjera insisted. "Where were you traveling? Tell me."

Mato hesitated, trying to remember a thought that had fallen through a hole in his pocket.

"Tell me, sweet boy," she repeated.

"I was going… I was going…" Mato stumbled through the cobwebs. Finally, Mato opened the correct file.

"Australia, Baba," Mato said proudly. "With the kangaroos."

"Good boy. Thank you," Vjera whispered, and breathed no more.

Kata's Father

✳✳✳

A few weeks later, in a far off place, near the Yugoslavian border that hugs Bulgaria, there is a small, almost pitch black room. Adjacent to this overtly poorly-lit room, there are a dozen exact spaces, all equally sharing the awful darkness. All the rooms are in fact the same size, and same in their purpose. Each of these rooms is there to make a building. Very few, except those in very high places know about this building. This is because the building is deep under the ground. Even those who know about it keep it deep down in their thoughts, because these rooms and this building is not something anyone really wants to think about, let alone mutter about in public places.

Each room is awfully small, no bigger than five by seven feet, with a low ceiling, no more than six feet high. The walls are covered by a thick plaster, chipped and cold. Sound does not come in or leave these small boxes. Nor does the odor. Each box is filled with a rank stench of despair and of the unwashed. A long time ago, each of the unwashed once were men, with hopes and dreams. Now, each body is just there, occupying a box underground, waiting. Waiting because though no one could call this living, they are not dead, yet.

In one of the rooms, for instance, resides a figure that was once a man. Blinded by darkness, he has forgotten simple things like the warmth of the sun. He has forgotten the autumn breeze. He has forgotten what his right hand looks like in front of his face, or that this hand has a birth mark. More dreadfully, he does not remember he once had hopes and dreams. That he is loved. He has even, from time to time, forgotten he once had a name.

All he knows now is the dark. The room on most days is so dark, so lonely. So awful. Every minute, each breath, every second, each moment the darkness haunts him. It taunts him. It mocks him. It makes him despair. And through this despair, the darkness teaches him who is in control, and who is not. It is a painful lesson that he is learning well. Too well. The darkness is the worst and best teacher there ever was, and ever will be. It has taught this being, that he has lost, and they have won.

But today, there is a little hope! This room has captured a little light. Today, a candle was smuggled in with a letter. All those in confinement are not supposed to receive candles and letters, but despite darkness's best efforts, both are here all the same.

With each word of the letter, the corpse is slowly once more becoming a man, who is perhaps in his early twenties. He can smell himself for the first time in weeks, and though it makes him gag with disgust, his eyes keep reading. The candle is small and will not wait. The news in the letter sparks his mind to a million memories of the life he once enjoyed and endured before he was put into this pit. Only as he gets to the halfway point of the letter does his broken soul gather that the words before his eyes are expressing gravely sad tidings. The letter is from family he forgot he had. Tears that he did not know he had left, well up within him, teaching the man a new lesson of pain; that regardless of your new sufferings, older, more painful grief, can live deep down for a long time, even after the mind forgot their existence. This lad, this boy, this child of legal age is feeling the worst of loss. This loss is complete once he reads end of the letter;

And with that Vjera Pavlović closed her eyes and let out her last breath. On her Father's day of rest, her soul left her body to be with Him. I am so sorry brother. Baba is gone.

We buried her on a Wednesday. How she wished to see you again. She held out for so long, but her heart and body failed her. I am so sorry. I pray we might see you soon and grieve together.

With all my love,
Your braco,
Mato.

Tears and torment filled Mirko's lungs. Sprawled on the prison floor, every point of his body was hit with the need to wail and howl.

Kata's Father

Mirko tore the rags that covered his chest, hoping that might relieve the cacophony of pain that spread instantly. Alone, without a friend in the world, Mirko was a wounded mountain dog, suffering the worst of it.

And yet, trapped in that box, underground, there was no one to hear him, not even the person in the next room. No one heard his violent screams. No one heard the ripping of his cloth. No one heard anything. No one saw his pain. Not a soul. He was all alone. His pain was only his to endure. And it kept going, and going. It would not stop. There was nowhere to hide, not in this darkness, especially once the candle expired. The pain was more than he could bare and he hated himself for it. In fact, he hated everything.

-12-

Zašto?[1]

It was Sunday evening and the frigid rain left Verka near freezing. Her heart sank, and her eyes dropped, but it was not from the deluge.

"He promised to be here," she muttered to herself. "Why, Mama? Where is he? He promised!"

Verka had been so certain of everything. From the time she first woke up this morning, her mind had mapped out the entire day, and excitingly filled her with such hope. Things however turned out quite differently. "Why Mama? Why didn't he come?"

Despondently, Verka dragged herself back up the mountain. Stepping to her front door, she unexpectedly found it cracked ajar. Though this might have surprised the young lady, finding her father asleep at the dinner table, snoring as if all was well, did not. Scanning her surrounds, Verka could tell the homes appearance was clearly disheveled. Chairs had been thrown off its designed alignment. Plates and glass cups were laying in shattered pieces on the timbered floor. Verka was appalled, but unsurprised. She knew what had happened, because it had happened before.

"Tata," she muttered, revolted. As Verka moved delicately across

1 Why?

the small house, something in the corner of the far room unwittingly caught her eye.

"Oh no!" Verka gasped, as her heart crashed downwards, and laid in pieces with the broken cups and plates.

Earlier that very morning, Verka's eyes opened before the new dawn, awaken by a soul singing a happy song. Her heart, so full of hopeful excitement, could not wait to begin her day.

Verka had just turned sixteen, but by all accounts already very much a beauty. Perhaps she was a little too lean and too pale from not having all that she needed, but anyone with a clear set of eyes knew she was a vision. Not that Verka cared about her appearance. Her hair was constantly unkempt and her fingernails usually were crusted by mud, sweat, and even blood. You see, Verka was too busy seeking the approval of her mother, Janica. And what her mother loved was the highlands and its music.

For Janica, the high country of Kopjari was a special place. Janica new its secrets well, and because of her mother, Verka knew them too. Its secrets spoke of a power that lived in the soil and its waters. Some would say that Kopjari was the first step toward Heaven's doorway. Others remarked that centuries ago giants occupied these lands, and from these highlands they disbursed the world's thunder, lightning, rain and hail.

Verka dismissed these stories, but she never denied that beauty was everywhere to see. You only had to spend a little time in this very country to suspect it was special. The trees were massive. The fruit grew bigger in Kopjari than anywhere, except perhaps in the lands promised to Joshua long ago. The grasses were the lushest of emeralds. Spring rains grew plants into trees, seemingly overnight. But these facts were just the cosmetic reality of an untapped power. If you looked closer, beyond what was humanly possible, you might witness a deeper attention to detail, perfected for the wisest to view.

Chapter 12

Then, and only then, could you truly view the highlands in its real grandeur. Reds, browns, greens, yellows, and blues were sharper and bolder, as if created for royalty, and not the peasants that lived there.

"Never forget what you see," her mother instructed her daughter. "Hold on to what you see. What you hear, and what you taste. Hold it dear. It is for you, so hold it close."

And Verka always did. Perhaps, this was why she always awoke a good thirty minutes before any villager or celestial light had dared dawn the new day.

And so it was on this day, much like any other day, about a quarter mile away from a cluster of dry homes, Verka sat in the midst of a morning rain. She sat all wet, tending a small band of sheep happily bleating in the new day, between their numerous tussles of choice grass. As the sheep ate, regardless of how soaked she got Verka knew today was going to be a good day.

For today was Sunday! Church and the long walk down to the Kraljeva Sutjeska would earnestly begin. But, before she could embark down the mountain, the sheep, goats and the cows neither knew, nor cared what day it was, and wanted their needs met.

With that in mind, soon each household would be sending out their selected family member into the green fields, to attend to their flocks and wave their hello's to Verka and her covered secret weapon. And while all the boys attended to their chores with long staffs to protect themselves and their flocks from what lived in the midst of the large trees, Verka went out to meet what may with her greatest gift. This was the real reason why Verka got out of bed with ease. It was a gift that allowed her to continue hearing her mother's voice: her violin.

It was once Janica's violin, before influenza took her six winters ago. It was Janica who introduced Verka to music, through that violin. The violin had been in Janica's family for four generations, created lovingly by Verka's great-great grandfather. Until grasped by Janica's delicate fingers, the instrument was no more than a delightful family keepsake. But she brought it back to life. Even though she was a wee little thing, she did more than learn to play. She practiced and practiced some more. She studied composers, learned their life stories, their struggles, and learned each saga behind their compositions, and through her most earnest efforts, their songs become her muse.

Janica had fleetingly wanted to go to university and study music, but had not the means. This lack of formal education did not stunt her musical pursuit. Instead, determined to inform the world that they could not stop her love of song, she practiced even more. And then when Janica had a family of her own, she ensured her knowledge would not go to waste, passing it on to her only offspring.

Janica cultivated and focused Verka's passionate pursuit of music at a very early age. When Verka first was being instructed, so small was she, it was difficult to see if Verka held the violin, or if the instrument held the child. But, because of a patient teacher, and persistent player, Verka learned how to bring each note and each story to life.

"Every real artist would live and die with each note they created," Verka would often hear her mother say. "This is so, because these composers knew their music had power," she would continue. "Music created properly is as close to heaven as we common folk can get, even in the high country," Janica said with all sincerity. "Especially in improvisation. Remember, the Bible says, that the Father loves a new song," her mother had told her over and over again. "Both love and hate know this to be so," Janica would remind her charge.

Verka's zeal for music only increased with Janica's passing. This could be heard best when Verka performed the classics. Like her mother, Verka played Mozart with power. Verka also performed Vivaldi with beauty, and with Paganini, her fingers dared to dance with a touch of madness. Oh, how Verka loved Paganini, because her mother loved Paganini. Her mother taught her an array of Paganini the summer before she passed. She had taught her to read his music, and feel each dangerous note the crazy Italian scribbled on the page. Verka knew the stories that Paganini preferred to play guitar, but that his real gift was his ability to control the stubborn whims of a violin. Verka even was told by Janica of the rumored reason of Paganini's unbelievable prowess was because the virtuoso had sold his soul to the devil.

Chapter 12

"Was that true, Mama?" Verka asked.

"Never!" Janica retorted. "Every good thing comes from God, whether we believe it or not."

With Janica's untimely passing, the instrument went to Verka. She named it Janica, and once again both Verka and Janica were inseparable. Verka played the violin while she completed her chores. While she walked around the village. She even tried to take it to school, but the teachers would not allow it. At eleven, when Verka stopped attending school - as was the norm - while other class mates were saddened because their schooling was over, Verka was glad. "More time to spend with Mama," she noted happily. A lot more time, in fact. Verka would play, and play and play, until her fingers bled. In fact, Verka would do more than just play. She was speaking to the instrument, and with each fingered note, she would often hear her mother's sweet reply.

It had been a week since the Hasikovanje spent with Mato, and since then mother and daughter had spoken a great deal. Today, she would see him again. Vivaldi's "Summer" strummed from her mother's voice approvingly, setting Verka further at ease. Nothing could upset her. Not her constant chores. Not the wet weather. Not even her father, and his affair with drink. Again that morning, she had tiptoed past him as he slumped snoring at the dinner table, while cuddling two empty rakija bottles. Since the death of Janica, this was where she often found him. But Verka knew her mother's death was not a true catalyst for her father's inebriated state, but rather a convenient crutch. One day, Verka thought, she would have a family of her own, and be away from problems.

So Verka played on, and with each conversation had with Janica, she could almost see her future. With each song she felt safe, loved and protected from any evil.

There were many examples that confirmed this protection. Only two summers earlier, a wolf pack dared to come upon the village flocks. Even the bravest boys ran to get adult assistance. But not Verka! Her adult protection was already there. Verka stood her ground, and spoke truth that was whispered by Janica many years ago. Verka stood firm, weapon in hand, demanding the pack leave in God's name, while stringing "*La Campanella.*"

Though the pack of devils mortally wounded half a dozen of the neighbor's flock, they bolted in the hearing of Verka's play, thus keeping herself and her small flock safe for another day. The rest of the village could not believe what happened. But Verka did. She was certain her mother was watching out for her. Nothing could hurt her.

With her morning work completed, and having spoken with her mother through a wide array of songs, Verka returned home, hoping to find her father still sleeping off his evening. The last few years had been brutal to Stjepan, and he to it. His plot of land, with minimal care could have been far better, rather had fallen into further disrepair. It in fact had become smaller, as he had sold almost half it to neighbors to pay for his preferred occupation, which was being the village drunk.

"Where are you going?" barked Stjepan, as Verka stepped through the door. "And why are you wearing that dress? Are you going to a wedding?"

"Tata, why it's Sunday," Verka replied, hiding her startled disposition as best as she could. "I am going to the Kraljeva Sutjeska. Would you like to join me?"

"Out in this weather, girl? Are you luda?[2]" he bleated. "I need to you to stay and make me breakfast!" he threatened.

But Verka was ready for this. "I knew you would wake up hungry. I have already made pita and the *prava kava*[3] is ready for you too. Now, do not fuss. Eat and drink," she said with trepidation.

"I want meat!" he pronounced. "I said, you're not going anywhere!" Stjepan took a step towards his increasingly frightened daughter. "Why are you cowering?" Stjepan demanded, as if his demeanor was nothing but friendly. "You want to go? Fine. *Idi!*[4] I don't care!"

---

2 Like lud it means crazy.
3 Prava kava, or proper coffee is what Bosnian's named Turkish black coffee. The stuff it so potent it can keep an unsuspecting novice awake half the night just by breathing it in.
4 Go!

Chapter 12

Verka did not wait for a formal invitation. She rushed to her bed, and placed her violin underneath it, promising to return to her mother as soon as she could. She picked up her Bible, and rushed towards the door, forgetting her small pack of food she prepared for the day's journey.

"I'll be back soon, Tata."

"Why must you?" demanded Stjepan.

"It's Sunday, Tata," replied the girl again, angering Stjepan further.

"Cowards go to church. Are you a coward, daughter of mine?"

"I'm nothing, Tata, but I still must go," she noted with her very last fistful of courage. Quickly, Verka turned towards the door, readying to leave, despite hearing her father crash to the floor, his feet a tangle of table and chair.

"Bjezi![5] Magarice![6] Konju![7] I don't care. Ungrateful!" Stjepan bellowed through the door while on the floor. "*Gubi Se!*[8]"

Verka had heard it all before. She knew he would eat and drink and then start drinking once more, and then finally fall asleep, most likely in the same place she had found him that very morning. Shaking her head, to dust off the awful moment, Verka did not wish to focus on things she had seen hundreds of times before. Verka wanted to hear a new song. Wiping her feet on the grass and refusing to look back, she consumed a deep breath of ratified air, and joined up with a small group of Sutjeska travelers.

"Nice dress, Verka," one of the young companions giggled.

"Thanks," Verka laughed, blushing.

Down the mountain they went, to the white palace of worship on the great hill. Verka loved church service. She loved that people came from so many villages, all over the mountain to be together. It reminded her that there was a great big world out there that started

---

5 Scram. Go Away. Go, be gone. Get!

6 Donkey. To call someone this is to state they are as stupid and dumb as one. A most degrading of insults, donkeys aren't viewed as the smartest of animals.

7 Horse. See explanation above.

8 He is asking her to lose herself! But a far more insulting variation, perhaps when yelling at an animal of little esteem and regard, like an old horse or donkey.

just down the road. It reminded her that things were different, perhaps even better than in the mountain she knew. Though she loved Kopjari, it was not an easy life. It made her think that maybe somewhere else could be better, and maybe a little easier.

The walk was long for those from Kopjari, but thankfully, as always conversation flowed freely. Usually Verka was in the throng of it all, but today she was mostly silent. She had other reasons to be excited. Mato promised to meet her. She had promised to meet him. The entire way down the hill, Pachelbel's "Canon" one of her mother's favorites, played in her mind. Verka was so very happy.

"What have you done?" Verka cried, surrounded by despair and the dark. "*Why? Why?*"

All church service Verka was agitated. She could not focus. She kept looking around for him. Verka knew this was wrong and she would have to give penance for her wanton distraction. She barely noticed the Priest discussing something about Matthew 6, Verse twenty-something. She barely noticed the scores of kinsfolk that surrounded her, or the fervor of their combined worship. Verka was swept up in what might happen. She was lost in the Hasikovanje. She hoped Mato was too. Lost in nervous foot taps and excitement, forty-five minutes felt like months.

But finally service ended. Even before the final "amen," Verka jumped quickly from her pew, rushing to and fro, cutting off other worshipers without noticing the inconvenience she was creating. She was lost in her thoughts and in her hopes. The hope of finding her new friend.

But she could not find him. Through the throng she bustled

and stomped, hoping to find her friend, but lamentably, Mato was nowhere to be found. She looked everywhere. At first, she repeatedly visited where they sat the previous week, but he was not there. Not knowing Mato's family or who his friends were, Verka quickly began to despair. After a while of unsuccessful seeking, Verka even mustered enough courage to ask strangers if they knew of Mato. Alas, they did not. She would have kept asking, but each "no" was another dagger in her gut.

It was getting late, but Verka could not leave, even after her companions left. Verka needed to see Mato. For hours she kept on looking. But it was no use. Despondency filled her heart. It was if she had imagined the previous week. What if she had?

Hungry, and fully aware of the lateness of the hour, Verka resigned herself to a miserably wet–for the sky opened up once more–and lonely walk. Each step was heavy and filled with pain. Verka attempted to hum Pachelbel's "Canon" once more, but even that did not help. She reasoned that something could have sidetracked Mato's plans to meet her. She reasoned that he too would have otherwise woken up just as excited to see her, but something must have happened. But that did not help eradicate her of her fears. It simply further confused and upset her. Not even trying to talk to her mother helped. She felt so alone.

Anger and sadness filled Verka's heart. She was inconsolable. Having returned home, she found her face was wetter indoors than it had been when facing outside's new evening rains.

"Why? *Why?*" she continued to wail.

Stjepan, finally awoke, his unconscious state interrupted by his daughter's cries. "What is the matter?" he asked, groggily.

"How could you do this?" she bawled.

"What? What did I do?" he asked, grouchily. "Why aren't the lamps lit?" Stjepan could see something was terribly wrong, but he had no idea what. He barely knew what time it was, or what day it was. His vision was blurred and his mind was a dark fog. He suspected it was late, but regardless of the hour he did not really wish to deal with parental burdens right now.

"Let's talk about this later," he suggested.

"*No, No, No!*" Verka yelled, through her mountain of tears. "Why? Why did you do this?"

"What are you going on with, child?" lambasted Stjepan. "What is it?" he demanded once more.

"Look what you've done," Verka announced.

Stjepan knew his daughter was furious. Furious like his wife used to get. This realization made him wince. But also it focused his feeble attention. Finally, looking directly at his daughter, Stjepan was shocked by the sadness he saw, and it hurt. Her visible pain made him want a drink, but he knew, perhaps for the first time in long time, he should not. Finally, he noticed Verka was holding something.

It was at this point, the fool understood. Horrified, he saw the truth! He saw Verka, and he saw her hands holding the remains of her most prized item. He saw her violin, the gift of her mother, the gift of his wife, shattered into a million splintered pieces, beyond repair.

"Why, why?" was all Verka could wail, over and over again.

Tears filled Stjepan's eyes. Now sobering, he saw the carnage his drunkenness had brought. "I'm so sorry, my dear child," he wailed, sincerely. "I don't remember why. I don't remember anything."

-13-

Sutra[1]

For three months, a darkening winter grew over the Pavlović household. It did not go unnoticed. Somehow, Mijo knew it was more than just the alarming early winter that found them that year. Interestingly, he was glad when the snow came, for it returned on the day they put Vjera in the ground. Some said winter's arrival was a sign, that the mountain was paying its respect. But with its return, something unwanted came with it.

For much of the past ninety days, Mijo watched the growing presence. He studied it and waited, wondering where it came from, and when it might leave. For three months he hoped it would, for he could taste its bleak bitter gift. Worse still, Mijo knew the rest of his family was slowly but increasingly being tormented by the tempest's presence. Lamentably, Mijo had yet to discover if there was a way to stop this brewing storm.

Within their home, Mijo watched Mara as she continued about her daily business, but now with a glumness that did not sit well with her or her husband. So concerned was Mijo, his chair was often stationed at the first floor dinner table. During those times, often the couple would lock eyes and Mijo would feebly offer an uncertain

---

1 Tomorrow

smile that was meant to be more reassuring. Mara would reply with a similar offering, as if both were attempting to acknowledge the possibilities that things would be alright, and both also proving they were not sure how.

The house had become colder, quieter, and lonely. For Mara, the weekdays were too quiet. With Mato at work all week, for the first time in their marriage, it was just her and Mijo. The walls had consumed too much commotion over the generations to now sit so still. Mara missed hearing someone else who liked to talk, for Vjera was a talker. She missed having someone else sing in the home, for Vjera was a singer. And she missed having someone else pray with in the house, because Vjera had lived to pray. Still, Mara could garner solace that Mirko had to be returning soon, if only on a furlough. But this left Mara worrying as well. Mirko would be returning to a changed home. An emptier home.

Mijo watched for three months of Sunday's as Mato returned from another week in Vareš, consumed with fatigue. Mijo knew how much his youngest had given of himself, and saw the quiet grief he carried. Mijo worried. Certainly, Mato was too young to act so old, even though he just had another birthday, his sixteenth, which he insisted be celebrated without any fanfare. Since Vjera's passing, nothing seemed to provide his youngest pleasure.

If he cared for calendars, Mato would have noticed twelve Sundays had come and gone since his grandmother had left. The only Sunday he cared for was Vjera's last. It replayed over and over in his mind. He could not help it. Mato was stuck. Everything else, it seemed, had been put on the shelf. It had been twelve Sundays since he last attended a Hasikovanje. The thirtieth was the following day, and he had no intention of visiting that one either. He had thought about going a couple times since, but he could not bring himself to go. Even the thought of visiting Verka, so to explain his delay could not force his attendance. His father asked him about again visiting *"the Talk"* seven Sundays ago, "Maybe next week, Tata. If it's not so cold," Mato replied with a wistful sigh. "Maybe next week."

But next week had yet to come.

Chapter 13

So Mijo sat and waited, and he attempted to ponder what was happening to his home, his village, his family. He wondered how they might go on without their rock, their fortress. Though not a young orphan, he wondered how he might go on without his shield. But what Mijo did not realize was through these baby steps, he returned to his old favorite game of Mijo *the philosopher*.

The return however did not last long. Future planning would flood back past promises, leaving Mijo's mind quickly exhausted. Mijo wanted to understand tomorrow, but his heart and tears could not vanish Vjera's last words, and her last gift. Mijo had made a solemn oath. He promised to take care and share that gift. He questioned whether he was ready. On this night, Mijo shook his head. As fate would have it, until Mirko returned Mijo knew none of this would matter.

So on this particular Saturday, the end of the twelfth week since Vjera's passing, twenty minutes passed the sixtieth hour, Mijo was readying himself to snooze the rest of the day away. Mara was downstairs, cleaning up an area that was already clean, and Mato was snoring the fatigue of the past week from his being. Each was a million light-years away. That is, until both adults heard a series of violent attacks upon the front door. Its banging coupled with a deeply boisterous voice shook the unwitting Pavlović cocoon. It appeared the voice on the other side of the door was totally put out by the barricade before him, angered that it had the temerity to be locked.

"Open this door, Pavlović!" the soul begin with a resonating voice. "I'm here! The prodigal has returned. Open this door! *Požurite*, I'm freezing out here!"

Finally, it occurred to the occupants of the home who had arrived. "Mirko!" Mijo exclaimed, jumping up to adhere to his son's calls. A smile leaped upon Mara's face. Her son was home! Her son was home!

Mijo yelled across the way. "Mato, wake up! Wake up! Your brother is here!" Mijo was a child, lost in excitement of a million Christmases celebrated all at once. His boy was home. "Mara, get the door!" Shocked, Mara could do nothing but stand up, so completely in a tizzy. Mijo rushed down the stairs to aid his dazed wife.

"Aren't you going to get it, woman?" mocked Mijo, as he got to the door before her.

"Oh," Mara began nervously, all the while beginning to fuss with her hair. "You get it."

"Open up, family, I am here!" continued the bellowing voice from beyond the barricade.

Mijo unlocked the door. "I am sorry son, the door should not have been…"

Mijo sentence trailed off at the sight of his firstborn. There before him, Mijo was overwhelmed. Mirko was home, and Mijo was glad for it. Until then, Mijo did not know how much he missed him.

"My boy," Mijo mustered, barely beyond a whisper.

"Greetings, Tata," replied Mirko formally, offering his hand, which Mijo gladly took, dumbfound.

As Mijo's flesh grasped Mirko's, a million past Sundays flashed upon him. Each Sunday Mijo ever had was a set of crashing cymbals. Mijo never wished to weep more in his life. His firstborn was before him, and thankfully if tomorrow would come, he would have another Sunday with him. There were times in the past two years that Mijo believed he would never again have this pleasure.

Mijo studied the returning boy before him. He had changed. Mijo could tell Mirko had seen something of life, but he had yet to conclude if this knowledge was for the better. Mirko looked thinner. His lips, and his hair were thinner. Mirko's cheeks clung closer to his jaw. His eyes were dark, further developed by a dark rim that surrounded them as if they carried heavy bags. Mijo did not wish to look surprised by Mirko's appearance, and wanted to cultivate a stream of conversation, but before he needed to find something of value to say, Mijo was gratefully interrupted.

"My *dechko*, you have returned," wailed an overjoyed Mara, pushing past her husband to embrace Mirko. "Son. How are you?"

"Managing," Mirko offered, while being squeezed zealously by Mara.

Chapter 13

"You're so thin," continued Mara, not concerned that the statement might hurt his feelings, in a way mothers never are. "You look tired. From your journey, I mean. Come in and get something to eat. Mijo! Move, out of the way. It's cold outside."

"Oh, of course," stammered Mijo, jolting himself back into the moment.

"No I am alright, I'm not hungry," offered the firstborn. "I'm a little thirsty though."

"Would you like some water or coffee?" asked Mara, forgetting the young man's age.

"Well, I was wondering if Tata had any…"

"Woman, you're talking to a man now," interjected Mijo, knowing Mirko's meaning. "Get him a rakija. Please, dearest," Mijo offered with a cheeky smile. "Allow me a little one as well."

As the two men sat, they both looked towards the set of feet crashing down the stairs.

"Look Mato, look!" continued an excited Mijo. "Your brother has returned."

Mato looked at his brother. He also noticed Mirko's increased appearance of age, but at the same time he also looked smaller to his eyes. As Mato walked right up to his brother, he did not know what to say. So much time had passed. What do you say to someone you have not talked to for two years? And though it was nobody's fault, time had built up unwanted awkwardness. Mirko stood up next to his younger brother. If everyone in the room had not noticed it before, it was now obvious Mato had grown. If a measuring tape had been handy they would have found he was five foot seven. Just like Mirko. But Mato looked taller. He looked wider. He ever looked stronger. Healthier too. As the two brothers each looked the other over, in a weird way Mato did not feel as tired anymore.

"Wow, braco, you have grown," Mirko said, stating the obvious. "But don't worry, I could still whoop you, even in a foot race!"

They embraced, and for a minute, things were as they always were.

"Don't be so sure," Mijo replied, in defense of Mato. "He hasn't lost a race around these parts for quite some time, have you boy?"

Mato shrugged, somewhat embarrassed by the fuss his father was making. He wanted to change the subject. "So when did you get back to the Sutjeska?" Mato pondered.

Mirko grabbed the glass, consuming its contents in one gulp, as if he had done it before a time or two. "*Hvala*, Mama," Mirko began, giving his mother thanks for the drink. "Um, I was discharged a few weeks ago. I got back to Vareš, um, last Tuesday," he stammered.

"Five days ago!" Mato exclaimed disappointingly. "Why didn't you see me in town?"

"I am sorry, I really wanted to see you all together, at once, brother," Mirko offered, while grabbing the bottle to refill his glass. "I had much to do before I could return. You know, to work out my job situation and meet up with a few friends, and friends of friends, so to deliver some letters and such. It is difficult to get letters through to love ones when you are serving, if you gather my meaning."

"Of course we do," Mara injected, without understanding at all.

"Discharged," continued Mato. "So, does that mean, you are not going back?"

"That's right," answered Mirko uncomfortably. "I'm not."

"Oh," Mijo answered, perhaps a little too happily. "Really. What happened?"

"Much," Mirko answered bluntly.

"Tell us," Mato pleaded, not noticing the awkwardness that this stream of conversation was creating. There was much he wanted to know. Much he wanted to understand. "C'mon, what was the Navy like? Your letters said so little."

"Not today, braco. Another time, perhaps, okay?" requested Mirko.

But Mato would not let go. "Please, tell me a little," Mato, asked once more, diplomatically.

"Ah, leave him be, Mato," requested Mara. "Can't you see your brother is tired and just got home? There will be plenty of time to catch up. Here is some more drink, my sweet boy."

"It's okay," Mirko noted, resigned to explaining a little. He bit his bottom lip and closed his eyes for a second so to recall what story to begin with. "Ah, the Navy," he began as if he was about to create a tale. "The boats were big. The waves and spray on my face were what I imagined. The sea, even in the colder months, was what I expected. Wonderful," he continued without a hint of a smile.

Mirko from there began to weave a two-year collection of thoughts and moments. Firstly, Mirko summarized basic training, and how difficult it was.

"Some of the boys really struggled with it, but not I," Mirko pronounced, in a manner that brought forth a beaming smile of pride from Mara.

From there, Mirko continued to discuss training and living on a frigate, where servicemen from all walks of life, from all over Yugoslavia, clamored upon the vessel's hull and slept within its belly. He talked about swabbing decks, completing drills and taking orders, while running back and forth. He mentioned sleeping only few hours each night, weeks at a time so "to ensure we didn't die because we were never sure when we were dealing with another drill, or the real thing," Mirko mused. With each word Mato was enamored. He felt so happy for his brother. Mirko had lived his dream. He had sailed. He had tasted the waters on the edge of their homeland. Mirko had traveled further than any of them. Mato was so proud.

"And then we were responsible for, I was responsible. For…" Mirko stopped, losing himself mid-sentence, without appearing to be able to find it again.

"And then what happened?" Mato interjected, hoping to retrieve it for him. "What were you responsible for?"

"Oh, um," Mirko continued to stumble. "I was responsible for a lot of things. A lot of important things, brother. Most of them classified," he noted with a cheeky grin, as if he regained his wanton train of thought. "That means I am not to profess them to anyone, on pain of death, braco."

Mirko laughed at saying this, and so did Mato, then also did Mara. Mijo offered an uneasy smile, so not to be left out.

"It sounds like it was great," Mato concluded. "But why aren't you going back, then?" The question hung heavy in the air. It was the twelve-hundred-dinar question that only the youngest was brave enough to ask.

"Well, you know," Mirko churlishly began. "You can have too much of a good thing. I did my part and wanted to come back. I did not wish to hold the next kid in line back, you know? And besides, well it was…" Mirko again ending his sentence, before it was done.

"It was what?" Mato wondered, frustratingly.

"It was too much of a good thing, you know?" was all Mirko could offer.

Mato nodded in approval, without being satisfied by Mirko's answer. But before he could prod his brother once more, Mara interjected. "That's enough for now," defended Mara. "Can't you see Mato that Mirko is tired?"

"Actually Mama, I am a little hungry after all," added Mirko, glad to change the conversation.

"Yes, yes, of course," Mara fussed. "I will get you some bread and sour cream. Sorry, no meat today, but the pita will be ready in about thirty minutes. If I knew you were coming today, I would have had it ready a long time ago."

"That will be great, Mama, thank you," Mirko replied.

Mirko sat and ate, and for the rest of the evening said little. Mara fussed over her returning boy, filling Mirko's plate before it could even become half empty. Mijo sat, watched and listened intentionally. He listened to what was said and what was not spoken. Mostly, Mijo listened to an excited Mato prattle on about life's comings and goings, giving a complete account of the past two years of mountain events. Finally, after telling Mirko about everything and everyone, Mato asked another unfiltered question that was on everyone else's lips. "Why didn't you let us know you were coming?" Mato continued to press.

"Oh, again, brother, you are right. I should have," Mirko conceded, while he finished off his fifth glass. "I wasn't sure when I was going to be released, and letter writing was hard, especially out at sea. Sorry."

"No bother," Mara replied for the rest of them. "You're here now."

"Yes, yes, you're here now," Mato said excited. "We're glad for it. I know Baba would have…" Mato's words trailed off, knowing he had crossed a line towards the sorest of subjects. Graciously, knowing Mato could not have meant anything by it, Mirko raised his hand, and grinned, as if to say it was alright.

"Son," Mara began, in an attempt to shift conversation once more. "Why don't you get some rest, and we can pick it up all later. It is getting late. It's already dark out."

Time had come and gone quickly that evening. Naturally, at the suggestion of slumber, Mirko yawned, and agreed that sleep might not be a bad idea.

"I can say my greetings to everyone tomorrow at the Sutjeska, I suppose," Mirko noted. "I think that will be great idea, actually. It has been a long time since I was there."

With this settled, each agreed that sleep would be the best course of action for each of them. Tomorrow was a big day. It would herald the next day of their lives.

Mato went to bed, excited that his big brother was back. He could ask him all kinds of things. About his time in the Navy. About what he was going to do next. But mostly, Mato could ask him for advice. He had a lot of questions that needed answering, about many things. He might even ask him about what to do about Verka. Mato smiled for the first time in over twelve weeks, wondering if everything might be alright after all.

Mara was glad her eldest son was back. For the first time in twelve weeks she fell asleep as soon as her head hit the pillow.

Mirko could not believe he was back in the old house. There were times the past two years he wondered if he would ever set foot back in it. There were times when he doubted he wanted to. Part of him was still unsure. But here he was all the same. But regardless of his concern, Mirko slept sounder than he had on any evening these past twenty-four months.

Mijo was the only one unable to go to sleep. He tossed and turned for twenty minutes, finally giving up and removing himself out of his warm bed and out beyond his heavy covers. With an exaggerated deep sigh, he lumbered over and sat into his chair, near the upstairs fireplace and stoked a new blaze. There was much to think about. Mijo worried for his returning son, but he could not put his finger on why exactly. Perhaps they might discuss it more tomorrow. Maybe it was the right time to deliver on the promise he made to Vjera. He nodded his head as if his body agreed with his mind. "Not now though," he mused. "Tomorrow," Mijo smiled.

Mijo smiled, glad there was going to be at least one more tomorrow.

-14-

Izgubljeno/Nadjeno[1]

Sunday came with a rapid thaw! Quickly, as if by magic or perhaps seasonal clemency, the snow left. Winter's abrupt departure appeared grossly premature, leaving behind a barren landscape, not readied for the arrival of Sun's stronger sting. But it had been decided, and the seasons complied. Snow's cousins, Ice and Cold also left in such a hurried huff, they barely said their goodbyes, while the dormant and the hibernators, plant and animal life alike, would stay behind and taste Spring's alarm.

The unseasonal warmth kicked Mirko out of bed earlier than he might have hoped. However, it wasn't simply the new warmth that shortened his wanton sleep. Military time was not yet out of his system.

"You're up early," spoke a familiar voice that stiffened the hairs on the back of Mirko's neck.

"*Stari*[2], you startled me," replied Mirko to his father.

"Stari," begun Mijo with a gruff, but welcoming smile. "*Stari, je tvoj ćaća!*[3] Come sit down with your old man, and have some coffee."

"Prava kava?" asked Mirko, as he eagerly sat, ready for plenty.

---

1 Lost/Found

2 Old, old man. In general, as used here, it is a cheeky term of endearment.

3 The old man is your father. This response is often used to show there was no offense to being called "stari" (old). The saying also works as a reminder that though your father is old, he is still your father, so don't forget it.

"*Da*. Strong, and black," he confirmed. "You're up early," Mijo said once more, eager to strike up a conversation.

"Da," confirmed Mirko, while lathering up some bread in sour cream. "I bet you did not sleep at all, huh? What time is it anyway? It feels later than it probably is, right?" Mijo had slept, but only a little. The weather's warmth slugged him like boxing gloves, knocking him out of his dormancy. Unlike his firstborn, Mijo was glad for his alert internal clock, as he had always been enthralled by the changing of the seasonal guard. It was Mijo's belief, that only in the mountains could you go to bed in one world and awaken in another. To miss the beginning of a new dawn and sun was unthinkable.

"It is early, but it is already warm outside. The time, well it's only five-hundred hours, Commander."

"I did not get beyond Petty Officer, Tata," corrected Mirko. "But, thanks for the promotion. Is there any more bread?"

"Da," affirmed Mijo. "You know where it is."

Mirko ventured without word or thought towards the larder, returning quickly with an additional healthy chunk of loaf. As he sat, Mirko started to pass half to his father, who quickly declined, rubbing his full belly to signify that there was no room left at the inn. Mirko was glad for his refusal. Mirko's once-suppressed appetite was growing with each lump he placed in his face. Mijo just sat and watched his son gorge himself on yesterday's extras, trying to learn what his son was thinking. "I guess Tito did not make bread like you're eating now, huh?" ventured Mijo.

"You could say that," Mirko offered, while munching through two cheeks full at a time. "There was much he didn't provide."

"Oh," Mijo queried, wondering if this was his wanted opening to learn more. Quickly, the room went quiet, as it might when conversation shifts into an area of awkwardness and when there is still more bread to consume. Mijo had forgotten how Mirko could eat and eat. Mirko ate as if he hadn't eaten in two years. So Mijo did the honorable thing. He held his tongue a little longer, returning to the larder and got some more bread and slices of salty prosciutto, to further whet his son's palate. Prosciutto was a rare larder gem in the mountains, only brought out on the rarest of occasions. As Mijo pulled out the cured ham, he ventured that his son's return after a two years absence was probably the rarest moment of his life. Mijo wanted very much to learn more about Mirko's adventures. In fact, during the past two years, he had grown to hope that it turned out well for Mirko. This, of course, was not always the case. Mijo, after all, had thought Mirko wrong for having left in the first place. But that was the past.

As Mijo returned to the table, and continued to watch his son eating as if his life dependent on it, the gravity of Mirko's disposition confirmed his worst suspicions. Mijo might not have the exact details to what led Mirko to this point, but whatever they were, *Stari* knew they weren't good. He saw how feebly Mirko attempted to hide his heavy torment. Mijo wanted to be his needed help. But how? If only he could show his son that he understood, and had had his own hardships. Mijo pondered, maybe Vjera's solemn final request could help. "So," Mijo ummed and erred. "So, did you find a place in Vareš to work, then?"

"Yes," Mirko mumbled, not looking up from his plate, as a crumb of bread escaped from his face.

"Good," Mijo replied, while looking around the room for a follow up question. "When do you start?"

"This is good prosciutto. Um, Tomorrow."

"So soon," Mijo replied with disappointment. He hoped that Mirko might put his feet up with them a little longer. "Why hurry?"

"I know it seems sudden," replied Mirko, with another full mouth of cured meat and bread. "But I have to start earning my keep, you know?"

"I suppose," continued Mijo. "Um, son…" stopping before he got started once more.

Mirko looked up, and briefly stopped chewing "What is it, Tata?"

"There is something we have to talk about."

"Oh really?" replied Mirko uneasily, clueless in the turn breakfast was about to take. "About what?"

Mijo took a quick, deep breath. "Well, it's something your baba..."

"Good morning son!" rushed in an excited Mara, hugging Mirko around his neck, while in unison planting an earnest kiss on top of his head. "Good heavens, you boys are up early. Did you eat anything Mirko?"

"Yes Mama," Mirko replied, happy to return conversation back to his stomach. "Tata gave me some bread and a little pro..."

"Stale, old bread, from yesterday," Mara chortled with disgust. "We can do better than that, just wait." Mijo smiled at Mirko and shook his head, perhaps as relieved as his son that their conversation was interrupted. He got up from the table.

"I'll leave you to enjoy your mother's doting then," started Mijo.

"Yes, yes, good," hurried Mara. "I'll have something much better in no time. Is it just me, or is it really warm today?" she asked, without even caring to learn the answer.

Mijo looked at his son. "We'll talk later then."

Mirko nodded. "Sure."

✳✳✳

"Where did all the snow go?" Mato could not believe it. He had never seen it leave so fast. "It's February, and I am not even wearing a sweater!"

Spring was attempting to catch up, having been badly caught on the hop by winter's retreat. But to nature's credit, life was sprouting in abundance all around, ensuring the Pavlović family was garnering quite the science lesson in fauna's proficiency in rapid organization. The entire world in this once quiet place was in a desperate hurry to go somewhere important, almost a blasphemy being it was the Sabbath. Shoots of green were venturing out of their slumber without fear that the cold might slap them back. Winter's mysterious still silence, a mountain staple just as recently as twenty-four hours ago, was now replaced by feverish action. Warblers could be heard fluttering and chirping to each other. Grand old trees were stretching towards the newest affectionate rays, all hoping to garner hues of green to shade their branches. Water was yawning through the once-glassed streams.

It was as if yesterday was a million months ago. Winter was gone and Mirko was back! But still, it was a shock to the system, especially to Mato, who had never sat comfortably next to speedy alteration. But like the sun on this first spring day, Mato was warming to everything that was changing around them. All of these new happenings had to be a sign, thought Mato. For the first time in a long while, he felt good. A little like his old self, and perhaps because of this, it began to rekindle old interests.

"So you wanna race me to church?" Mato asked Mirko, grinning.

"I would," began Mirko, looking for a way out of the challenge, "but our mother forced me to consume two weeks' worth of meals this morning. I'm carrying bricks in my belly."

"Aw c'mon," protested Mato. "I'll give you a healthy head start."

"Not today, little man; I'll give you the beating you deserve another time."

They both laughed at themselves, and Mirko quickly turned conversation towards a topic of greater interest to him. "So after church," Mirko began, "You're going to the Hasikovanje with me, right?"

Now, Mato wished he had the ability to laugh off a subject, as his brother just had with his. "Um, probably not," was all he could stammer.

"No, no," mocked Mirko. "You're coming. You're not scared or something?"

"No, not all," Mato defended. "I've been plenty. I just don't think I want to go, that's all."

"Ah yeah, really," Mirko continued cackling. He was clearly enjoying himself. "So what's the problem then? You got a girl there you like or something?"

Mato was startled with Mirko's apparent insight, and began to blush at this line of questioning. "Well, yes, I mean no. I mean, I don't know."

Mirko laughed, and turned to his parents, who were walking close enough behind the boys to enjoy their son's conversation. "Mama, did you know?" Mirko began. "Did you know your youngest has a girl?"

Mato stepped towards his brother, seething, fists clenched. This made Mirko laugh even harder. "I don't have any girl, did you hear?" Mato bellowed.

"Okay, okay, brother," offered Mirko, with hands open-faced, up in front of his face in surrender. "I was just trying to find out what was going on. I haven't been around for a while, you know," he offered as an apologetic explanation.

"I know," Mato replied, cooling his tracks. "You know, you might know more of what's been going on, if you wrote more often. You never wrote."

They continued walking with the last words hanging in the air for a good while. Finally, Mirko sighed. "I wish I did write more. It can't be helped now. I am here now, though. So what happened with this young woman of yours?"

"I told you she is not mine," Mato replied, once more becoming annoyed.

"I know, you said that, but what happened?" offered Mirko, eager to learn the truth.

Mato blew out a strong, deep breath that puffed both of his cheeks. "Baba."

"Oh," was all Mirko could offer, in reply, knowing there was nothing more to say.

Church had come and gone. Many people were rushing up to Mirko, especially since so few had gotten word of his return. Mato looked over at his older brother. He was glad so many people were sincerely happy to see him again. Mirko's return made Mato feel better about things in general as well. His brother's return steadied his own ship, and made him more certain of the way it should go. Mato however,

Chapter 14

was walking away from the throng, already beyond the outskirts of the courtyard. He had decided about five minutes into mass that he was not going to stay for the Hasikovanje, regardless that it might concern his father, and bring future ridicule from his returned brother. It was a price he was willing to pay. Mato had somewhere more important to go.

Lost in the growing crowd of greetings and backslaps from well-wishers, Mirko had impatiently been looking for Mato, but he could not find him. "Coward," Mirko muttered dismissively, guessing he had left. The Hasikovanje had already begun, and Mirko did not wish to miss any of it! It had been too long. His belly for the first time in an age was full, and perhaps because of this, his mind was starting to remember the sounds and smells of the Sutjeska. Surprisingly, right at that moment, he welcomed them. Younger brother or no younger brother, Mirko was going to enjoy himself. But before he could throw himself into the fun, Mirko saw in the corner of his eye, his father motion for him to come over.

"You seen Mato?" queried Mirko.

Mijo shook his head. He had a more singular reason for meeting up with his boy. "Son, you have fun tonight. But, remember when you come back home later, we need to talk, okay?"

"Okay," Mirko said in a somewhat dismissive manner, which was difficult not to notice.

"It's important, I promise." Mijo noted reassuringly.

"Okay," Mirko answered once more, so to appease his persistent father.

"You promise?" asked Mijo, suggesting he was not convinced.

"Sure," Mirko answered, while his eyes looked at the throng of young people before him.

Again Mijo noticed his son's distracted eyes. "Okay, go and talk the Hasikovanje. Go have fun."

With his father gone, it did not take Mirko's eyes long to match his mind's wants, because within moments he noticed a pretty young lady, perhaps fifteen yards directly in front of him. In noticing her, he also noticed it appeared that she was looking for someone.

"*You look lost, but now you are found,*" offered Mirko in the Hasikovanje way.

Surprisingly, the young lady did not seem to want to play *"the Talk."* In fact, she had barely noticed the comment floating her way and almost rushed right past.

"Oh sorry, I don't wish to disturb you," persisted Mirko, in the general conversational style, "but I am looking for someone too. Perhaps we can look together."

Finally noticing Mirko, the girl seemed unimpressed. She was anxious to go about her business.

"I doubt we are looking for the same someone," she offered.

"I was actually looking for my brother," retorted Mirko, ignoring the lady's dismissive tone. "He seems to have disappeared, a bit like the Sutjeska snow."

"Oh really?" smirked the young lady, disbelieving Mirko. "You're looking for your brother, but to find him, you stop to talk to me!"

"*I didn't know having fun in the Hasikovanje could be considered bothering someone?*" begun Mirko, returning to verse. "*I always thought the square was for those who wished to talk, not stalk.*"

The young lady blushed, knowing the young man before her had a point. It was part of the rules after all. The square is for talking. Mirko knew he had the young woman over a barrel, and plus he was the only one who had even attempted to rhyme any of his sentences since they began chatting.

"So, I think you're harassing me, to be perfectly honest," further defended Mirko. "Like I said, I am looking for my brother, but because of the rules, it's my duty to talk. But in regards to my mission, *my brother appears to be a bit shy to play. I think all the women in this mob, like you no doubt, have scared him away.*"

The girl smirked. She thought the male before her was funny, and perhaps charming.

"Well," she began to reply, starting to warm to this different type of game. "I suppose we cannot be looking for the same person. Because, the one I am looking for talked pretty freely to me."

"Oh, really?" replied Mirko.

Chapter 14

"Yes, really," she confidentially replied. "So if you please, excuse me."

The young lady attempted to step aside and around Mirko, but without the success she expected.

"Can I help you sir?" she exclaimed, feeling further put out.

"Yes," replied Mirko, enjoying himself far too much. "Leave if you must, but I must have your name first. It is only polite."

The young lady was getting quite cross with the situation. "Only polite!" she huffed. "What do you know of politeness?"

"A little," Mirko offered, ignoring her annoyance. "Your name, please."

The young lady again shook her head with dismay. "Boys," she muttered to herself.

"Your name," the man demanded once more. There was no getting around it. If the young women wanted to move on across the bridge, she would need to pay the toll.

"*My name is Verka. Verka is name. Simple and plain. But if you don't mind, and let me go my way,*" she curtseyed, and strove past with purpose, believing she had gone beyond her traditional requirement. But Mirko was not satisfied, once again stepping in front of her. "Now what?" Verka demanded, curtly.

"*No, not yet,*" Mirko lectured. "*You have to ask me for my name, and then you can pass. I think it is my duty young lady, to educate you on the complete rules of the Hasikovanje. You appear sweet, but your talking manners, like dirty feet, are distressingly foul.*"

"I am *what?*" Verka retorted.

"I am sure the young charge you are looking for would approve of what I am saying," Mirko continued, either oblivious to Verka's consternation or simply not caring. "You need to ask me my name. After all, it's only polite." he repeated.

Verka was growing more agitated by the second, deciding that she had more than enough of this young man's company. "You let me pass, or I will scream!" she yelled.

Mirko laughed with nervous embarrassment. "Oh, I am sorry. I was only playing. I meant no offense." Mirko shook his head. First night back, and he was already annoying the locals. He began, perhaps for the first time all day, to feel awkwardly out of place.

"Please forgive me," he offered once more, looking to make a quick exit.

Now it was Verka who felt embarrassed, wondering if she made more of it all than necessary. Now she stepped in front of him. "Oh, I am sorry," she stammered. "I was looking for someone, and I am just in a hurry. I did not wish to be rude."

"That's alright," Mirko offered, lifting his eyes to meet hers. Mirko at this moment again noticed how pretty they were.

"So, what is your name?" Verka offered with a smile.

"My name," he laughed. "You want my name?"

"Very funny. Yes, your name," giggled Verka. "You have mine. Now let me have yours."

"My name is Mirko," said Mirko.

"Okay, Mirko what is your family name?" continued Verka.

Mirko noticed that Verka asked, even beyond what he did. "Why should I give that? You didn't give me yours!"

Verka had a ready answer for this. "*Perhaps it is because I know the rules of "the Talk" too, and I am attempting to educate you,*" she laughed. "No, really what is it? I am curious. Mirko, what?"

Mirko laughed. "You got me," he surrendered. "My name is Mirko. Mirko Pavlović,"

Verka stopped smiling, stopped walking and even stopped breathing. Verka stopped so suddenly she almost had two other talkers run right into the back of her.

"What did you say?"

"Pavlović" Mirko replied with a shrug. "Why?"

"Your brother," continued Verka. "His name isn't Mato, is it?"

"You know him?" asked Mirko, surprised by her change in countenance.

"Where is he?" she asked.

"I don't know," Mirko blurted. "Like I already mentioned, I was looking for him."

Chapter 14

Verka was flush with panic and need. "You have to take me to him!" she demanded.

Mirko returned home, exhausted. The evening moon shone so brightly upon everything, that the star's duty appeared demoted to drab decoration. Mirko thought it was grossly unpleasant, reminding him of a barrack's grilling under a set of awful lamps. Mirko opined that thankfully he had survived the first day back in the Sutjeska, if only just.

He was glad to be going to work tomorrow. Another day like this one might have finished him off for good. Thankfully, tomorrow, he would be back in Vareš, and away from small village life for good. That was another reason Mirko was glad he was going. He had yet to tell his folks that he would not be traveling back and forth each weekend, and now he was not sure he wanted to. Besides, he had much to accomplish beyond regular working hours in Vareš. This would occupy almost all of his free time, making traveling back-and-forth impossible. He was eager to begin it without unnecessary conjecture from family that surely would not understand.

As he opened the front door, Mirko found his father sitting in his chair, surprisingly drinking a glass of water. Mirko could tell he was waiting to speak with him. "Son, you are home?" eagerly pronounced Mijo.

"Yes," answered Mirko, with each growing minute increasing his longing for Vareš.

"Good," Mijo mentioned, "I want to talk with you, son." Mirko felt the request to talk was the same as all the unwanted commands he endured the past two years. But this one, he did not fear to deny.

"It'll have to wait *Stari*," rebuffed Mirko.

"Who are you calling old?" replied Mijo, less playfully than he had earlier that day.

"It doesn't matter," said Mirko, also unwilling to play along. "We have a guest," Mirko looked towards the direction of the opened front door, "Come in, Verka."

Mijo was incredulous. "Who is this? At this hour! Is this a friend of yours?"

"Not exactly," Mirko offered, sheepishly.

Tu i tamo[1]

Boldly, Mato came. Back up the mountain he traveled, most satisfied with his evening. Mato spent the day alone speaking with the wind, and it had soothed him. After service, having avoided detection, Mato went to meander with the new spring and his thoughts as his only company. There, he pondered each inkling and notion and their possible ramifications. The conclusion of this action was profound. After months and months of fret and regret, he dared to hush the worries of the past and ready himself for tomorrow and reclaim the future that once beckoned.

While he was musing, Mato had for the first time since her passing, talked things over with Vjera. And knowing that she could hear him as clear as the bright sky, Mato was certain that not only would she understand, she would approve.

With each stride, he felt better about everything and everyone. His mourning was over. A new day shone and it all seemed so clear to him. Everything seemed right. As he questioned the wisdom of all of what he had decided, even an old owl swooped close by with a loud hoot. Mato took it as providence. Mato concluded that for too long he had been a shadow of himself, a lesser creature, demanding less

1 Here and there

from himself, and simply stewing in his daily sameness. That Mato was done, he decided. He was going to be his old self again!

And this newfound thought of the future included Verka. He was very ready to see her. He needed to and wanted to see her. But in making this decision, uninvited anxiousness swept over him; the type of fretting he thought he had just learned to completely conquer. What if she did not care about him any longer? After all, it had been over three months since their Hasikovanje. They had made plans, and regardless of the reasons that thwarted their completion, Mato knew he had broken them. And he had kept on breaking them every Sunday since. What made his anxiousness worse was Mato knew he would have to wait another week still before he held a hope of seeing her once more.

But thankfully, after a few moments, Mato's newly befriended stoicism returned, once again shackling his despondency. Just as he concluded earlier things were going to be better, because he again wanted them to be better. His mind, for the first time in an age, fluttered and flittered with new ideas and notions. He had even started thinking of maps again, albeit of ones slightly closer to home.

"*Perhaps, I will detail a map of our greater community*," he internalized, as a million other possibilities readied to dance upon him.

While he walked, and before the new moon adorned the sky, dusk had thrilled Mato, leaving him awestruck by the parade of oranges and reds in the atmosphere. These colors brought the mountain's cliffs and crags into prominence with its many browns and grays a dramatic contrast. Mato shook his head, wondering why he never before noticed how beautiful multiple shades of gray could actually be. Each differing hue served its purpose to exaggerate the peak's edges and crevasses. Mato, not ready for the evening to end, paused for many minutes. And while staring at the cliffs that had been there his entire life, perhaps for the first time, Mato could not help but ponder what manner of creatures might call those beautiful high up nooks and crannies home. There was so much of the world to explore, his mind ventured, and a million worlds to discover just out one's door. This notion made him smile more and more. He was looking forward to creating his world map. For the first time in too long a time, Mato Pavlović was again looking forward to tomorrow.

With that happy thought complete, the night took center stage and Mato galloped home to get out of the moon's light. On arrival, and without slowing down, Mato opened the front door with gusto, eager to taste every second of his future.

"Hello Pavlović family, I am home!" he proclaimed. "Mama, I'm…"

The thought stopped dead in its tracks, stunning Mato by what, or rather who, stood before him.

"Hello, Mato," proclaimed Verka, with a disturbing calmness.

Slušati[1]

"What, are you doing...? I mean, how did you...?" stammered Mato, flummoxed by everything that swirled around him. Finally he settled his poor mind enough to string a single continual thought. "Verka, it is so nice to see you."

"Is it?" she sneered.

Mato looked around the room. The rest of the Pavlović's were there. To Mato's astonishment, his entire family was all enjoying the circus before them.

"Jeste[2]," Mato, chirped, convincingly. "Shall we go outside to talk? In private, I mean," Mato added, hopefully. He moved towards Verka, hoping to lead her toward the front door. However, Verka recoiled. Now that she was here, in front of the person she had searched for these many months, anger and disappointment filled her heart. She began to wonder if coming was a mistake.

"Actually, I need to be heading home," she announced. "It is getting quite late, and I have a long walk."

"And I will then come with you," Mato quickly retorted. "To make sure you get home safe."

1 Listen
2 Yes, it is

"That's a wise idea, Mato," chimed Mijo, sitting across the room. Mato looked at his father. He had a weird smile on his face that Mato did not understand. "That is, if the lady does not mind putting an old man's mind at ease, of course," Mijo added.

Verka gently curtsied. "If it is your wish, Sir," she replied, with a genteel politeness. "That will be fine."

"Shall I go too?" offered Mirko. "To make sure they both get home safe."

Mato cringed. "I'm not a child, Mirko!"

"Would you, Mirko?" asked Verka, gladly. "If it's no trouble?"

"No, no. You should stay Mirko," chirped Mijo. "We've much to chat about."

"It's no trouble at all," Mirko responded. "Tata, we can talk later. Let's go, children."

"Well, I'll pack you a food parcel, for your journey home Verka," offered Mara.

"Oh, there is no need, really," responded Verka, not wanting to be any trouble.

"Nonsense, it won't take more than a moment," insisted Mara. "And you'll take it, Verka, for my sake." While the two ladies continued their battle of generosity versus politeness, Mato shot Mirko a stern glance of disgust, which made the older of the two chortle.

"Don't worry brother," he began, in a way that left Mato concerned. "I won't be in the way. Promise," he added in a way Mato struggled to believe. "Shall we be off then?"

Before they could hike Verka home, at the behest of his mother, Mato headed to the second floor, to grab one of her warm shawls, just in case it became cold for Verka during the journey.

"Mama, I am sure she'll be fine, the weather changed," reasoned Mato.

"Hush, and do as your told!" Mara demanded, ending the subject.

Within seconds, Mato hurtled southward three stairs at a time, with shawl and satchel in hand (for the shawl). His mind was already racing, lost in the midst of the upcoming journey. In a daze, Mato could not believe it! His chance to rekindle their talk was about to happen right now.

This led to panic! Everything was moving so fast. Was it too soon? Though Mato had wished to embrace the challenge before him, now he was not so sure. Only an hour ago he had so much to say, but now, he dreaded having to go through any of it. Perhaps, Mato surrendered to himself, Mirko should just take Verka home, and he could go to sleep. Mato rubbed his head, hard. Fatigue from over appraisal and downright fear was overcoming him. Mijo could see the dread building to dangerous levels. "Son," Mijo called. In a trance, Mato did not hear him. He could hear nothing but the doubts that were yelling at him to run. "Son!" Mijo called once more, with additional force that nudged Mato back into reality.

"Yes, Tata. I guess I've got to go. They're waiting," Mato muttered, reluctantly.

"Son, she's a nice girl," Mijo noted approvingly, with a smile of reassurance.

"Tata, I know," Mato agreed.

"Do you?"

"Yes," Mato said, with so little confidence, even he noticed it. "Yes, I really do, Tata. I know," Mato repeated once more, with more effort, but not enough to convince Mijo.

"Really, I do!" Mato said a third time, with a forced confidence.

"Good," Mijo said finally. "Then, I have two bits of advice for you."

Mato sighed. "Really? C'mon, Tata. They're waiting!"

"First," Mijo began, ignoring Mato's anxiousness. "First, before you go outside, I want you to do something."

"Do something?" Mato repeated, confused.

"Son, I want you to breathe," Mijo noted with all seriousness. "Take a deep, long breath. The type you can taste all the way down to your stomach. I want you to really breathe. It will be good for you."

"A deep breath?" Mato said, unbelieving. "That's your big advice. To take in air. Really, is that all?"

"No, that is not all, boy!" Mijo mocked. "And secondly, after you have taken this important deep breath, make sure you tell her the most important thing."

"Well, what is that?" Mato puzzled.

"The truth," Mijo chortled. "The truth, boy. And I don't mean some of it. I mean all of it. Every single speck of it. Otherwise…"

Mijo paused, waiting for his son to interrupt again. But this time he wanted him to. Mato, anxious to get the entire evening over with, duly complied.

"Otherwise, what?" Mato repeated crankily, while moving his left hand in a circle like motion, suggesting his father hurry.

"Otherwise…" Mijo continued. "In this race, you'll lose." After Mijo's pronouncement, a vacuum of silence filled the house, as if both kernels of given truth finally resonated between Mato's dull ears. Seeing his son was finally listening, Mijo hammered home his point. "Will you do these two things, son?" he asked.

"Yes, Tata, I think I will," was Mato's earnest reply.

"Good," Mijo pronounced. "Then go!"

Mirko was glad to be outside, especially since he was alone with Verka. Eager to break the silence, Mirko quickly came to the point, at least as he saw it.

"So," he began. "You and my brother, huh?"

Verka gave a nonplussed answer, with a shrug of her shoulders.

Mirko quickly took hold of her non-commitment. "Are you sure Mato is that interested?"

Verka did not like Mirko's tone and the conversations direction. He was being too forward for her liking. "Why do you ask?" she offered bluntly.

"Look, I like my brother, but you need to know something about him."

"What is that?" she asked.

"He's a runner," he offered, matter-of-fact. "First sign of trouble, he runs. He's always been that way."

"Oh, and you're telling me this because…?" Verka retorted, seeing unwanted reasons behind this conversation.

"Well, some are runners and some are fighters, that's all," Mirko continued.

"And I guess you're a fighter, I suppose?" answered Verka, placing Mirko's meaning into the light.

"I'm just saying," Mirko coyly noted. "I'm not going…"

But just then, Mirko was cut short by the creaking of the door.

"Are we ready to go?" Mato proclaimed.

-17-

Gore, Dolje¹

Up the mountain the three mice scurried. The trio's bond, though a result of the Hasikovanje, now conjured zero conversation to pass the time. No funny stories. No explanations, questions or sayings were spoken. Only the shuffling of feet, and the occasional coughing splutter could be heard.

Within this muted company, Verka felt alone. Each fluctuating emotion was bittersweet. All these months she wanted to see Mato, and now their re-connection left her despairingly disappointed. Within her heart, Verka thought the festering misery would evaporate just by seeing him again. But it didn't! Somehow, it made everything worse, leaving her confused, and uncertain. As they walked in silence, Verka thought about the constant searching and seeking she had endured. All to find Mato. And she did! But now, the payoff left her dour and befuddled.

But, at this most morose moment, Verka realized an important truth. She had done all of this searching and seeking, and it got her feeling completely lost. So, Verka wondered if it was time to stop and keep still. Maybe, she had done her part by finding Mato again. If this were so, the rest would be up to Mato to show her that the past three months were not wasted time.

1 Up and Down

Furthermore, Mirko said Mato was a runner, alluding he was nothing but a scared little boy. Verka doubted this was true, but she needed to know the truth. She took a quick glance over her right shoulder, and allowed herself the pleasure of the smallest of smiles. Mato was there! That was a small start, but not enough. "*Yes*", she began to mutter in the four corners of her mind. "*The rest would be up to Mato.*" He would have to fix this, however he saw best, thus proving her right, and Mirko wrong. Verka could not stop smiling. Her recent revelations were making her feel so much better.

So further up the mountain Verka went, silently leading the way, which was perfectly natural since she was the only one who knew the path back to her village. However, both Mirko and Mato were a step behind, not just because they did not know the way, also because Verka was moving at a pace they struggled to keep.

Mato's breathing was labored. The night warmth weighed heavily on his chest, however, how to break the silence weighed much more on his mind, rendering, for the first time in his life, his feet useless. He took his second big, deep breath of the night, to couple the one he took for his father's benefit, before heading out the door.

Ready to try to engage an angered Verka, Mato nudged Mirko, in the hope his older brother might take a step back and give them relative privacy. But as Mato edged closer to Verka, Mirko walked closer too. Frustrated, Mato motioned for his older brother to acquiescence, but surprisingly, he would not. Mato yelled through whispers, mouthing "*Bjezi!*" but Mirko refused to yield. "Wouldn't get in the way, indeed," Mato whispered with fired fury.

Finally, after moments of continual hand gestures, and numerous pulled faces that expressed Mato's strong disgust, Mirko buckled under Mato's consistent pressure.

"Fine," Mirko mouthed angrily, which left Mato shaking his head. "*Nobody asked you to come,*" Mato thought as loudly as he could. Mato could not believe Mirko, but right now, none of that mattered. Mato did not have time to care about his weirdly-acting brother. He had greater mountains to climb.

Chapter 17

"So, Verka," Mato fumbled. "I suppose you're wondering where I have been?"

"Why would you think I care about that?" she began sternly, further increasing her pace.

Mato gulped, and his pace slowed. Instantly, he felt defeated. But just as he was about to give up, his father's words leapt forth. *"Just tell her the truth,"* rang in his ears, as he almost stumbled over a stone that stuck up from the dewed grass.

"I know you're angry," Mato sighed. "I know. If you only knew I had promised myself to see you next week, so to put everything right and tell you everything. But now," he reasoned, "because you found me first, none of that sounds true."

"No it doesn't," Verka retorted in agreement.

Mato was no savant to the inner workings of a young woman, but even he could see her hurt.

"Verka, I'm sorry. I really am," he lamented while looking over at her. "I hope during our walk, I can at least offer a complete explanation."

"I don't think it will matter, really. You lied to me," Verka blurted, still looking straight ahead.

Verka was so angry, Mato was certain it was over, even before it begun. And yet, though Mato's cup filled with grief, surprisingly, his lamentations freed his mind from considering any concealment of the entire story. Mato now knew it could not get any worse than it already was. Though Mato could say nothing or everything, he realized that at least with everything, he could live with himself.

"Just tell her the truth."

"I know it won't matter," Mato agreed. "But, I think I owe you that much anyway."

Mato took his fourth long deep breath, and took the plunge. He told Verka everything! He told her about how excited he was after their first meeting, and how he looked forward to seeing her once more. He then told her about the depth of sorrow that gripped him, and how it felt that life stopped with his baba's passing. Not just for himself but for the entire family. Going forward felt impossible without their dear Vjera.

Mato did not stop there. "*Tell her the entire truth,*" Mijo told him, and he was resolved to do so. He told Verka about how when he was young, he dreamed of faraway places, and how he loved to imagine visiting them. He told her about how he loved learning about these distant lands, about their cultures, and about their deepest passions. But now, with each day on the job in Vareš those dreams seemed so far away to the point he stopped thinking about them any longer.

At this point, Mato stole a quick glance at Verka. For her second, Verka's unchanged countenance made him hesitate, but the nagging phrase given to him by his father would not let up.

"*Tell her the truth!*" Mijo had said. "*Tell her the truth!*"

It was then, with a deep sigh, Mato began to tell her why these dreams really stopped, informing Verka of the most important story of his life. He told her about being chased by the pack of wolves and how he had to spend a night up a small little tree that felt fifty feet high. It was here, Mato informed Verka, that he had spent each of the past twelve Sundays at this saving tree.

He did not stop there. Mato then explained that his night at little/big tree changed his life for the better and worse. "I had never felt such emotion," Mato began. "I was so tired, so scared, so relieved, so angry, and so happy all at the same time. Each feeling was so alive. Maybe, each emotion felt like this, because at that moment, I was glad I was still alive. I should have been dead!"

As Mato continued, though Verka would not show it, she could tell a human being was pouring out his soul. He spoke in a way that had meaning beyond simply wanting to patch up a friendship. He spoke as if his life depended on it.

There was more to say. "*Tell her everything!*" yelled his mind. Mato continued discussing that fateful night in the trees. He talked about being hunted each of those waking hours, with nothing for company but the trunk of a tree and the snow falling upon his scalp. He spoke of how the night was so intense, it felt as if the wolves had a personal vendetta against him. At this point, Mato then spoke of their pack leader, who he called *The One*. "He really wanted to get me Verka, I do not lie," Mato exclaimed with a passion, drenched with dread, as if the original ordeal had just concluded moments ago. "He wanted me dead, so much so…"

Mato paused. He knew what he was about say was going to sound crazy. He took a deep breath.

"Tell her the entire truth, son. Tell her the truth! Tell her the truth!"

"…So much so, I thought I heard the wolf pack leader speak to me."

At that, for the first time during their hike, Verka completely turned to meet Mato's face. "You heard him speak to you? You're kidding, right?" Verka said, disbelieving.

Mato gulped again. "No, I'm not," Mato answered steadfastly. "I didn't say I'm sure he spoke. I said it seemed like he did. I don't know if I dreamed the conversation, or I was in some kind of trance, but that's what it felt like."

During Mato's entire story, Mirko was close enough to hear bits and pieces, but far enough away for them not to notice. However, Mirko heard enough to know what was going on. Especially, when Mato began discussing his ordeal with the wolves. Mirko could not help but smirk at that point. Disbelieving his candor, Mirko thought Mato sounded ridiculous.

"And though, I really did want to see you over the past few months," Mato began to conclude. "With everything I have seen, done and been through, I just couldn't until I was sure."

"Sure of what?" Verka queried, uncertain of Mato's meaning.

Mato took his fifth deep breath of the evening. They were in the high country now, and the air felt good. He felt awake and refreshed. He felt happier than he had all night.

"I wanted to make sure I was ready, and well, that I might be good to you," he said shyly. "I wanted to make sure, you know?"

Under the cluster of the highland's heavy evergreens, though the Pavlović boys held small lanterns, the darkness cocooned them. And yet, Verka could still see Mato was blushing. This made Verka feel very special, like one of those Hollywood movie stars. It also made Verka remember why she liked Mato in the first place. "I see," Verka replied, not giving anything away.

Nervously, Mato's heart jumped. These were the first words of niceness she had directed toward him all night. Was there hope? Though he shared everything out of need to say sorry, a spark of anticipation dared to grow. "I know you might not forgive me," Mato concluded, "but now, I hope you at least understand."

Verka paused, leaving Mato to hang on an emotional edge a little longer, punishing him a little. Verka mused, Mato had made her wait three months so he could wait three seconds for her answer. "I might," she toyed. "But only under one condition."

"What is that?" Mato panted, becoming desperate to learn her truth.

"This tree of yours. I want to see it," she demanded.

"My tree," Mato began, dismayed. "Why do you want to see it?"

"I want to, that's why," Verka proclaimed.

✳✳✳

The boys returned late, neither having said a word to each other during the entire uneventful return flight. As they arrived, the silent brothers found Mijo sitting downstairs, awaiting them, near an old black leather cover book. Mato knew it was Baba's old Bible.

"How did it go boys?" the old man asked.

"Good, I think," proclaimed Mato. "After a few long deep breaths, at least."

Mijo smiled. "Good. Good night, Mato." Quickly, Mijo's attention turned to his other son. "Mirko, do you have a minute?"

Mato could tell this was his time to depart the scene. "Well, goodnight then."

"Laku noć," both Mijo and Mirko proclaimed.

"Son, do you have a minute?" Mato asked once more.

"No, not really Tata," sneered Mirko.

"Well, I want you to," he persisted. "Sit!"

Mirko complied, unhappily. "What do you need to say, Stari," he blurted unkindly. Mijo sighed, knowing Mirko was attempting to pick a fight. Moving closer to his son, Mijo took his open right hand, gently up to Mirko's face, hoping to cup it lovingly. But, Mirko jerked back. Though disappointed, Mijo believed he had to keep going. He made a promise to his mother. It was now or never. Unabated, Mijo started to say what he needed to.

"Look son, I know you don't want to talk about what happened to you these past two years. That's fine. But I know things did not go well there. I know it. If you don't want to talk to me, fine. But, there is something important I need to share."

Mirko attempted to take his mind elsewhere. He was grossly uncomfortable. He did not ask for this conversation, nor did he wish to have it. He wanted to get out. He knew he needed to get out!

"What is Tata, *What is it*?" he shouted, his face flush with rage.

"Your grandmother…" Mijo began.

"I don't want to talk about this!" interjected Mirko.

"Your grandmother," Mijo continued. "Before she died, gave us all something. It was for your brother, you and I. She gave us a gift."

He picked up the old Bible off the table, and stretched out his hands towards his first born son.

"She said it would help us. Me, Mato and you too, Mirko." Mirko was incredulous. He did not know what Mijo hoped to achieve by any of this. Nor did he care. "You think her old book will help me?" Mirko blurted.

Mijo shrugged. "Your Baba thought so."

Mirko vehemently disagreed. "What would Baba have known about what I was going through?"

"I don't know," Mijo answered honestly. "But, before she died, she said she knew."

Mirko had had enough. Enough of this conversation. Enough of being told what to do, what to know, and what to think.

"You want me to talk?" Mirko seethed. "With who? Not you! Not with someone who never talked anything over with anyone."

"This is not about me son," defended Mijo.

"Of course not, Tata," Mirko continued sarcastically. "Still one set of rules for you and one set for everyone else. What happened to your Father, huh? You never talk about that."

Mijo knew this was going very badly. Mirko was so defensive, so quick to anger. He seemed so scared. But Mijo knew he had to keep Mirko talking. He knew it was good for him, even if it was not good for them. "That is a different conversation, son," Mijo answered.

"Of course it is," Mirko blurted, as if this was now a game, a death match to win. "So let me ask you, did you look into Baba's book and get help from it?"

Mijo did not respond straight away. He did not have a satisfactory answer to this question. Mirko quickly surmised the answer anyway.

"No, I didn't think so," Mirko continued with disgust. "As usual, one set of rules for you and another set for everyone else." Mirko did not want to talk. He only wished to fight. He was enraged, a pit bull latched onto its prey until the end. He thought he had Mijo right where he wanted him. "Let's do this then old man. I'll look at your book, once you have read it from head to foot. How do you like that?"

Mijo looked at his son. He felt bad for him. All he wanted to do was help, but at that moment, he realized he could not. He looked at Mirko once more, and began to mourn for him. Even though Mirko Pavlović was still a living, breathing entity, Mijo knew he was not alive. "That's what I thought, old man," concluded Mirko, with disgust. "Laku noć." With those final words, Mirko stormed up the stairs and slammed the door. Mijo took a long deep breath, slumped to the floor, and wept.

-18-

Feste[1]

Mato found himself running at full speed, almost out of control! Though uncertain where he was running too, it had to be better than his current predicament. Mato sensed a great danger everywhere! With nervous courage, Mato glanced over his right shoulder. Though he had a growing lead, Mato was startled to hear the purser beckoning over and over, as if he was right next to him, in language he did not understand.

Mato did not wait for a translation. Through the throng he flew, darting in between the trees, hoping this action might shake what was trailing him. On and on, our scared charge ran through the forest.

Within seconds, Mato's effort appeared to pay a dividend! The trees disappeared into a blur, leaving him in new surroundings that owned a large openness of nothing. Its vastness surprised him. Its lack of noise left Mato uncertain. Not even the wind hitting his face dared to whisper. Maybe Mato thought the chase was over.

That thought unfortunately was an untruth. Though he still could see nothing, Mato quickly sensed the purser's voice was there. Worse, Mato now knew its voice had always been there. "What do you want?" Mato yelled, desperate to get out of this place.

1 Affirmative or as mentioned earlier, "yes, it is."

"What does it take to make a person happy?" it asked, in a deep, calm, but sinister voice. The voice owned a power that made each follicle, strand, and fleck of stubble on Mato's body ache with cold.

"Truly happy?" the voice asked again, in a manner that suggested it knew the answer. "If one knew, they would be rich, rich, rich."

"Are you rich?" Mato asked, daring to speak.

"Am I rich?" it asked Mato. "What do you think?" This time, Mato hesitated. The voice did not like this delay, and perhaps because of it, its tone changed. It was more biting, angry, and frightening.

"My customers gain satisfaction, and so do I!" it boomed, inching closer to Mato with every syllable.

"What do you sell?" Mato sheepishly asked.

"What do you want?" the menacing sound replied.

Mato dared not say.

"It does not matter," the voice reassured. "I know what you seek. You cannot hide. I know."

"Arrghhhhhh!"

Mato screamed, awaking out of breath. Sweat poured from his scalp. The booming voice of this newest nightmare was a continuous wave crashing upon rocks. Seven nights, seven nightmares! It was somehow always the same booming voice, coming to him in different scenarios and in different form. Scarier still, the voice owned a familiarity Mato dared not pinpoint.

Mato got out of bed, hoping to remove the lingering notions of trepidation. It was still dark. Sunday was almost upon him. Mato smiled through the lingering effect of the nightmare. Seven days had come, and seven days had thankfully left. Though they put up a fight and scared him out of his needed slumber, only hours stood in front of him and today's destination of seeing Verka once more.

Groggily, Mato trudged down the hallway to see how many hours were left in the night. Rubbing his eyes, Mato noticed it was eighteen past three. It was early. There was nothing for it but to go back to bed. At least each night had only afforded Mato one terror. He could rest easier knowing his ordeal was over, for this night at least. Tomorrow's problems could wait. Mato was in no hurry to rush past this day, but he needed more sleep. As Mato turned to return to his room, a deep blast resonated from the direction of Mijo's chair, spooking him terribly.

"Argh!" Mato gasped, before realizing the noise was nothing more than his father snoring from his favorite spot. Shaking off the double fright, Mato went over to his slumbering father. As Mato approached, Mijo opened one eye powerfully, further frightening the already disheveled son.

"What time is it?" Mijo asked.

"Late. Early. Just after three," Mato answered.

"Oh," Mijo replied. "Why aren't you sleeping?"

"I was," Mato started to answer. "But I had another dream that woke me."

Mijo chuckled. He knew today was a big day for his son. Mijo believed Mato's inability to sleep was down to nothing more than jitters.

"Son, it will all be okay. Get some rest."

How does one rest when the heart is the one dreaming? Church service was complete. Now all Mato had to do was wait at their decided meeting place, the spot on the square where they first talked *"the Talk."*

It was a beautiful spring day. All week, the commotion in Mato's heart and mind, was only matched by the villager's efforts in further cultivating their fields. Planting, hoeing, and curating were happening all over the mountains.

In the outlining areas, the field grass had grown tall, each strand dressed with many wild flowers in its hair, ready to meet the nuzzling bees. Bushes and trees were beginning to flower too, but in these instances they were the first sign of nature's giving. The flowers that would one day provide strawberries, blackberries, and plums, were pushing through. The aroma of spring was permeating everywhere.

Life was abounding, begging all celebrate its return. And all were! That is, except for Mato. He stood, on his prearranged spot, waiting anxiously. He could not help it. Each night for the past seven days dreaming had come at a cost. Now very much awake, Mato understood the risk. Perhaps because of this, until Mato's eyes met with Verka's, his nerves were going to be on guard.

But everything was arranged. Mato and Verka agreed that after church service, they would wait at the square's edge until the other arrived. Mato was glad he got there first. In the past three months, Mato knew he had made Verka wait long enough. So he slipped out after service. Not too early. He simply edged closer to the exit with the final calls of "amen" bellowing from the congregation. Mato was not only first to reach their rendezvous, but he was in fact the first person to make it to the square. For the first time in his life, Mato walked the square's pavement and could hear the sounds of footsteps. As he pounded its cement, he felt strangely powerful.

But he also felt alone. Each moment took an age to pass by. His aloneness worsened as the church began to empty, and people began to flood from the Kraljeva Sutjeska. As people began to converge, Mato stood on his toes, hoping to get the first comforting glimpse. Anxiousness drained his ability to comprehend time. Each second felt like a minute. As the moments mounted, Mato's ability to compute worsened. A second was five minutes and then ten. What Mato did not realize was that he had been out there longer than that. Twenty minutes had passed. But, Mato was ready to wait, for however long it took Verka to appear.

Verka could not wait to see her friend. Over the course of the past seven days, her smile beamed equal to the new spring sun. Each word Mato had confided during their walk up the mountains, now danced within her mind. It was the closest thing to music she had heard for a long time.

With the service over, however, she was so excited she first needed to visit the ladies room. This annoyed Verka to no end, because she did not wish to keep her friend waiting, but Nature does not confer with best laid plans. Unfortunately, as it is with any large crowd, there was a long line to use the ladies room. Unable to hold, impatient minute after impatient minute passed and went. Finally, relieved of her unwanted duty, Verka rushed for the square. Stress levels were irritatingly high. Verka did not want Mato to think she was punishing him for the past. Each of the past seven days glistened with forgiveness. Oh, how she just wanted to see Mato right now! Out of the church she ran, out through the halls, and down past one of the building's major walls. Just around one more corner, past a flight of stairs and the rest of her day, and her life could begin. Just as Verka was about to bound past the final corner, when an eager hand grabbed her arm, stopping her in her tracks.

"Hi Verka," resonated a newly familiar voice. Coupled with the voice, was a newly similar face.

"Hi Mirko, have you seen your brother…?"

"No, no," Mirko quickly interrupted. "They don't know I'm here. Anyway," he continued, "I didn't come to see them. I came to see, well…"

Verka got his meaning, and blushed uncomfortably. "Look," she began, "I'm going to meet Mato."

"I know," Mirko continued, "and that is fine, but I was wondering if…"

"If what?" Verka asked, impatiently.

"If you would rather walk with me?"

"But, he's your brother!"

"I know," Mirko responded, almost apologetically. Verka looked at Mirko. *"Why me?"* she mused. *"Why not someone else?"* It did not matter, though. Verka had chosen someone else, and she liked her choice. Verka liked why she liked Mato, and did not wish to change this fact. Not now. Verka decided she wanted to make this evidently clear.

"I don't have a lot of time, because Mato is waiting," she began. "So let me ask you a question."

"What is it?" Mirko smiled.

"When you were younger, what did you want to be?"

Mirko froze, his smile quickly disappearing. "Why'd you want to know that?" he asked defensively.

"C'mon, I'm interested, that's all," Verka pressed. "What did you want? What was it you needed?"

"Um, um," Mirko stammered, "Me, well not a lot. I didn't. I mean. I wasn't into much, you know?"

Verka looked Mirko dead in the eye, and knew the truth had not left his lips. "I have to go," she said, her voice trailing as she flew, toward a newly exhaling Mato.

Through the woods the two walked, hands clasped tight, as if they always belonged together. There was much to talk about. Everything seemed new and important. It was as if it was the first time they had ever been in this forest, or any other. It was the first time they saw a spruce or birch with new leaves. The first time they saw fresh mountain grass, or heard a bird singing.

Each wanted to share everything. Verka talked about the first time she saw a hawk soaring. Mato talked about his first sighted eagle. Mato warned Verka about the vipers that could be baking in the new sun, and Verka in turn warned him about the possibility of black bears, as if just mentioning these things would keep them immune from their differing dangers. Their conversation bounced all over the place. Verka asked Mato questions he never would have thought of having an answer for, like what was his favorite flower? Mato in turn, prattled on about foreign places, and the different languages they spoke there. Verka thought Mato to be very intelligent. Mato, in turn, was fascinated how Verka saw things in such a different manner, unlike anyone he'd ever met.

They were long lost friends that had only just met. Conversation turned to the slight differences of their upbringings, and what they loved best about each of their experiences. Verka fondly recalled that when she was about seven, she witnessed a parade of deer and their babies nuzzling the grasses near her home as if there was not a care or gun in the world. In turn, Mato talked of the many rabbits he and his brother caught when he was not yet ten. Verka bristled at the sound of Mato talking about Mirko, but kept her feelings quiet.

Verka looked up at the sky and was glad. The weather was a continuation of the spring bliss that had enraptured the mountains for the past week. Except for scattered clouds, which were a fluffy white, it was a perfect day. The temperature was delightful, and though the clouds were low enough, or perhaps the ground was high enough to ensure the cotton balls in the sky provided moving shade. It truly was a beautiful day to go on an adventure.

Mato was having the time of his life. He was glad to be with Verka, though nerves danced within him, multiplying with each step closer to the most secret aspect of his life. Questions also were having their way with him. Mato wanted to know so much, all at the same time. So, to get the ball rolling, he posed the same question he asked of Verka, when she first expressed an interest in his tree.

"Because," was Verka's short reply. But Mato pressed again for additional detail.

"Well, I want to see where you survived. Because, well if you didn't…"

"What if I didn't?" Mato queried.

"If you didn't make it," Verka continued. "We would not be here now."

"Right," Mato giggled nervously, as did Verka. They then both laughed some more, even though neither thought it was that funny.

After about twenty minutes of additional uneventful walking, Mato pointed in the direction of a thicket of trees. "It is right there!" he proclaimed. "C'mon!"

The two friends ran onward, though there were only a few dozen steps to go. Verka wondered if Mato did this each time he arrived to his sacred place. The answer to this unasked question was yes. Each time Mato ran to his tree, he would remember the terrible and terrific night. Mato truly loved this place. Nothing could hurt him in his tree. With his tree he was safe. He was at peace.

Within seconds of sprinting, they were standing within a clump of trees that appeared to be unnaturally close. Verka scanned the trees before them. Two of them were strong and powerful, full of life, with complete foliage a real possibility within a few days.

"Which one is it?" Verka asked.

With this question Mato took two quick strides and bounded upon what appeared to be a tree of the sickliest disposition. "This one," Mato announced proudly as he stood on the lowest and thinnest of branches. Verka was stunned how his lowly perch could withstand his sturdy frame.

"Well," Verka began amazed. "You weren't kidding about it being small. "So," she continued, "Which branch did you sit on all those hours?"

Mato pointed to three branches above the one he stood on. "That one!" Mato climbed to the next branch, rubbing its trunk with great affection, especially a section that appeared to have some writing on it.

"What is that?" she asked.

"Oh," Mato said. "Just something I carved into it, after the night was almost over."

Verka wandered around the base of the tree, amazed at how little and thin the tree was. Then, she got as close to the tree as possible, and hugged its very trunk, while breathing it in. "What are you doing?" Mato wondered.

"Oh, nothing," Verka responded, dismissively.

From there, at least to Mato, Verka continued to act quite strange. She proceeded to circle the tree several times, each time muttering the words, "Very interesting, indeed." After this, Verka pulled a small amount of the trunk's bark and smelled it. Then she tugged one of its few leaves off, taking a deep whiff of its fragrance. "Now," Verka proceeded. "Do you mind giving me a hand up?"

"Sure," Mato answered. "But, I don't think the tree is built for two."

"Oh, she'll manage," Verka confidently replied. Verka climbed up to the second branch, where Mato had just been. Mato, continuing to disagree with Verka's assessment, decided not to strain his little tree, and instead sat where its base met the grass. While

Chapter 18

Verka stood higher up, Mato surveyed the surrounding areas. Pulling at some new tufts from the turf, Mato began to recognize something different about his woods. Shadow was forming, making his place on the ground colder than it had been less than minutes earlier. Mato looked up into sky, and noticed the number of clouds had multiplied and were forming into darker shades.

"We should head back," Mato called up to Verka. "It could rain soon."

"Sure, in a minute," Verka replied, while returning to her work, which continued to puzzle Mato.

"Hey, what are you doing up there anyway?" he inquired.

"Oh, nothing much," she surmised. "Just looking at...the... view."

Verka looked the tree all over. She was fascinated by the little tree's beauty, looking beyond its poor size. She continued to play with the bark, realizing its pattern looked like an oversized fingerprint. As Verka continued to scan over Mato's tree, she made an even more startling discovery. On one of the higher branches, a glint of a gold-like substance captured her attention. Quickly, Verka pressed upward, now about fifteen feet above where Mato sat on the Sutjeska's surface below. Getting as close as she could, Verka reached up towards the yellow gleam. "Mato" Verka called.

"Yes," he replied, without paying much attention.

"When you were a child, did your mother or grandmother tell you stories?" Verka asked.

"What kind of stories?"

"You know," said Verka. "Children stories like nursery rhymes, or fables?"

"Sure," Mato answered, weirded out by the question, but playing along as he did earlier. "What, like Ivica and Marcia who got locked up in a gingerbread house, or something?"

Verka laughed, "Something like that."

"Why do you ask?"

"Just wondering."

"You like to ask random questions, don't you?" stated Mato.

"I guess," Verka replied, all the while reaching toward golden-covered branch. She stretched and stretched, until finally her fingers connected with what was a most sticky substance. Smiling, Verka brought her right hand down to her nose to smell it. "Wow, is it?" she asked herself, while readying an answer. "Tisovina." she muttered with a smile.

"What did you say?" Mato pondered, without looking up.

Without replying to Mato's query, Verka tasted the yellow substance. It tasted wonderful! Taking another taste, Verka closed her eyes, allowing the honey like product to make its way down her throat. All at once, a million emotions entered her heart, all centered on a single topic. Each and every thought, all one million raced towards her mother, and of her violin. Verka opened her eyes, and for a second forgot she was so high up. "Mato," Verka cried. "Please. I need help getting down!"

In a flash, Mato was up the stairs of his tree, as if the wolves had returned, steadying Verka's balance.

"Are you okay?" he asked, sympathetically.

"Yes," Verka replied. "I just got a little dizzy, that's all. Are you ready to go?"

Mato was more than ready. "Sure," he confirmed. "You think you can get down alright?"

The clouds in Mato's mind were darkening even more than those above their heads. Something was stirring, and it felt unfavorable. Just then, far off in the distance, a thunderclap crashed the heavens.

"We will need to hurry," Mato mused.

Then the thunder crashed and crackled again. A third, then a fourth time it arrowed with force, each time appearing to be gaining on the couple. The fifth time it erupted, it destroyed the last fragments of peace that had only moments ago dominated the sky, startling both young man and woman alike. But this was nothing, when, real terror struck their ears.

"Hooooowwwlllllllllll!"

Fear gripped Mato. But before it took hold, he resolved himself to action. "C'mon. Let's get out of here!" he bellowed.

Chapter 18

The two quickly dismounted the tree, if somewhat clumsily, with Verka stumbling to one knee as she returned to terra firma. As they readied to sprint for their fates, they both heard and then saw a nearby shrub rustling violently, as if it caged a frenzied beast ready to break free.

Neither Verka nor Mato wished to wait around to find out what had been residing within it. They bolted as the crow flew, not once looking back. Through the thickets and brush they pushed, fending off cuts, scratches and a caning along the way. There was nothing for it; they could lick their wounds later. They ran as fast as they could, past thousands of trees that now held no interest to them. Only once did Mato hesitate his pace, and that was to collect a solid looking branch, that had fallen during last winter, a forest made weapon just in case something was about to nip their heels.

Gladly, within fifteen minutes of hard running, at least on this day, Mato's branch was not needed. Once they entered the clearing, even Verka knew it was okay to exhale. They were safe, except for the frayed nerves, cuts, bruises, and their disheveled imaginations. "Are you okay?" Mato wheezed.

"Yes," Verka panted - so much so it hurt her stomach.

"That was fun. Not!" Mato laughed.

"Yes, quite," Verka continued, trying not to laugh, as that hurt as well.

After a few minutes of gasping, wheezing, and feeling like they might puke, Verka turned around, and faced where they had come from. This sent her mind back into the forest where her thoughts had centered on memories of her mother, her violin, and thoughts of her music. For three months, she had tried to block memories about this painful subject. But now, she could not! They always seemed ready to burst back into the forefront of everything. This realization forced up uncontrollable tears. She didn't want to cry, but she could not stop them. Not now. As Verka continued to blubber, at least she thought her tears would be safe in Mato's company. Not that Mato, at this moment understood, thinking the tears were his fault. "I'm sorry, Verka," Mato offered. "It's okay. We're alright."

"I know," she offered, though the tears continued unabated. Mato removed a handkerchief from his right pocket, passing it to her.

"Do you want to talk about it?" he asked gently.

Verka looked at Mato, and thought about telling him what was going on inside her, like he did with her. At this moment, Verka learned how hard it was to share ones darkest secrets. This realization also increased her admiration for Mato's courageous recent retelling. "Ask me another time," she replied, while retaking his hand, and leaning on his shoulder.

Rain began to trickle. The rain was cold; the last holdover of winter's bite, but neither seemed to be in a hurry to get out of out of it. Both were perfectly content to stand in their newfound freedom. "Verka," Mato began, "I want to ask your father something."

Verka looked at Mato, and smiled. "You don't have to ask him," she announced. "You can ask me."

"Okay, I have something to ask you," Mato began, nervously.

"My answer is yes, Mato," Verka interrupted, before he could properly begin. "My answer is yes!"

Part III
Tito

-19-

Promjenjivo vrijeme[1]

The clock struck, and a joyful hurrah leapt from both hearts. Plans were made. Preparations were set. Bonds were united. Foundations were laid, and futures were understood. Mato and Verka were to be married! Each was so happy and so nervous, that in danced a million other emotions in equal measure. Mato thought he could hear a tamburica playing somewhere. Neither could recollect a happier moment. They were making the most important decision of their lives, and both were glad that they had each other to lean on. Mato looked at his beloved as she sat on a tuft of hilly grass before horizon's sunset, his heart swelled with jubilant glee. The moment was perfect, as if time itself was satisfied in their choice.

Mato and Verka talked through the intermittent rain, and beyond the setting sun, cueing conversation about everything and anything. All portions of their dreams needed to be covered, even fears and concerns. For example, Verka wondered if Mato's parents would approve. Mato laughed, "Don't worry Verka, Mama will love you," he said with certainty.

At this, Verka went very quiet, lost in her next thought, leaving Mato worrying out loud if everything was okay. The silence stayed

1 Changing weather

for quite some time, but Verka finally whispered, "Good. I'm good," putting Mato at ease with a growing grin. By the time her smile was at full tilt, Verka had changed the subject to whom they thought might come to the wedding, and the moment of worry was a vapor. Cheekily, Mato wagered that he'd have a family member travel the longest distance to join the party.

"Wager?" Verka laughed, mocking Mato's empty pockets. "You have to have some money first."

"You're right," Mato gulped. "Perhaps, I should look for a better job over the next few months, or maybe get promoted or something," he mused. "Oh well, It's not like we can get married for a little while."

"Oh yeah, that's right," Verka giggled at herself, having forgotten her young age.

Both were still awaiting their seventeenth birthdays, and eighteen was the magic number. Although Verka was three months older, eighteen was still nineteen months away for Mato. While looking at his wife-to-be, he smiled. The harsh winter that had been his life these past few years was receding away. But not totally. Not yet. The last few years had been so hard. Having to cruelly work so far from home at such a tender age. The racing from the fangs of death. The despair of misplacing his hopes and dreams. The void left by Baba's death. All of these moments had torn at his very being.

But, somehow, he also realized those difficult times had prepared him for this beautiful moment. It gave Mato a resolve to know that whatever came his way he could tackle it. And best of all, Mato knew, Verka would be there to help find the right road.

This confidence on the future set his mind ablaze into a greater level of speed, a rushing locomotive ready to have its fires fueled to the hilt. Mato could not wait to board the next stage of life. He felt ready for it. He wanted it. "Why couldn't we be older?" Mato lamented.

Verka looked at the young man sitting next to her. His happiness gave her strength. She knew over the next nineteen months, she would need this. But at the same time she did not wish to rush anything. There had been so few happy days, and today was one. Verka wanted it to last as long as possible. Quickly, she reminded Mato there was nothing they could do about it anyway, so there was no use fighting it. Verka told Mato how her mother used to say, "even if you plead and beg, time will never hasten, nor budge from its consistent tick-tock. Time, despite its ebbs and flows, is never in a rush."

Mato nodded, thinking Verka's mother must have been quite the wise lady.

"Well, I guess it is not a bad thing to have to wait a while, right? It does give us plenty of time to plan everything," Mato reflected.

"Not as much time as you think," Verka replied.

As it happened, Verka was to be proven correct once more, for the past moves faster than the present, and the future arrives when it chooses.

Seasons shifted. Warmer weather came and future responsibility joined the fold. After a few months of enjoying their delightful secret, they broke, informing Mijo and Mara of their choice. As Mato predicted, they were overjoyed! Especially Mara, who was finally gaining the daughter she always knew God would give her. "Oh my," said a stunned Mara. "I get to help plan a wedding!"

The days continued to fall by the wayside, like the leaves in autumn. Monday to Friday, Mato continued to work in Vareš, saving like a miser, working like a horse, and praying like a priest for the promotion that had yet to come.

As winter blew in, invitations were sent to the four corners of Yugoslavia. Mato continued to work, still with no promotion, and with few prospects. Time's consistency continued to remind him that it was less than a year before the Kraljeva Sutjeska's priest would say 'Man and Wife' in his direction, leaving him worried about the future. Ah, such is the life of a man.

Mato and Verka's lives moved with the seasons. One winter came and went, but another would have to do the same before their day could take center stage. Spring and summer moved in and moved out quicker than ever before, taking the months given to its seasons with them. Autumn barely stayed for a chat. By late September, winter was once more muscling in. Mato wondered where the time went. He was only four months away from being eighteen. Verka's birthday was next month! Everything they had talked about was soon to invade their reality.

Though time continued to move, it hadn't changed Mato's high esteem for the happy arrangement. In fact, he found himself so content in it, that he hadn't visited his little tree since he first showed Verka. Initially, he had wished to go back to it, but Verka never seemed to want to, and after a while, Mato realized he did not need to. This was not the only long absence from Mato's past. It had been fifteen months since he had seen his brother.

Mato had looked for Mirko all over Vareš, especially early in their estrangement. He longed to find him. But alas, Mato never once even caught a whiff of his older brother. After a full year of searching, Mato started to doubt whether his older brother was in the city any longer. None of Mirko's old acquaintances had heard or seen of him for months. He certainly had not been back to Pavlovići. Mirko hadn't even found the time to scrawl a simple letter, just to let the family know he was still alive and well. Over time, Mirko was slowly becoming a forgotten thought, as it appeared was his wish.

Tired of looking for someone who did not wish to be found, Mato's Monday-to-Friday focus returned to work. He even picked up the habit of working additional shifts. Mato wondered why he had not done this before. Held ransom by Vareš five days a week, why shouldn't he reap its reward as greedily as his body would let him?

His schedule on Sunday also was set. Of course, he spent it with Verka, where they would accompany Mara and Mijo to church and then back to the village for refreshment, pita and additional wedding planning. During this time, Mara also ensured Verka knew everyone in the village, so that Mato's world felt like hers.

That left Mato with one free day, and he did his best not to make it free of activity. In the past, Saturday would be used as a day of rest, but Mato's future hopes did not afford him slumber. Mato and sleep were not on the best of terms anyway, but regardless, he had made arrangements for Saturdays, and he was going to stick to these plans! These plans, different than those confirmed on Sunday, were fulfilling another lifelong ambition that existed long before Mato ever set eyes on a pretty young lady. In fact, Mato was making and *then* implementing plans! Long-held plans. These plans saw Mato laying his eyes on the land, and locating worlds he had never known. He was traversing catacombs, while scouting the darkest valleys. He was exploring the woods and all of its plunder, with only a knife for protection and his wits his only guide.

Mato was map building!

Not just one, but an entire book of them! Mato could not believe he was writing a book, albeit one with mostly pictures. Traveling all over the mountains, Mato found that each stride across Sutjeska's landscapes stirred unbelievable purpose. After only a few months of trekking over the country, Mato had scores of topographies drawn on the thinnest paper, prepared with care for posterity. That thought made Mato smile. One day he would show them to his sons and daughters.

The journeys across the Sutjeska thrilled all of his senses. During this time, Mato had discovered lost kingdoms within his walking sphere. He drank from hidden streams. He found caves that once housed bears, built for hibernation. On different occasions, he had seen both a stag and doe within range of whispers. He even saw an eagle swoop to kill its prey. Each experience left Mato with overflowing contentment. Each day was new. Each adventure was his own that strengthened his passion for tomorrow. Furthermore, these hard travels harden and flexed his growing muscles, and cleared his expanding mind. Though Mato would leave early and come home late, and despite the hard distances traveled, he felt refreshed and rested, ready to tackle another workweek. This was something Mato needed, because the weeks in Vareš were becoming a heavy burden.

While Mato's dreams during his waking hours appeared to be going to plan, nighttime was another story. A terrible, awful story. The nightmares were coming thick and fast. They were always different, but somehow eerily felt the same. Each night terror always had Mato always running from something. The second similarity was the awful, booming voice that always threatened him. He hated that voice most of all. Many of the dreams awoke him with terrorized screams pouring from his lips. Also, Mato found he had begun grinding his teeth as he tried to sleep, leaving his jaw painfully clenched each morning. The crazy thing to Mato was, the nightmares only appeared while he was away in Vareš. This is what probably made it so easy to work extra shifts. With each week, getting any sleep was an impossibility that deep down Mato knew would get worse.

It had been like that, one non-particular Wednesday. Winter had arrived unseasonably early, like an unwanted relative who planned to stay for an extended period of time. The nightmare from the night before lingered, leaving Mato sullen. Even the early snow falling upon the cobblestones in the city did little to refresh his spirits. The snow had fallen heavily the past week, seeing the town folk hastily shovel the powder to the street's edges that conjured images of a three-foot high foamy ocean wave stuck in time. Mato had always liked the snow, but this shoveled variety, moved to allow horses and vehicles to pass, was dirty with street and soot, making it look ugly and uninviting. It looked nothing like the snow that fell in his village. Mato thought the city made the snow look like trash.

Like any other night, with his shift over, Mato shuffled back to his small weekday room. With his mind stuck on morbid hauntings, he did not know what to do. Mato had struck upon the idea of writing a letter to Verka about it, though he wasn't sure that was the best thing to do, as he did not wish to worry her. Attempting to be rational, perhaps he just was not feeling well, and was coming down with something unpleasant. As he opened his door, his features tightened with shock and surprise, as there sitting on his small bed, was a being he had not seen for a long while. "Hello brother!" the figure exclaimed. "Long time no see."

Finally calming from thinking he was about to be pounded by an intruder, Mato looked at Mirko, unable to say a word. As had happened last time he saw his brother, Mirko's appearance shocked him. He was thinner, a fact exacerbated by a black leather coat he wore that appeared to be two sizes too big. Mirko looked pensive and scattered. Mirko's eyes squinted with suspicion. There was no doubt Mirko had once again changed. Mato mused; perhaps Mirko just looked unrecognizably older, which happens when you don't see someone for so long.

"How did you get in?" asked Mato, moving passed pleasantries.

Mirko laughed, "Pretty easily, actually. It is a good thing you have nothing worth stealing."

It had been a long time since each brother had seen each other, but there was no happiness in this newest greeting. Truth be told, Mirko's timing could not have been worse. Mato was tired. He was feeling sicker by the moment. However, Mirko did not notice. "I hear congratulations are in order," Mirko continued. "I am happy for you, brother."

"Thank you," Mato replied, with a wince. Mato grabbed at his stomach, as if attacked by a thousand swords from within. Mato's brow was clammy. He felt exhausted and overtly warm. He felt unsteady on his feet. Mato did not wish to be rude, knowing it had been so long since he saw his brother, but an awfulness was plaguing him.

"Hey, Mato, are you okay?" Mirko asked with a real sincerity. "You look like you're about to pass…"

"Brother, I'm sorry but, I don't feel too well," Mato blurted, at the very moment he fell towards his bed, blanking out in his brothers arms.

Pitanje[1]

Hours passed. For most of his slumber, Mato's sleep was peaceful, but it did not last. Once more, he awoke, startled by another terror! Mato could not remember a single thing about this latest night drama, but he knew he had had it before. Still, he just could not put his finger on it, which troubled him further. Mato muttered that he would get to the bottom of these unwanted dreams.

Slowly moving out of slumber, it took Mato a moment to remember where he was. He was still in Vareš! The darkness of the room clued him in that it was the evening, though uncertain how long he had been asleep. And then Mato remembered what had happened. Hearing a familiar voice further confirmed that some of it was not part of his subconscious.

"You feeling any better?" asked Mirko. "You gave me a bit of a fright."

"Yeah," Mato groaned.

"What happened? That was weird."

"I don't know," Mato answered honestly. "Just tired I guess. Hey, what time is it?"

"It is six forty-six."

---

1 Question

"I've only been asleep twenty minutes?" Mato asked, confused.

"Yes. Well, twenty minutes and a day," replied Mirko "But don't worry about missing work. I informed your boss. A nice German man. Didn't know there were any. Oh, what was his name?"

"Nico Gruber," mumbled Mato, still groggy from his marathon-length slumber.

"Yes, that's it!" exclaimed Mirko, with a slap of his left knee. "Nico. Very good. Nico, that's right. I was never very good with names."

Mato slowly forced himself to sit up. He smacked his lips. His mouth tasted of bad breath. His stomach was a pack of growling dogs. Getting out of bed, Mato headed towards his bread tin. The remaining piece he found was smaller than he remembered. "Sorry, I had a little," Mirko offered.

Mato began to mutter. He was annoyed that he had missed a day of work and the pay it would afford his pocket. He was annoyed that each night's sleep was being interrupted. But mostly, Mato was annoyed that his brother had out of the blue come for a casual visit like all was well. Over the many months he did not understand why Mirko disappeared. But now that he was here, Mato understood even less why he had returned. He got directly to the point. "What are you doing here?" he demanded.

Mirko, not the first time in his life played it coy, "Can't one brother visit another?" he suggested.

"Sure, but I haven't seen you in ages," mentioned Mato. "What? Twice in three, going on four years. That's not visiting."

Having finished his diminished hunk of bread, Mato got up to find a piece of fruit he stored in the small cupboard adjacent to the bread tin. That too was gone, and Mato did not need to ask how or why it was missing. "Has it been that long?" asked Mirko, more to himself than his brother.

"Jeste," Mato quipped. "I didn't know you were in Vareš anymore."

"Da. Pretty much the entire time," laughed Mirko, like it was no big deal. "I have been really busy." Mato hated when people said that. He found it insulting, that everything Mirko had done these past fifteen months was more important than seeing him. That stung more than the long absence.

"So," Mato began again, once more. "What are you doing here?

"I wanted to wish you congratulations," Mirko announced, cheerfully.

"I thought you did that yesterday?" replied Mato.

"Oh, yes. I did do that yesterday. I was not sure you'd remember," said Mirko, through a nervous smile. "There was another reason I wanted to see you. I wasn't going to, but I thought I should, you know?"

Mato was puzzled. "Oh, what about?"

"Um, I have to tell you something," Mirko stammered, repeating himself.

"If it is about you making a move on my girl those many months ago, I don't care about that anymore," Mato offered.

Mirko laughed at his brother's explanation. "Oh wow, I almost forgot about that! She got around to telling you, huh?"

"No, never," replied Mato.

This surprised Mirko. "Then how did you find out?"

"From you, just now," remarked Mato.

Mirko sat, with his mouth slightly opened, wanting to say something, but unable to find the words. Finally, after a few moments, he gasped, "Oh, you got me. Wow!"

"Yeah, I did," smirked Mato, very proud of himself.

Silence again filled the room, making Mirko uncomfortable. "Actually," he stuttered. "I am really sorry about that. Sorrier than you might believe. I was foolish. Please forgive me. "

Mato nodded approvingly, but through clenched teeth. He tasted the rising conflict within him, and it was bitter to his stomach. With every additional minute, Mato's gladness for Mirko's return was growing, as he always owned a soft spot for his brother. As children, Mato had not just lived in his shoes - he had often borrowed them. Because of this, Mato thought he knew him so well, and in turn, he thought Mirko knew him.

But, Mato also knew time had changed them, ensuring he did not trust that old fondness. As Mirko spoke, Mato's heart was shooting alarm bells throughout his veins. Mato sighed, overcome by a new truth. What was between them had gone. It had been gone for a long time, only he had just realized it. Neither of them were children anymore, running in the fields, and fishing the streams. Mato was not sure who his brother was or wanted to be anymore. The seafarer was lost. Who sat before him was a mystery, a mystery he was unsure he cared to solve. "Thank you brother. But, this is not why I have come," Mirko finally began, breaking the silence. "I came to ask you a question."

"You come to ask for some dating advice?" Mato laughed.

"Very funny," Mirko said, without even breaking into a smirk. "No, I was wondering, when are you going to serve in the military?"

Mato was going to begin to answer, but paused and diverted into a question. "Why do you ask?"

"Your eligibility opens in a few months. So when you do enlist, I want you to know that I have friends that can help you," offered Mirko.

Again, Mirko's constant use of half answers left Mato more puzzled, and actually less interested in the answer. But still he asked, "Help me with what?"

"With the transition, of course. And when you come out," replied Mirko. "Because after you come out, you'll know that there is much work to do."

Mato was getting more annoyed by the moment. He felt Mirko was talking in half sentences to appear smart. Mato really wished he would get to the point.

"What work are you talking about?" Mato sneered.

"Important work," offered Mirko.

"What work?" Mato bellowed once again.

Mirko refused to answer. It was if he was sizing up Mato's answers, and trying to learn if he could trust his younger brother. This further annoyed Mato, because he could tell Mirko did not.

"Brother, you need to get the point!" exclaimed Mato. "I am tired, and I have to get ready for tomorrow's work and then the journey home. You remember home, don't you?"

Chapter 20

At the mention of home, Mirko sighed and rolled his eyes. "Everyone doing fine back in the village?"

"Da," Mato shot back. "Nothing's changed. A few new babies born, the Tomašic heifer died. But other than that, all's the same."

"Good, good," Mirko nodded.

"Look Mirko!" Mato jumped in. "If you have something to say, say it! Otherwise you need to drop it. I'm tired, and I want to go to sleep." Mato did not really want to sleep. Really, all Mato wanted was for Mirko to get to the point. Mirko scratched his face, as if he was attempting to figure out where to begin.

"We need to fix things, Mato. It is up to us to do it," Mirko blurted.

"Fix what?" Mato noted, more confused than ever.

Mirko took a deep breath, and finally, after so many year's began to share the thoughts that lived in his mind.

"Tito is ruining everything!" Mirko began.

Mato rolled his eyes. Tito this and Tito that. He had heard these types of conversations before, usually from the older workers, who had had a few too many evening refreshments. But now, to Mato's dismay, the older worker was his brother, and he did not appear to be drunk. Thus Mirko began. For the next twenty-five minutes, Mirko cursed and verbally charred the name of Tito. He even proclaimed that he doubted Tito was a Croatian, and nothing more than a Serbian stooge that was scourging the lands owned by real Croats and Muslims. "Everything is a lie." Mirko continued, in way Mato wondered if he would ever stop. Oh, how Mato wished he would stop! Mato could not take it anymore, taking the bait to finally respond.

"What are you talking about?" he mocked.

"Everything!" Mirko proclaimed.

"Everything?" Mato repeated with the shake of his disbelieving head.

"Yes, everything!" repeated Mirko steadfastly. "You don't believe me, but you need to understand Mato. Everything is a lie. The notion we are a community is a lie. There is no such thing as community, not in Tito's Yugoslavia, not in Vareš, and not even in Pavlovići. People don't really know one another, or themselves for that matter. You said it yourself, that you didn't even know I was here in the city. What sort of community is that? This notion that we are united in a common cause for the betterment of all is the biggest lie of all. And everyone has bought it. Everyone. Hook, line and sinker!"

In finishing this statement, Mirko folded his arms in contentment, as if he dropped a jewel of wisdom for Mato to pick up. Dumbstruck by everything his brother said, Mato just looked back at him and laughed. "What's so funny?" Mirko blurted, unimpressed with his younger brother.

"Oh, that was the first time in ages I had heard you used a fishing phrase," Mato replied.

"What?" Mirko sneered, bemused.

"Hook, line and sinker," Mato repeated.

"Oh," Mirko offered. "Yeah, okay, I get it." Annoyed, Mirko return to the subject at hand, "So can we count on you, when the time comes?"

Finally, Mato realized that Mirko was attempting to recruit him for something, leaving Mato worried about what his brother had gotten himself into.

"I don't know Mirko. I am to be married in a few months," he began nervously. "I will have a family one day. There is much to think about." Mato, in truth, was attempting to be diplomatic. He did not care to think about it. Mato simply thought his older brother sounded foolish, as if he jumped into the deep end, and retrieved nothing but a discarded secondhand political science book.

"Okay, fine, if you're not interested now, one day you might be," replied Mirko, leaving the door ajar for future conversations. "Especially after you serve. So let me ask you again, when will you join Tito's grand plan?" Again with that question, thought Mato. This time, Mirko's persistent use of Tito's name peaked his interest, "Why do you keep asking me that?

A worried look blanketed Mirko's face. "Because when you do, you have to promise me something. It is very important."

Chapter 20

"What's that?" asked Mato.

"Promise me, you'll do the right thing," Mirko replied.

"What do you mean?" Mato said, not getting Mirko's meaning.

Mirko looked ashen and grave, and very afraid. It was at this point Mato realized Mirko looked afraid for him.

"Look, they will ask you a question. To them it is the only question that matters," Mirko, said. Mato noticed Mirko's hands were trembling. "To them, this answer is life and death. You must understand, to them there is no middle ground. There's a right way and wrong way to answer this question."

Mirko paused, licking his lips, "Hey Mato, do you have anything to drink?"

"Only water," Mato replied.

"Never mind then," Mirko said, fidgeting more than ever. "You asked me why I came," he pronounced. "It is because of this question. Promise me you'll answer the question properly."

A fire was blazing in Mirko eyes that ensured Mato was afraid for his brother. Deathly afraid.

"Promise me you'll answer the question properly, okay?"

A gravity hung over the two brothers. Both were afraid for each other, scared what life might do and was doing to each of them. Mato had never seen his brother so petrified. He was a little boy scared of the dark and its shadows. For the longest minute, not a word was muttered, as if all had already been said. But Mato knew that was a lie. Finally, the younger brother stepped forward and asked the only question he had ever wanted his brother to answer.

"What did Tito do to you?" he asked.

Vrag[1]

Verka did not like secrets. But for the past fifteen months, she lived a clandestine existence. While celebrating her engagement in the open with Mato's village, Verka had yet to say a word to her father.

Every day she hoped and wished to, but with Stjepan so busy with his liquid occupation, he never gave Verka the proper opportunity. At one time, Stjepan considered himself a part-time drinker, but since destroying Verka's violin, he promoted himself to a full-time role. Showing an overt commitment to his destructive cause, he often worked overtime as well. This left Verka a difficult decision to make. As repulsive as her father was, surely, Verka asked herself over and over again, even he would be happy for her, right? The answer to this question always appeared uncertain.

In the past, when unsure what to do, Verka would begin playing her violin and wait for the music to float heavenward, where her mother could hear. Then after a few moments, advice would always drift back down again. But her music was gone for good and without it, Verka had no way to hear what Janica wanted to convey. Because of her father, Verka's music was dead. Because of her father, her mother was really...dead! This made each moment in Kopjari very lonely.

---

1 Devil

Chapter 21

To her credit, Verka knew lamenting her plight would not change anything. She knew the time to become the adult her future required had arrived. So for many weeks, she pushed away her personal misery and sat with her sheep and pondered what had to be done. It was not easy. Through rain and snow, she waited and waited for the right answer to strike her. It felt as if it would never come.

Seeking an answer without her music was so unnatural. Occasionally to offset this, she would hum one of her favorite pieces. But lately, to her dismay, Verka would often forget what was supposed to come next. Not just the next note, but complete chunks of the tune.

Anger would seethe with every forgetful occurrence. Feet would stomp. Tears would well. But the songs still would not come back. With each occurrence, as she returned to the ground in a huff, still without the lost notes, or a reasonable solution to her original problem, Verka would be reminded of what she had lost with her mother's passing, and what she never had in her father.

Strangely, Verka suspected her inability to remember began when she met Mato's tree. She suspected this because since tasting from it, the hurt resulting from her mother's death had worsened by the day, as opposed to healing with time. How Verka wished she could just see her mother for one more minute. Perhaps just one more second. At least, Verka wished she might live an entire day without mourning her so. Verka was so sick of crying.

So one fateful occasion, as she continued to search for hidden answers, Verka closed the faucet to her tear ducts and refused to let go of the water. Amazingly, for once, the tears cleared. As they vanished, Verka's mind flashed back to happier times, and there she saw her mother. As her mother watched on, Verka saw herself playing her beautiful violin.

And as she played, Verka noticed something important. She was playing with her eyes closed. Verka forgot that her mother would often use this tactic to trick Verka's dominant senses. Verka giggled, and for a fleeting moment, with her fading memory as a guide, she went back in time, and let the music dance. "Mama, I know what to do," Verka blurted, while she reopened her eyes.

In the midst of a happy daydream, it came to her! She had always known. Verka's disdain for her father's drinking had not changed. She had always hated how he was when drunk. She hated how he loved the drink more than her.

As a result, Verka decided Stjepan would only find out under one condition. He would have to be sober. And not just for a fleeting day, when his bottles ran dry. He would have to be sober for a stretch. Long enough, where he didn't just look sober, but he acted sober too. This was the only way. Her amazing news would be soiled and tainted otherwise. Until then, Verka decided, she would sit on her secret. Stjepan would make her wait a long time.

Weeks became months. Then seasons passed. Winter became spring. Spring danced to a hotter season's song, and then faded once all of the leaves turned brown. Winter arrived once more, and still Stjepan had not provided Verka with the satisfactory scenario. The calendar was losing pages, and Verka was running out of open dates to share her joyful secret. Or rather, as Verka continued to reaffirm, Stjepan was running out of time to learn the truth. Only four months were between her and matrimony. Verka was resigned to leaving without telling her father, if he unwittingly did not keep his end of the bargain. As the days flew away, it seemed as if her father was giving Verka no other choice. Mato, on a number of occasions wanted to march up the mountain and tell Stjepan himself and save her from it all. But Verka refused, saying that she knew best on how to deal with her father. Mato doubted the wisdom in this, but out of respect for his bride-to-be relented.

However, the secret's weight was still burdensome. Verka hated what her father was doing to himself and in turn, to her. She was tired of all of this pain. Yesterday hurt and today was anguish. All that was left was the future, and she knew, as her mother told her many times, you could not rush towards the future. This unwanted despair created a new sadness, because Verka knew she was putting pressure on her future husband to make everything alright. But, she could not help it. Verka could not wait for tomorrow to begin.

Tomorrow held everything she could want. In Mato, she was going to garner a person to love her forever. Secondly, she was going to get a real family, with both a mother and a father. Mijo and Mara were very sweet to her. Their home felt like her home. Excitingly, each day brought her closer to their village, and further away from the high hills and the high hurts of Kopjari.

Stjepan was a blind drunk, but he was not blind. At first, the truths of Verka's engagement were simple whispers. People around the village heard rumors and as a small village does, they moved them along. Fortunately for Verka, at that time, since all Stjepan did was sit at his kitchen table in the company of a bottle, neither of them, traveled in circles that would collect the passed along murmurings.

However, as conversation became louder, not even Stjepan the drunk at his kitchen table, could miss them. Compounding this, Stjepan noticed how distracted Verka was. She had always loved Kopjari, but now her eyes betrayed her. They were always somewhere else.

Stjepan began to put pieces together. Each Sunday, he noticed the earliness of Verka's leaving, and the lateness of her return. He knew something was up, but what? Then as Stjepan pondered these thoughts in-between bottles, he thought about his deceased wife. He thought about when he first laid eyes upon her at the Hasikovanje many, many years ago, and how his life changed.

Through a cascade of tears, that's when Stjepan knew. She had fallen. Though he was unsure of when, just as he was unsure what day of the week it was, Stjepan realized that she had been in love for a long time.

Stjepan raged at Verka's betrayal. Janica left him, and now his daughter was going to leave him too. He tore his shirt in despair, knowing from experience, there was nothing he could do but show his teeth and growl at the pain. For weeks Stjepan carried the truth, hoping it was not true. But finally, on a typical Tuesday afternoon, after Verka had returned from tending the animals, Stjepan spoke his mind, and fear gripped their little world.

"Djevojko!"[2] he began loudly. "Djevojko, where have you been going each Sunday? And don't lie to me about it being about church!"

Verka held her breath, knowing the hidden truth was finally about to come forth.

"I don't know what you mean, Tata," she replied coolly. "Where could I be going on a Sunday, but to the Sutjeska?"

Stjepan seethed. He knew Verka was concealing much. "Where else have you been going, girl? I know something is going on!"

Verka sighed. There was no point pretending. She was to be married within months. Verka doubted her father was sober, but guessed he must be lucid enough if he could discover something big was going on. So Verka, stuck between Kopjari and Pavlovići, informed her drunkard father the beautiful truth. She told him about how they met. She told him how delightful a young man Mato was. She told him how hardworking he was, and that he came from a good family. Verka even told him how Mato wanted to speak to him from the beginning, but she had dissuaded him a number of times, "so please don't be mad. I wanted to be the one who told you." She continued telling him the truth, about how happy she was, happier than she had been for a long time. Verka spoke for what felt like an age. She spoke more to her father in that one conversation, than she had in years. Verka spoke with passion and care. She spoke about love and life. She spoke about being free.

But Verka had made a mistake! She dared to open her heart to the most heartless man she knew, and Verka was about to learn that the heartless always find a way to hurt us. The result shattered the last vestiges of the most fractured relationship. Stjepan wanted to rage. He wanted to destroy. He did not hear a word his daughter expressed. He did not care. He looked within himself, and only saw his wants, and his drowning sufferings. Combining the full force of the hate and despair, Stjepan shook the sky, and shuddered the earth.

"You went behind my back, *and did this*!" he yelled. "You are not permitted to do this. *I forbid it.*"

---

2 Women, used here in an unflattering manner.

Chapter 21

Verka took a step back and almost fell to the ground, so great was her fear. After steadying her legs and feet, she took a quick second to close her eyes. And then Verka remembered. Verka remembered who she was. She remembered her mother, and her love. Verka remembered her music, and for a fleeting moment it made her heart dance.

Furthermore, she remembered she was going to be Mato's wife in a few months' time. In that very moment, while surrounded by the worst of winter storms, Verka felt the kiss of the summer sun, and beamed. "No Tata, I am getting married," she pronounced with a grace of highland royalty.

Stjepan continued to yell and hurl insults. But Verka held her ground, unafraid. Her strength just made Stjepan madder, and more foolish. He threw furniture! He crashed cups and plates! He threatened. He cursed. He looked like he wanted blood. He wanted destruction. There was no turning back, and his anger knew just what to do.

"Get out," he demanded. "BJEŽI. IDI, GUBI SE! GET OUT, GET OUT, AND NEVER COME BACK!"

Brodolom[1]

"You really want to know?" tempted Mirko.

"Yeah. I really wanna know," Mato retorted.

The old Navy man sensed his sea monster closing in. His instincts wanted to lift anchor and flee. For the past two years, Mirko's safe port was a secluded room, preferably far from all windows, doors and threats. And with only himself to worry about, it had worked well enough.

But tonight, the usual plan was insufficient. Mirko pondered Mato's future, and saw only pain. Having carried the burden of Tito's new world, Mirko hoped his suffering was sufficient penance for both of them. But it was no use. With Mato's service at their doorstep, Mirko knew he was trapped. Only he could prevent the worst now, and that thought scared him most of all.

And yet, as the voices of fear and dread gripped Mirko, a tiny voice, unknown to even his deepest fears leaped up, speaking of the terrible cost about to be brought upon his brother. The small, strong voice spoke of desperately dark quarters that housed a living death that destroyed hope and disregarded all mercy.

"*He's your brother. He's your brother,*" the unrelenting voice

---

1 Shipwreck

harped, until Mirko realized if he did run he would never be able to face his brother again.

"*He's your brother,*" the little voice continued, until Mirko knew of a small amount of resolve. Enough, at least, to look his brother in the eye. Mirko did not know the name of the voice, but he sensed its peacefulness. It spoke in a soothing manner, never wavering, until it convinced Mirko what must be done. Finally, he understood. Though Mirko believed his doom was sealed, that did not need to be his brother's fate. It reminded Mirko that there was still time to put things right.

"Okay, fine," Mirko grunted. "But not here."

Mirko zigzagged through the cold streets, and speedily past the throng and their colder demeanors. Left, right, left, right they went. Desperate to keep up, Mato was flabbergasted by the voracity of his brother's city stomping. It looked like Mirko was on skates, gliding around effortlessly, while everyone else was stuck in mud. Though Mirko's feet moved powerfully, his eyes were far away, traveling a joyless journey all alone. Mato could not help but look on his brother with concern, for the deeper they traveled into the city, the more Mirko carried the gloominess of the others they passed.

The *Dark Section*, as Mato dubbed it, was foreboding. Deep in the city's belly, its darkness was distinct, as if sadness shaped it. The air hung heavier, as if it did not know its purpose. Mato quickly realized he had not sensed fear like this since his night in the trees.

Mato doubted their location's appearance was helping Mirko's countenance. Its collection of unkempt rubble looked shunned even by Tito. Glancing skyward, the gray buildings appeared to stalk each morose pedestrian. Through the grim night, Mato tried to imagine its buildings had once held stores and provided jobs. He imagined they once held histories and complete family trees.

But cheerful imaginings could not live long in this sullen atmosphere. The longer Mato walked, the more he began to believe his eyes that harkened ghost shanties and evil catacombs. Just as Mato believed he was about to go mad from fright, Mirko turned towards his panicky brother.

"We're here," he muttered. "Keep your head down, okay?"

Mirko stormed directly to a heavy gray door; its purpose was to be unwelcoming. Above it hung an old wooden sign, with the faded heading, *The Jewel and Its Captain*. Mirko punched twice upon the door, providing it a dull echo. Instantly, Mato saw a slot at the top portion of the door angrily slide open. Within the slot, two red bulging eyes glared towards them.

Abruptly, the slot closed. Before Mato could decipher what might occur next, the sound of the lock echoed its release, allowing the large barricade to career inward. As light poured from the opening; the doorway was blocked by a massive obelisk of a man with the least happy disposition Mato had ever had the displeasure to witness. Naturally, Mato gulped with fear. The colossus could have beaten both brothers simultaneously with a simple flick of his pinky finger. Instead, he leaned towards Mirko, and whispered something inaudible to Mato's ears. "Ivan, this is my brother Mato. He's cool," Mirko offered.

"*Dobra večer*[2], young Pavlović," Ivan grizzled. Again, Mato gulped, while forcing a short nod of greeting.

"You coming?" Mirko asked his young brother, already beyond the enclosure's gate.

Slowly, Mato inched within the structure's walls, tip-toeing past the fearsome doorman. Instantly, Mato was drowning under the pungent tang of cigarette smoke. His eyes stung instantly, reminding Mato of that awful first day, many years ago at the factory. Maybe that is why Ivan's eyes looked so red? Mato noted, a thought comforting enough to diminish his nerves.

Oblivious to Mato's sufferings, Mirko walked confidently deeper within the *The Jewel and Its Captain*, as if he had been there every day of his life. Mirko sat at a booth, motioning for Mato to do the same.

---

2 Good evening

Chapter 22

Gaining his side of the booth, Mato scanned the room, wondering why Mirko brought him here. It was not for its appearance. The plaster was chipped. Decoration was spartan, with only a few portraits spread without reason of old faces Mato failed to recognize.

The small space had a dozen small tables clustered together, hugged by either two or three worn chairs. Unsurprisingly to Mato, these seats sat almost empty. The booths, situated on the west and east of the tavern however, were filled, by groups of equally somber patrons who focused on their distant thoughts and drinks. At the southern side, a tired-looking jukebox sat beside a small, lonely dance floor. The box shook violently, scratching out Chuck Berry, Everly Brothers, and Elvis Presley tunes. Not that the cheerless souls cared to notice the upbeat music. It seemed the appearance of pleasure was frowned upon.

Mirko sat, tapping his fingers nervously on the table. He still looked grave. Mato was beginning to question whether they should continue. But, there was nowhere to run. Not now. He was trapped. That's when Mato realized what he did not like about the tavern. It felt like a prison. Maybe, Mato mused it had been.

As Mato shuddered at that awful thought, a waitress, dressed like a 1950s extra from a James Dean movie, stood over them. She wore a short leather skirt, her hair coiffed to its maximum height, and the chip on her shoulder even bigger. To Mato, the waitress seemed annoyed any customers were there, each a misuse of her time. Mirko, however, looked right at her without even a causal greeting and ordered a large plate of *ćevapi*[3], bread and two *pive*[4]. The waitress huffed, refusing to scribble down the order.

"What is it, *Ženo?*[5]" Mirko grunted.

"Your date here," she mused. "He ain't old enough to drink here."

---

3 Ćevapi is a delightful three mincemeat meal, usually lamb, pork and beef, mixed with garlic and onion. Rolled into mini sausages. They are served with ketchup, bread, and if you are really adventurous, green onions.
4 Beer
5 Ženo means women.

"Really," Mirko chimed. "Since when?"

The waitress was unmoved. "Do you want me to get Ivan to decide who's right?"

"Fine," Mirko relented. "Get the kid a Cola, and the two ales can be for me."

In a huff, the stern waitress stormed off, shouting in the direction of the kitchen.

"Sorry about that Mato," Mirko began with a laugh. "Rule number one. Don't date the help at your place. Not even once, because they will hold a grudge."

Mato laughed nervously at Mirko's attempt to break the ice. "So, what is this place?" he asked.

"It's quiet and doesn't ask questions," Mirko replied, returning to his trail of thoughts. "But tonight we're going to make an exception, aren't we?" he asked, more to himself than his brother.

Mirko glanced up at the ceiling. A swirl of smoke chased the tail of the fan's fluttering propellers, as if it was stuck in a vortex or a hamster wheel. It made him dizzy. Mirko could not believe he was about to share his story. He never thought he would. He was not even certain of what he was going to say. *"Maybe,"* he pondered, *"It did not matter."* He had been hiding for so long, and its suffering was almost worse than the story itself.

Mirko looked at Mato, and forced a smiled. It might be okay. *"Yes! This might work,"* he mused. Mirko lowered his head to steady himself, bringing his hands together as if he was about to say grace. Instead, he violently cracked his knuckles, and muttered, "Alright then."

But, with the beginning on his lips, the stern waitress interrupted, slamming both of Mirko's drinks down, and the "bottle of Coca Cola; for the kid."

"So, how do you like Vareš?" Mirko asked Mato, further ignoring the server.

"Um, it's okay."

"You like it that much, huh?" Mirko chuffed. "Fair enough. You might wanna know I just caught wind that a mine near home is looking for crane experts."

Chapter 22

"Which one?" Mato asked, knowing their mountain held dozens.

"*Haljinići*," Mirko replied nonchalantly.

"The coal mine!" Mato exclaimed. "I don't know. That mine's trouble."

Mirko rolled his eyes. "There's no reason to be scared of being underground. With your trade, you'll be driving topside, while the rest are digging," he continued with a laugh. "Plus, you'll be home every night, if you listen to me."

Mato pondered Mirko's notion, wistfully. Home every night! That would be a wonderful dream. A dream that would allow him to sleep better. As the idea dug deep into Mato's mind, Mirko sleeved beer froth off his face, and asked "You want to know why I didn't, no rather, why I couldn't write to you much brother, especially at the end?"

"Sure, I guess?" Mato shrugged.

"You guess," Mirko blared, agitated. "Mato, I have never told anyone about all of this, okay?"

"I know," Mato replied, respectfully.

"You ever heard of the pit?" Mirko began.

Mato shook his head. "No, I did not think so. But don't feel bad, I hadn't either, until…" Mirko noted, stopping mid-sentence, wanting to begin his story again. "Remember when I couldn't tell you about certain stuff because it was classified? Well, the pit was, is classified. It's an underground building. Where exactly, I don't know, but it's there. I know it! I have seen it. It is dark, barren, and devoid of life, though there are people in it. They put them in there. In little dingy cells. Like rats, these people live, scratching against the wall, without cheese, without hope. They store us people to ferment. They store them for punishment. How long? Does it matter? A day, week, month, year! Time does not live down there, and then forever loses its luster by the time you're out, because even when you get out, you're not out!" As Mirko talked, he could not be sure what he just said. His head and heart could not hear a thing, but he felt the dangers of the words, because each and every word cut at his vocal cords.

"I was there, Mato!" Mirko muttered, with rage in his eyes. "I was there for a long, long time. All because of the question."

"What question?" Mato butted in.

"I'm coming to that!" Mirko snapped, finishing off his drink. As he did, the waitress returned with a half loaf of sliced bread and the largest plate of ćevapi Mato had ever seen.

"Oh, good," Mirko noted, his countenance completely changed with the arrival of food. "Dig in Mato, please. To make up for the bread and fruit I ate. Oh, and dear," Mirko continued, turning to the server that owned hate in her eyes. "Could you bring another coke and a favorite for me? Thanks."

The waitress sulked away, stomping off with mutterings in her mouth, while Mato grabbed an edible envelope, and stuffed it with ketchup and meat. "She is a nice girl, if you dare to get to know her. Or so I hear, anyway," he joked. "Now where was I?" he pondered, traveling further back in time than ever before. "I spent months in that hole, maybe longer. Like I said, I cannot remember. Awful does not explain it, Mato. I was all alone. Except for the others in the nearby cells. Not that I could hear them, of course. The walls were too thick. It made every day down there so eerie, so, so…" Mirko shuddered. After a lost moment, Mirko picked up his trail of thoughts. "Thankfully, I had friends on the outside. They took great risks for my welfare. That's how I got your letter, and found out about Baba."

"You got that letter, while in there?" said a startled Mato.

"Yeah," Mirko continued nonchalantly. "I lived with an empty belly, a bucket of feces and a heart-filled note. Thank you brother," Mirko noted, sincerely.

Mato shook his head, waving off Mirko's gratitude as unnecessary.

"I was one of the lucky ones," Mirko paused. His eyes were red, and not from the tavern's smoke. "If not for that letter, I thought," he stammered. "I thought I was… I thought I was dead."

Mato sat in shock. "Why?" he began. "Why did they do this? What did you do?"

"Didn't do, brother," Mirko mused. "It's what I didn't do."

Chapter 22

"Okay, what didn't you do, then?"

"I said I'll get to that," replied Mirko. "It wasn't always like this, in the beginning at least. Ah, at the start, Mato, it was a different dream. A dream that teamed with the fantastic," he recalled fondly. "Remember, the story I told you and Mama and Tata, about my time in the Navy, about how great it was?" Mirko asked.

"Yeah, I remember."

"I know you think everything I said that night was a lie, but that's not so," stated Mirko. "A lot of what I said was true. The first few weeks, the first few months were great. When I first arrived, I was given the typical rank of Seaman, Second Class. I was stationed on the school ship, *Galeb*[6]. It's a traditional sailing craft, with sails and everything," Mirko laughed. "The only thing I needed at that point to feel more like an old pirate was a peg leg and an eye patch."

Mato looked at his brother. His face was changing right before him, once more. He looked... happy. "We were posted off the Adriatic Coast," Mirko beamed. "Mato, you couldn't believe it. Here I was, a Bosanac finally in our heart's homeland. I was in Croatia. I was one of the mighty, defending its shoreline, like the soldiers of old. Nor just on the water's edge, but sitting amongst it, on a proud vessel, worthy of its role. The spray, the smell of the ocean breeze, was, ahhhhh," he said, letting out a satisfied breath. "It was everything I thought I ever wanted. And guess what Mato? Guess what?"

"What, brother, what?" Mato asked, playing along.

"I was good at it. Sailing. Being on the water. Doing what was needed. I was real good," he noted with pride. "Quickly they noticed. The Lieutenants, the Commanders. Those in charge, they noticed. Within days, they moved me up to Seaman, Class One. This was a big deal. No one ever got moved up so quickly. It was unheard of. Within months, I was moved up again, to Petty Officer. I was given responsibility and told to dish out orders. At mealtime, I was even given a little more. The food was horrible, but my belly was full, so I knew not to complain. Mato, I was going places. I was where I

---

6 Seagull

wanted to be. All those years of dreaming, hoping, and praying. All of it was coming true."

Mirko stopped right there, scanning the dank bar, as if he was looking for his next words, or at least, the angry waitress to get him another beverage. But she was nowhere to be seen. He picked up a ćevapi, but his complete lack of appetite compelled him to fling it back down. With nothing for it, he proceeded.

"And then it started," he noted, in a dark manner, leaving Mato fearful of what was coming next.

"A Rear Admiral, with a bunch of medals pinned to his left chest summoned me, and began singing my praises. I'd never met him before, but he knew everything about me. He told me I was going places. He was flattering me, and I liked it. He said he led a Koni Class Frigate. It was one of the biggest and best ships in the fleet. Strategically, it was very important to the defense of Yugoslavia. The Rear Admiral told me that he got to handpick his crew. He only wanted the best. He was calling me the best, Mato. Do you know how that feels?" Mato could only shake his head, having never been bestowed this compliment. "Well, because I was the best he wanted me to come along," Mirko said, pausing once more. "But, the Real Admiral only wanted me to come along under one condition."

Mirko took the napkin off the table, and wiped his brow. He felt awful, and if he had a mirror, or asked Mato, both would have told him he looked a shade of putrid green. "What was it?" Mato pressed.

"Communism," Mirko forced. "I had to become a Communist."

"What did you say?" Mato asked, not quite sure what this meant.

"I told him I thought everyone in Yugoslavia was automatically one," Mirko continued, his hands shaking. "The Rear Admiral laughed, and said that was a good answer. He rephrased, asking whether I wished to become an official party member. He said it was a great honor."

"What do you have to do to become one?" Mato jumped in.

"You don't know either, huh?" Mirko continued. "Good, I don't feel so dumb. The Rear Admiral, at first, gave me the line of protecting the nation. Of serving under his command, and under direct authority of Marshal Broz Tito, blah, blah, blah. At this point, everything he said didn't seem so bad, but I knew that couldn't be all. Something told me, you know?"

Again, Mato did not, so Mirko tried to explain in a way his younger brother might understand.

"Mato, everything in Yugoslavia, whether in the military or in other work, like your steel factory, has rules like this. No big deal, right?"

"Right," Mato repeated, finally glad to know something his bigger brother was saying.

"Wrong, brother!" Mirko retorted. "I thought like you once. Until they asked me the question."

Mirko stopped. Mato thought very prematurely, so he pressed. "Asked what?"

Mirko steadied himself. Standing on the edge of life, without a net, he tried to ready himself to take the plunge. "He asked… he asked… He asked whether I believed in God."

Mato was dumbfounded. "That's it? That's what he asked?"

"Yep," Mirko muttered.

"What's that got to do with anything?" Mato blurted, confused.

"That's what I asked him," Mirko responded. "He looked at me with cold, harsh eyes, saying only true members could join his boat. It was then I understood."

"Understood what?" Mato pressed.

"The old medal-bucket was saying," Mirko said, still stung by the words he was repeating, "that if you believed in God, then you couldn't be a true Communist. I disagreed of course, and I told him so. I wanted on his ship, but I could not lie. I told him what I believed in."

Mirko leaned back in his chair, as if he had nothing more to give. He hoped his retelling would allow him to feel better, but it didn't. He still was haunted by the entire ordeal. Even worse, though he could tell Mato felt awful for him, he did not appear to appreciate the gravity of the situation. Frustratingly, though he wished to stop, Mirko knew he had to keep going to make him understand.

"And with this question answered," Mirko wheezed, "the Rear Admiral sailed into the sunset. He actually looked a little disappointed, or so I thought at the time. Though I did not know it, because I was too stupid, my answer changed my life forever. And because of this day, because of this answer, they threw me in the classified pit, to die like a decaying flea-infested dog."

Mato said nothing, stunned. He had forgotten he had been holding onto a sandwich for so long, the bread was falling apart, and the ketchup was oozing out.

"Wait one minute. You got thrown in the pit because of the way you answered?" protested Mato.

"Jeste," Mirko answered steadfastly.

"Right after that, they threw you in?" Mato persisted.

"Well," Mirko began. "Not exactly."

Mato folded his arms crossly, feeling if he had been taken for a fool.

"Wait a little," Mirko defended. "There's more. After I said yes to God, I never saw the Rear Admiral or had any further meetings with the high-ranking class. The promotion chance was gone. To further insult, others with less ability got promoted. They got my promotions," Mirko noted hurtfully. "I stayed a Petty Officer, and that seemed like the end of it. But then things became worse. I got transferred from my beautiful Croatia, and joined the worst soldiers far away in Montenegro on the *Napredak*[7]. There, I found the most unruly lot. Awful manners. These weren't sailors. They were barely men. They got promoted over me as well!"

Mato could see Mirko's anger rising. For the first time that night, his whispers were breaking free, building into growls. People from the other booths were beginning to unhappily notice. Not that Mirko seemed to care. He needed to finish what he had started.

"Party men got promoted, and the rest got the raw end of the stick. Then conditions got even worse. The ship's provisioning was so bad we'd have to wait to get back to shore, and go to the nearest village to buy something decent with our meager wages. Not that

7 Progress

the leaders wanted us to do that. We literally would get into trouble for buying food. What sort of world do we live in?" he asked Mato, and the rest of the room. "Even the water was really poor. It made me sick on more than one occasion. But the infirmary was worse than being sick in the hull. Especially since everyone seemed to know the way I answered. It was as if I was wearing a Star of David on my uniform.

"And then, they stuck me on the torpedo boat, *Crvena Zvezda*[8]. Just its name was a constant reminder of what I was up against. I had been in just over a year at this point. I had had enough. I could not take it anymore. I tell you, I had to get out. I had to get out!" Mirko said once again, slamming his glass bottle. The glass shattered in his hand, cutting the skin. Mirko looked down at the mess he made, without flinching. Balling the hand into a fist, the blood oozed in multiple trickles.

The stern waitress stormed over, unimpressed. "Mirko Pavlović!" she shouted, while throwing him a clean napkin for him to dress his bleeding hand. "Keep your voice down, do you hear? Or we won't need Ivan to kick you out, 'cause everyone else here will do it for him. Do you get me?"

"Sorry," interjected Mato. "We'll keep it down, promise."

The waitress chortled. "You really should listen to your date, Mirko."

"Woman, where's my drink!" Mirko barked, but the waitress stepped away again, without a reply.

"So what did you do?" Mato asked spellbound.

"Huh?" Mirko muttered, lost in his past.

"What did you do, Mirko?" Mato asked emphatically once more.

"Oh," Mirko stammered. "The only thing I could think of. I stopped obeying orders. I flatly refused. The clowns in charge would get real mad," he laughed. "They'd shout that I was making them look bad in front of the bosses. But I didn't care. They demoted me, but I didn't care. So they threw me in the brink. I still didn't care.

8 Red Star

But then they fixed me. Real good. After that, I wished I cared. But it was too late."

As Mirko's words trailed off, the retelling took an energy-sapping toll. In a desperate attempt to renew, Mirko picked up the bottle he finished an hour earlier, slurping at its dregs.

"Then one day, they said there was a fire in the hull. Now, a fire on a ship is no joke. Well, one of the stooges said I started it, but of course I didn't. But it didn't matter what I said. They all knew it was lie too, because if I did do it, they would have thrown me into a real prison, or had me shot. Instead, they threw me in the pit, to keep me quiet and out of the way."

Mato sat with his head down, in silence. It was only starting to hit him that the awful story was not just a story, but that it actually happened. And to his brother. Mato did not want to hear any more. He hoped it was over. But before it was, Mirko had one more thing to say.

"So you see," he queried. "That's why I wanna know when you are going in."

"Why?" Mato muttered, almost too upset to speak. "What does it matter?"

"Don't you see?" Mirko pleaded. "Don't you get it? Why all of it happened? The question. It's about the question! You got to answer the question the right way or they will ruin you!" Mirko continued, now with tears in his eyes. "You need to understand they're vultures. All of them! They'll find people like you, and will make an example of you, *slatki* brother of mine."

Astounded, Mato finally understood what Mirko was saying.

"God will understand," Mirko continued, at the top of his lungs. "Answer no. Tell them no! He will forgive you. He will understand. *Please, brother, you must! Please!*"

-23-

A što sad?[1]

Mato ran. And ran. And ran some more. There was nothing else for it. He needed to. The wolves of Mirko's past were chasing him.

It had been twenty-four hours since hearing the dreadful saga, and Mato's anguish refused to relent. Mato had thought nightmares only came during sleep, but now he knew different. After departing from Mirko, a terror was awoken, with each and every flicker grabbing and clawing at him, the fangs refused to let go.

That is why as soon as the factory whistle blew, Mato began his escape. He ran out of the door. He ran down the streets of Vareš, and he kept going. The running was neither easy nor enjoyable. This left Mato lamenting for the old days, when he ran for pleasure. Would those days ever return? Right now this did not matter. He just needed to keep going because his mind was burdened with a collage of emotions and fractured opinions that added to his turmoil. Until his mind eased, his feet needed to keep going.

His legs struggled to keep the required pace. It did not help that he now had a right hip bruise; the result of landing awkwardly after Mirko's loudness got them both kicked out of the *The Jewel and Its Captain*. *"Boy could Ivan throw a person a long way,"* Mato

---

1 What now?

mused as he ran. Though this pain was Mirko's fault, Mato could not, and would not be angry with him. Not anymore. Maybe never again. Mato felt a deep guilt. All these years he had wondered what had happened to his brother. For too many years, Mato prejudged his disappearing act as awful and selfish. Now, the truth stared him in the face, and he was too ashamed to look back at it. What made it worse was Mirko did not seek pity. Rather, Mirko opened up as a warning, striving for Mato to beware and prepare for the fates that would soon be knocking at his door.

As he ran, Mato could feel the grief swelling within him. Strangely, it was like the grief he lived with when Vjera died. What Mato could not reconcile was why his suffering felt even worse now, even though Mirko was still very much alive.

That's why Mato ran. He needed to go forward, and quickly. Thankfully, Mato was running with his eyes wide open, for his hasty journey was the primary ingredient of a good plan. Mato hoped the conclusion to his plan would give him peace, but first, the running needed to add the hope. Mato was not just running away from something. He was also running towards something, too. He was running to a place that unshackled questions, and had always provided clear council. With determination, Mato Pavlović was running towards his tree.

Mato was running deep into the wooden dark despite its risks. Being in the forest at night was always a dangerous proposition. Almost becoming the main course to a wolf feast had proven that. Though Mato eagerly wished for a better, safer plan, he knew there was not. There was nothing else for it. Mato would go to the tree, and hope all would be fine. After all, he only wished to spend a short while there. In the past, just a few moments in the tree's presence were often enough to soothe his mind and focus his thinking. As Mato ran towards his tree, he was certain the solution would come to him as soon as he sat on his favorite branch. Then, he'd be home only a few minutes later than usual, no worse for wear.

So Mato ran, never daring to stop. So much was needed to be understood. So much was still to be decided. Over and over,

Chapter 23

Mirko's story, and his demands shouted their way within his mind, deafening Mato's ears. So loud were his thoughts, on more than one occasion Mato thought Mirko was running right alongside of him, yelling in full voice. The underlining dilemma was not just his brother's story, or his job in Vareš. Or his impeding wedding. Rather, what was truly plaguing him was how each part seemingly wove itself together, right into Mato's future. Mirko had asked when he was going to serve at Tito's pleasure. Mirko had asked it over and over again, to the point of annoyance. The problem was, Mato did not know. That is why he did not, or rather could not tell Mirko. It is impossible to speak of an answer that did not exist. Its decision was acutely more difficult, knowing he would be leaving a new wife behind. Mato knew this was going to be a difficult parting for everyone. But at least Verka would be safe. What would happen to him at this point was still uncertain. Forced military service would change everything, most likely for the worse. All of this frightened Mato greatly, but his hope was not yet dead. That was why Mato knew he needed to get to his tree.

"*There, I can work it all out,*" he mentioned within himself on more than one occasion.

However, fear was whispering. As he got closer to his wanted destination, Mato's running mind was becoming dominated by a different force beyond the voice of his hurting brother. This added presence gave his shoulders a chill. The gray cold that was present the day he showed Verka the tree, seemingly, had returned. It did not seem to matter how fast he ran, Mato could feel the ill wind moving ahead of him. Dread was stalking, rising in strength. Mato could taste it all around him, and it tasted bitter in his mouth. What scared Mato most was he knew what the dread was, though right at that moment, he just could not put his finger on its name. Mato wanted to close his eyes to block it all out, but he knew that would stop him dead in his tracks. He had to keep going. He was almost at his tree. Onward he pressed, running faster than he thought possible. Still, the gray menace closed in, filling the air with a deathly sadness. It brought with it a hurt that was unbearable. Though surrounded by trees, for a moment Mato thought he had returned to the darker section of Vareš.

Yet, Mato was only a few hundred strides away from his goal. Thankfully, he was getting closer and closer. Suddenly, the bushes to his east rustled violently. Mato halted abruptly, his fear surging to even greater heights. Mato's fists clenched in readiness. Then, in the clear open, to Mato's shock, stepped out a small wolf. It could not have been more than a six-month old puppy, but Mato could tell that its eyes knew the face of evil. The young menace glared directly at Mato, doing the most astonishing thing. Though Mato later on would say he imagined it, the wolf smirked at him. It smirked as if it knew something Mato needed to know. But, before Mato could discover its secret, the young wolf turned dismissively, and returned back into the shadows.

Mato could not believe his luck! He thought he was a goner. Though a monstrous stitch developed at his right side, thus adding to his long list of ailments, Mato's determination would not let him waver. Not now. He was so close. Mato knew he just had to keep going, even if he needed to drag himself on hands and knees.

Then, despite his resolute commitment, for the second time in minutes, he stopped. He stopped, and could not travel any longer. A new torment shot through him like a revolver, defeating him. "Who did this?" he howled. He looked to the ground. There before him in the midst of a bunch of very healthy forest, lay Mato's little tree. Even in the dark, he could tell it had been cut down to the ground.

Mato was undone, his heart cut down like his tree before him. Grappling on all fours, snow, snot, and tears lived as a mixture over his face. He lay upon his falling comrade, ready to wage war upon who had slain it. Mato stretched out near the scratched markings, placing his fingers to his mouth and then touching the surface of his carved initials. As Mato stayed there, a conclusion grew within him.

"How could you?" Mato whimpered. He knew he could not lie there long, though he did not want to leave. Then, Mato's senses heightened to uncomfortable levels. The rustling wind startled both

Chapter 23

him and the surrounding leaves. Mato knew he could not linger. Fear brought him back into action. Without sufficient time say goodbye to a dear friend, Mato leaped into full gallop away from his tree. "How could she do this?" Mato yelled, directly into a whistling wind.

-24-

Tamo, ovamo (Papir)[1]

In the midst of the cold snow, Mato raged. With hostility his fuel, Mato ran with a directness he had never known. His focus was completely on finding the individual who had done this to his tree. Nothing else mattered.

Mato knew only two people knew of his tree's exact location: his father and his future bride. The thought that either of them had done this cut Mato in two. Mato did not understand why either could have done this, but he had his suspicions. On more than one occasion, Mato heard Mijo complain his tree visits kept him away from activities considered more acceptable to a boy his age, like the Hasikovanje, for example. Perhaps, Mato thought, now that he was going to be married, Mijo did not want him to venture towards what was considered a childish crutch.

While Mato considered this, another more awful possibility, that Verka chopped his tree down sprang up like lava. "That's why she didn't want to come back to the tree!" Mato yelled, his voice shaking the forest like thunder. Mato knew Verka hated his tree. The last time they both saw the tree together stomped on his mind. Mato remembered all the different ways Verka studied it. The bizarre

---

1 Hither and Tither (Paper)

ways she looked upon it. It seemed weird to him then, but now as his beautiful tree lay dead, it all made perfect sense. Mato concluded Verka was studying his tree so to cut it down.

His wrath continued to grow. Since that day they visited, Verka had continued to act strangely whenever the tree was mentioned. Especially whenever Mato had suggested they return for a visit.

As he ran towards home, the fury that ran with him made plans. It readied its attack upon those who brought Mato pain. Fury prepared Mato to attack those he loved. Part of him wanted to go all the way to Kopjari that very night and have it out as soon as possible. But before he could head northward, the wind groaned from deep within its belly, bringing a storm surge of snow, that quickly reminded Mato how wet and cold he already was. He knew the elements were making him wait at least one more day.

Into the village he ran, without slowing down. It was late, and Mato was wet and miserable. As he often did, Mato charged towards the door of his parents' home. To his surprise, on this occasion, Mato saw a vision. "Hello Mato," said Verka. In an instant, Mato forgot his furious companion. The anger, the hurt and the pain, were all gone. Mato did not care whether she had cut down his tree or not.

"What are you doing here?" he blurted, through a smile of happiness. "Not that this isn't a beautiful surprise."

Verka didn't say anything, leaping up from her seat, towards her beloved with a desperate hug.

"Hey," Mato noted with surprise. "Are you okay? You look like you have been crying."

Mato learned why Verka had been crying. He learned of what her father had done. He learned that Verka cried all the way down the mountain. With only the smallest bag, carrying a few feeble possessions, she had cried into the village, and right up to Mijo and Mara's door. He learned that she had been crying until the very instant he had opened the door. A new rage built within Mato. A new wish to go up to Kopjari grew, so to meet the man who did this, and have it out once and for all.

Kata's Father

✳✳✳

"Don't worry," Mara began, in between coughs. "It is all arranged, Mato. She gets Baba's old room until you marry."

"Yes, it is all arranged," chimed Mijo.

Mara turned, and looked directly at Verka, "This is your home, dear girl of mine."

"Are you unwell, Mama?" Mato interjected.

"Oh it's nothing. Don't interrupt me over a little cold," Mara snapped. "She's our daughter, and that's final."

"Good," Mato nodded. "Thank you."

"It's nothing," Mara insisted. "She's ours, and so are you."

Mato looked over at Verka, hoping to put her mind and tears at ease.

"It is going to be okay, Verka," he pronounced. *"Ja volim tebe.²"*

"I know," Verka said, with hurt eyes.

The young couple sat for a long time. Both Mara and Mijo got up after a few moments, and left the two of them alone. Finally, Mato looked over and Verka, while sifting through his right jacket pocket.

"What are you looking for?" Verka asked.

"Something. Something important," He mused. "Ha-ha-ha, there it is."

Mato pulled out his hidden hand of the pocket, holding a small piece of paper, which he handed to Verka.

Verka unfolded it. On the paper there were eleven scribbled words. Each letter was in UPPER CASE print. Each line had two words, except the third line, which had five. Each line had words separated by an = sign. The note looked like this;

> GRAND = AWFUL
> BEAUTIFUL = TERRIBLE
> CONSIDER = PRAY, or PRAY FOR
> GLAD = SCARED

---

2 I love you

Chapter 24

"What is it?" Verka asked.

"It's code," Mato replied.

"Code for what?" Verka asked, all confused.

"It's a bunch of code words for when I go away to service," Mato mused. "I've made a decision. I wasn't sure, but now I am. Six months after we get married, right before winter, I am going to begin my service"

"Oh," Verka began, tears returning to her checks. "So soon."

"Yes, my dear, so soon. It's no use ignoring it. It was going to come anyway, so let's be done with it. But don't worry, I'm going to see you a lot before I go."

Verka stared at the floor. So much was coming at her so quickly. "What do you mean?" she blurted, tears readying to reappear.

"I heard that there is crane work nearby," Mato continued. "I am going to find out about it tomorrow. Then will be able to be home every night. We will see each other every day."

In hearing this, Verka allowed herself the smallest of smiles. "But, you'll be gone two whole years," she lamented.

"I know," Mato noted, fighting the tinge of defeat in his tone. "My family will look after you, my dear, while I am gone."

"I know," Verka agreed, while trying to make sense of the piece of paper that had been placed in her hand. "But, what's this note?"

Mato smiled. "I will need you while I am gone," he began to explain. "The only way we will talk is via letters. I will need your letters, Verka. I will need them more than we both know right now. I think you will need mine too. The words on the note are code. I will give Mama and Tata these codes too. This is to make sure Tito's stooges don't catch wind of what we are all really saying to each other."

"Oh," Verka noted. She looked at her future husband, nodding in understanding. Verka looked at him with pride. Mato looked older to her. He looked stronger. He looked readier for what the future might bring, in any time she had known him. He also looked sad.

"Hey Mato," Verka began kindly. "What's the matter? It looks like you have been crying."

"It's nothing," he said, dismissively. "I love you."

"I love you too," Verka replied. "Hey, you," she continued, nervously. "We are getting married really soon," she giggled.

"I know," he giggled in reply.

They giggled a little more, and for the first time that night, they both felt better. Verka leaned in and put her head on Mato's shoulder. Each of them looked nowhere in particular, staring at their futures. Both knew their lives were never going to be the same again.

Stolica¹

The woods know real darkness. In the belly amongst its thickest trees, it develops shadows upon shadows. Bleakness begets further bleakness. On the most morose nights, even the bravest critters question the sanity of their nocturnal preferences. Wisely, they retreat to their hollows, far from the evil's sanctum, awaiting the safety of the next day's blinding light.

Mijo did not know why he was up. His body knew it was late, but sleep refused to find him. He looked everywhere for it without success. Mijo even looked outside in the darkness, though not for long. There, he sensed an eerie sky out not wanting company. Even the moon could not be found, having slipped away hours earlier. This left Mijo not knowing what to do with himself. Dizzily, with an impetuous huff, the old man slumped into his old chair.

For years, Mijo had sat comfortably in his chair, by the second floor fire. During those many nights, Mijo would ash away hour after hour. But that was a long time ago. Sure, Mijo had from time to time reacquainted himself with its company, but these moments were fleeting and without purpose.

---

1 Chair

Yet, something strange was happening. Mijo could not or did not wish to move. Mijo could not remember the last time he sat in his old thinker's chair, and yet despite the hour there was no other place he wanted to be. To test this internal notion he attempted to stand, but he found he simply could not. Mijo took a deep breath, tasting a surprising elixir of uncertainty, beheld by mystery. A mystery that wanted his attention.

It appeared Mijo's surroundings knew this night would come. As he looked towards his old fireplace Mijo found something startling, for there was a ready blaze he did not remember making. He looked down at his hands, and found his fingers held a glass of rakija he did not recall pouring. In disbelief, Mijo looked at it once more, noticing it was full to the brim. He had yet to drink a drop, and strangely, he had no intention to do so. Mijo put it down on his side table, feeling an awful sense of déjà vu. "This is not logical," he muttered. "None of it is."

Mijo rubbed his jawline, fiercely moving against the friction caused by course stubble. He sat there thinking about his illogical night for a long time. As he continued in this way, with the wood's crackle background muse, the game of world pondering returned to Mijo for the first time in an age. And because of its rejoinder, moments quickly turned the clock deeper into the night. And as it moved simultaneously down chasms and beyond stratospheres, one, two, three minutes become one, two, three hours. Not that he noticed, because within moments Mijo lost track of time. But, as it once was, Mijo did not care if it was found. His journey back, back, back into time began.

Mijo quickly went to a place that was alive in him. Though it was dark in Pavlovići, the sun shone in Mijo's mind and excitedly his heart yelped. It yelped with memory that danced firstly towards a gateway born six months ago. It was a date of buoyant glee. Not just for Mijo, but everyone. Mijo would readily admit that six months ago was the happiest day in his life. Six months ago they'd had Mato's and Verka's wedding! It was six months ago that Mijo saw the mountain bow before the young couple, as their majestic

Chapter 25

procession paraded down the simplest dusty path, back towards his humble village. It was as if six months ago, the grand Sutjeska was created just for them.

Mijo looked back, as if they were the only memories he had ever known. Every reflection was perfect. The weather was bright. The grasses green and the birds chirped with full fettle. Mijo remembered how Mato wore the traditional garb that he had given him. Verka, in turn looked beautiful as she wore her mother's wedding dress. Though the clothes were borrowed, the smiles and laughter were new. Mijo was proud to be a parent in the Sutjeska. As he looked upon the warming fire, Mijo saw his son, and his new daughter. He remembered his wife, and how good it was to see her so satisfied.

Then, as Mijo sat, he studied his Mara's face. Through the happiness, however, she also seemed tired. At this, Mijo paused. He paused because he did not remember noticing this during the wedding feast. But now, it left Mijo searching for answers why. Perhaps, it was a spring cold she had not completely shaken. Perhaps all the planning and preparation just plain wore her out. Perhaps it was just a byproduct of his overworked imagination.

Mijo then again remembered Verka. The new bride. His new daughter. She looked so happy. As Mijo remembered all and every moment of six months ago, he knew the last six days were very different. Mijo's mind leaped, washing the color from his face. Mijo looked upon Verka. Her face was flush with tears. These were hot, red tears that erupted and would not stop.

Just as Mato had promised, six months after the wedding he left for military service. The entire family knew he had to go. Mijo knew Mato had to go. Even Verka knew he had to go. Tito would not wait much longer. But that did not stop the deluge of sadness. Not even Mara's kindness could comfort her, so great was Verka's misery. Mijo did not know what to do, but to question whether it was fair that newlyweds must know such parting?

As thoughts drifted toward his departed son, sadness was ceasing this night's enjoyment. But, just as Mijo was about to get up from his chair, he took his right hand to his left shirt pocket, finding a small folded memory. Instantly, Mijo remembered its purpose. Mato told him the note contained code words. This notion made Mijo shake. Mato expected him to write? Mijo was not much of a letter writer. What was he going to write to his son? Not of Verka's sadness, or his growing fear for Mato. Mijo knew what forced service had done to Mirko, turning him into a ghost of tormented memories. Mijo was afraid that Mato might meet an equally awful fate.

As Mijo sat, he tussled uncomfortably. The fire jumped, with the largest log splitting in two, it thrust Mirko to the forefront of Mijo's mind. Mijo was not certain, but he remembered thinking he caught a brief glimpse of his eldest at the wedding, standing at the perimeter of the square, talking to Mato. At least he dared himself to think that maybe his eldest was there. Mijo was not sure. The figure looked a little like his boy. At the time, Mijo had wanted to rush over to the two of them, but a long list of guests had slowed his ability to get to them. By the time he did, whoever Mato was talking to was long gone. Mijo had promised himself to ask Mato about it, but somehow until now, he had forgotten all about it. Lamentably, Mijo knew now it was too late! Mirko was nowhere to be seen, and hence six days past, Mato was so very far away. Dejected, and feeling very alone, Mijo wondered if he would see either of his sons ever again.

Mijo sighed, while looking around the room. He still did not know why he was sitting in his chair. Mijo scanned his familiar space for answers, as he had a million times before. With further despondency, Mijo noted that nothing ever changed in the midst of his space. And yet, while carrying a heavy melancholy, he knew everything differed. This made him long for a drink. Mijo looked over at the double that sat on his side table undisturbed. The little glass looked right back and beckoned him. But, just as Mijo was about to be overpowered with this need, he noticed a new unexpected item.

It was the third detail that jumped at him with surprise. Sitting patiently was a very old black leather-bound book. It was a book he had not noticed for quite some time: it was Baba's old Bible! Its presence surprised him, because like the drink sitting nearby, Mijo did not remember placing it there. As Mijo looked at its cover, the

Chapter 25

book reminded him of older memories and newer promises. Each of these left Mijo further tormented, and conflicted, a squirming wreck in his once comfortable chair.

Quickly, Mijo returned his aging eyes back upon the fire, a feeble diversion from the discomfort growing in his mind. Mijo realized the chair and fire were allies, thwarting him from finding either pleasure or peace. Each spark, each flicker only introduced him to new tears. Tears for Verka, for himself, and for his sons. Every new moment now reminded Mijo of the service both Mirko and Mato were required to give. This notion of service begot Mijo of much older, hidden memories. Memories that Mijo really did not wish to think of, but was never allowed to forget.

Overcome by the future, the past had him surrounded. Kidnapped by dusty memories, they refused to let him return to the present. The past stalked him. These were not pretty moments of spring wedding days. Rather, they were harsh. They were brutal. They lived in the deepest caverns of his past. With a gut-wrenching dread, Mijo could see it all. Every horrific moment. Terror was everywhere. The sparks of fire enhanced their intensity. There, in supposed comfort of his chair, Mijo saw mortar, fire, bombs, bullets, and death. Mijo witnessed engines swooping powerfully overhead. From the crackling of wood, overpowered by flame, Mijo heard voices barking frantic orders. Each living thought was at war. The Battle of Sutjeska was being waged once again, this time on the second floor of the Pavlović household. For twenty years it was a battle that knew no end. It was the battle for his father's soul.

Again Mijo was there. As he looked on, he appeared younger than he remembered, and even less prepared. His hair was black, like the mood of the Sutjeska. War was at their doorstep! This was no surprise, because war was banging on every door across the globe. Now sitting in his chair, Mijo could smell hell and hot blood. He could smell the powder of the heavy guns. He could smell the petroleum in the tanks and warplanes. His senses surged with a beckoning call of fury. The offensive known as *Case Black* was in full earnest.

At the time of battle, Mijo thought living in a small village made it difficult to know what was right and what was evil. But in hindsight, Mijo knew the truth. It did not matter that new enemies were hurling bombs and destroying cities. The trumpets of both the Red Menace and the Swastika blared so close by that thinking was almost impossible. Still, the people knew who the evil was. They knew.

Mijo remembered. Up till then there had always only been one enemy. And at the dawn of battle, once more the Chetniks were coming! This time they came with Tito on their shoulders, leading the way. Mijo could see them. He, like all of his friends, was ready. Thousands of them were all ready to defend and die for the homeland. The might of the 369, the Legionaries, were ready to kill all evil.

But not everyone was certain this was the right course of action. With this uncertainty, doubt whispered. The Peasant Party, the historical voice of many villages like Pavlovići, spread concern. They whispered a warning. The English, they said, would be against them. The Americans too, they said, would be against them. But Mijo recalled, most did not care what Churchill or Roosevelt thought. They did not care, because they knew what they had to do. The people, they said, knew who evil was.

As Mijo sat, he remembered. Now he remembered that he was so young, but still so certain. What he had to do was fight! He must fight! Mijo loved his homeland; his home in the high hills. Looking back, Mijo remembered, that he was ready to defend it against everything and everyone. He had to! He had a young family to protect. He had a young wife who was about to have their first child. Even from his small little home, high up in the mountains, he could hear the enemy coming. As now, as he sat in his chair, he could hear the tanks, and battalions stomping closer and closer. Up the Sutjeska, the anticipation rose. The noise became so loud Mijo could not stand it anymore!

Chapter 25

Mijo remembered. Mijo kissed his young wife. He kissed his mother, and headed straight for the door to find war. There, he found his father. The father he loved.

As he sat in his chair, Mijo stared at his father. Branko was larger than life. Many considered him an unmovable object, like the Sutjeska's themselves. Branko was only two inches taller than his son, but it seemed so much more. Branko was all muscle. Branko was all might. He could work all day, without sweating. He never got sick. He never slowed down. Branko wore a tan in the winter and a resolute sternness that suggested he knew exactly what was going on at all times, even before it happened. Mijo could hear him now. "Where do you think you're going?" he pronounced.

Mijo remembered how he responded. "To fight."

"To fight," Branko mocked. "To fight for what?"

"For Sutjeska," Mijo responded.

"You want to kill Serbs, huh?" Mijo's father asked. Mijo remembered the way the question was asked. He remembered that his father didn't say they were evil, or they were the enemy. Branko did not even call them Communists or Chetniks. Branko said 'Serbs,' making Mijo feel his words. In one sentence, Branko made them seem human. He made them neighbors, from an adjacent village. Remembering his father's words, Mijo felt ill.

"You're not going anywhere boy," Branko announced. "You have a young family and a village to protect." Mijo remembered how this statement cut at him. Made him feel small. Made him feel less of a man. He also remembered how stupidly he responded.

"I don't care, Tata. I must go. My homeland needs me."

Mijo remembered how Branko laughed. Laughed right in his face. "*Za dom spremni?*[2] Your homeland, huh? Come here," he mockingly demanded. As Mijo obliged, Branko Pavlović continued.

---

[2] "Ready for the homeland." This was once a traditional phrase of pride, has had its meaning reshaped and hijacked by firstly the Croatian Ustasha forces during WWII, and then later by the communists and other controversial groups during and after the Balkan wars. Unsurprisingly after decades of misuse, the phrase continues to divide.

"*Gledaj!*[3] Look around where we live, where you live. *Slušaj!*[4] *Sinko*[5], this is your *dom*[6]. Your Fatherland. Right here is your *Život*[7]."

"But I must defend it," Mijo pleaded.

Mijo remembered the way his father answered. Branko responded by punching his son in the jaw! Down Mijo fell. In many ways, he was still falling. As Mijo remembered, he rubbed his jawline against the stubble growing on his face like he had just been hit, his heart falling further and further through the floor. "Fine, my son, I understand you want to go," Branko began, standing over his fallen son. "But you cannot. I forbid it. Your family needs you. So, I will go."

Mijo looked back, up from the floor, and remembered. Mijo recalled his pleadings and how his father refused to listen. Mijo remembered that once Branko Pavlović made a decision, it was final.

"Your job is to stay," Branko continued. "This is your place. Never forget that, my Sinko. Never forget."

Mijo remembered how the echo of his father's voice cut him. It cut him still.

"I need you to stay," he continued. "Protect your family. Protect your village. Never forget what I have told you. Never forget."

Sweat dripped from Mijo's cheek, while a chill completely covered him. His hair was soaked as if he had dunked it into the nearby stream. With Branko's last words refusing to stop bouncing around the room, all Mijo knew was he wanted to go back in time and change it all. Mijo wanted to join and fight, despite his father's demands. Then maybe things could be put right.

Not knowing where else to turn, Mijo looked once again at the fire. He could see Branko marching away, with a rifle slung over his shoulder. Tears poured down Mijo's cheeks. Now as he looked on, hindsight was screaming at his father to stop. Screaming for him to come back! Hindsight then became bold. It told him that they were

3 Look
4 Listen
5 My son or daughter
6 Homeland
7 Life

wrong! That he was wrong! That during this time the Croats were wrong. That they were the evil. That they were the enemy. Mijo's heart yelled at his father to come back before it was too late. Mijo needed him to come back, before each and every one of them signed their names in blood over to the world's greatest enemy. But it was too late.

Mijo's throat stung with an awful bitterness. With the aid of hindsight, Mijo saw evil lose. And though the world would rejoice at it, happiness could not enter his ashamed heart. Much was lost during the world's evil war. Mijo lost much too. He never saw his father again.

As Mijo continued to look out into his fire, he questioned how great a personal price he would have to pay. He lost his father. Was he to lose both of his sons too?

Overcome with grief, he picked up his glass, downing its contents with a desperate gulp. Mijo could taste terror all around him. The rakija burned his throat, adding fuel to the internal cauldron. In disgust, Mijo hurled the glass into the fire. It shattered on impact, rousing the flames to their highest possible point. These higher flames conjured a sinister grin upon Mijo's face. He liked the fire's power a little too much. He wanted it to be bigger! Stronger! Before he realized what he was doing, Mijo picked up the next closest object, and hurled it towards the fire as well. As he let the object go, a bellow of "Noooooooo," left his throat. But it was too late: Mijo had inadvertently thrown his mother's last gift into the furnace.

Panic engulfed him. In foolish desperation, Mijo grabbed the tongs, hoping to salvage something of the gift. Tears wailed. Self-pity combusted. "How could I be so stupid?" was repeated over and over.

Though Mijo knew it was a lost cause, he gripped on what possibly could be the charred remains. Somehow, as if by a miracle, Mijo clasped onto a remnant. "It's not totally gone!" he wheezed. Pulling it out with haste, in between the blackened tongs, was Verka's black-covered Bible. Stunned that any fragment could possibly be intact, Mijo quickly released the charred book from the hot metal, plonking it to the floor. Covering his hand with his shirtsleeve, Mijo touched the book. It did not feel too hot. In fact, it was not warm at all! Mijo blew the ash that clung to its envelope, hoping to find something underneath that was still there to behold. Amazingly, the ash was not from the book itself, but chars of wood that just found the book as a resting place. Confident that it was not hot to his fingers, Mijo picked it up off the floor. He could not believe it. The book was whole and unblemished! Mijo brought the book up to his face, giving a quick thanks that he was not punished for his mistake. Taking a breath in, Mijo somehow thought he smelt the scent of honey.

Thinking his smeller was simply playing tricks, or his stomach wished for an early breakfast, Mijo put the book on his lap. Closing his eyes, his thoughts drifted upon his dear old mother. Mijo thought about her last words, and what he promised. Mijo recalled his promise to Vjera to look after the book. Mijo shook his head, with disappointment. He almost failed. If not for a minor miracle, he knew he had failed. As Mijo let the book sit in his lap, he looked at his surroundings, and out the nearest window. The morning's new sun had arrived: Mijo had stayed up the entire night! The strength of the sun paraded all around him.

Mijo got up out of his seat, to put out the fire that now served little purpose. With it snuffed, Mijo returned to his chair, and return Vjera's book to his lap. Thinking about his last conversation with Vjera, Mijo knew that he had failed in what his mother really wanted him to do. For too long he had been putting it off. So finally, after all those years of procrastination, Mijo opened his mother's little black leather bound book. As he opened its pages, Mijo found himself surprised with what he found. So surprised, that he smiled a big happy smile.

Lijevo ili desno[1]

The speeding locomotive blurringly ca-clanged down track after track. For hours it beat to a rhythm opposite to that of Mato's heart, aiding him to forget which noise belonged to which chest. Mato did not wish to go on, but there was no stopping fate. New unwanted worlds awaited our wayward explorer. Mato felt ill. Everything he once knew now never existed.

Over the next two months, the ca-clangs continued in the direction of the small alcove of Kocani, near the Bulgarian boarder. There, each day, dread sat next to Mato, at the edge of his small bed, one of the many gifts, compliments of Marshall Tito. As soon as he arrived, Mato longed to get away, but he knew he did not have the ticket to punch his way out. Trapped, he sat, waiting. Waiting for something to set him free. Thankfully, Mato discovered a small respite: a pencil. When coupled with paper, it allowed his heart to fleetingly dance.

> *December 10th*
> *Dearest Verka,*
> *Life continues though we are parted. It must be snowing on the Sutjeskan hills. I have never missed them more than now.*

---

1 Left or right

Kata's Father

How I wish to trample over the thick blanket of snow, toward my father's little home, back to you. Please let my folks know that I will write them also. However, it would please me if you might also convey in detail how both Mama and Tata are doing. I hope each of you are enjoying each other. Though I wish to be there too, I am glad that I'm able to complete my grand mission. Life here continues in a beautiful manner, which I am becoming accustomed to.
Please consider me and I look forward to seeing you soon.
Love, Mato.

Quickly, another page was filled. Mato looked satisfied. Not because of his prose, for each of his recent letters was mostly identical, so myopic were his thoughts. Rather, while he wrote, Mato was not sitting in an army uniform on the edge of a small bed near the Bulgarian border. He was home.

With another letter done and sealed, Mato perused his enforced quarters. His eyes found what he had located each of the past sixty days: that he was surrounded by a group of young boys, barely men that surprisingly looked like him. That acted like him. They were him.

Sure, instead of letter writing, some played chess, while others read or slept. Maybe, some come from Croatia, or Bosnia, while others were from Slovenia. Surprisingly, some were born in Hungary. Some were fisherman. Others were peasants. A few were even part of the educated bourgeoisie, whose mind's Tito would use after their bodies were worn out. But that did not matter to Mato. Too him each looked somber and detached, longing to be anywhere but here. Regardless of where they were from, in Mato's eyes it made them all the same.

Mato sighed. This mutual understanding sent his mind back to the only topic he cared for: Home. Lamentably home felt like a desert mirage, as Mato had already sent a million letters homeward, and yet not a single page had yet come back his way. Not one! Not from his mother or father. And not one from his young wife. This fact stung him the hardest. Mato clung to the notion that it was not their fault. He strained to convince himself that this is simply the way of things, that getting mail through would take time. But this reasoning was not working. Mato did not know it, but after only two months, the ca-clangs were starting to grind at his resolve.

But somehow, his pencil knew. So Mato wrote and wrote, tearing at sheet upon sheet. Each time he connected lead with paper, for a few seconds, hope was availed. His heart lightened, even if his earnest longings were written in his very limited code.

> *December 16th*
> *Dear Tata,*
> *The army really treats us beautifully. The quarters and food provided is really grand, and more than I could have ever expected. Basic training is going very well. I am learning a lot, and expect to be asked into leadership soon. This leaves me very glad for the way of things. I hope I am up for the challenge to do what is right. Please consider what I have said. I miss all of you very much. I hope you are all writing me many, many letters, that I might read really soon. Then I will sit while looking upon the Osogovo while imagining the Sutjeska.*
> *I love you very much,*
> *Mato.*

> *December 18th*
> *Dear Verka,*
> *Camp continues beautifully. I'm wondering how the festive season is proceeding without the one who loves you. Eat and be merry, and think of me. I'm making many friends, many who are moving onto more beautiful situations. Please consider them, and the beautiful choices granted them. I'm so glad for them all.*
> *Love,*
> *Your husband,*
> *Mato*

Though Mato felt safe writing in his code, deep down, he knew they were all being watched. Though danger lurked, its awful truth was right in his face. Sadly, Mirko was right! People he had only just met were disappearing. Zukovic, a Croat was there one day and gone the next, replaced by whispers and rumors. Some said it was because he refused to carry a weapon. Others said because he refused to swear an oath. Mato guessed the real reason, and it filled him with fear. He knew because his brother's claims grew inside of him each day, wondering when his day might come. Mato also knew Zukovic was not the only one to meet this awful fate.

The ca-clang rumbled on. Mato pulled another piece of paper. Next to Mato's bunk, a Slovene, Franković, recognized Mato's haste.

"Another letter, huh?" Franković smirked.

"Da," Mato offered.

"To who this time?"

"It doesn't matter." Franković nodded, understanding. Mato returned his eyes to his blank page. As he was just about to connect pencil to page, Mato was interrupted with a loud bellowing call.

"Pavlović!" the voice boomed.

"I am he," Mato offered, standing at attention.

"Letter for you," the voice replied.

Mato looked over towards Franković. They both smiled, in quiet celebration that one of them, any of them, had received something of home. Mato sprang towards the carrier, and greedily ripped it open.

"Well," Franković began, "what does it say?"

Mato smiled, eager to share. But, before he could, another voice engulfed their peace, shouting out two words.

"Franković! Pavlović!"

"Yes sir," the owners of the names replied, both at attention.

"The General wishes to see you both," the voice boomed. "Now!"

With rapid haste, each of the little lemmings readied themselves, engulfed by their newly given orders. Both were properly preened within moments. Still, Mato dared to be annoyed at the orders timing, stuffing his letter into his right pocket. He was so miffed at having to delay its reading, he did not notice Franković's pensive disposition. Nor did Mato notice Franković hide a small item under Mato's pillow. He barely noticed the bellowing Corporal's return, and his demanding their departure once more.

On they went, side-by-side, behind the Corporal who walked with certainty. Not a sound could be heard, except for their shoes clip-clopping upon the polished floor. With each step away from his bunk, Mato's mind shifted from the letter, to the realization his summons could not be good. It never was. After zigzag through the maze of sheeny floors, they stopped at a nondescript door.

"Wait here," the Corporal announced.

Both Franković and Mato glanced at each other, and smirked nervously.

"So, who is the letter from?" Franković whispered.

"I don't know," Mato shrugged.

"Have you got it on you?"

Mato nodded.

"I would like to know who's it from," Franković offered. "Pull it out and 'ave a look."

"Why?"

"*Molim te²*. Just do this for me, okay?" Mato looked up to ensure the coast was clear. While never lowering his head, Mato pulled the letter out of the envelope, and immediately recognizing its sender. Just as quickly he put it back where he found it.

As he did this, the door thrust open. Out walked the Corporal. "Franković, the General will see you first," he commanded. "Pavlović, you wait here." Franković looked at Mato with a quizzical look, as to ask him once again about the letter.

Mato understood, and motioned his mouth in silence. "My brother." Franković nodded his understanding and proceeded through the door. Quickly it closed behind him, leaving Mato very much alone. Mato sighed. A letter from Mirko left him underwhelmed. He hoped it was from Verka, or his parents. But, alas, it was not from any of them. Still, Mato shrugged, a letter was still a letter.

2 Please

As he continued pondering his pocket's contents, the excitement returned. And as it did, the temptation to read it was far too great. Quickly, Mato re-stuffed his hand into his pocket and re-pulled it out, determined to garner a longer glance. Disappointingly, the letter was short and to the point, without any news.

> *November 14th*
> *Brother,*
> *I hope you are well. You should believe me by now. Remember*
> *to do what I told you.*
> *Mirko.*

The excitement of receiving the letter was gone, with each of Mirko's words attacking Mato on all fronts. Worse, it brought him back to his new reality. Fear gripped him. He was standing behind a door, where he would learn his fate. He did not know what to expect. He knew he was to find out soon. Sooner than he realized. The door flung open, signifying the Corporal's return. "Let's go, Pavlović," he muttered.

Mato tucked the letter in his left pant pocket, doing what he was told. There, Mato found an enormous chattel of a man sitting behind a very large desk. Mato wondered how big he might be if he got to see him stand. At least six foot four perhaps, and easily 300 pounds, he mused. Beyond being large, Mato thought he was a hairy swath of a being, his arms covered with a natural sweaty-looking sweater. Though amused by the General's appearance, Mato was unable to calm his gangling nerves. These were worsened with an awful realization. Where was Franković? He came through the same door, and yet he did not come out. What happened to him? Did the General eat him? That made Mato chuckle internally a little, but the awful questions remained. Did he make him disappear? This question was not funny, because Mato knew that generals could make people vanish. The truth was right there out in the open. Franković was nowhere to be seen.

"Sit," the mountain of man motioned towards Mato. He obviously did what he was told.

Chapter 26

"Private," the behemoth began, "I am General Vukovic. I will get to the point. It has come to my attention that your performance to this point has been good. And that is very good," he grunted.

"Thank you, Sir," Mato replied quietly, attempting to play the role of a good soldier.

The General seemed unimpressed. "I need men I can promote. Can we count on you, Private?"

Mato hesitated, not knowing how to respond. His mind was becoming overcome by a ca-clanging in his chest. He asked himself once more where Franković was, but grimly, Mato already knew. Mato knew Franković had just received the same question. He must have answered in a manner not to the General's liking. Mirko's foreboding warning was rising within him. Mato now felt that he had been backed into a corner. A corner he could not run from.

"Can we count on you?" General Vukovic growled.

Mato rushed back to his quarters. He was miserable. Someone in the room called out to him, asking where Franković was. Mato did not respond. He was shaking uncontrollably. "What just happened?" he asked himself, over and over again. As Mato flopped onto his bed, his head hit a surprisingly hard surface, living under his very thin pillow. Without sitting up, he pulled up the feeble cushion, to find a small package, with a note attached,

> *Pavlović.*
> *My time is coming to an end. Take care of this little package. Hold onto it. Or at least make sure it gets back to my family. I have enclosed the address.*
> *Franković.*

Mato unwrapped the brown butcher paper that hid the item from his eyes. There, in his hands sat a small leather-bound bible. Guilt swept over him. "What have I done?" Mato said, as he began to quietly sob. Just then, Mato heard someone shout his name.

"Pavlović, mail!" the voice boomed.

"Really?" Mato replied, hand breaking his tears.

"Yes, Pavlović, mail," the courier replied.

As Mato forced himself out of his bed, he was handed a massively large package.

"There's an entire tree trunk of paper in it," the courier commented.

"Thank you," Mato replied, not wanting to be chatty. Mato slumped back on his bed. To his astonishment, the package held letter after letter. Dozens of them. It was if everyone from the Sutjeska had written him more than one. Mato's heart broke. For months, he thought he was alone. But like an answered prayer, scores of family and friends, rested in his grip, ready to talk and comfort him. Heart filled note after heart-filled note from souls who wished him well. "If only the letters came yesterday," he mused. "It might all be different. What have I done?" he blubbed. Mato's mind could hear the howls. He had made a decision, and it had already begun to plague him. Mato already hated himself for it. As he wept, Mato concluded God would hate him too.

Postanska torba[1]

Day after day it continued. Letter after letter was sent, and received. More and more, Mato, a tormented soul, liked little of his days except when receiving notes and packages. Because of his accepted role of leadership, delays were minimal. And though a grave guilt grew with each letter, at the same time, nothing else mattered but hearing from home. At least for a few moments, that is.

> *September 16th*
> *It has been two minutes since you left our door, dear husband of mine. How I miss you already. I wonder if you know how much.*
> *Love,*
> *Verka*

> *November 12th*
> *Dearest Husband of mine,*
> *I hope you have received my many letters. I know it's not always easy to get them while you complete your grand mission. Just know I have you always close to my heart. Lately, I have just not been feeling well as I would like.*

---

1 Letter bag

Love,
Verka
PS. it's nothing to worry about.

November 16th

November 16th
Dear boy, it's your mother. How I miss you. We are doing well,
though I have a little cough.
With love,
Mama.

December 2nd
Dear son,
I miss you very much. I hope to write more, once you reply. I am
sure you have written much. I look forward to reading each letter.
Love,
Tata

December 26th
Dearest Husband,
I got the first of your letters. Thank you for finding the time
to write. Christmas has come and gone. It was a lovely affair,
if somber with you not being here. I still feel a little ill in the
morning, occasionally. Your mother and father are taking so
very good care of me. Mara has been sick the last few weeks,
but does not allow us to make a fuss. Your father dotes on me
with loving care. That is, when he is not going for long walks,
or pottering around in his workshop. Mara says both of these
activities are strange for your father. Is that so? He seems to be
having a wonderful time with all of his additional activity. He's
always in a good mood, though a little secretive with where he
is going or doing. Again, your mother says that this is weird for
him, but neither she nor I complain. He is amazingly happy,
though sad at the same time, with you living so far away.
Love you more than you know,
Verka.

Chapter 27

February 24th
Dearest Verka,
It was lovely to receive your note, though it's always a hardship to have to wait between your dear letters. Things are going grand. Though I am dreaming very vividly, like I once used to. I've been promoted quickly and have 25 men in my command. Conditions are beautiful, though never as lovely as you are.
Love. Mato.

March 18th
Dear Verka,
How I would love to receive another letter from you. I miss you terribly. I'm eating well, and sleeping in grand comfort with beautiful dreams, as I have mentioned previously keeping me company. Please consider.
Love,
Mato.

April 1st
Brother, I hear congratulations are in order.
Mirko.

April 19th
Dear Father,
I've inherited great responsibility over the past few months, with many men under my authority. It's a grand gift I don't deserve. Still it leaves me glad, because I'm considering the future. There's a beautiful price in doing Tito's most beautiful work. Please consider all my words, and write soon.
Love,
Your son, Mato…grand dreams

May 15th
Dearest Husband,
Much has been going on to occupy our minds. Your mother is

recovering from another chest cold. I don't wish to burden you, being that you're so far away, but I hear and see your father's concern. However, Mijo continues to work with the zeal of a younger man. He works the fields, and after a hard day, still finds time to take his long walks, or do his woodworking. I think of you often. Oh, I didn't mention, my illnesses are thankfully gone.

Lovingly, your wife,
Verka

June 1ˢᵗ

Dearest son,

I received your grand note, and pondered it greatly, over the course of many days. It had a profound impact upon me, as I garnered much understanding from it. It left me knowing that I must convey some advice to you that I wish I'd sent to your brother, when he too found himself in a similar situation.

Dear son of mine, who I love, so much of life is lived between our ears. It's here where love, hate, happiness, daydreams and fear play. I know this, for I too feel and see my inadequacies. These shortcomings are alive, whether creeping close to the surface, or festering deep down inside. Still, I know they're there, for at times they chart even my course of action, and then make things worse, by determining our reflection.

But here is the good news. If these items live in us, then we've been given the right tools to be their masters. And if we are their masters, we can decide what song our ears listen too. My dear son, conquer all, and live. Consider.

Your Father, with love, always.

July 21ˢᵗ

Dearest Tata,

Thank you for your needed note. I have a question though. What if I played a beautiful song?

Love,

Chapter 27

Mato
PS. I haven't gotten a letter from Mama or Verka for a long time. Could you get them to write?

August 3rd
When you sing a beautiful song, my son, don't forget you're always able to start from the top of the lyric sheet again.
With love,
Tata.
PS. I'll get you the letters you crave.

August 14th
Verka,
Could you please write? My dreams are often of you and are so beautiful. It's if they're really are happening.
Please. Mato.

September 13th
Verka,
Could you please write? My dreams are so grand. They're often of you and our family. Again they're so grand. I love you.
Mato

November 14th
Dear Mato,
I'm sorry I haven't written. So much has happened! I have a surprise! Mato, you are a father. Kata Pavlović was born a few short months ago. Your father and mother asked me to consider this name. And after telling me why, I thought it a splendid idea. She's such a healthy, beautiful baby. I have included a photo. I kept it secret until now, because I didn't want you to worry, knowing you have so much to focus on. Your mother says Kata looks much like you when you were a baby. Again, Kata and I are well. So is your father, who is so happy. Your mother has been suffering from another recent cold, but is in good spirits.

I love you so much.
Love,
Verka and Kata

November 14th
Son,
Life's gifted you a great burden. Remember, each day starts
delightfully new. Like a newborn babe, each is a wonderful
gift, given freely.
 Your father, with love.
PS. Thank you for making your mother a baba.

Mato sat, rubbing his chin while staring at the photo in his lap. So much had changed so quickly. For the first time in months he allowed himself a smile. Then a knock came at his door. "Letter, Sir," said the Corporal.

"Good. Give it to me please," requested Mato.

"Will there be anything else, Sir?"

"No, you may leave," Mato replied, already lost in the note's possibilities.

November 15th
Dear brother,
 Congrats. Leading 75 men. Good.
Mirko

Mato rolled up the note, and seethed. He looked around the room. He was alone, but for the constant whoosh provided by a circulating fan. Mato cringed, burdened by his self-created mess. Over a year of service was completed. Only one to go, and yet it seemed too great a price. He looked up at the fan above. Again, he could hear the ca-clang in his chest. Worse, he could see his nightmares of the wolves chasing him. So many thoughts mired his mind. His father's letters. Why was his mother seemingly always sick? And then he heard it. He heard a baby crying. And then he realized, somehow, he knew it was

Chapter 27

his baby Kata crying. "Kata, I'm sorry, I now know what I must do," Mato muttered to himself, wiping tears with his sleeve.

December 9th
Dear Mrs. Franković,
This is your son's bible. He asked me to keep it safe a few months ago. But, my time to do this has ended, so I return it to you. Consider me as you consider your son.
With the greatest respect,
Sergeant Mato Pavlović

December, 9th
Dearest Verka,
How wonderful it was to receive your letter and the photo of our little Kata. How cheeky of you to keep it secret. However, I understand your reasons and thank Isus[2] that you are both well. Much has gone on here over the past year. The grand mission has shaped my thinking in a grand manner, leaving me glad about what it has done to me. But I have considered it all, and am ready for whatever beautiful thing comes next. I'm prepared, though the cost of doing what is right in Tito's army isn't always easy, but it's always worth it. Until that wonderful day, when we might see each other again, kiss Kata for me. Love my parents, and tell them to consider me.
Your husband,
Mato.
PS. Inform father that I have considered his advice, and have decided to pick the song I listen to from now on.

June 14th
Dearest brother,
I'm not sure you'll get this letter, but I write with candor, because now it doesn't matter. Why'd you do this? You were safe. You were in. You would have been a great benefit to us all down

---

2 Jesus

the road. If you get this letter, I know where it finds you. Are you enjoying your new quarters? There's no need to explain, for I know them well. I don't understand why you changed your course of reason. Your two years would have soon been up, but instead you sit and rot. Stupid! How much longer will you sit? I'm not certain. Six months perhaps? I hope that this is the worst of it, but who knows if you'll see light of day again?

I write though, hoping to give you some important news, because I doubt you have gotten any. This letter will find you late, but at least, because of my connections, it will find you.

I hear congrats are in order. A daughter, wow! I have paid my respects. I mention this because I know it would please you, though anything pleasing you where you are is dangerous for your future survival. Still, I know Kata's mother is doing well, and that father, I hear, is a proud grandpa, though I have not seen him. I know Mama was glad for the occasion also.

It is about Mama I write. Dearest brother, you once wrote me with sad tidings. Regretfully, I write in a similar vein. I don't know how much you knew, but Mama had been suffering much over the past eighteen months. She had become weak… too weak…and she could not fight any more…As of last May, she passed on from this world, dear brother. I'm sorry. You would have found out sooner, if I had the power to make it so. I hope to see you soon.

Why did you do this thing?

Mirko

Mato sat in his hole by the flickering light and wiped his nose. The note said June, but it was not June. Nor was it July. Mato was not sure what month it was. Perhaps it was October, or maybe November? It had been a long time since he saw the light of day, let alone a calendar. Either way, the news was months old. Mato rubbed his jawline. His mother was dead, and his heart ached. He missed her greatly. He began to weep, uncontrollably. But as he did, Mato thought about Verka. Mato thought about the last letter he wrote her, before he

Chapter 27

stormed into General Vukovic's office, where he recanted his answer on what he believed, and who he believed in.

As Mato sat in the pit, he questioned whether it was worth paying the cost for righting past wrongs. But as he pondered this notion, his mind kept bringing him back to those he loved. Mato thought about them all, but especially his daughter, Kata. He wondered if she knew how to walk or talk yet. Each was a real possibility. Though he was not certain when he might finally get to meet her face-to-face, at least when he finally did, he would be able to proudly look her in the eye.

Mato then thought of Baba, and what she might think. He also thought of the wolves that had chased him once. That chased him still. Each time he saw them, they looked happy. Happy at his lot. Happy at his suffering. The notion that wolves could be happy made Mato laugh. He laughed a mighty bellow of a laugh that felt so good it hurt. It was at this point, his thoughts returned to the mother he would never see again. "That's okay," he noted defiantly, through the pain and hurt and darkened howls. She, like Baba will be okay. Whether, he would be too, Mato was less certain.

Part IV
Kući

---

1 Homeward

-28-

Tata[1]

Mato looked up at the sky. There wasn't a cloud to witness. Mato looked down at his watch. It was three minutes past the hour. As much as Mato wished it might stop ticking, the minutes, hours, days, months, years kept moving at a draining monotonous pace. Mato sighed.

It had been three days since he was dishonorably discharged, and placed on a train away from Kocani. It had been three hours since his body arrived to Vareš. Leaving town quickly, he was less than three miles from Pavlovići. However, it had been three minutes since Mato stopped and sat. This might seem silly to most, since he was almost home, but he needed time to ready himself. Mato could tell his senses had yet to embrace his new reality, and time was running out.

Surrounded by a multitude of spruce and pine, with swallows chirping at the sun, Mato's eyes were telling him he was out! The darkness was gone. He had escaped the grave dug by Tito. And yet it was clear, though the pit might have been over 600 miles away, Hades was still too close for comfort.

---

1 Dad

Chapter 28

Mato paid a hefty price for his insolence. He was still paying for it. A lifetime! Well, at least a lifetime of a young child: Mato's own child. Mato looked down again at his watch, and noticed the date. Mato calculated that Kata had turned three only a few months ago. It did not seem fair. Three years had come and gone. Mato had spent each of Kata's first three birthdays singing salutations in solitude. For three years, surrounded by darkness, Mato attempted to imagine what Kata looked like by taking the photo in his mind and trying to age it. Time and time again he failed.

When not thinking of his newborn babe, Mato thought of his Verka. Remembering her in that awful place was brutally difficult. Just remembering her voice in the cell of silence or attempting to recall her smell in the midst of the pungent, musty odor was impossible. Mato had forgotten what her laugh sounded like. He had forgotten the way she said his name. He had forgotten much.

And now, though he was so close to seeing them, speaking to them, holding them, fear gripped him. He wondered if he had forgotten the way home. He knew it was an irrational fear, but most fears were. With these fears, came awful questions. The type of questions that never have rational answers to combat them. After all this time, would Verka still love him? How was Tata without Mama? Would Kata know who he was? How could she? Would she warm to him? Would Mato warm to her? With each awful question, Mato fretted, and fretted some more. So much so, he closed his eyes to block it all out.

As Mato sat with eyes closed thinking the worst, somehow behind his eyelids, he gained a fresh realization. From behind the darkness that his now closed eyes created, Mato could still hear the swallows. Mato could feel the slight intermittent breeze. And, most importantly, Mato could feel the sun's warmth. While he sat, Mato stretched out his arms and began soaking up the Sutjeska's rays. Thankfully, Mato could feel its grip bind to his flailing soul, energizing his hopes. Within thirty minutes, Mato stood up, recharged and ready to go on.

Surprisingly, with this new energy, Mato felt the urge to run. For the first time in years, Mato ran over one hill, two hills, and then a third. Within minutes, his lungs were burning hotter than the heat of the summer day. And as sweat poured off his brow, for at least three seconds, Mato smiled. Instead of fatigue, Mato was consumed by a comforting, satisfied tiredness, happy to be reminded of a time before the pit and its lurking evils.

As Mato shuffled closer to his Sutjeskan nook, he felt the urge to pluck a thick bunch of wildflowers and smell them in. It was then Mato knew it. He was almost home. But before he could complete his long journey, there was one more thing he had to do.

Mato walked past the Gaj, the wooden section just north of the village. As a child, Mato had played in, hid in, fought in, and ran through these bushes and trees each day of every summer. As he continued, to his left, Mato could hear and see the moving stream. This was the same stream where Mirko caught trout, set off boats, and dreamed of conquering oceans.

As he pondered his brother, these thoughts were interrupted by an overactive curiosity. Beyond the direction of the stream, Mato thought he noticed something scurrying in the long grass. Mato took a few steps in the supposed figments direction, so to get a better look. However, his effort was to no avail. Whatever he thought he saw, it was no longer in view. Shrugging it off, Mato returned back into the throng of trees and his plan.

The Gaj was not deep or wide, and quickly Mato pushed through towards the final brush and nettle, meeting a wooden fence. Hurdling it with little trouble, he arrived at his point of interest within three strides. Before Mato could visit with his future, he needed to nod to his past.

There, right before his feet and eyes, laid the tombstone of Vjera and Mara Pavlović, his dear grandmother and mother.

Mato stared at both tombstones. The reality of life traveling without his witness engulfed him. This really happened, drummed unabated inside his heart. It was if his mother had died at that very moment, so new was the pain. Needing to move beyond these hurts, Mato took the bunch of flowers, and split them into three smaller parcels. Placing a handful lovingly before both tombstones, Mato's set of wobbly legs forced him towards the ground, where his tears drenched the grass.

Moments, minutes, maybe hours passed. Mato could not be sure, for in total exhaustion, he had fallen asleep. Surprisingly, despite sleeping on the moist ground, Mato felt refreshed. He mused; this was a supposed benefit of sleeping on the cold floor all these years, no doubt. Mato again looked at his watch. Brushing himself off, Mato knew he needed to move on, but he needed the right words first before parting. Finally, after a frustrating few moments, Mato simply whispered, "*Draga moja Mama,*[2] I'm home."

At peace in paying his deepest respects, the excitement of what was next started to sink in. But, as Mato turned away from both Mara and Vjera to go see Verka, Kata and his father, Mato was met by one family member he did not expect to see. "When did you get home, brother?" asked Mirko, jumping past cordial greetings.

"Hello, Mirko," answered a startled Mato. "Just now. What are you doing around here?"

"Oh," Mirko replied. "You didn't hear. No, I guess you wouldn't have. I transferred to the mine at Haljinići."

"Oh. The underground, huh?" Mato replied.

"Don't worry," Mirko began. "So far, it hasn't been that bad. It's kind of fun to blow up stuff inside the mountain."

"You back home, then?" Mato asked.

"No. I live right by Haljinići."

"Oh," Mato replied. "Haljinići, huh? I guess I need to go see them about my old job."

"No need," Mirko injected. "I already did. You're on the cranes, of course, this Tuesday. It's the least I could do."

"Thanks," Mato offered. "Hey, it is good to see you, but I need to go…"

"I understand," Mirko interjected. "They'll want to see you."

Mato motioned to pick up his belongings. But before he could, Mirko stopped him with one last question.

2 My dear Mom

"Mato."

"Yeah."

"You look tired. Are you...okay?"

Mato looked over at his older brother. Hearing his concern, Mato pondered the question sincerely. Finally, he answered with a shrug of the shoulders. Mirko smiled at Mato's honest response, nodding in acknowledgment, both understanding each other better than ever before.

"Go get some rest. You need it. I'll see you around," Mirko noted. Mato again stooped down to collect his thoughts, feeble belongings, and the last of the picked wild flowers. But as Mato stood up to say goodbye, surprisingly, Mirko was already gone. Mato concluded that did not matter. He knew he would see Mirko soon, probably when he least expected it. With Mirko's departure, Mato again glanced at his watch. Hesitating, he looked once more. Then a third time. Why? Because it appeared to stop working. Mato put it to his ear, and heard no ticking. Mato shook his wrist, but still nothing. He attempted to resuscitate it back to life by winding the side mechanism, but regardless of how many times Mato twisted the little knob, the watch gave Mato nothing.

Throwing the item off and into the Gaj with contempt, the stopped watch created a level of panic Mato had not felt for a long time. He needed to see his family, and now! Mato had dithered for too long. Within seconds, Mato ran as a hard and fast as his frail body could muster. He ran past so many things he longed to see again, past houses and people he had known his entire life. But now, Mato cared little for those memories. All he was concerned about was getting home. He needed to see his Pavlovići. Right at that moment, Mato needed to be faster than time.

Running right up to the front door, as he had in his youth. Surprisingly, Mato paused, unsure of what to do next. He had lived this moment every minute of every day for three years, and now, Mato froze. He was home, but he felt like an intruder. Should he just walk in? Should he knock? Should he turn back?

But Mato's hesitation was of little consequence. In the midst of his confusing doubt, the door opened and out burst two figments of

Chapter 28

a once desperate imagination. One of the two beings was completely caught unawares, until she was struck still by the sound of his voice. "Hello, Verka. I'm home," Mato offered, pushing out the flowers for his bride to take.

Verka turned to face the voice. To face her husband. Struck mute, Verka was unable to say a word. Fortunately, a little creature that stood up just past her knee knew exactly what to say. "Tata. Tata. Tata!" Kata cried. Mato stood there and cried too. It was at this moment, that the mountains finally allowed time to halt.

-29-

Opet¹

It was late. Mato noticed it was almost three o'clock, but sleep was far from his mind. Sleeping had become tiresome. It had become dangerous. The dreams were worse. More violent. More gruesome. Too vivid. This is why Mato sat, and sat, and sat. At least while Mato sat in Mijo's old chair, rustled up next to a warm blaze, his hands and feet were comfortable. Though he could not sleep, he was not facing danger. He felt safe.

Glancing up, Mato looked over at a small calendar he hung nearby. The weather did not know it, but April was upon them. Mato wondered where the time had gone, without a satisfying answer. He rubbed his chin, musing that almost four years had come and gone since he returned home. Four full calendars! This notion made Mato shake his head. Over the course of his adult life many calendars were given. Many more calendars were simply taken.

Verka rolled over in her bed, her subconscious awoken by being all alone. Again! She sighed. Mato was not there, but Verka knew where he was. Where he always was. He was sitting just outside the door, in Mijo's old, frayed chair, waiting for the sun to rise. She rolled back over, in solemn silence, and attempted to return to her

---

1 Again

pitiful slumber, worried for her husband, while also concerned for her future.

Fixated by the hypnotizing blaze, Mato wondered where all of the days went. Kata was already seven years old. Seven calendars were given. Seven calendars were lost. Mato again shook his head, but this time in wonder of his firstborn. It took little time to realize that Kata was a skinny-limbed spitfire, a blur of ready-made opinions. Even Verka, who did not like to have such an opinionated child, was glad for the laughter. It killed the quiet that lived in the Pavlović home most of the day.

That was, except when his son, Pepan, was not crying for something to curb his want. Mato smiled. Life had given him a son. It gave him one almost three calendars ago. Mato smiled knowing he was there to see his son being born. He was allowed to see his first steps. Mato got to hear his first words.

But, even these happy thoughts were mixed with sadness. He could not help it. Every moment of bliss, reminded Mato of the old pain. He longed for the lost years. He wished he could go back.

Mato sighed. He would have to get ready for another shift shortly. For four years, Mato worked the cranes at Haljinići. Each day, Mato could sense, and could feel the insides of the mountain's darkness calling all into its belly. The dangers of mining in Tito's Yugoslavia were there to see, if you dared open your eyes and value each life. Though his role was above surface, occasionally Mato would have to go under. He was never sure which day his supervisors would demand he go below, filling each shift with dread. As Mato sat, he recalled each time he had to go into the devil's lair. Mato concluded that each moment was worse than his time in military prison. There at least, he knew one day, he might get out.

Verka once again awoke, and once more found herself alone. She sighed, and readied herself to be rejected by her love once more. Getting out of bed, she peered her head out there door. "Mato, are you coming to sleep?" she asked forlornly.

"Oh," replied a startled Mato, not expecting conversation so late at night. "Um, sure in a few minutes. Just waiting for the fire to die down."

"Okay," Verka answered, disappointed. She returned to her covers, and shook her head. The house seemed much more quiet since Mato returned. As she lay there, Verka reminisced of her childhood, and all the music that surrounded her. She missed her violin. She missed her mother. She missed Mara. Even though he sat only a few feet away, Verka missed Mato most of all. As quietly as she could, Verka wept herself back to sleep.

Mijo, in what was once Vjera's room, was also awake. It was not because he could not sleep, rather he was often up by this time. Sleep was something, like the old days, Mijo did not need.

He awoke with family on his mind. Family was driving him back and forth, from one side of his room and back again. As his feet shuffled north and south, north and south, Mijo's mind traveled freely in all directions. Each thought, pleasant and cruel did not daunt him. Mijo was truly grateful how his life had turned. His eyes watered with pride at the thought of his growing family that now lived in his house. The house that was once his father's home. Mijo loved being a father. He loved being a grandfather. As he paced, Mijo's thoughts drifted towards Mato. They often drifted towards Mato. He knew Mato was sitting outside his door in his old chair.

Mijo knew that instead of sleeping, Mato spent many of his nights there. Mijo also knew what was drawing him to his chair. It was what once drew him there. Even without the exact details, Mijo knew Mato suffered and was suffering alone, and that these burdens could be unrelenting.

As Mijo paced, he planned his next move. He knew he had once tried to help one of his son's before, and it had backfired badly. He did not wish to make the same mistakes with Mato as he did with Mirko. Standing there, in the middle his mother's old room, Mijo closed his eyes, and said a prayer of thanks. As Mijo opened them, his reasoning brought forth a peaceful clarity. He knew he was better prepared this time around. Mijo was confident about his next call of action. It would be just what Vjera would have wanted.

-30-

Knjiga[1]

For three nights Mijo sat on his decision, waiting for the right moment. For three nights Mato was awoken by a terror that decimated his sleep, and sent him escaping to his father's old chair. For three nights, Verka awoke abruptly, to notice Mato was not there. She then spent the rest of each night forlornly fretting about feeling helpless, until she whimpered herself back to sleep.

On the fourth night, everything came to pass. It was about eleven o'clock on a Saturday, and Mijo was once again pacing, wondering whether tonight was going to be the night. As he headed to the southern corner of his room, he heard a scream and crash coming from Mato and Verka's room. Mijo could hear Verka asking Mato, "What's the matter?"

"It's just another nightmare, Verka. That's all," Mijo heard Mato reply.

Mijo heard their door open. He opened his, finding Mato already in his old chair and Verka searching her husband with melancholy eyes. "Mato," Verka muttered. "Please, come back to bed?"

"In a little while, Verka," Mato answered, while looking straight ahead at the unlit fireplace. "I'll be there soon enough." Mijo looked over at Verka, and noticed her frustration.

---

1 Book

"Don't worry, *sinko*[2]," Mijo whispered. "Let me help."

Verka sighed. "Alright Tata, if you think you can."

Mijo stepped toward the turmoil and angst sitting in his old chair, while Verka closed her door. If Mato noticed Mijo pull up a chair, he did not show it, as he continued to stare at the fireplace.

"You know, I used sit here quite a bit," Mijo began.

"Oh, hi, Tata," exclaimed a startled Mato. "I didn't hear you creep up. Did you want your chair back?"

"Oh, no, "Mijo replied. "I was saying I used to sit here quite a bit. But I would generally only stare into the fireplace if there was a fire going on."

"Oh, yeah, I see your point," chortled Mato. "Should I start one then?"

"I think you should," Mijo chimed. "You hungry?"

"Da."

"I will be right back then."

Within minutes the blaze was burning and stomachs were being filled with pork and bread.

"So son," Mijo began. "Another bad dream, huh?"

"Da," Mato quickly replied, in an effort to minimize the conversation.

"They happen almost every night, huh?"

Mato looked over at his father, answering as before, "Da."

"They happen every night, right?"

"Da," Mato replied for the third occasion.

"What are they about? A slight change, but basically the same, right?"

Mato was about to answer "Da" once more, but his father's question tripped up his thoughts, "How'd you know?"

"Just a guess," Mijo confessed. "Son. Tell me. What are they about?"

Mato wanted to tell his father. He wanted to tell him it was always about a pack of wolves, led by the One. Sometimes they were chasing him, often chasing his wife and children. And tonight was

2 Child of mine

the worst. The wolves teamed up with all manner of evil creatures, including vipers. The vipers were almost worse than the wolves. It was awful. Twenty minutes after being awoken by this awful nightmare, Mato still was overcome by the shakes. He felt like a feeble child.

"Come on, tell me. What are they about? I know you know," Mijo persisted.

"Oh, the past," Mato sighed. "The future."

"I see," Mijo replied.

"You do?" Mato answered, surprised.

"Yes I do," Mijo answered confidently. "The past has troubled many men. It can shake confidence. Shake foundations. It can cloud everything. Even one's future. In fact, it already is, right?" Mato looked at his father. When he had first returned, Mijo's change had surprised him. But four years on, there were moments when this change left him stunned. This was one of those moments. As Mato continued to look over his father, he studied his face. Mijo looked so well. It was as if he had gotten younger each of the past four years. Though it was late, Mijo did not look fatigued. His color was rosy. He looked rested. Mato envied that rest. He wished he could share in his secrets and partake in this peace. It was at that moment, Mato noticed Mijo pull out a very worn old black book. Mato recognized it instantly. "Wow, Baba's old bible!" Mato proclaimed. "I haven't seen that old thing since, since…"

"That's right, Mijo interjected. "Since the night Baba died. That's what I want to talk to you about.

Mato began to panic, uncertain which direction their conversation was about to head. "I don't know Tata," stuttered a nervy Mato.

"Don't worry," Mijo responded, sensing Mato's trepidation. "I'm not going to make you do anything you don't want. I just want to tell you something, and then I am going to leave you to it, okay?"

"Alright," answered his wary son.

"Your grandmother was a very smart woman. We'd all agree to that, right?" Mato nodded to the basic truth spoken. "Well," Mijo continued, leading his son down a path. "She left us this book, for reasons she at first only knew. Well, after she died, I held onto it. And held on to it. But I wouldn't go anywhere near it. You know why son?" Mijo asked Mato, who could only shake his head.

"Well, for a long while, neither did I. But then I realized I was afraid of what I might find. Silly, huh? I was afraid. That I might find something. Something, good or bad. I was so afraid, I tried to pass it over to your brother, and make him look first. But, Mirko was too smart for that. He found me out, and left me with it. And left us," Mijo added with sadness, but he kept on.

"And for many years I still sat on it, until one day, I dared to be bold. I opened it, and read it. I read all of it, my boy, and all I can say is…all I can say is…"

"Say what, Tata?" Mato wondered.

"All I can say, is your baba was an amazing woman. We were fortunate to know her."

"You read it all, huh?" Mato asked.

"Da," replied Mijo. "Every page. And because I have, I leave it to you."

"I don't know Tata," doubted Mato. "I don't think I can."

"Why not?" queried Mijo.

"I don't think it is for me."

"I understand," Mijo began. "Except your grandmother said it was for all of us. She knew. She knew it could help."

Mato pondered this. No one could doubt Mijo was a changed man. A changed man for the better. "You say it's all because of the book?" he asked, doubtfully.

"Da," Mijo replied with confidence. "All of it. And I mean all of it is for you."

Mato looked incredulously at his well-meaning father. "I don't think it is for me," he muttered, with a tinge of shame. "Because of what I have done…" Mato paused. He had let out more of himself than he wanted. But Mijo understood.

"Son, the truth will not put you back into prison," he began reassuringly. "The truth is a gift, to let you live." Mato listened to his father, heard what he had to say, and began to cry. He cried and wept some more. He could not stop. The floodgates opened. The River Bosna could not have held all of Mato's tears.

"But Tata, I'm a bad man," he blurted through the sobbing. Mijo got up and keeled before his son, grabbing his face with both of his hands as gently as he could muster.

"Boy, no you're not," Mijo stated definitely. "Only a honorable man knows when he has been bad. It's because you know you've been bad, that there is still hope for you." Mijo stood up, and passed Mato the book. "Your grandmother gave this book to me. I have read it. Now I give it to you. Do with it what you will, but remember it was your grandmother's wish that you read it. Be tender to it, and I promise it will be tender to you. Laku noć, son of mine."

"Laku noć, Tata."

With that, Mato sat, holding the book passed on from beyond the grave, unable to do what he was told. It was not out of disobedience, but because of guilt. Guilt for what he had done. Mato had once said he was an unbeliever. It did not matter to him that he had gone back on his first statement. It did not even matter that he had paid a great penance. The facts did not change. Mato knew he had fallen short, and he could not let go of it. But as Mato dwelt on this truth, other truths seeped into reckoning. Mijo had changed. Changed for the better. And now, his father was saying his change was because he read an old tattered book.

"Could it be all that simple?" Mato whispered.

Mato took his thumb to the right hand cover, and hesitated. "I can't," he muttered. He had been so bad. But Mijo told him he was not bad, but rather he had just done a bad thing, and made a poor choice. Mato could not believe this. He dared not believe it. For so long he had believed the entire opposite. But his father told him different. It was then Mato remembered his promise to his baba. He had promised to look after the book. The book that was in his hands.

Mato remembered when he returned from prison, and visited his baba's and mother's grave. He had told them both he was home. But as Mato sat, he knew that was a lie. His body was home, but his mind was 600 miles away, in the pit. Knowing this reminded Mato what Mijo had once written to him, that so much of life was lived between the ears. That seemed right. For too long Mato had lived with wolves, vipers, screams, and terrors. He wanted to come home. He needed to come home.

As Mato held the book, he noticed a piece of red string sticking out of it. Mato knew this to be its built-in bookmark. Interestingly, this old bible uniquely had two. Mato thrust open the bible at the first bookmark. There he found a verse underlined, at Acts 2:17;

> *And it shall come to pass in the last days, Says God*
> *That I will pour out of my spirit on all flesh*
> *Your sons and your daughters shall prophesy,*
> *Your young men shall see visions,*
> *Your old men shall dream dreams*

Mato thought little of what he just read, and quickly moved to the next bookmark. There, Mato's eyes darted towards another underlined verse. As he began to read, Mato wondered if Baba would get into trouble for drawing in a bible. The underlined verse was 1 Corinthians 4:1;

> *Let a man so consider us, as servants of Christ and stewards of the mysteries of God.*

Without additional strings or bookmarks, Mato randomly flipped though the next few pages, without stopping. His interest in the book was lagging. But as Mato was about to put the book down, he flipped one more page. As he did this, a little booklet fell out of the bible, and onto the floor.

"What's this?" Mato mused.

Ono što je unutra¹

Mato picked up the mysterious booklet. Its cover held the same two verses that were bookmarked in the Bible; Acts 2:17 and 1 Corinthians 4:1. Additionally, Mato noticed written under these two verses was a little note exclaiming,

> *The contents found within its pages is a gift given freely to me so I may give it too.*
> *Love,*
> *Vjera Pavlović.*

Mato looked over towards Baba's old room. Here in his hands was a piece of his Baba's life. A piece he never knew existed. And yet, she told him about it years ago. Why was he only looking at this piece of history now? What would it mean to him? What did Baba want to say? Mato excitedly turned the page. Upon it, was a piece of poetry, with the heading in what appeared to be in Latin:

> *Lumen est.*

---

1 That which is inside

"I wonder what that means?" thought Mato. But, without pondering too long, he read on,

> *I was brought to the banquet.*
> *Me, the Mountain's young charge*
> *To be nourished*
> *By a banner that spoke so large!*
> *About who we longed to be*
> *In the Sutjeska!*
> *The table was set.*
> *Decorated with cakes, pita and promise.*
> *Because verse and supper are always prepared.*
> *And I wanted to eat deeply*
> *For I knew I needed to.*
> *And though not young anymore*
> *I was homesick.*

Mato struggled to read on. The poem went for about four more pages. He could not make head or tail of it, so confusing was it to his eyes. It felt a bit like something that might have spouted during the Hasikovanje. Mato chuckled, concluding he would have jested any talker for speaking so flowery.

Mato turned past Vjera's prose, thinking he could always return to it later. Gladly, the following pages instead of poetry, held portraits. Firstly, Mato saw a picture of a young man, working in a woodwork shop. The man's face owned a deep seriousness, as if he was studying the wood before him. Mato grinned, for he liked the picture. Then it hit him! It was Tata; at least, it was Tata when he was younger. Mato wondered what he was making in that picture, as the project appeared to be in its infancy.

Eager to see what was next, Mato flipped the page. There he found Mijo once more. He looked a little older, but not too much older. The drawing found Mijo in his old chair. Mato saw a tinge of sadness in the drawing, as the still young Mijo was staring at the fire. It was a large blaze. Strangely, within the blaze itself, it appeared as if the opposite sides of the fire were waging some kind of battle. Within the fragments of flame, Mato could see opposing armies. Mato wondered what this picture meant. He wondered if Mijo knew.

Thoroughly enjoying the diagrams, Mato turned to the next one, finding a depiction of a stream, surrounded by meadow, trees and mountains. Quickly, he summarized it was the stream just beyond the Gaj. There, at the stream was a younger Mirko. In the picture, a smiling Mirko was about to put one of his boats in the water, while nearby, three lines floated, hoping to catch lunch.

The next page, Mato found Vjera had drawn a picture of a large ship with huge sails. The ship was in the midst of heavy storm. Turning the page once more, Mato saw an image of a solitary figure on the ship, but the drawing was set too far away to make out who it was. Hoping to learn more, Mato turned once again, and there on this page, it focused on this single person. It was Mirko! At the age of when he went to the navy. Mirko looked so sad. So helpless. Mato paused for a moment to ponder what he just saw. His grandmother had drawn Mirko's awful military experience. "*But how could she know?*" he questioned. "*She died before he came back to tell us what had happened.*"

Mato pressed on since he was unable to come to any conclusion. Over the next few pages there were detailed drawings of hawks, buzzards and even a vulture. Next, Mato found two drawings of vipers, similar to those found in the forest during the summer. One in particular made Mato shudder, as it looked exactly like the one he saw in a recent dream. But again, thinking nothing of it, Mato once more turned the page. However, he turned to a page that almost made him drop the booklet, its contents scaring him out of his wits. "What?" he muttered. "How?" he questioned. Mato could not believe it. He did not wish to believe it. On the page sat a clear, concise, vivid depiction of it. "This isn't possible," he proclaimed with certainty.

But as Mato looked on, the picture that sat comfortably between his two tensing hands was of the sharp fangs and beady green eyes owned by the One. The wolf that chased him so many years ago, and was still chasing him was in his grandmother's book! Its vividness was profound. The drawing's accuracy was staggering. The picture before Mato was not just Baba's depiction of the creature, but rather a perfect portrait, down to the finest detail. Vjera even caught the One's exact snarl. Every hair was in its perfect place. Its teeth, and the way they protruded out its mouth were exact. It was as if Vjera was there the night Mato was chased. "I don't believe it," Mato confessed. "I cannot!"

Too frightened to stay on the page, Mato turned once more. But there, Mato found another page of the One, and its minions. Spending little time on that page, the next drawing found the pack on the move, chasing someone. Mato discovered whom the pack were chasing; Him! There on the page was the younger version of himself at the time of the great chase. Mato looked at the picture of his younger self. The picture showed uncertainty in his eyes. Mato did not remember feeling like that, but yet in looking at the picture now, he could not disagree with it. It was as if Baba, while drawing all that occurred that day, drew Mato's expression and feeling based on a different time altogether.

Unable to peer into his own past self any longer, Mato again turned the page, hoping to find respite. However he did not. Instead, the newest page left him awestruck. This page had a picture of his tree. The tree that saved him all those years ago. Under the drawn diagram sat a single word: Tisovina. The word seemed vaguely familiar, as if he had heard it before. Again, Mato could not understand how Baba had come to draw an exact portrait of both his tree and his wolf. She had never gone to the tree with him, nor even discussed the topic in any great detail. And yet, the pictures were there all the same. Mato was amazed by the pages, but worry drenched over him. He clearly was curious how Baba knew so much. Mato hoped the next few pages might answer some of these questions. So he read on with rapid need. However, the next few pages confused him. To Mato's dismay the newest pages contained the diagrams of what appeared to be little bug like creatures. The first page had a detailed version of one of them. Under it again was just one word;

Wisp.

On the opposite page, was penned a short verse,

> *Through their kiss*
> *They bring wondrous bliss.*
> *But if they bite,*
> *Or sting,*
> *Remember*
> *It is still a gift.*
> *Bringing both*
> *A joy and suffering,*
> *To you and your offspring.*

Vjera's writing confused Mato. He was even more confused by the drawing that accompanied it. And yet, all Mato could do was press forward and hope for a explanation. The following page, it appeared that these Wisps were all around a tree. It was his tree! Flipping forward, Mato then found many of these bugs flying over a mountain. Mato recognized it to be the Sutjeska Mountains. Mato began to become agitated, for he was beginning to piece the puzzle together. Mato turned the page once more. In the next picture, again Baba had drawn these bugs, these Wisps. On this page, Baba had drawn lots of them. Hundreds and thousands of them. They were all flying through what appeared to be a thick snowfall. And the midst of this flight and snow stood a single person. It looked like the silhouette of a woman. As Mato studied this picture, Mato recognized the woman. It was a younger version of Baba! The bugs were swarming all around her. Yet, instead of being terrified by their attack, to Mato's disgust, Vjera looked extremely happy.

Mato turned the page once more. On the next two pages, there was a depiction of two children. Two young children. The first diagram was of a toddler-aged child. The child was in bed, asleep. And as the child slept, the bugs were around him too. To Mato's surprise a name appeared under the child's bed:

Mirko.

On the opposite side there was a picture of a newborn, with the bug like creatures around it. Above it was a date.

February 17.

"*That's funny,*" Mato mused to himself, "*that's the day before I was born.*" It was when Mato noticed, that right under the babies left foot was another name:

Mato.

Mato could not believe it! The baby was him. He had never seen an image of himself as a child of any age. Shaking his head, Mato turned to the second to last page. There, Mato saw one of these little bugs either feeding Baba some kind of food or giving her a kiss. Either way, he thought it ridiculous.

Finding himself at the final page a rage was growing. Mato felt as if he had been had. On the final page, Mato found more poetry, like the type he had been subjected to earlier. He read on, ready to heap scorn upon it.

> *And yet*
> *The evening hangs.*
> *A remembrance of the price.*
> *Till the day breaks*
> *I will go my way.*
> *Into the mountains and foray.*
> *With hope not provided*
> *By swords or spear*

Or victories cheer.
But by a new stronger banquet
Of the first and the final tense.
And without blood on my hands
Satisfied.
I can run
And perhaps once more a Kolo I will dance.
However, beware!
I say Beware!
For I have learned first hand
The shadows
Is only a day away.
Unspeakable vultures, wolves and crows!
Longing and yearning to take flight
With a new fear.
On the lips of the unknown future and the foregone.
If you dare to listen,
Listen, Listen, Listen.
They mockingly proclaim,
"Nothing is going to be the same!"

Mato slammed the Bible and the pamphlet shut. He finally fully grasped what the booklet and in turn, his baba and now his father was saying. They were both expecting him to take fairy stories as the absolute truth. Mato shook his head. He could not believe it. He refused to believe any of it.

He looked over at the side table that was holding his empty glass and the bottle of rakija. He quickly poured a glass, drinking its content, before any of it had a chance to settle to the bottom.

C'mon," Mato cringed. "This is not logically possible, is it? No, it couldn't be," he answered defiantly. "*Gotovo.*"[2]

---

2 And that's final

-32-

Vjera[1]

Sunday met Mato where he sat, for he did not move from that spot the entire night. He just sat and sat, staring directly at the cover of Baba's old tattered bible. All night Mato pondered the fantastically unbelievable story that was put before him. He did not know what to believe. But, Mato understood what he was being asked to accept. He could not help but shake his head. "Ridiculous," blurted from his mouth.

"What's ridiculous?" replied Mijo, as he came through his door.

Embarrassed that an inner thought was out in the open, Mato still knew he needed to challenge what was presented before him. "Tata, you can't believe this?" Mato asked, hoping this was some kind of cruel ruse.

"Can't believe what?" Mijo asked innocently.

"The book," Mato replied indignantly, picking Vjera's bible over his head. "The book? All of it. You can't believe it. It's not possible."

Mijo looked over at his unbelieving son. "Logically, no. Of course not. But…"

"But, what?" Mato blurted.

---

1 Confession, faith, belief, trust, persuasion, devotion

"The mountains aren't constrained by our logic, are they boy?" Mijo concluded.

Mato knew what his father was alluding too. He was talking about Mato's experience with the wolves.

"I don't know Tata," Mato replied, hanging his head.

"I know son, but that's okay." Mijo paused, and then changed the subject. "You want to come to church today?"

For years Mato had not gone, but today felt different. Today, he needed to go somewhere. Anywhere. He needed to get out, and away from unbelievable fairy stories that surrounded him.

"Jeste," Mato answered.

At Mass, Mato was a swarm of conflicted reports. He did not know which way to run. So he did what he thought best; he sat still. Even after mass was concluded, Mato sat. What did he sit for? Mato could not even say. Maybe he was hoping to make sense of everything, maybe at least something. Maybe he was hoping to garner divine intervention. Regardless, even after everyone else was in the square enjoying the afternoon festivities, Mato could not and would not get up.

As Mato sat, though he did his best to focus on the subject at hand, he could hear the echo of footsteps clapping towards him. As they arrived at the foot of Mato's stoop, a quiet voice reverberated.

"*Dobro jutro*[2], my *slatki*[3] son," a voice said. Mato looked over at the voice. It belonged to a priest, much younger than Mato.

"My son!" Mato scoffed. The priest laughed, getting Mato's meaning. "I suppose you're right. It's a force of habit. Much of what we are required to do is born of habit. My name is Father Pero," Pero offered, sticking out his hand in greeting, which Mato took. "May I sit?"

"Sure," Mato added quickly, "If you wish." Mato squirmed in his seat unsure he wanted the company, while at the same time, unsure he wished Father Pero to leave. Besides, Mato wondered if

---

2 Good morning

3 Remember it means sweet, perhaps innocent, and sensitive. Even thoughtful...all of these words together

you were allowed to refuse a request from a priest in a church. Pero noticed the anxiousness of his guest.

"Is there something you need to share?" he pressed, getting right to the point.

Mato glared, "I don't think so," he began, "I was just looking to sit somewhere quiet for a few minutes."

"Pah," the priest scoffed. "I doubt that."

This bruised Mato's feelings. "Why?" Mato asked sternly. "What is so surprising about sitting in a church and looking for peace and quiet?"

Pero shook his head. "You didn't come here for peace and quiet," the priest began confidently. "Maybe, if you live the city that would be reasonable, sure. But in the mountains, there are a million quiet spaces. No, no. People come here because they wish to confess. You have something else on your mind."

Mato thought about where he used to go for quiet. Mato sighed. He longed for his tree. That's where he would have gone. But today, Mato had nowhere else to go. "I don't know. How old are you?" Mato asked, attempting to change the subject.

But the priest saw through Mato's redirection. "Old enough to know some things, and young enough to know nothing," Pero chuckled. But he got serious in a hurry, coming back to the subject at hand.

"Look, I think you have something to say. If you wanted to talk to one of the older priests, that's fine, but you could have sat in a confessional, and been done with it an hour ago. But here you sit, with something on your mind."

Mato sighed once more, having been found out. "You're right," he offered.

"You don't need to confess, you just need to talk, right?" Pero asked.

Mato nodded.

"Okay, then talk," Pero demanded. "And, I'll listen."

Mato thought about the ridiculousness of the story he was considering to express.

Chapter 32

"I don't even believe the entire thing myself," Mato began. "Maybe that's the problem."

Mato for the second time in his life told his entire story. He told the priest about the wolves and their chase and his tree. But now, that part of story was only half the amazing tale. Then he told the priest about his baba's bible, and the additional book that lived inside. He told him about the wisps and the gifts they give. He told him about how she believed them to be real. That she believed his tree to be more than just a tree. Then Mato explained, to his dismay, his once hardheaded father now believed in all of this nonsense too, and expected him to believe it as well. "And that is my story," Mato concluded. With the story complete, the Priest simply sat there staring out in front of them, in a contemplative state. "Well," Mato sneered, "Lud, right?"

"Fantastic," the priest muttered. "Fantastic."

Mato become slightly nervous at the Priest's response. "Too fantastic, right?" Mato asked, almost hoping the priest would laugh at him and then leave him be.

The priest continued to sit and ponder the situation. And after a few moments, he spoke. "You know, what?" Pero began, "Many people say they believe in God and the Bible. But a lot of them, even in this congregation, say that some of its content is unbelievable. What do you think?"

Mato shrugged his shoulders, unsure of the way to answer.

"Fair enough," Pero mused. "Since you seem undecided, do you mind if I share what I think?

Uncertain of what the Father wanted to say, Mato politely nodded.

"I like the whole book. Even the parts that aren't easy to understand."

Mato looked at the priest incredulously.

"Smirk if you want," Pero continued. "But not every part of the great book is very clear to everyone. At least not to me. After all, God is a mystery. But like I said, I like all of it."

Mato straightened up. He remembered that the second verse

Baba quoted had the word mystery in it. This left him intrigued enough to continue.

"Okay, Father, why do you like all the books then?"

The priest smiled. "Thank you for asking, Mato. I'll tell you. I kind of think God's an all-or-nothing type. I think He likes us to believe or not. He didn't make us incomplete. He made us all pretty much the same. Sure, we have a few little differences to keep things interesting, but my point is God wasn't making us one day, and just decide to stop half way."

Mato shook his head," I don't understand."

"You don't huh?" Pero scoffed. "My point is if He didn't complete us halfway, then why would He commission some of the books we like or understand, and with others outsource them to some confused stranger? No, I think those books are all real." In finishing his statement, Father Pero had a question. "Can I share another thing with you?"

Mato had never met a priest that liked to talk so much. Nor had he met one he liked more. "Sure," Mato mused.

The young priest pulled an old tattered bible out of his pocket. "This was my father's. I like it because I can carry it around with me." He flicked through the pages, to the end of the book. "Ever read Revelation?" Pero asked.

Mato shook his head.

"It is very interesting, even though many find it confusing. It's confusing because it about the future. It is a story that focuses on what heaven looks like," the priest explained. "Now, where's the verse? Ah ha, here it is. I'm reading from Revelation 4:8,

And the four beasts had each of them six wings about him;
And they were full of eyes within: and they rest not day and night, saying,
Holy, holy, holy, LORD God Almighty, which was, and is, and is to come."

Mato looked at the priest. "You believe those animals exist?"

It now was Pero's turn to look incredulous, "Of course, and do you know why?" he asked.

"No, why?" Mato blurted.

"Because of elephants," Pero answered.

Chapter 32

"Elephants?" Mato mocked.

"Yes elephants," Pero repeated. "When I wonder about those creatures in Revelation, I think about the first Europeans in Africa, and I wonder what they believed in, and if they thought those verses were crazy, before they set their eyes on elephants. But you know what Mato, it's more than that."

Mato edged forward in his seat.

"I believe in those creatures. I believe in the beginning of the book in Genesis, and the ending in Revelation, because herein lies the full mystery of God. The mystery is we don't know everything. We haven't seen everything. There are so many amazing things. In Heaven, and sometimes, here on Earth too." The priest let those words hang for a while. And then continued. "Let me ask you one more thing, Mato, and then I'll leave you alone."

"Sure," Mato offered.

"It's about your grandmother. Was she a God-fearing woman?"

"Very much," answered Mato with certainty.

"Did she pray, fast, and praise God?"

"Yes, every day."

"Did she live in a manner that wanted to please God?"

"Da,"

"Was she nice to you, and your family?" the priest continued.

"Very much."

"Did she give you good advice? Did she take care of you?"

"Da," Mato answered, wondering when the supposed one question might end.

"And other people in your village too?"

"Da,"

"Well, then, there it is," the priest surmised. "The Bible says you will know Christians by their fruit."

"Okay?" Mato asked, confused.

"Matthew 7:16 my boy! Let me speak plainly so you can be done with me. By your very own account, your grandmother was a brilliant woman. You could almost say she was your family's Tisovina." It was then Mato remembered where he heard the word

Tisovina before. That was what Verka once called his tree. It was then what the priest had been saying hit him like a ton of steel.

"Yes. She was either a Tisovina, or she was crazy! And if she was crazy, then that would make your father crazy too. And finally, if they are crazy, then you might as well call yourself crazy as well and get it over and done with. But…" the Priest paused for less than second, "I wouldn't call you crazy."

"Oh," Mato began scoffing at himself. "What would you call me then?"

Pero laughed.

"Somewhere in between foolish and blessed," he mocked with total seriousness.

-33-

Karta¹

Even after Pero departed, Mato remained entrenched, contemplating every aspect of his sticky situation. Like a toad on a lily pad, he just could not *"riddup, riddup"* even after his family had decided it was time to go home.

Finally though, as fate would have it, it smacked him right up the head. Dizzily, Mato realized the state of things and summarily accepted it. With this tucked under his hat, Mato removed himself from the pew, crossed himself with the sign of a sword, and then muttered, "I know what I'm to do." With the words hanging in the air like incense, he walked out into the dark.

As he hopped down the road, Mato kept nodding to himself, as if to confirm what he was thinking. Mato occasionally repeated, "I know what I must do." The more he did this, the more Mato walked with a focused purpose.

With what felt like only minutes, but obviously was not, Mato returned to Pavlovići. There, Verka greeted him, with a voice filled with anxious worry. "You're finally home. Are you well?"

"Yes, dear," Mato began. "I've never been better. Where's Tata?"

"I think he's in his workshed," she replied, somewhat confused

---

1 Map

by the excitement in Mato's voice. "He said he needed to grab some things for you. When we got home, he started acting quite strange. Even more so, I mean."

"There's nothing wrong with him. I need to get some things too," Mato noted.

Verka could tell Mato appeared distracted. "What is going on, Mato?"

Mato walked over to his wife, and kissed her on the forehead. "You'll know soon, enough. I'll be upstairs. Call me when Tata comes back inside."

Just as Mato started up the stairs, Mijo walked through the front door. "Mato, your father's inside," Verka said sarcastically.

"Where you going son?" Mijo asked. "Going to pack?"

Mato stood, looking at his father, surprised. "How did you know?"

"Never mind that," Mijo replied. "I've got some things for you. Here."

From behind Mato's back, he pulled out a rather large book. It was covered with a heavy binding, covered with thick hardcover, wrapped in old paper and string. Mato took it from Mijo's hands. "Open it," Mijo pleaded. "Don't worry, it won't bite." Mato took the oversized volume.

"I lot of hard work and love went into that book," Mijo proclaimed.

"Who wrote it?" Mato asked. "Another book by Baba?"

"No, it's not. Open it and look," Mijo suggested.

Mato sat at the kitchen table and scanned through it. Within seconds, he knew whose book it was.

"How did this happen?"

"Well," Mijo began. "You worked so hard canvasing out all the different aspects of the Sutjeska, I thought it was crazy just to leave them lying around in heaps." Mato looked intently at his father. The book was all of Mato's maps. "I placed them in order as much as I could. I hope it's okay?" Mijo offered sheepishly.

"No, no, don't trouble yourself. It's perfect." Mato gushed. "How did you…?"

"Oh, why did I put it together? I figured one day you might need it. You're going after it, aren't you?"

Mato looked up from his book with a focus. The reality of what Mato was about to embark on hit him with full force. And what more, from the way he asked, his father knew.

"Yes," Mato answered directly.

"When?"

"Tonight."

"Where are you going?" Verka asked, incredulously. She had been standing off to the side, attempting to garner some semblance of understanding. The room was waiting for Mato to answer Verka's question, but he just left it hanging out to dry.

"Where are you going tonight, husband of mine?" Verka asked once more.

"He's going after the wolf, Verka," Mijo interjected. "And honestly, it's about time. But he isn't going yet. Not without some necessary supplies."

Verka wanted to shriek at Mato! And at Mijo, who seemed to be in total agreement with what was about to occur. Verka didn't understand. She feared for her husband, and for herself. While he was in the army, and then in military prison, Verka dreaded the worst, haunted that Mato might not return. And now, as she looked over her husband forlornly, Verka wondered if he ever did. That was when she realized what she had to do. Verka got up out of her chair and sat next to her husband. And while squeezing his hand, she said in the calmest voice she could muster, "Look, I have only one question, and the question is why?"

Mato looked back at her, with watering eyes. He wanted to tell her that the One had been hunting him long before the night in the tree, and it had been hunting him ever since. That perhaps it had been hunting his family for generations. But Mato did not know if she was ready for another verbose tale, however factual it was. He doubted he had the energy anyway. Mato knew he was in no shape to go after the One. He was not the young man he once was. He had not run over the hills for years. He had not hiked in the forest or added to his book of maps for an age. But, as he contemplated his options, Mato knew he had no choice. Not now. He could not wait any longer. The truth stared at him, and called him by name. He had to go! Vjera's book confirmed it. Mijo's actions confirmed it. A priest did not dismiss it. And because of all of this and more, Mato could not stubbornly fight off the need to do this any longer.

"I must go Verka," Mato began with a desperate whisper. "I need to go, so tomorrow night, I might finally rest."

Verka looked at her Mato, and she completely understood. "Okay," she muttered, fighting tears. "You go then, and come back to me safe, you hear?"

"Yes, I will," Mato noted, with complete conviction. The two embraced with sincerity neither had felt since Mato had first gone into the army. Somehow, for perhaps a fleeting moment, her sadness was replaced with a flint speck of joy. This however was interrupted by a cough.

"Well, I don't want to disturb," Mijo began, showing a cheeky smile, "but we have work to do. Did you look over the maps?" he asked.

"Tata, I don't need to," Mato mused. "I know where the coward lives. Up beyond the gray crags."

Mijo nodded in agreement. "Good. But before you go, you'll need some arms."

It was then Mato and Verka noticed Mijo's hands were loaded with items. Firstly, Mato passed along a relic of a rifle. "This was your grandfather's," Mijo began. "It's old, but I have taken great care of it, and it will do the job if need be." Mato slung its strap over his shoulder. It felt heavy on his back, but it also felt strong.

"Good, I am ready then," Mato, proclaimed, eager to go.

"Not so fast," Mijo replied. "I have other things for you." Mijo handed Mato a bow and a quiver of arrows. Mato's eyes lit up. They looked brand new.

"Where did you get these?" Verka asked with astonishment.

"What do you think I have been doing in my workshop all these years? Sleeping? I made them. From good wood, too." Mijo looked over at Mato. "If it gets too cold tonight for my Tata's gun, then these will do the trick."

"Thank you," Mato offered. "This is a brilliant gift."

"I have one more thing for you, son," Mijo noted, as he ran out to the door. "It's in the workshop. I will be right back."

As Mijo leaped out the door, Mato was astonished by the spring in his father's step. Mijo looked like he was having fun. Too much fun.

"I wonder if he refurbished the Sutjeska canon, too?" Mato offered to Verka. They both laughed.

Just as the two of them finished their little joke, Mijo returned with what looked like a staff of some kind.

"Son," Mijo offered, with what Mato thought looked like trembling hands. "I hope this staff keeps you safe once again." Mato took the staff and looked it over. It looked, somehow vaguely familiar. "Tata, what do you mean a…?" Mato began, but he stopped mid sentence, for something caught his eye. On the staff, there was an inscription,

"*M.P > WOLF,*" Mato read with a whisper.

Mato looked up at his father.

"Where did you get this? How did you…?"

"Where it lay, son," Mijo offered. "What you're thinking is right. The staff is made of the wood from your tree. So is the bow and arrows. I hope you don't mind?"

Mato dropped the staff, and embraced his father, harder and more intently then he had in his entire life. But an awfully troubling thought sprang upon Mato. It was then Mato wondered if it was his father who cut the tree down after all? Before he could ponder this notion any longer, he shook it off. These concerns were further brushed away as his father spoke with boldness. "Verka," Mijo began. "Prepare your husband some food. He's going to need it. He's going hunting!"

Within ten minutes, Mato was packed and out the door. He looked up at the sky. It was gray like the crags he was setting forth to reach. There was a bite in the air that Mato had not felt for weeks.

"What's the matter?" Verka asked, standing by the front door.

"It's about to start snowing," Mato replied.

"Really? It's the second month of spring, Mato," Verka exclaimed.

Mato turned to face his wife, "Tell that to the snow."

Just then, the heavens opened and down fell winter's late coming deluge.

"I guess you're not going then," Verka suggested hopefully.

Mato stretched out his arms, and embraced the elements falling onto him, and smiled. "You're not going still, are you?" Verka asked again, more forcefully.

"Verka," Mato began. "Wake up the children."

"Why?"

"Wake them up and dress them so they can come out and play. It's not often it snows like this in May."

As he waited for his little ones, Mato continued to study the sky, allowing the flakes to collide with his exposed face. Stretching out his arms, Mato soaked in the elements, and embraced what the mountains wished to give him. Mato understood Verka's reservations. Finding and then killing the beast was going to be difficult enough, even without winter aiding the enemy. In reality, Mato understood his mission would be nigh impossible. Sure, he knew the mountains, but the creature was going to know them far better. Deep down, Mato knew he was grossly outmatched. He knew there was a chance he was not coming back.

But tonight, none of these facts could matter. Mato would not allow fear to shape his mind. "*If it lives in us, then we have been given the right tools to be its masters,*" Mijo had written. And tonight, Mato knew it to be true. Just then Mato turned around, distracted by the sweet sound of his daughter's excitement. "Tata, Tata, It's snowing!" Kata squealed. "It's snowing a lot!"

It certainty was! An inch had already accumulated. Scooping a handful, Mato hurled it playfully toward Kata, missing on purpose, but showing his intentions. "Tata," Kata exclaimed. "That's not nice."

Mato laughed. "Sorry, *Sinko*². I promise not to miss next time."

"Oh, Tata," Kata proclaimed, gathering her father's meaning.

---

2 An affectionate way to refer to your daughter or son

Chapter 33

She ran towards Mato as fast as her shorter limbs could muster, tackling him to the snow. On the ground, Mato tickled his daughter unmercifully, until she could not take it any longer. With this, Mato suggested they should build a snowman. Eagerly agreeing, while the rest of the village slept, two generations enjoyed the gift the mountain gave as if it was just for them. For the next thirty-five minutes they worked feverishly, as if nothing else mattered. After their work was done, they both stood silent, hand-in-hand looking at their efforts.

"Not bad," Mato offered. "What do you think, Kata?"

"What do I think? This!" Kata replied, launching a snowball that hit Mato in the right shoulder. "Ha, Ha. I got you!" she laughed.

"Why you," Mato said with fake crossness. In a single stride Mato swooped up his daughter, and once again began tickling her. This wonderful silliness continued for a few moments longer, until Kata became very solemn.

"What is it, Kata?" Mato asked with concern.

"You going to go kill some wolves now?" she asked.

"Only one, dearest," Mato replied.

Kata paused and pondered what she was going to say next. Finally, she asked the only question that mattered. "Why, Tata?"

"Well," Mato began. "Because I must."

Kata looked at her father and considered his reply with confusion. "I don't understand," she confirmed.

Mato laughed. "I did not expect you to."

"Hey, Tata?" Kata exclaimed. "Have you ever noticed that when the snow falls, it looks like it is dancing in the sky?" Mato smiled. He looked at his daughter. He always knew she was beautiful, but there was wisdom in her eyes he had not noticed before. It was a wisdom that reminded him of his grandmother.

"No," Mato said with wonder. "No I haven't. Would you like to dance, Sinko?"

"Da," Kata replied with love. And the two of them proceeded to spin and spin, like a Kolo of old.

"Hey, Kata," Mato began, as thoughts drifted upon the other members of his family. "I wonder where your mother and brother are?"

"We are right here," Verka offered, having appeared upon the front porch with Pepan sleeping in her arms. Mijo also was with them. "It's time for Kata to come inside."

"And it's time for you to go," Mijo offered.

"Da," Mato said, nodding in agreement.

Dva puta[1]

Mato was ready! As he set out with the staff in hand, he could not help and think about how he now carried the Tisovina that once carried him. As he continued to ponder his long journey through falling flakes, Mato could see another being coming his way. Surprisingly, he knew who it was. "Good evening Mirko," Mato offered.

"More like good morning," Mirko, replied. "Weather's crazy, right?"

"Da," Mato replied. "What are you doing out so late?"

"Ah, visiting friends in Pavlovići. We're cooking something up, for tomorrow."

Mato looked at his brother bemused. "What?"

"Something we should have done a long time ago. Stirring the pot, stirring the pot," he laughed. "Where are you going, little brother?"

Mato pointed towards the gray crags. "Into the mountains."

Mirko's grin turned into concern. "Are you sure? Nothing good lives up there."

"I know," Mato noted.

"I wish you wouldn't."

---

1 Two roads

Mato could smell fear on Mirko's words, "I won't go, under one condition."

"What's that," Mirko asked with curiousness.

"I won't go if you call off your planned mischief," Mato answered.

Mirko quickly shot down the offer. "Sorry, brother, I can't do that. It can't be stopped now anyway." Mirko reflected. "You can't stop the machine."

"Me either," Mato replied with sadness. "Hey, why you so concerned about me anyway? You don't even know where I am going."

"Maybe I do, maybe I don't," Mirko replied. "But I bet it's something to do with your old tree."

Mato put his right arm on Mirko's left shoulder. "Don't worry. I'll be fine."

Mirko nodded. "Brother, please take care. I will see you later, right?"

"Sure," Mato replied, noticing even in the dark, a tear trickling down his Mirko's cheek.

With that, Mato continued his journey past Mirko, for a few seconds at least. After about twenty paces, Mato understood! He understood everything. The tears. The apologies. He turned towards the direction of his brother.

"It was you!" Mato shouted through the falling white wall. "You were in the bushes when I was there with Verka. You cut it down, didn't you? *Didn't you?*"

"I am sorry, Mato," Mirko bellowed back into the darkness. "I was there. I followed you. I wanted to taste from it. I knew what your tree was, even though you didn't. I thought it would be good, but it wasn't. So I had to chop it down! I had to. I had to. I'm so sorry!"

Rage built up within Mato. After all of these years, it was Mirko. It was him! Mato clenched his fists around his staff, ready to inflict pain upon him. With the anger reaching its zenith, Mato charged towards Mirko, ready to do whatever came to his mind first.

But when he reached Mirko, literally in seconds, his anger was gone. Before him stood not his older brother, but a feeble, scared

Chapter 34

little soul, frightened he was about receive what he deserved. At this, Mato remembered meeting General Vukovic face-to-face with his truth, and he wondered if he looked like Mirko looked now. With this realization, only understanding and pity remained.

"I am sorry, Mato, I thought the honey was going to be good, but it wasn't," Mirko whispered.

Mato breathed the apology in. It felt better than he expected. With understanding, its acceptance gave him new clarity.

"I know why it wasn't any good Mirko. I know," Mato exclaimed, while resting his arm on Mirko's shoulder.

"Why?" Mirko asked with a whimper.

"Because, Mirko," Mato began, finally understanding the truth about the Tisovina. "It wasn't your tree. It was mine."

Lovac[1]

Leaving his brother to go his own way, Mato strode, further and further up into the wild. There was much to conquer. Both in action and in thought. With each step closer, Mato was ready to reclaim what was his. With each embedded snow print Mato was closing in on his future. With each footprint, he was more certain of his past.

Mato knew each stride brought him closer and closer toward his prey. Carrying his grandfather's gun for the first time in his life, Mato was the hunter. A hunter, who felt the strength of his family, whether alive or long passed. Mato knew they were all with him, even in this desolate place. It was then Mato truly realized what he was embarking on.

One way or another, he was changing the course of future Pavlović history. Mato sensed the surrounding area knew it too. He could smell a difference in the atmosphere; a frightened panic lived there. Mato knew the fear grew because of him.

This fright added a pop to his step. Without realizing it, Mato's walk had become a trot. Within moments, the trot had added haste. Mato was running! Mato was running up and up. And though Mato's

---

1 Hunter

eyes had never been to this portion of the Sutjeska before, he knew exactly where he was going.

Further up and further in Mato drove, passed the last of the small trees that managed to grow, despite their brittle appearance. Beyond these feeble trees, the area was devoid of life.

"So much closer to the sun, so much further from its warmth," Mato shuddered, realizing where he needed to go. To comfort himself, Mato held his staff more tightly. He was glad his tree was with him once more.

Mato looked up at the horizon. Miles off, the dawn of the new day, and its beautiful work of clear blue sky was readying itself for its daily victory. Yet, the stark reality continued to live above. In this lifeless place, night was still king. Its final twilight was menacingly morbid, hatefully holding onto the darkness. Brownish-gray clouds were enslaved to their position, ready to pour their poison. This threat caused Mato to laugh. Despite the lurking fears, he was ready.

Within eyeshot, he spotted a cave. Without hesitation, he ran right towards it. Within a few dozen strides of its entry point, not a sound stirred, but it did not fool him.

"Come out," he bellowed. "I know you're in there. Come out!"

With Mato's cry, the cave's insides stirred. Mato's senses heightened, imagining a large creature from his terrifying nightmares was lumbering closer. Fear was attempting to return, but he fought against it. "They're my emotions, and I will control them," he muttered to himself. "I must."

Impatiently, he hollered once more. "Dog, get out here now!"

These words rustled the beast and a maundering growl echoed from the cave. Mato readied himself, pulling his grandfather's gun from his shoulder, and cocked it.

"I know you're in there, dog!" he yelled. "Come out and face me!"

"What's your hurry, little Pavlović?" a booming voice growled. "Too scared to wait?"

Mato shuddered. It was the One! He'd forgotten how powerful its voice was. He did not just hear it with his ears, but within his heart and mind. Instinctively, he took a step back, but still with a grim determination to see the night through.

"Come out, dog!" he repeated.

"There's nowhere to hide this time boy," the voice warned.

"I'm not the one who's hiding," Mato replied. Steadying himself, he hoisted the rifle into position. Despite the lingering darkness, it was now or never. With a determined zeal, he pulled the trigger!

Click!

But, nothing happened! Startled, he pulled the trigger once more. *Click!* Again, nothing happened. The rifle refused to fire. A bellowing laughter rose from the cave. A few mangled, deformed wing creatures perched nearby the cave entrance flew away, startled by the growing echo. On and on the laughter went, filling the entire surrounding airspace, and adding unwanted dread in Mato's heart.

"What happened, little Pavlović? Your grandfather's toy didn't work? Hah, no rifle can kill me!"

Mijo could not sleep. He knew morning was coming, but on this day, he would have liked to slumber a little longer than usual. Sitting up, Mijo suspected it was because of a paternal concern for Mato. But as he pondered that conclusion, Mijo knew Mato would be fine, regardless of what met him. Logically, Mijo concluded it must be something else. Still, uncertain of what left him so leery, he removed himself from his room. He was startled what he found. "Verka, draga! What are you doing in my old chair? And with a fire no less!"

"Oh, hello Tata. I couldn't sleep," offered a worried-sounding Verka.

Mijo pulled up a chair and sat by her. Picking up Verka's hand, he attempted to offer comfort.

"You know he will be back soon?" Mijo noted confidently.

Verka clearly was not so certain. "Really?" she reflected. "How can you be so sure?"

Chapter 35

Mijo smiled. "Because I know. You should get some sleep, Verka. The children will be awake soon."

Verka shook her head, "It doesn't matter."

"Really?" Mijo replied, despairing at her pain. He knew he had to act. "Wait here, I'll be right back." Verka nodded in recognition, without removing her fixation on the blaze. Though warm and dry in the comfort of that old beat up chair, Verka was drowning, fearing the worst had befallen Mato. But within moments, Mijo was armed with a life vest to rescue his daughter.

"Verka," he began.

"Yes Tata," Verka offered with minimal notice.

"Verka, please look at me," Mijo requested. "*Ja vas molim.*²" Verka turned to face Mijo, startled that an elder begged anything of her. "You asked why I know Mato will be okay. I'll tell you," he proclaimed confidently. "Living in the mountains, its gifts sometimes seem really, really strange. It took me a long time to get that."

"What does that mean?" Verka interrupted.

"I am trying to explain, dear," Mato continued. "We all have a gift. I have one. Mato has one, though it might seem very strange, it is very real. Verka, you have one too."

"Oh, what is mine?" Verka blurted, doubting Mijo's reasoning.

"I wondered that," Mijo mentioned. "A long time I have watched you. And you know what I have learned, Verka, daughter of mine? I have learned you don't like silence. It's your enemy. And when it stays too long, it brings sadness." It was at this point Mijo picked an item off the floor. Verka was not sure what it was, as it was wrapped in deep red cloth. "I was hoping to give you this once its box was completed, but I think you need it now. Please take it." Verka unwrapped the given item. Within moments her countenance drastically changed for the better.

"How did you know? I mean, how could you?" Verka stammered.

"It's the same reason I know Mato will be okay. Do you like it?"

Though tears filled Verka's eyes, she held the item to her lips, and kissed it. Verka looked at it with disbelief. There in her right

2 I beg you

hand was a meticulously-crafted violin. "Where did you get it?"

"I made it from the same wood that your husband now carries. Do me a favor, Verka."

"Anything," Verka blurted through a stream of tears.

"Play for me, draga Verka," Mato requested.

"But I need a…"

"A bow," Mato laughed. "Here you are," as he passed it over. "Play. Play until your heart is filled with song. Play!"

✹✹✹

Mato looked down at the gun. As he suspected, the cold got to it, rendering it useless. Mato's older instincts for the first time that night, made themselves known, begging him to run. But his heart and feet refused. Something at that moment filled Mato with peace and hope. Mato did not know where it came from, but he knew it gave him the strength not to back down.

"Come out and get it over with. Or are you afraid, wolf?" Mato growled. The cave snarled, adding to the smile on Mato's face. "Ah c'mon dog. You're afraid of me, aren't you?"

Mato could see the creature coming out of the cave slowly. Amazingly, though Mato knew the creature looked like the One, it appeared so much smaller than before. He wondered if his eyes were playing tricks, or whether his youth added dimensions at their original encounter that were never there. Suddenly, another more pressing notion occurred to Mato. "Wolf, where are your minions?"

The question hung in the air unanswered. Mato quickly realized the truth. "Don't tell me you are all alone, wolf?" Mato mocked. "Did they all leave you?"

The beast again snarled, baring its teeth. But this time, it had no effect. Alarmed by the lack of a fearful response, it was the wolf that now looked frightened.

Mato peered at the creature, bemused. It appeared to be aging before his very eyes. Could this really be the creature he was looking for?

Chapter 35

"You can't kill me," barked the wolf once more. "It is I who destroy. It is I who hunt. It is I who debilitate. It is I who haunt. I do, because I can," The One howled.

Mato chuckled. Collecting his bow and arrow, Mato readied a shot. "Not anymore," Mato remarked with defiance.

But the wolf was still cunning. It noticed Mato's strength. So it did the only thing available to it: it fled. Towards a cluster of boulders and rocks it made its attempted escape. Surprised by this tact, Mato chased after it. Quickly, Mato jumped into high gear, as if he returned to his glorious youth. Though mindful of a trap, Mato knew the wolf's tact proved it was weakening, and time was on his side. Mato was ready to run for however long he needed.

Down and down the mountain Mato ran. Away from the stark gray crags, and back into the woods and closer to lands and nooks that he knew well. Mato could tell he was slowly but surely gaining on his four-footed foe. On and on he ran. Mato ran like his life dependent on it, or the wolf's death dependent on it. He could not stop now. Though his aging lungs and legs did not wish to go on, Mato refused to allow his effort to wane. As he ran, he took a moment to look at his surrounds. He had been in this place before.

Just then, Mato saw it. The One was a hundred meters away. Mato ran right towards it, bow and arrow at the ready. As Mato stalked in closer he could tell its breathing was labored.

"Do you know where we are, boy?" the wolf wheezed, seemly unable to go on.

Mato looked around once more, recognizing it at once. "Yeah, this is nearby where my tree once lived."

"That's right. Before I had it knocked down," the One mocked.

"It wasn't you," Mato replied. "I know who did it, but that's over."

"It's never over!" the One gasped. "There's always another tree. Another time. Like your brother's boats. Like your dungeon."

"Mato shook his head, disbelieving. "How do you…?"

"I know," it sneered. "That is why you can't kill me."

The beast mustered one last charge. But Mato was ready. He flexed his bow back as far as it would bend. He was done with conversation. He was done with the lies. He was done with the evil's reasoning. Mato was ready to shoot.

Verka placed her violin up to her chin, and placed the bow upon its strings, ready to play her muse.

"Tata, this is Paganini's "*La Campanella,*"" she pronounced, with tears still in her eyes. Verka pulled back her bow. Mijo smiled.

✳✳✳

"I already told you, boy. You can't kill me," the wolf mocked in seeing Mato's bow. "Especially with your little twig shooter." Unperturbed, Mato let an arrow fly. With haste, Mato readied another. But before Mato shot his brace, the wolf slumped to the floor.

"How? What?" it gasped. "I can't be killed by any little twig."

"That isn't any twig," Mato corrected the wounded brute. And as he did, Mato let the second arrow rip through the air, hitting the wolf right between the eyes.

"I can't be killed," the wolf yelled definitely. "I can't be…"

Mato ran up to it. The One slumped deeper into the surface, and lay there, defeated! In disbelief, Mato quickly got out another arrow, just to be sure. But before the arrow danced into flesh, the beast shriveled up, and turned into a small mound of greyish dust.

Mato exhaled. "It is done," he said, not yet believing it. Within moments, his words spoke a resonating truth. "It's done! All done!" he yelled, scaring a dozen finches off their perch. Jubilant, Mato began to dance for joy. Around and around he circled, yelping with glee. "It's done! It's done!" Mato repeated, over and over. Faster and faster he circled, until he collapsed with dizzy tiredness.

Settling himself on the turf, Mato noticed a tussle of trees about twenty yards away. Three trees stood out in particular. Two of the trees were strong aged spruces. Between them, stood a little tree that seemed less than a few years old. "No, it couldn't be?" Mato rushed up to the cluster. "It is!" he exclaimed.

Amazingly, in the spot where once sat his Tisovina, was a newly growing tree. Though it was not more than ten feet high, it looked like a smaller version of the tree that once saved his skin. Mato had to climb and sit in it. Though its limbs did not look particularly sturdy, he believed it would be deceptively strong. And thankfully, Mato was right!

Mato sat halfway up, amazed at his evening's outcome. The wolf was dead, and his tree was alive! But, was it his tree? It sure looked like it. Mato laid his head back on the trunk, and did an amazing thing. At least for him. He fell asleep. Mato slept in a way he hadn't in ages. His sleep had dreams. They were not sadistic nightmares of terror and turmoil. They were pleasant. They were adventurous. They were of faraway places. Of lands and possibilities. His sweet dreams were of new cultures and different languages. Of countries Mato once pondered and hoped to visit. While nestled in the young tree, Mato slept for the first time in over twelve years. In this new sleep, Mato was introduced to peace and gladness. He slept the rest of the morning away. Even when the sun arrived, he continued to sleep and the mountain was glad for him to do so.

Mato slept, that is, until he heard and awful crash in the distance. This crash, made him fall out of the small tree, landing him hard on his side. Gladly, there was still a small filament of soft snow ready to break his fall. It however, did not break his curiosity. "What was that?" he wondered. This question terrorized his heart, as answers came crashing in.

"Mirko, what have you done?"

To što je on učinio[1]

"Please," Mato pleaded with the wind, "Please don't let me be right. *Jas vas molim.[2]*"

Mato tore towards Pavlovići. He knew where the crash came from. Disaster stuck the mine! Nothing else could make such a horrific sound. Worse still, Mirko's notion of needed mischief plagued Mato's speedy travels. Tears and dread hurtled down the fields. The parading flowers looked so innocent and oblivious to the new way of things.

Though tiring, within minutes, Pavlovići was in sight. From it, Mato could hear the sounds of panicked neighbors. No doubt they heard the blast from the pit as well. As Mato rushed into Pavlovići's boundaries, he could surprisingly also hear Mozart being played on a violin. Mato burst into his home, he hunched over, his lungs begging for air. As Mato looked up, he found Verka standing upright, holding the aforementioned instrument. Mijo was sitting nearby, with both the children at his feet.

"Verka," Mato gasped. "Where did you get the violin?"

"Mato," Verka beamed, rushing over to embrace him. "You're alive. You're well?"

1 What he had done
2 I beg you

Chapter 36

"Da."

"Tata," Kata interjected, from across the room. "Did you get it?"

"Yes, I did, and I'll tell you all about it, later. Tata," Mato said solemnly, turning to his father, "The Mountain, it erupted."

"I know. Haljinići."

"Have either of you heard any news?" Mato asked.

"No son," Mijo confessed.

"I need to know. People from this village might be hurt."

"Please be careful," Verka demanded.

"I will."

As he dropped his returning belongings, Mato left only holding his staff. As he was about to re-exit the front door, Mato turned to his father. "If you hear from Mirko, tell him to meet me at Baba's grave."

"Why would I hear from Mirko?" Mijo demanded.

"Just do it. I'll explain later."

Towards the exploding mine he shot. Mato ran like Mirko's life depended on it. Looking towards the mine, a massive blackened gray cloud hung near its peak. Forlornly, Mato knew this tragedy would stay long after the mountain winds pushed the smog and haze away. Though miles away, Mato could hear alarms and sirens that yelled fear and terror. The graveness of the situation was growing within his belly. As each stride brought him closer, Mato knew he was running towards a war zone.

At the scene, pandemonium reigned. Men wrapped in madness, were shouting frightened phrases towards all points of a compass. Everything was out of control. Despite the chaos, Mato focused. With his Tisovina still in his grip, he sprinted towards the mines main entrance. Young boys, in old military uniforms, were barricading it. Beyond the standard garb of authority, each of them was armed with weapons, and a visible disposition of wishing not to be there. As Mato ran right up to them, he knew this was the most dangerous thing of all. One of them, a lad whose face Mato doubted had ever visited with a razor, stepped forward, curtly reminding Mato that he was not permitted to move beyond them. He also disliked Mato's staff.

"Hey, drop that weapon!" he barked.

"It's not a weapon; it's my walking staff, that's all."

"I said, *drop it*!"

Mato laid it down, informing the increasingly agitated soldiers that he worked at the mine, and that his brother could be down there. As Tito's finest continued to verbally accost Mato, he saw the severity of the wreckage. The army soldiers did not need to be there to begin the cover up, as the entry point was completely blocked. Boulders bigger than those carried by Atlas lay where a gaping hole used to be. "Somebody has to be digging out that opening!" Mato bellowed.

It was at this point the soldiers began redefining Mato's visitation rights. Their boisterous leader prodded Mato to move back. Knowing bodily harm was fast approaching Mato knew it was no use. Mato reasoned with himself that the answers to his questions lived elsewhere. So while never taking his eyes off them, Mato slowly backed away from the newly protected tomb, picked up his staff, and bid them a good day. Then after ten back-shuffle paces, Mato hastily turned, and fled.

Quickly, Mato found his next point of interest. Thirty yards away, he saw a makeshift tent; he knew often played the role of a temporary mess hall. Leaning on a hunch that scraps of food had been replaced by morsels of information, Mato quietly slipped inside.

Rapidly, Mato wished he had not gone in. In the tent, he saw more of the mines destruction. A dozen bodies lay upon tattered fabrics that were acting as makeshift gurneys. Covering his face to block the nauseating odor, Mato selfishly scanned each stretcher. Guilt swept over him as gladness swelled; Mirko was not in there! However, Mato recognized a face from the village. Josip, an older cousin, who lived four houses down, regretfully was. Mato knew he was in bad shape. Blood coursed through a bandaged head wound. His limbs were covered by coal and more blood. As Mato moved over to him, Josip noticed his visitor, and strained unsuccessfully to sit up. "Please lay back down, Josip," Mato insisted. "Can you talk?"

"Da," Josip blurted, through clenched teeth.

"Josip," Mato began, knowing time was running short. "What happened?"

Chapter 36

"The fools," Josip said, through a hoarse cough. "Fools. Idiots! We told them the levels were too high. How many times, Mato? How many?"

Mato nodded, knowing the number was numerous.

"Da, da, many times. Just last night too," Josip continued. "Again, the gas levels were too high. But they didn't listen. They never do. They sent the next shift in anyway."

"*Bože moj*,[3] help us" Mato replied. "How many were down there?"

"At least fifty," Josip replied, through another coughing fit. This time his coughs brought up an unhealthy mixture of coal, spit, and new blood.

"Mato, you need to tell my wife, my children," he wheezed, grabbing Mato's hand.

"Josip. You'll tell her later, over a rakija with my Tata," Mato interjected, refusing to listen to fears.

Josip laughed. "Your father never liked my rakija."

Mato smiled, knowing that was true. He asked one last question. "Tell me, how many are still down there?"

"I don't know," Josip whispered. "Some got out in time. How many? Not enough."

Mato was frantic, thoughts of his brother hammered against him.

"Mirko!" Mato blurted. "Have you seen Mirko?"

"No. Not since the explosion," Josip replied. "I don't know. I'm sorry."

As Josip continued to cough and sputter, a pushy stranger in a white coat demanded Mato leave at once, blurting that his presence there was upsetting the dead. Mato wanted to remind the quack that it was the explosion that had done this, but as it was with the soldiers, arguing was futile.

"Josip, get some rest old man," Mato noted in the direction of his wounded neighbor, knowing those might be the final words Josip heard.

---

3 "My God." As it is used it is a not a curse, but rather a sincere call to the divine.

Undaunted, Mato continued to scrap for information. In the following hours he had rushed from place to place, it was confirmed that seven were dead, and a dozen were unaccounted for, most likely trapped inside. The twelve from the mess tent, including Josip, were sent to the local hospital, possibly to die in more sanitary confines. An equal mixture of sadness and hope danced within Mato. Mirko was not officially accounted for.

With no more to be done at the front, Mato rushed back home, hoping his family had gotten better information. As he returned to Pavlovići, each face Mato saw told a story of grim despair. Returning exhausted, his family rushed upon him for news. Giving them the fragments he knew, Mato in turn learned that Mirko's whereabouts were still unknown. Mijo fell to the floor, sobbing. Mato, however, would not have his brave father succumb to the notions of the worst. "Tata, I will find him," Mato promised. "I know he's alive. I know it!"

Without knowing his exact course of action, Mato flew back out the door. A headless chicken, he inquired of every soul he bumped into. Alas, nothing came of it. Nobody knew anything more than he already knew. When those Mato met learned he had been at Haljinići's door, they understandably demanded news about their loved ones. Everyone was in such a panicked state. It was dreadful. Mato began to doubt his belief that Mirko was alive.

He needed to think it through, but every moment was a second too valuable. Mato's desperation demanded action. His frantic running found him out beyond the main square, and near the Gaj, right by the stream. He ventured closer to the water and threw some liquid on his face. Mato felt mildly revived, enough at least to repeat this action until his shirt shared in his face's drenching.

In this quieter setting, Mato's mind began to relax. He stood up and looked over at the cluster of the Gaj's trees. Then he remembered the graveyard, and how Baba and his Mama lay there peacefully. Mato needed to be somewhere where peace reigned. Maybe, Mato thought, Mirko would need the same thing too. His insight or perhaps the search for peace served him well. As Mato approached the tombstones, he found Mirko right before Vjera's grave, with a flower in his hand, fast asleep.

As younger brothers do, Mato playfully wanted to ruin Mirko's slumber. But, before he set his plan into attack, Mato was alarmed to find a viper slithering right for Mirko. Still holding his Tisovina, Mato sprung towards the beast, and as if he was swinging a sickle, struck evil with all mustered force. Mato's successful effort flung the monster high into the air, as if it unnaturally gained the ability of flight. Watching it carefully, Mato saw the rules of gravity return the creature to its normal station. A clunk confirmed that it heavily struck against a healthy spruce, some twenty feet away, slumping upon the Sutjeska's surface, devoid of life. This action finally awoke the sleeping beauty. "Mato," Mirko began. "Good evening."

"Good evening," Mato replied, full of agitation. "What did you do? Do you know what happened?"

"Yes, I know," he answered calmly. "Horrible day."

Mato looked upon his brother. He did not like Mirko's calm tone. He did not like finding him sleeping, as if the entire world was fine. He got to the point. "Your pot stirring. Was it at Haljinići?"

"Yes," Mirko replied, regaining his footing. Mato boiled; his mountain was ready to burst. Springing forward, with complete disgust, for the first time in his life, he struck his brother. Back down to the ground Mirko fell.

"How could you?" Mato asked, shaking the pain off his hand. "How could you?"

Dumbstruck, Mirko wiped the trickling claret from his growing lip.

"What was that for?" he demanded.

"How could you?" Mato raged. "People we know. People we lived with? Haljinići."

"Yes Haljinići," Mirko puzzled, "And Kakanj, Vareš, Pavlovići, and even Sarajevo. We hit them all." Mato did not understand. "What are you talking about?"

"What are you talking about?" Mirko replied.

"The mine, it blew," Mato answered.

"I know," Mirko replied. Then he began to understand. "Wait, you think I had something to do with that?" he asked.

"That's what you just said," Mato replied.

Mirko staggered to his feet. It was then Mato noticed an empty bottle of rakija.

"You've been drinking?" Mato proclaimed with disgust.

"Yeah, but don't worry. I poured most of it out," Mirko confided.

Mirko began to walk away from Mato. Turning, he asked if his brother, "was coming?"

"Where? " Mato protested.

"Come, you'll see," Mirko replied, without even looking back to answer.

Mirko walked ahead without saying a word. Mato followed, with a million choice phrases bouncing in his mind. They walked back towards the village, right toward the middle of the square, where the magistrate's office resided. Mirko stopped, and pointed towards the office door.

"There," Mirko said.

"What are you talking about?" Mato replied, not attempting to hide is agitation.

"Look," Mirko demanded.

So Mato looked. He squinted. It was late, making visibility difficult. When he finally took a few steps forward, Mato saw a poster on the door. He stepped even closer to read its words.

Tito, Vani! Bosna nije tvoje.[4]

It was surprising to see this on the office door. Mato turned to Mirko, to find him looking ashamed.

"That was the big mischief," he began. "This is what our big band of brave rebels came up with. This was our big effort all over Bosnia. Big deal, right?" Mirko asked and then answered with the shake of the head. "So big a deal, the authorities didn't even take it down. What a joke we are."

"So you didn't?" Mato began.

"What do you think I am?" Mirko replied, disappointed that his brother could think that little of him. Mato did not have the words

---

4 Tito out! Bosnia is not yours.

to answer this question properly. And before he could muster them, a vehicle, a rarity in the mountains, came roaring towards them. Its abrupt presence startled both brothers. The car screeched to a halt, and out jumped three military police. One of the officials blurted out a name.

"Mirko Pavlović," he barked.

"I am he," Mirko replied calmly.

"We need you to come with us," he commanded.

"Why" Mato blurted with fear.

"Haljinići," he answered.

"But," Mato stammered.

"Don't worry, Mato," Mirko interrupted "It will be fine."

Mato did not believe him, but he knew he had to relent. "Okay, I'll wait for you here," he offered.

Mato waited. For six hours he waited. There was nothing more for it. He refused to leave. His promise was set in stone. However, this promise did not stop sleep overcoming him. Mato's slumber sent him traveling far and wide, just as it had earlier in the day while he rested in the new tree. In Mato's new dream, he recognized that it was Christmas time. And though it was a Wednesday, he was not at work, In fact, no one was at work. Each family was enjoying the day's celebrations. What further surprised him, though it was Christmas, there was no snow on the ground. It was actually quite warm. Mato could see he was wearing a short sleeve shirt. The children were wearing skirts and shorts respectfully. Verka was wearing a pretty flower dress.

As Mato's dream continued, at the edge of their festive celebrations, Mato could see white sand and blue sea. Furthermore, strange creatures he had never seen before were upon this sand, making the entire family giggle with glee. And as they shuffled towards Mato, they said hello to each family member. Just as Mato was to answer the creatures, his subconscious was rustled, alerting him that someone was nearby. Mato knew who it was. "Mirko," he blurted, opening one eye. "They let you go?"

"Da, just a little while ago. So," Mirko smirked. "You couldn't wait up, huh?"

"What time is it?" Mato asked, disorientated.

"It's almost daybreak," he replied. "Let's get you home. The family will be worried."

Both fatigued, the brothers shuffled slowly side-by-side towards their childhood home. The sun, as it always had done, crashed upon the sky's darkness, demanding the beginning of a new morn.

"Mirko, what did they want?" Mato asked, breaking the ice.

"They wanted to know what I knew. Everything is fine," Mirko replied.

"Mirko." he began, nervously.

"Yeah,"

"I beg you for your forgiveness," Mato offered sheepishly. Mirko stopped walking, forcing Mato to do the same. Mirko looked at his brother and smiled. He ruffled Mato's hair.

"Don't worry about it, okay."

"Okay," Mato said, with a relaxing smile.

It was then three neighbors rushed upon them, interrupting their peace. So much that so Mato almost sprung upon them with his staff, until he realized they were all crying. "Hvala[5] Mirko. Thank you, thank you, thank you," they all wailed simultaneously. Mato was shocked. One planted kisses all over Mirko's face, while the other two were shaking each of Mirko's hands. Having seen enough, Mato demanded to understand the meaning of all of this.

"Oh, you don't know," one replied. "Your brother's a hero! He was the one who ran into the mine and warned the men to get out. Because of him, twenty-four got out alive."

---

5 Thank you

Novi Dan[1]

For the next three years, the appearance of normalcy returned. After the cleanup, Mirko and Mato, having no great alternative, returned to the mine. They worked on and under Haljinići, despite its dangers. Of the awful incident, evidence was brought forward that found the foreman and supervisors guilty of gross incompetence, causing the loss of twenty-eight lives. Eight of the twenty-eight who died were from Pavlovići, including Josip. To honor him, Mijo promised never to drink another drop of rakija again. The national party honored the dead by sending the management to prison, but then quietly released them only two years later. It was rumored their release was because of good Communist behavior.

Events at Haljinići dug up criminals and local heroes in equal measure, particularly Mirko. Not that his efforts were ever officially recognized. After all, the state would not award a medal of bravery to former military felon. Not that Mirko cared. People from all over the mountains, from all of the local villages showered him with wines, plum brandy and all manner of foodstuffs. His larder was so full that he wondered if he ever had to purchase another crumb again.

---

1 New Day

Life continued for every member of the mountains. Each day, Mato went to Haljinići with prayers on his lips and the Tisovina staff in his hand, hoping that each might keep him safe for another day. Then every night he slept soundly, with a smile on his face, as he dreamed of distant places. The rest of his time he spent in his mountains with his family. He would explore, racing eagle or deer across the hills with youthful glee.

Mato was glad to learn that both Kata and Pepan loved to run and explore their surrounds. Every second Saturday the three of them would gather their belongings early and trek far and deep into the hills. They would traverse. They would hike. They would seek. Then they would sleep under a large oak. They would pluck lunch right off the branches. They would splash by the refreshing waters. All in all, the children were getting a hardy education and Mato was learning to love his home all over again. Once, Mato even took Kata and Pepan to where the new tree grew in place of his Tisovina.

"Whose tree is that then, Tata?" Kata asked.

"I don't know," Mato replied honestly.

While the three of them journeyed over the Sutjeska, Verka would be content at home with her muse. As she played, Verka thought of her past, and the increasingly delightful present. Every few moments, Verka would look at the floor and smile, to witness the new young heartbeat playing at her feet. Mara, born last summer, brought forth daily celebrations. Everyone said she was such a happy little baby.

As Verka played, Mijo would tinker in his workshop, plying his talents on the next hunk of forest. The six of them, all in all, made for a happy family. They were a satisfied home.

Then one fine summer Saturday, as each were completing their favorite pastimes, the mountain spoke. Mato was watching both Pepan and Kata, to see who could roll down the hill the fastest. But before Kata could celebrate her tumbling supremacy, Mato called to them, saying they all needed to be off at once. "But why?" complained Pepan.

"Because we need to get home, immediately."

Chapter 37

As the three of them ran home, Mijo heard the whispered calls. He closed his eyes, and took in a deep, yet sad breath. Dropping his chisel, he ventured inside, and returned to the house, finding Verka had stopped playing. She was crying. Mijo looked at his daughter with understanding. It was at this point Mato returned. All three looked at each other, and embraced. Mijo broke the silence, as was his right. "It is time then?" he asked.

"It appears so," Mato replied.

Mijo nodded, in total agreement. "Good. The Sutjeska has spoken." However, one item puzzled him. "But how is it going to happen?"

It was then that Verka spoke.

"Mirko is going to help us."

Mato smiled. "And I know where to find him right now."

Mato trekked across the village road that had yet to change once in his three plus decades. Holding onto his usual traveling company, his Tisovina walking staff, Mato breathed in his life. His journey had not been easy. But he was here. More importantly, his family had endured. Mato sighed. Almost all of his family. Mato's one lament was Mirko. Mato was glad to be seeing him today.

Into the Gaj, Mato walked. Through the trees and bushes that had grown considerably over the past few years. As he walked to the graveyard, there Mirko was paying his respect.

"*Dobar dan*[2], dearest brother, Mato proclaimed. This introduction caught the elder brother off guard. Mirko wiped his eyes and nose with his sleeve. He obviously had been crying.

"Mato," Mirko blurted. "What are you doing here?"

"Coming to see you actually," Mato offered. "I need you to help me with something."

"Me?" Mirko said, surprised. "With what?"

"Let me ask you," Mato began. "You still have your contacts in the State Department, right?"

Mirko scratched his head, looking perplexed. "Yes, a couple. Why?"

Mato handed him a piece of paper, which Mirko immediately opened. It was not a note or a letter one might send to a friend or

---

2 Good day

family member. It looked very official. Very proper. Very important. As Mirko continued to glance over its contents, he understood what this was, and was staggered.

"Are you sure you want to do this?" Mirko asked.

"Da," Mato noted. "We are all in agreement. Even Tata thinks this is best for us."

Mirko shook his head. "Okay, then."

Six months later, the summer and autumn months fled from the mountain's sight. Another winter was harkening its changing of the guard. One nondescript day, as often happens upon a door, the Pavlović's heard a harsh tap-tap against it. Mato opened it and was shocked to find Mirko facing him.

"Mirko, it's good to see you," Mato said with exuberance. "What are you doing here?"

"I have something for you," he answered. "Something you have been waiting for. Do you have a minute to come outside?"

"Don't you wish to come in out of the cold?" Mato offered.

"Not today. Please, have you got a moment?"

Mato grabbed his coat, and though they weren't traveling but a few feet outside, he also grabbed his staff. The two brothers walked less than twenty paces, and stood facing each other. Mato was curious what this was all about.

"So what's going on, brother?"

Mirko looked up at the clouds merging and blending their shades of gray. "It looks like snow," he said.

"Yes, snow is probably going to fall some today," Mato agreed, impatiently.

Mirko smiled, knowing Mato's curiosity was getting the better of him. Mirko dug into his right jacket pocket. Pulling his hand back out, he passed Mato an official-looking envelope.

"Here," Mirko blurted. "This is what you have been waiting for."

Mato smiled. "Really?" he asked.

"Da," Mirko sniffled, ready to go on his way.

"Mirko, wait," Mato pleaded.

Agitated, Mirko turned, with a gruffness blurted, "What?"

"Take this," Mato pleaded, while offering Mirko his Tisovina staff.

"What do I want that for?" Mirko mocked.

"It's not that you need it," Mato began, "but rather I need you to have it. Please. For me."

Mirko stepped forward, and nodded his head in gratitude. As he took the staff from Mato, he could not help but smile.

"I'll see you soon, yes?" Mato asked.

"Da, soon," Mirko replied.

✷✷✷

Mato glanced at the letter, and exhaled long and hard. Its contents forced him to rush back through the door. Mato was eager to share the letter's contents. Verka was right by the entryway, with her curiosity getting the best of her.

"Mirko handed me this," Mato explained.

"What is it?" Verka asked, wanting to get to the point without reading it.

"Look," Mato said, with a smile. "Read it out loud."

"Okay," Verka said. "Um, the letter looks like it is from Belgrade. It looks like an official document," she offered, by looking it over. "From the State Department."

"Just read it," Mato said once more.

"Okay, okay, I'm getting there," Verka, joked. "Okay, it says. To Mato Pavlović, from Pavlovići, Yugoslavia. This letter, hereby decrees, that you and your family, which includes your wife Verka Pavlović and each of your three children, Kata, Pepan and Mara will hereby depart on May 18 from Sarajevo International Airport, to Frankfurt Germany, whereby your following flight from Frankfurt

Airport on May 19th will arrive…will arrive," Verka said with tears in her eyes.

"Read on, dearest," Mato asked lovingly.

"The flight will arrive in Sydney International Airport, Australia at eight hundred hours on May the 20th. The cost of the flight will be…"

Before Verka read the rest, she threw the letter in the air in euphoria. Mato clasped his hands together joyfully. Kata asked what the letter meant. Verka explained that they were going on a long trip on an airplane. This made Kata shriek with glee. But after a moment, Kata asked about their family's future. "But what about *Djed*[3]?" she asked, wanting to know if Mijo would come as well.

"No, my dear one," Mijo began, his tears flooding his checks. "My place is here. And besides," he continued with more hope and understanding. "One day, my family just might move back to the mountains. I must be ready for their return."

---

3 Grandpa

Stara/Nova Pjesma[1]

Mato awoke early that morning. He ventured down the stairs, finding five suitcases patiently waiting by the doorway. Each of these cases shared portions of his entire life, proving the future needs little of the past to keep going. Pondering all that he had been through, the reality was that the Pavlović family was packed. Their small number of belongings were ready for the great journey. Hearing the sound of steps venturing towards him, Mato grinned, seeing Kata with additional items in her hands.

"Tata, I didn't have room in my case for these. Can I just carry them?"

Mato picked up his daughter. "What did your mother say?"

"We only get one suitcase each," Kata replied glumly.

Mato smiled. "Don't worry. When we get to Australia, we'll get whatever you need," he noted confidently.

"Really?" Kata answered hopefully. "Even new shoes?"

"Yes, even new shoes," laughed Mato.

At this time, Verka also was coming down the stairs, holding an awake Mara. Though the sun was yet to truly arrive, the finality of their decision was upon them. Tomorrow's new world was dawning.

---

1 Old/New Song

There was nothing to stop its arrival now. And yet, as Mato looked upon Verka's face, he began to fret. She appeared to carry a great burden.

"Are you okay?" Mato asked.

Verka nodded her head.

"You know, we don't have to go," Mato said. "I don't need us to go."

Verka looked intently at her dear husband. "I know you don't," she noted. "But we do."

Mato nodded. "So are we already then?"

"Not quite. I have a couple of things we still have to do."

"Oh, like what?" Mato asked.

"I need to go for a walk," Verka announced. "Would you like to go on a walk with me?"

"Sure," Mato replied. "And the children? What about Tata?"

"They're all coming too," Mijo answered, as he sprang out the door while holding Pepan's hand. "So where are we going?"

"Everywhere," Verka replied.

✳✳✳

Finality makes everything important. As the sun rose to greet them on this early spring day, the family was already walking beyond the village borders. They had strolled past the Dol and the Gaj. They walked past the stream, where Pepan once took an impromptu swim in its still freezing waters.

Then, the family walked up to both Mara and Vjera's place of rest. As Pepan and Kata climbed their tree of choice, the adults hugged each other and wept, as if each funeral was occurring for the first time. Mato sobbed most of all. This was the last goodbye.

As they lingered, Mijo took the reins. "So, where shall we go next?"

"Let's go to the Kraljeva Sutjeska," Mato suggested. "I need to visit someone before we go."

Chapter 38

Eagerly agreeing, the group meandered as if time was on their side. Each furlong provided them a reason to stop. An old neighbor speaking blessings for their journey. The children running off in random directions. Mijo pausing to explain some old family context with each section of the beaten path. And yet, though they seemed determined to avoid their actual destination, by mid-morning, they finally arrived at the square. "You coming in?" Mato asked of Verka.

"I think you need to go yourself," Verka replied. "I'll stay with the children."

Agreeing, Mato went alone.

As he stepped inside the iconic white relic, Mato was amazed that after all these years he continued to find its interior awe-inspiring. Minutes melted off the clock. Mato began slowly spinning, so to soak in the entire realm. Each spin allowed him over and over to look at each glass window, each statue, and at each old wooden pew. Losing track of time, Mato's continual spinning caught the attention of one of its priests. He was an elder gentleman, gruff in appearance and action. The priest took a dim view of Mato's spinning display. "Young man, this is not a playground," the priest remarked sternly.

"Oh, I am sorry," Mato began. "Maybe you can help me. I am hoping to see Father Pero. Is he here?"

The priest appeared perplexed at Mato's request. "Who do you wish to see?" he crankily asked.

"Father Pero," Mato replied, more loudly for he feared the priest before him was deaf.

"*Čovječe²*, there is no need to shout!" the priest proclaimed indignantly. "There's no one with that name."

Mato was disappointed. "So how long ago did he leave the Sutjeska? And where did he go?"

"You don't get what I'm saying." the collared curmudgeon barked. "I don't remember the last time we had a Pero here."

Mato could not believe it. "But I spoke to Father Pero just a few years ago!" he protested.

But the priest was not having it.

---

2 Man. In English lexicon, it is the equivalent of "look dude…" or something like that.

"You calling me a liar? You couldn't have talked to him," he replied definitively. "There is no Pero. You must be confused." Mato smiled, befuddled at the priest's answer. He so wanted to continue arguing, but he resigned himself that it was no use.

"Well, thank you for your time," Mato answered, reluctantly, with a tip of his hat.

Out of the church Mato bounced, wondering what just happened. Then it hit him. Mato looked up at the sky, and wondered to himself, "*Wow! The mysteries of the mountains never cease.*"

"Everything all right?" Verka asked, as Mato returned.

"Da," Mato said with all sincerity. "Everything is great. Where else do you wish to go, Verka?"

"One more place, if you don't mind," she replied. "It's a little further up."

Up and up the entire clan went. For one hour, two hours and then more. It was slow going, especially with the children, but no one complained. The weather was fantastically mild. Though the sun was bright and warming with each hour, a cooling breeze kissed them so very slightly ensuring each generation of the party was in the best of spirits.

Besides, the mountain appeared to be putting on one last parade. A doe and her offspring pranced past them. An eagle swooped high above a little later. Scores of its chirping relatives were heard while they passed each new batch of trees. It appeared that on this day none of the creatures had a care in the world. It was at that moment that Mato knew, though everything was going to change, he did not have any either.

For hours they walked on and on. Towards the land of bigger plants, and far bigger trees. Trunks so big, that all of the Pavlović present could not have danced a Kolo around it with held hands. Not that Kata cared for the trees. Her attention was caught by bushes filled with her favorite fruit. "Look, at those strawberries. They're huge!" she exclaimed.

"Yes, they are *dijete*[3]," Verka agreed.

3 Child

Chapter 38

Those bushes meant they were close. They were close to a place Verka had not been in a long time. Verka had finally brought her family home to Kopjari.

"Are you sure about this Verka? Mato asked, noticing her evident nerves.

"Jeste," she replied, while rushing to take her husband's hand. "It is time," she said with certainty.

Releasing Mato's grip, Verka put her satchel on the ground. Pulling out the contents, Verka pressed her violin under her chin. She took a deep breath, and began to play. She played songs that had become strangers to her. But true old friends love you even when you are absent. And because of this love, each note rushed their return, flooding the highlands' airwaves with the most heartfelt story.

Within the first stanza, old faces rushed out to greet the new music. Each set of ears, whether they belonged to a Croatian or Muslim knew who the fiddler was. As their eyes saw what their ears already knew, their legs ran to greet her. "Our Verka is back!" they cried, "Our Verka is back!"

Tears, embraces and greetings engulfed them all. Verka introduced her family. They in turn, introduced theirs. Each new face was embraced as old friends. Kata's and Pepan's cheeks were pinched more than they could stand. Mato looked over at his dearest wife. She appeared overwhelmed with happiness, and he was glad for it. Seeing his wife in her old environment further enhanced his understanding of her. Gladly, it made Mato love Verka even more.

After the initial greetings and celebrations simmered down, the Pavlović family walked further into the small village. As they slowly walked, the entire village, bar one, followed. And they knew where the last one hid; in only other house Verka's life had known. "Are you sure?" Mato asked once more.

"Da!" Verka replied, with even more certainty.

"Hajde mi sviraj,[4]" Mato remarked.

Verka nervously brought her mountain gift into position. Anticipation was in the air. Not a voice, whether owned by small

4 Then my love, play.

313

child, or bird made a flutter. Verka closed her eyes, so to hear nothing but the music. With a deep exhale, the bow danced. It danced to the whims of Paganini's "*Caprice Number 24.*" Verka did not just play with her hands and fingers that day, but with her soul. And with each note, it felt cleansed. With each note, Verka could hear her mother speak soft words of encouragement. In turn, Verka told her mother about her brave husband. She told her about her three children and the differing aspects that made them special. She told her about how Kata's passion, Pepan's love of football, and how Mara was at an age where she was getting into everything.

Verka played and played some more. Finally, Verka informed her mother, that she was going away. Far away. And as she told her mother this difficult news, a stirring murmur could be heard from inside the old house. Tears flowed from Verka's eyes, as its front door opened, and out popped a frail, somewhat odd-looking man. "Verka, is that you?" the old man creaked.

"Da, Tata," Verka replied stopping mid note. "It's me."

The old man smiled, showing the few teeth he still owned. "Hvala," he remarked. "Thank you, my girl."

With the sun setting, the Pavlović family returned to their village. Each child was floating in a dream, being carried by a different set of adult arms. Mijo, Mato and Verka were tired, but happy. It had been quite a day. As they got to the town's edge, Mato turned to face the forest perimeter. He looked into its throng wistfully.

"You know, there's time to go and look at your tree if you want," Verka remarked, reading her husband's thoughts.

Mato smiled, and kissed Verka on the forehead. "No, that's alright," he said, sincerely. "My tree is not there anymore. I was just thinking about it all, you know?"

"Are you sure you don't still wanna go, for old time sake?"

"Da, I'm sure. Let's get home."

Chapter 38

"Home," Mato thought. Tomorrow, home would look very different.

Thirty minutes later, all three children were in bed. A late supper of pita was being warmed. A promise of Tablici and songs were hanging in the air for after supper. But Mato was restless. He wanted to smell in the night air one more time. As he stepped outside, he caught a glimpse of a familiar figure, motioning for him to come over.

"Mirko," Mato muttered. Mato ran over to his lurking brother. They greeted each other warmly.

"So, tomorrow, huh?" Mirko asked.

"Da,"

"Then that's it," Mirko noted, sadly.

"Yeah," Mato remarked. He changed the subject matter a little, hoping to lighten the mood. "But maybe you'll come one day, too?"

"Da, maybe."

"You know they have really good fishing in Australia," Mato smirked. "Not that little stream stuff either. Ocean fishing."

"Maybe, one day, but…" Mirko said, stopping short.

"But what?" Mato asked.

"Someone's got to look after the old man, you know," Mirko offered.

Mato put his right hand on Mirko's shoulder and smiled. So did the mountain.

-39-

Hajd' idemo[1]

Mato sat uncomfortably on a plastic seat at Frankfurt International Airport, his mind a whirling dervish. On his lap, his eldest slumbered deeply. The other two children shared Verka's lap. All three of them were visiting their own dreams. It had been an overwhelming day of new adventures.

Until this moment, Mato had little clue that his Kata snored and mumbled while she dreamed, but he was glad to learn it. *"Even as children sleep,"* Mato mused, *"you can learn much about them."* As she slept, Mato looked down at Kata's newly-fitted feet. They weren't even there yet, and his children were being given items the mountains could never provide. Mato wistfully smiled. His dreams were already coming true, but he wondered at the cost. It was probably more than the price of the new shoes. But the risk was worth it. It was what the mountains wanted.

As Mato continued to sit, he was amazed at the amount of people rushing back and forth. "Where were they all going?" he had asked Verka. She of course had no answer. Still, Mato thought it was amazing. Life truly was going to be very different.

As Mato continued to look in all directions, the empty seat next to him was taken by a priest. The priest wore a warm smile

1 Let's go

and rosy cheeks. The two men made eye contact, and cordially greeted each other with a nod. "Good morning to ya'," the priest noted, enthusiastically offering his hand. "Name's Father Peter, from Ireland. Where are you off to this fine day?"

Mato could only shrug his shoulders, not understanding the collar's meaning. He guessed the priest had probably offered his name. Naturally, the Bosnian, offered his. "Mato," he said, grinning with a smile.

"Mato, is it?" Father Peter continued. "And where are you flying today?" Peter continued, while waving his arms around like a plane. That did the trick.

"Oh, Australie," Mato offered.

"Australia! Very nice." Peter laughed. "I have an aunt that lives in Melbourne. If you see her, say hello for me, will ya?" Peter looked at his watch. "I need to be going now. God be with you." And with a tip of his hat, the priest left.

Mato smiled and waved his hand, wondering if he had somehow seen that priest before. As he shook off that illogical thought, Kata awoke with a startled expression. "Tata, I had the most amazing dream!" she exclaimed, with pure youthful exuberance.

"Oh yeah, what was it?" Mato asked.

"Well it was of Djed Mijo, and he was walking into the forest," she began.

"Oh, yes," Mato replied, in a condescending manner that only parents can.

"Yes, it was of Djed. And he was walking at nighttime. And yet, somehow it was really bright, as if a light was following him around. Well, he was walking and walking with a big, big smile on his face. As he was walking, he went deep into the forest, right out of Pavlovići, up to a bunch of trees. Three trees to be exact."

At this point, Mato, who was not really paying attention, was jolted into the throng of the story.

"What did you say?" Mato exclaimed.

"Three trees, Tata," Kata continued to answer. "Two of the trees were old and big, but the one in the middle was smaller, younger, but it was amazingly strong. I could see its roots. They went very, very deep. All the way to Australia. Anyway, Djed climbed that middle, smaller tree. I didn't know that Djed knew how to climb trees. Did you, Tata?"

"No, I didn't," Mato replied, amazed.

"Well, anyway," the young child continued. "Djed climbed, until he stopped at a certain spot. There, he reached out to grab something. The thing he grabbed looked sticky. It looked tasty. And do you know Djed ate the sticky stuff? Just then, after Djed ate it, there were all of these bugs all around him. And guess what, Tata?" Kata asked.

"What?" asked, a staggered son, a staggered father.

"One bit him, and then somehow at that moment, I was in the dream too, and it bit me too. But don't worry Tata, because you look worried, it somehow didn't hurt. Weird huh?"

At the completion of Kata's story, Mato tickled his daughter, and then playfully hugged her tightly, rocking her back and forth. Finally, stopping before her giggles awoke the rest of his family, Mato smiled and answered Kata's question.

"Perfectly and logically weird," he said.

Dosta[2]

---

2 Enough

Acknowledgments

I once foolishly believed a writer embarks on a lonely journey of discovery with only ideas and conclusions tagging along down their dusty highway.

In writing *Kata's Father* I've discovered that's false, with plenty of new and dear old friends keeping me company, and often coming to my rescue. Each friend has been a trusty set of jumper cables keeping me chugging down the road.

In writing a story about chasing hopes and dreams, I've been reminded that, like telling a story, these are gifts bestowed by our Creative Father to be shared. What a blessing it's been to share this creative journey with so many people far more talented and giving than me. Not only is my book so much better because of all of you, but I have also learned a great deal about who I am as a person and what I should be. Thank you.

First, Donna Kinley, who volunteered for the (I think) awful task of editing my much, much longer first draft. With care, you gave my writing much needed coherence while keeping its soul intact. This is a rare ability.

To Kate Baum, for the additional final edit. It is because of you I now know how to adhere to proper formatting rules. Surprisingly, these things *are* important.

To Jamila Hutchinson, for encouraging me to re-start writing *Kata's Father* back in late 2012 after I put it away in frustration for almost two years. You reminded me there was a story that needed to be written. I hope you still think this way.

To artist Josh Garrels, for *Jacaranda*. Your music became this journey's soundtrack. As soon as *Lake Yarina* kicked on in each of my 486 listens through your *album* (yes, that many), I was always transported to the little world in the *high hills*.

To the entire Mill City Press team, particularly project manager Ali McManamon, for patiently answering my many, many questions; Biz Cook for knocking my cover out of the park and Athena Currier for the beautiful interior design that complements my story so well.

To Wayne Crowe, for designing the *Hullabaloo Bookery* logo. You are a dear friend and a great talent.

To everyone who invested in my Kickstarter campaign. I was standing on a tightrope and each of you became my net. Every prayer, social media shout-out and every investment amazes and humbles me still. I must mention Marko Sola, Mile & Kata Tomin who ensured we got over the line with plenty of room to spare. Particularly Mile, who I learned after the fact simply refused to allow me to fail. Tata, this continues to mean everything to me.

To my brilliant daughter Ivana, the inspiration for my logo (with a little help from her toy "Diggy"), and who wisely picked the book's cover. What I'm most grateful for was your infectious enthusiasm to hear the latest completed chapter. I love writing stories you love. My dear, you are a far better writer than I will ever be. I can't wait to see how God shapes, molds and directs your talent. Never forget (and this is for your much younger brothers too), if it is God's will, beautiful dreams do come true!

And finally, to my magnificent wife Shedell – we made it! On this road you were always there, even when I face-planted into muddy waters that dared bog me down. When I made it harder to pull me out of the mire you never wavered in coming to my rescue. Your honest critique and approval gave me confidence that I was not laboring in vain. You are my best friend. I love you.

And finally, finally to the people of the Sutjeska. I hope this book does you proud. I hope it shows that we who have journeyed far from your roads will never forget you. And maybe one day we might sit in each other's company and share some pita.

Hvala.
John M. Zurak